MW00653326

BETTER THE DEMON
YOU KNOW

DEBORAH WILDE

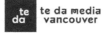

te da media
vancouver

Copyright © 2024 by Deborah Wilde.

All rights reserved. No part of this publication may be reproduced, distributed or transmitted in any form or by any means, including photocopying, recording, or other electronic or mechanical methods, without the prior written permission of the publisher.

Publisher's Note: This is a work of fiction. Names, characters, places, and incidents are a product of the author's imagination. Locales and public names are sometimes used for atmospheric purposes. Any resemblance to actual people, living or dead, or to businesses, companies, events, institutions, or locales is completely coincidental.

Cover by: Covers By Christian.

Issued in print and electronic formats.

ISBN: 978-1-998888-44-3 (paperback)

ISBN: 978-1-998888-43-6 (epub)

Chapter 1

Evil had a scent: lemon. It was bright and crisp and brought to mind colorful drinks with paper umbrellas savored in tropical climes after a successful drug lab bust in the jungle.

Well, at least the drug lab part was accurate when it came to today's mission. Shame about the rest.

In a sales pitch I'd since dubbed "Snow Job," I'd fallen prey to the lure of escaping Vancouver's December gloom and rain for a winter wonderland, with the added glory of stopping some Eishei Kodesh from producing a non-magic, yet illicit street drug called Crackle. And when Francesca, the level three leader on this gig, had shown me photos of the pools of steaming hot springs nestled beneath mountain peaks that was our reward once this mission was wrapped up, well, my temptation was complete.

Now, with the compound where we suspected the lab was housed within sight, I was also assaulted by the peppy citrus smell of the drug, taunting me with visions of a world with color rather than an endless sea of white whose glare in the moonlight was starting to induce blindness.

Interestingly, Francesca had left out several key details about this mission: how we'd be strapping on snowshoes (more like tiny torture contraptions than the lightweight paddles I'd envisioned) and trudging over uneven rural terrain, sinking into the snow with each footstep when we weren't skidding on frozen patches hidden under powdery drifts; the fact we'd be approaching the clandestine lab at night in subfreezing temperatures; and the double my body weight in outdoor fabrics that were slowly sous-videing me to death.

The only sounds had been the sharp crunch of our party breaking the crust on the snow with each step, my hot, damp breathing against the heavy scarf wrapped around my mouth and nose, and the wind that stung my eyes, groaning through the trees.

Francesca held up a gloved hand, her brown cheeks ruddy with cold. Edward, a buff Serbo Canadian and the first of our trio of level two Maccabees on this takedown immediately stopped, followed by me, and then Paul, an older operative who showed photos of his prize-winning Siamese with the same pride as a new dad.

I unsnapped the binding on my snowshoes with the manic relief generally reserved for getting through airport security and scoring coveted concert tickets and tossed them under the massive evergreen next to us with a sigh, rolling my ankles to stretch them out. Sweat ran between my shoulder blades, and my hamstrings and quads burned.

The last twenty feet between us and the barn was partially shoveled, partially tamped down from whoever worked here, and easily accessible.

Snow splatted off the tree branches, barely missing our party, but I didn't care, lost to a coiled excitement that flared up inside me. *Please let our quarries fight back.* This city girl was no match for Mother Nature, but most human opponents I could handle just fine, and I was raring for someone to look at me wrong.

Francesca indicated for Paul and me to head for the small barn, while she and Edward checked out the weather-beaten house on its left.

Paul and I bolted silently, keeping low.

Sadly, there was no cloud cover to hide us once we burst from the woods across the exposed ground. The sky was clear and the moon hung low in the sky, illuminating us like nature's searchlight.

Any chinks in the barn's siding had been patched from inside. They'd boarded up the windows and soundproofed it well since there was no faint murmur of voices or any sound of electric equipment like the condensers, evaporators, or heating mantles involved in the production of this synthetic drug. Not even the hum of a generator.

It was odd that they'd taken such care, given how remote this property was, and yet Crackle's lemon scent had managed to defy their other security precautions and ooze into the surrounding woods. I didn't have time to dwell on it, however, because Paul and I were too busy playing hopscotch through the blind spots of the security cameras.

He grasped the handle of the barn door and turned back to me with his eyebrows raised.

I stuffed my gloves into my jacket pockets, drew the weapon peeking out of the holster attached to my belt, and nodded.

The Zen Zapper was a new design combining electroshock technology with white flame magic. Not only would it physically incapacitate the target, it'd amp their level of calm into an almost compulsion-like desire to chill out and stay put.

I'd proposed the idea a couple of months ago after a case where a White Flame had relaxed a Prime vampire into remaining still long enough to be staked. This was the first working prototype, and if the magic failed, I'd still have its Taser-like capabilities.

After a late-night brainstorming session with the R&D crew generated a shortlist of names that included the Tranquilizer Thunderbolt, the Harmony Hammer, and the Mellow Magic Mallet, we went with Zen Zapper which we'd deemed the best of the bunch.

Paul flung the door open. "Maccabees! Freeze!"

His hands were raised, ready to deploy his orange flame magic, and I had a cool weapon, but there was no one to use it on. The barn was empty.

I gritted my teeth with a sigh, my pent-up disappointment and restless energy bouncing around inside me like a pinball.

The area closest to the door had been turned into a makeshift kitchen. An old stove held a large dented steel pot, ostensibly used to make the candy that formed the delivery mechanism for the chemical high. There was an open industrial-sized bag of sugar on the floor, while multiple mesh bags of lemons were thrown on the countertop next to bottles of yellow food coloring and a candy thermometer. It was almost quaint. Hardly food safe, but I guess that wasn't high on the list of priorities for drugmakers.

The lab area with its glassware, beakers, flasks, and solvents, on the other hand, was all business. Red jerry cans of gasoline were on hand to power the generators, and a couple of hazmat suits were thrown over chairs.

Piles of the rough round yellow candies were heaped on a long metal table, along with sealed packages of the icing sugar mixture containing the chemical compound that these candies would be dusted with, making Crackle the premier choice for the discerning partier.

The drug may have resembled old-fashioned lemon

drops, but sucking on one was more like eating Pop Rocks, hence the name. The euphoria that Crackle induced, however, was all its own.

Both Trad cops and Maccabees had attempted to get it off the streets for years but as with many drugs, it was a losing battle. We'd recently gotten intel that a group of Eishei Kodesh had ramped up production in a remote and rugged area not far from the border we shared with Alberta. Most cities in our province didn't have their own Maccabee chapters. When things got hairy, Vancouver operatives were deployed as necessary, hence the four of us on this job tonight.

The hair on the back of my neck prickled. All of the barn was visible and there were no other exits. "Where is everyone?"

"Is it a trap?" Paul sifted through a stack of the gold tissue paper used to wrap each individual dose, his expression wary. "Drug labs don't close up shop for the night."

"It looks more like they forgot milk and stepped out to the store. In any case, why leave the drugs out in the open with an unlocked door? And leave all the lights on?" I held a sealed bag of powder up to the light. "If they were expecting us and funneled us inside to a kill chute, it still doesn't make sense to hand the authorities evidence. They could have hidden the candies at the very least. Make a minimum effort to conceal their crimes."

"Unless they were positive we wouldn't be leaving again," he said dryly.

Added to my confusion was the fact that my literal inner demon, Cherry Bomb, the Brimstone Baroness, was showing a marked disinterest in the proceedings. I expected her to be excited to take down bad guys. Even if they were human, not demons or vamps, these drug manufacturers were still dangerous, but I was getting nothing off her except mild boredom.

Maybe snowshoeing lulled her into a coma and whenever she required satiation, I could hit the mountains for some Mother Nature time instead of secretly tracking and fighting demons.

Yeah, I couldn't rouse up enthusiasm for plan B either.

I surveyed the room yet again, as if it had transformed into a more exciting crime scene. Nothing. I sighed.

Then a bloodcurdling scream rent the night.

Now that's more like it. I sprinted outside, Cherry now wide awake, with Paul on my heels.

My first read of the scene inside the living room of the lone house on the property was that Francesca had been injured by the Eishei Kodesh engulfed in flames, whom she was attempting to subdue. Except her expression was frustration, not fear.

The fire didn't hurt the living tiki torch, so he was a Red Flame. *Kaden Scott*, my brain helpfully supplied from our intel report. Thirty years old, previous conviction of assault.

That was as far as I got with facts and rational thinking, my brain struggling to make sense of Kaden's unyielding determination to cave his own skull in. He bashed it against the wall with agonized cries, but also a dreamy smile. When his next strike landed with a reverberating thwack, I flinched harder than he did.

The house thankfully hadn't caught fire since Kaden's head was flame-free, but one wrong spark would incinerate the faded wallpaper or the wooden slats on the ceiling.

Francesca grabbed an iron fireplace poker and prodded Kaden and his fire magic away from the wall into the center of the room, but she didn't have a way to take him down that didn't involve getting barbecued.

The room stank of blood with the tang of lemon

6

running under all of it, while a man on the battered radio sang about rocking around the clock tonight.

Kaden switched up his assault and punched himself in the face until his nose flattened with a sickening crunching sound and the skin around his right eye tore. He hooked a flaming finger into his eye jelly deep in the socket and, with effort, plopped the entire eyeball out. His breathy sigh conveyed the pleasure he took from this, yet it ended on a pained howl that would haunt me to the end of my life. It was heartbreaking and horrifying to see him caught in this deadly thrall, torn apart in equal measure by bliss and agony.

Paul, a hardened Maccabee who'd also done military tours of duty in some of the roughest places in the world, gagged.

Shoot Kaden, Cherry urged gleefully.

To another person, my fine demoness's suggestion might appear as insane as Kaden. However, Cherry had great instincts, both for our self-preservation as well as ending battles quickly.

"Francesca. Down!" The second she stepped away, I squeezed the trigger, discharging the electromagnetic probes into Kaden's shoulder.

He seized up, his flames sputtering out, then he crashed onto the floor on his side, still spasming. His face went slack. Was that the same as calm and subdued? Had the Zen Zapper worked?

I ducked into my synesthete vision. I was a Blue Flame with the specific ability to illuminate weaknesses in people, the synesthete aspects of my magic manifesting as sight.

And what a sight he was.

Kaden presented as a human outline colored with jagged streaks of vivid blue along his entire nervous system, like a sugared-up preschooler had deployed their limited coloring skills.

His heart was a large fluttering blue dot while his head and face were a swath of blue, consistent with his physical injuries. Upon closer examination, his mesolimbic dopamine pathway, the part of his brain controlling addiction, was a darker navy than his physical injuries.

I reminded myself that Crackle was not airborne. The drug had to be ingested for it to take effect; we couldn't be harmed by inhaling its signature scent.

Though this wasn't Crackle's normal advertised happy high either. Had they changed the chemical compound producing a new Crackle that caused users to self-harm to outrageous degrees? I shivered. It was good that we were taking these guys out of the picture now.

But had Kaden eaten some of this janky batch? I narrowed my eyes. These guys were professionals. The equipment set up in the barn proved that. This was no rookie mistake. It was lunacy. This crew hadn't just lost it right before we'd arrived. They were methodical. They'd evaded local law enforcement several times. Why get sloppy now?

I retracted the Zen Zapper's prongs from Kaden's shoulder. "Francesca—"

Kaden moaned loudly. He rocked in a curled-up ball, the blood streaming out of his mangled skull mixing with the tears from his empty eye socket.

Francesca pulled off her gloves and placed her palms over his empty socket to cauterize it with her yellow flame healing, while Paul snapped magic-nulling cuffs on him. Better to be safe than sorry.

Kaden gripped my leader's hand tight, but at her gentle questioning, he simply stared dully into the distance, lost to pain and shock.

Francesca asked Paul to help her turn Kaden onto his side so she could assess the extent of his injuries.

Since they had this under control and Francesca

assured me the upstairs was clear, I headed into the kitchen. These people were clearly not fans of washing dishes, but the room was otherwise unremarkable save for the open door leading to the basement and who knew what dangers.

Let's find out! Cherry mentally fist-pumped.

I poked my head back into the living room. "Did Edward go down there?"

Francesca thinned her lips, her expression strained at my question, but her quiet "Yes" was carefully devoid of any anxiety about her team member. She trusted him to take care of himself, her professional demeanor ruthlessly honed through training and experience.

"On it." Keeping the Zen Zapper at the ready, I stepped through the trapdoor and into the darkness.

Chapter 2

I crept down the narrow staircase and along a short, dimly lit corridor, keeping my back to the wall.

Cherry nagged me to hurry up, but rushing could get me killed.

I peered around the corner.

The corridor was dank and cobwebby, but free of anyone wanting me dead. Unfortunately, there was a closed door at the end of it.

I pressed my ear against it, but when I didn't hear anything other than the faint strains of the Supremes singing "You Can't Hurry Love" from upstairs, I wrestled the door partially open from the bloated frame and slipped through. My legs buckled from the spike of excitement that punched through me, courtesy of the Baroness.

Something splatted against the wall above my head and fell onto the back of my neck. It felt like a warm, wet sponge and I yelped, batting it away as I slid on a patch of wet ground.

I looked down to see what on earth that had been and immediately wished I hadn't.

It was a freaking ear, with a gold hoop still dangling from it.

Cherry made a disgusted sound, chiding me to get my shit together.

Remember when that spider fell on the back of my neck? I suppressed a shiver. *Human ears are not better than spiders.*

The weak bulbs overhead were strung with a multitude of stripped extension cords. Did these people want a fire? Because that's how you got a fire.

I moved forward between the many shadows, the air in here so infused with that lemon stank that my eyes watered.

Maybe that was a blessing because it blurred the sight of the mangled bodies.

I sucked in a breath. Sure, the freezing temperature would keep the corpses from decomposing quickly, but what was wrong with the more traditional cellar offerings of canned fruits and winter vegetables?

Only one person in my line of sight was still alive, a woman—missing an ear. Jasmine Bakshi, a seventy-some-thing of Indo Canadian heritage, was the lone female and suspected mastermind of the group. The wiry senior was also providing her own soundtrack to this destruction, humming a peppy tune, which, if memory served, was from the Beach Boys' catalogue.

There was zero possibility that this businesswoman had voluntarily taken Crackle, and yet my magic sight verified that her mesolimbic dopamine pathway was affected.

I raised the Zen Zapper with a steady claw.

Claw?

I blinked three times rapidly, but it didn't turn my left hand back into human fingers or erase the frosted toxic green scales striping my skin.

Oh fuck. Oh no.

My teammates would be coming through the door any second now. My heartbeat spiked and the scales bloomed farther up my arm and along my hands, locking down into a protective armor.

Jasmine bit down on her thumb with enough force to tear it half off, snapping me out of one horrified stupor and into another.

I re-aimed my weapon at her.

She growled at me with a mouth full of blood, her thumb dangling off her hand by a tendon.

On the upside, she wasn't reacting to Cherry Bomb, but damn.

How had Crackle gotten into everyone's system and why was the drug making these people turn themselves into "some assembly required" humans?

I shot Jasmine with the electroshock/calming magic combo, but before I could rip the prongs out of her torso, she grabbed hold of the connective wires transmitting the electric current and wrapped herself in them, bucking off the floor like it was a mechanical bull in a country and western dive bar.

Ride 'em, cowgirl, Cherry snickered.

So not appropriate, I hissed back in my head, freeing Jasmine from the tangled wires.

Thankfully, her spasming was subsiding and the white flame magic had kicked in. She rolled onto her back with a glazed look.

Sadly, one of the Zen Zapper wires had broken. I dropped the weapon with a baleful glare, intending to have words with Maccabee R&D when I got back for not making it sturdier, and scrubbed a scaley hand over my face. I needed Francesca down here to heal the injured woman.

In my head, Cherry commanded me to breathe. *Do you trust our instincts?*

I looked from the door to my claw. *Yes.*

Okay, then, she said. *We practiced this.* True. It was a new addition to my personal training regime. *What are you going to do?*

I centered myself, letting my frosted scales armor the exposed skin on my face, and neck, though I didn't go into my full bulked-up shedim form. There was a moment when I almost changed my features all back because I'd never willingly shown any part of myself in front of humans.

As I always said, I was Cherry and she was me, and we had been working on trust and control in a whole new way these past couple of months. I could reverse it if needed, but for now, my protection stayed in place.

I twisted my Maccabee ring around—it was dim down here, and hopefully, if the pillbox compartment was hidden, the band itself wouldn't be a dead giveaway of my identity. Using a dusty towel that was flung over a box of Crackle wrapping papers, I triaged the zoned-out Jasmine and made a tourniquet for her hand. Her head was also covered in blood, but the flow had stopped, and the wound appeared shallow.

For her own safety, I snapped magic-nulling handcuffs on her.

A series of low, animalistic grunts sounded from a far dark corner.

"Edward?" I'd forgotten about the other operative.

There was an agonized cry followed by a rusty chuckle.

I hesitated, torn between escorting Jasmine up to Francesca and dealing with this new crisis. Swearing under my breath, I ran deeper into the cellar, my crimson hair whipping into my eyes.

The ground was uneven, and I had to mind my

footing and keep my horns from hitting the sloping roof, and then I was pulling up short in confusion.

A demon who resembled the unfortunate aftermath of a wild night between a sloth and a bratwurst sausage sat inside a tall cage made of thick iron bars whose door was secured with a heavy gold padlock. About three feet high, the shedim had bumpy brown skin and stumpy arms with long fingers. Long toes too. She looked dirty and small in the cage, but she was absolutely enthralled with the shivering mass in front of her.

It was a shadow, rocking back and forth—a man on his knees with his arms wrapped around his midsection.

Edward.

I lurched forward to help him, watching in horror as he straightened with a wet hiss of pain and held the small dagger he always carried aloft.

Then he stabbed it into a bleeding wound in his gut.

My stomach dropped into my toes. Were his actions a result of a demonic compulsion or the drug?

Crackle first hit the news back in the 1990s in Vancouver when an Eishei Kodesh rave turned into a horror show. Thanks to the testimony of the few survivors, it was determined that Crackle fucked with the synesthetic quality of our flame-based magic.

Partygoers destroyed themselves chasing the ultimate sensation. Red Flames, who experienced their magic as textures, burned people alive, seeking the feeling of velvet perfection against their own skins.

A Yellow Flame survivor described wanting to achieve the scent of umami, which is a taste, not a smell, but that didn't stop them from attempting it via cleansing magic, bursting eyeballs and shattering bones in other people in the process.

The partygoers not on Crackle, who were screaming and running for the exits, couldn't find their way out.

Orange Flames, whose magic use was temperature-based, entombed rooms—and bodies—in ice, chasing a glacial coolness in the hot, sweaty warehouse, while the few Blue Flames present, those of us who illuminated weakness, decided now was a good time to turn their synesthete vision into an underwater paradise in a million shades of blue. Which sounded poetic except they'd done it by illuminating tiny flaws in the building's foundation, directing people to the weak spots.

That in itself wouldn't have been a problem, but White Flames then stoked people's enthusiasm to turn the indoor event into an outdoor one. The crowd bashed on those places with fists and furniture, shifting the walls off their foundation until part of the ceiling in the main dance room caved in.

People were buried alive.

A thorough investigation by the Maccabees traced the drug back to a shedim (the plural Hebrew term, used conventionally for both singular and multiple demons, like the word "fish"). This demon, based in northern British Columbia, had infused its secretion into the candy to create this misery and chaos.

The shedim was hunted and killed.

I inched closer to Edward, who snapped at me with his teeth then licked the knife.

The drugs we'd found in the barn were one hundred percent evil organic and needed to be torched. But even with this organic version responsible for the violence these people had inflicted upon themselves, there was no way any of them—and especially not Edward—had taken it.

The shedim was locked up, so she hadn't physically forced the drug down their throats. Had she compelled them?

Why didn't she try to compel me?

On second glance, the shedim wasn't simply sitting

there like an evil voyeuse, she rocked back and forth so quickly, it was like she was attempting to get liftoff.

That did not make it better, but it did make me doubt she had any compulsion ability. Ergo, Edward was affected by the drug somehow.

Crackle didn't go away once the original demon was killed, but it did change into a non-magic, chemically produced version that produced a blissful high in both Trads and Eishei Kodesh—without the carnage.

The version of the drug that we'd expected to seize.

None of that helped me now. I stepped into a shadow, taking a circuitous approach to my teammate so as not to agitate him further.

The Maccabee's eyes were blank. He grunted each time he stabbed himself, the blade sliding free with a disconcerting slurping sound, but he didn't stop, despite now being so incapacitated that he'd collapsed onto his back and lay sprawled in the dirt.

I crouched down beside Edward. I'd never used my synesthete magic to suss out a partner's weakness unless they were so injured that they couldn't tell me how they were hurt, but when he didn't respond to me calling his name, I took that as a green light.

There were three parts of his body lit up in blue: his gut wound, his heart, and his mesolimbic dopamine pathway. It was scarily easy in my Cherry form to take the dagger away from my teammate, who had a good fifty pounds of solid muscle on me. He should have fought back hard at what appeared to be a new and different shedim disarming him.

The caged demon growled, her eyes glinting yellow. Not all shedim could recognize infernals, so her hostility could have been toward me as a fellow demon encroaching on her conquest. That would be better, since she wouldn't assume I was weaker than she was.

Edward didn't register my presence at all. His only reaction when he could no longer stab himself was to shove his fingers into his wound and try to rip himself open that way.

I slapped magic-nulling cuffs on him, overwhelmed by the carnage, but Edward was bleeding out and training took over. I tore off my jacket and pressed it against his wound.

"Like them submissive?" the shedim croaked and winked at me. She didn't have eyelids, so it was more one bulbous eye bulging farther out than the other for a moment, but I got the gist.

I screamed myself hoarse for Francesca and Paul, but my teammates upstairs didn't answer. Ice filled my veins as quickly as Edward's blood seeping through my jacket. I'd have reverted forms and checked why they'd gone silent, but I was scared to stop applying pressure to Edward's wound.

Awareness finally returned to his gaze. He flinched at the sight of me, his eyes wide and his skin draining of what little color he had left. Oh, for the good old days of ten seconds ago before he'd seen what I was. At least he didn't realize it was me, Aviva. Just another rando shedim.

I ignored the sting in my chest. "I'm not going to hurt you."

"Hurt! Hurt!" the imprisoned demon cried gleefully, her bumpy skin percolating.

The shedim-induced jonesing at the rave that made the drug newsworthy didn't match the damage tonight, because those partygoers hadn't turned their Eishei Kodesh abilities on themselves. Lethal as that original demonic form of Crackle had been, it didn't inspire self-mutilation.

So what accounted for the difference?

Bratwurst Demon kicked a chamber pot out of her

way, upending the full container of urine, which sank into the dirt. Gross.

I moved my jacket to check how badly Edward was still bleeding, and whether I could risk leaving him to get help. Why hadn't Francesca or Paul come down here yet? Even if they hadn't heard me calling out, one of them should have come to check on Edward and me.

Had they been ambushed by more Eishei Kodesh drug manufacturers? Our intel report had mentioned only four people. Weren't Sonny White and Jack Meister the two dead bodies down here?

A drop of sweat trickled down my spine.

Could the compulsion to self-mutilate also be transmitted by touching someone who'd been in direct physical contact with the shedim? Paul and Francesca had touched Kaden with their bare hands, and Edward would have attempted to assist Jasmine.

A thread of worry snaked through me. I'd touched them too. Then why hadn't I—

I looked at my scaley armour.

You're welcome, Cherry said smugly.

Yeah, all right. I glanced up at the dirt ceiling, praying Paul and Francesca weren't turning their bodies into their best deconstructed selves, then shook that dark thought off, and returned my focus to Edward.

His blood had slowed to a trickle. Like his breathing.

I wrenched my eyes to his. They were dull on the life force front, yet jam-packed with his lingering horror at my shedim form.

He took a final shuddery breath and lay still.

I stuffed my sadness—for Edward and this entire situation—down tight. I hadn't known him well, but he'd been a kind soul, always ready to lend a hand, and a committed operative. He deserved justice.

Retribution, Cherry amended silently, like it was a treat that would cheer me up.

I let out a deep breath at his blood soaking the knees of my snow pants. She wasn't wrong.

Jasmine was humming again, some slow tune that kept breaking into hiccuped sobs, but she was still alive. As were Francesca and Paul, upstairs.

I hoped.

Check on Francesca and Paul and leave the jailed shedim alive until everyone else was secure? Or take her on myself? I raced through the pros and cons of each but concluded that if my teammates were incapacitated or if touching the shedim (which we'd inevitably do when fighting) induced violent urges, then my armored scales placed me in the best position to take her down so no one else fell victim.

I found the keys next to a severed arm and unlocked the cage.

Bratwurst Demon didn't move.

"Get out," I snarled.

Instead of using the open door, she contorted her body like an octopus and slipped between the bars.

I lunged for her with my claws, longing to rip into her, but she sidestepped me.

"Stupid humans thought this would hold me," she sneered, crushing the gold padlock into a twisted mess. "Foolish children." No sooner had she dropped the lock into the dirt than her gumption drained out of her and her entire sausage-like body slumped. "Need to eat."

The shedim wasn't getting a last meal, but she was right about one thing: she was on death row.

Chapter 3

Garroting Bratwurst Demon with the broken Zen Zapper's wires was a great way to work out tension. Cherry even cheered in my head—and assured me that my scales would keep me safe.

I had to trust her because choking the demon out this way was a close-contact sport. With a grunt, I twisted the wires tighter by one last death-inducing millimeter.

The wires slid cleanly through the demon's neck. Or rather the section of her sausage body approximating that part.

Her skin smoothed back into place; the shedim was uninjured.

I stared dumbly at the wires in my hand.

She grabbed my forearms and flipped me to the ground, propelled by a rage-fueled adrenaline rush. Her repeated kicks to my ribs were no piece of cake to endure, and her long toes gripping my side briefly with each strike made me shudder, but I wasn't compelled to aid and abet her in my own destruction, so there was that.

I rolled to my feet, danced in close, and planted a swift right hook to her side.

She undulated and stumbled sideways.

I pressed my advantage, following up with two swift jabs between her eyes that made her jiggle like a bowl of jelly.

The shedim hissed and curled her long fingers into fists, but her arms were still stumpy, and it was like watching a T-rex go two rounds. She tried, bless her, she really did, but she'd never met a fight move that she didn't telegraph, and I easily avoided her clumsy attacks.

I wailed on the fucker, pouring out my fury at the pointless deaths. Those damn snowshoes I'd been forced to endure were also worth venting about. The drug producers could have plowed the single dirt road leading to their property, but nooooo. We had to do the trek from hell, while the criminals would get a nice, cushy helicopter ride back to HQ.

The shedim smashed her forehead against mine and I stumbled backward, coshing my skull. My ears rang, the room swinging nauseatingly around me.

I slammed the heel of my boot into what would have been the Achilles of a person, nodding in satisfaction when the demon crumpled to the ground, trying to protect that spot from further assault. Methinks I found her kill spot.

I debated using the Maccabee ring that I'd liberated from a half shedim on a previous case. Its owner, Maud Liu, turned out to be my slightly younger half sister. She'd requested the deathbed token from her Maccabee godmother under false pretenses, intending to use it to kill our father.

You know, the demon with whom my ex was running the Copper Hell, a dangerous gaming hall located on a megayacht.

The Brady Bunch, we weren't.

I'd used the magic cocktail in Maud's ring twice, with

two more doses available, but this was an official Maccabee assignment. Better to use my ring now since refilling it wouldn't raise eyebrows and save Maud's stash for hunting demons to feed Cherry.

I flung an arm out for balance because neither the ringing in my ears nor the dizziness was subsiding. If this damned shedim had given me tinnitus, I'd—

What? Cherry asked in amusement. *Hunt her down and kill her twice?*

Maybe, I thought petulantly. I ground my knee into Bratwurst's hip and readied my strike. The magic in my Maccabee ring would confirm the Achilles as her kill spot and end her.

She screeched and threw me off before I could activate it, causing me to bash my hip against the cage, and snatched up Edward's discarded knife.

I tensed, ready to block her lunge and strike, however clumsy it might be.

"I'm not going back!" She plunged the knife into the back of her foot.

Right into her kill spot.

I'd had many emotionally intense moments when time seemed to slow down: through anger, terror, even passion. Not once had disbelief been on that list, and yet I'd swear reality ground to a snail's pace. Every detail was as clear as if it was allowed its own moment in the spotlight: the blade sinking halfway into the shedim's foot, her mouth pressed tight in determination or pain, the cracks spider-webbing across her sausage-casing skin.

Time snapped back like a rubber band. The shedim exploded, brown bits hitting the ground like crispy pork fat before being sucked up by the dirt.

I toed at the spot where she'd made her last stand, my brows furrowed. There wasn't even a stain to commemorate her existence, so expecting answers was a stretch.

How about just one answer, universe? To one very perplexing question.

Since when did shedim commit suicide?

Yeah, her fighting skills were laughable, and she hadn't been able to compel me into hurting myself and weakening me, not even to boost her own strength, but still. She should have given her all to a last-ditch attempt to stay alive, because when it came to self-protective instincts, shedim had the market cornered.

With the threat gone, I returned to my human form, my ears ringing and my head throbbing.

A demon suicide unnerved the shit out of me. Their behavior was unpredictable, but in a consistently violent, chaotic, or at least mindfucky way.

Unassailable truth number one: they hurt others. Not themselves.

And what was with her final words? Where didn't she want to go back to? *Okay, two questions, universe. Get on that.*

I hurried over to Jasmine, who remained in shock but alive, and helped her to her feet. Through a combination of verbal encouragement and taking most of her weight, I half walked, half dragged her out up the stairs into the kitchen, her cuffs jangling with each step.

I wanted to rail against her for making this awful drug to begin with, never mind bringing a demon into the production chain for the worst version imaginable, but she was suffering and I couldn't harden my heart to her plight.

"Francesca? Paul?" I assisted Jasmine into the living room.

Whelp, I had my answer as to why the rest of the team hadn't come to our assistance.

Paul had used his orange flame magic to suck the heat out of Francesca's body. She was as blue as a Smurf, her teeth chattering, and her body bowed, but while she was down, she wasn't out.

She'd taken the creative route and reverse engineered her healing abilities to break Paul's right leg, which he dragged limply along. One of his arms was also twisted and bent at a grotesque angle.

Kaden was dead. Either Francesca's healing magic hadn't been enough, or she'd aborted the attempt when she became lost to those demonic urges herself.

I sat Jasmine down on a ratty sofa. She was so far beyond registering my presence that it was like moving the limbs of a doll, albeit one that now hummed "Only You" along with the radio.

"Hey, gang." I turned the radio off.

Jasmine began shrieking, so I hit the power button again, turning up the volume until she calmed down. Ooookay, no radio silence for this one.

Neither of my teammates reacted to the commotion. Francesca sluggishly prodded Paul and held up her hand.

The temperature around us plummeted and I coughed on the freezing air, my breath coming out in white gusts.

I sprinted toward them.

Paul forced the heat of the room into my team leader's fingers so suddenly and with such force that they shriveled like wieners left to burn.

How nice. They'd teamed up to better achieve their insane desires of inflicting maximum damage on their own persons.

I stepped forward then back, loath to hurt them further, but even more loath to let them finish each other off. Edward was dead; the rest of my team was getting out of here alive. And with my Zen Zapper a useless paperweight down in the root cellar, I had no way to stun them out of their compulsion.

Choking it was, a move that was more reliable than trying to punch them unconscious. I'd simply put each person in a sleeper hold to cut off the blood flow on either side of their neck and prevent oxygen going to their brains.

Risking that they'd be too far gone to notice my scales, I once more armored my hands and arms. Then I sidled up behind Paul, put my foot into the back of his knee, and lowered him down to my level. I tightly wrapped my arm around the front of his neck, grabbing my shoulder to secure the grip, and flexed my arms to begin oxygen restriction. My other arm got pressed behind Paul's throat, leaving no gap in my chokehold.

Confident there was no way for him to break free, I squeezed from the sides of my chest, arms tightening, while leaning slightly forward.

Paul coughed. Three seconds later, he was out cold.

Judging by Francesca's non-reaction to her subordinate choking out a team member, I could have taken my sweet time.

I lowered Paul to the floor.

Francesca prodded him with her toe, giving an annoyed growl that he wasn't keeping up his end of their mess-each-other-up arrangement. The new friends with benefits.

A moment later, I had two unconscious team members at my feet.

Was nearly asphyxiating your teammates mandated Maccabee training? Hell no. Darsh had taught Sachie and me these moves. A vamp was the perfect person to practice choking on until we were positive we could do it properly. We'd also executed the moves on each other to make sure.

Not fun.

I sprinted for the comms in our backpacks outside, along with a couple more pairs of nulling cuffs for Francesca and Paul, and some latex gloves for me to prevent any physical contact because I had to lose the shedim scales. At least that happened fairly quickly and easily.

The wait for our air evac rescue was interminable. I'd insisted on speaking to healers at HQ the second I sent my emergency request for assistance, and they talked me through all I could do with the first aid kits in the backpacks.

I split my time between Jasmine, and Francesca and Paul, who'd regained consciousness. All three were in shock and unable to process or respond to anything, save for Jasmine clinging to those golden oldies on the radio, humming along with empty eyes.

It was like sitting in a room full of zombies, set to an oddly nostalgic soundtrack.

Thankfully, none of the Eishei Kodesh tried to hurt themselves further.

When they were as stable as I could make them, I dragged Edward's body upstairs to be with the rest of us. I owed it to him, though I positioned him behind some curtains, out of sight of the others. They were traumatized enough.

I left the two other mangled corpses downstairs. Maccabee HQ was sending a helicopter with fresh meat to deal with the cleanup.

Cherry chuckled. *Nice phrasing.*

I winced, but I was too tired to feel bad. I slid down a wall onto the floor, gripping a half-empty bottle of water. My clothes stuck to me in cold, sweaty patches, my back throbbed, and my stomach was so knotted up in grief and worry that the power bar I'd been commanded to eat while waiting for the helicopter was nothing more than cardboard lumps in my belly.

I zoned into a loop of grim thoughts, examining every second of this mission for all the places where we should have made different choices. By the time the cavalry arrived, the whir of the rotor blades slicing the air, all I wanted to do was crawl into my bed and pull the covers over my head.

Yeah, well, that was not to be, because the second the chopper landed in the faint pre-dawn light on the roof at HQ in Vancouver, I was whisked inside for a debrief.

First, though, a level three Maccabee forensic tech divested me of my jacket, snow pants, and gloves, wanting to test for any traces of the demon secretion. If this shedim was the same type as the one who'd originally created Crackle, we were screwed because there was very little information on that first demon in our records.

It made a dangerous drug. Maccabees found it. Maccabees killed it. In hindsight, they should have taken the time to question the demon, but twenty-twenty and all that.

Our Maccabee tech would get fuck all from my clothing since I hadn't worn the jacket or gloves during that gong show, though I claimed to have had both on until after the demon was dead.

I'd worn latex gloves from the first aid kit while triaging the others, which kept me from making skin contact and being affected once I lost my scales. The gloves were in an evidence bag, which I also handed over.

Edward's blood was on my snow pants. I told the tech they could keep them.

A healer was also present to check me out. Her treatment of my mild concussion was worse than the injury itself, and I was almost grateful when Director Michael Fleischer showed up to personally take my report, given the gravity of the situation.

Michael led me to one of the interrogation rooms— supposedly because it was closer than her office.

Riiiiight.

I had no doubt that she'd listened to the medical emer-

27

gency details I provided when I first contacted HQ, but despite me hanging half-off the hard metal chair in exhaustion, she had me take her through every step of the events multiple times. To be fair, that was standard procedure and I recited everything as honestly as I could.

Emphasis on "as I could."

Finally, she stopped the recorder.

I yawned, then covered my mouth with an apology, but I was so ready for bed.

Michael clicked her silver pen, studying the yellow legal pad she'd made notes on. "Just a couple of clarifications."

"Sure."

There were more than a couple, but there was only one point she kept circling back to, slipping her reframed question in at different points like it would catch me off guard.

I should have caught on immediately when she took us off the record. There was a shedim involved, and a straightforward mission had ended in tragedy. I blamed fatigue for my taking so long to clue in.

"You're really fascinated by the durability of my clothing, Michael." I crossed my arms. "Looking for some advice for your next extreme winter sport adventure?"

She tucked a strand of silver hair behind her ear, her makeup impeccable and nary a wrinkle on her suit, despite the early hour. "I *was* thinking of doing some backcountry skiing on my next trip up to Whistler. Do you think the gloves you wore while fighting would be suitable for the conditions or would I need protective gear not traditionally found in stores?"

I leaned back with a tight smile. "Would it matter what you used so long as at the end of the day it kept you healthy and whole?"

"No, but if the rest of my party suffered from exposure, and I walked out unscathed, there'd be questions as to how I survived. Especially if one died."

My expression hardened. "I tried to save Edward."

She actually blinked. "I didn't mean to imply otherwise."

"No." I laughed bitterly. "You just meant to imply a whole host of other things, none of them being 'Thank goodness my daughter is okay.'"

She opened her mouth, but I held up a hand to cut off her protest.

"Sorry," I said. "'Thank goodness my *operative* is okay.' I know you don't like to be familiar at work."

There had been a short period of time on a case a couple of months ago where my mother believed I'd been killed when my car exploded. The first time she'd seen me afterward, I'd merited an entire shoulder squeeze. Apparently, that underwhelming gesture was supposed to speak volumes about her relief.

She didn't chide me for my snarky comment. But she didn't disagree either.

"To answer your question," I continued, shoving down the familiar flare of anger that she induced, "most people would chalk my well-being up to training and intelligence and leave it at that."

"Perhaps." She drummed her pen against the bolted-down metal table. "But I'm not most people. I'm responsible for everyone, and it's my duty to understand every element so I can make sure nothing like this happens again."

"I didn't make skin contact," I said blandly. "Not much else I can say." I failed to stifle a yawn. "With all due respect, Michael, Francesca and Paul will be out of commission for the foreseeable future, so you can grill me on protective gear, or you can let me go home and get

29

some sleep so that I can start investigating why the shedim killed herself."

Michael wrote a final note on her pad. "What does a demon taking themselves out of the picture matter?"

I groaned. The one crucial piece of evidence and she wasn't picking up on it. "Because that's not how shedim behave."

"If I've told you once, I've told you a thousand times, Aviva, do not anthropomorphize demons. She was badly wounded, correct?"

"Correct," I said stiffly.

"Was there any possibility of her escaping?"

I clenched my fists, my mother's patently patient voice setting my teeth on edge. "No."

"There you go. The shedim had no way out. She no doubt chose to die on her own terms than at the hands of a human. One last effort on her deathbed to assert power and sow chaos. What matters is that a credible threat is gone."

"But—"

"But nothing." Michael flipped the pages of the legal pad closed and set the pen on top, her expression inscrutable. Not for the first time, I wished that my mom was an open book, free and easy with her praise and with her sorrows. If she wore her heart on her sleeve, I wouldn't have half the problems I did with her. Then again, she wouldn't be the intelligent role model who, for all her parental failings, I admired the hell out of.

She'd used her yellow flame purifying magic to root out a decades-long systemic corruption here in Vancouver and became one of the youngest Maccabee directors, with a reputation for being a bastion of righteousness, fighting the good fight on every front.

Sucked for me that I was included in that last part.

"One of my operatives is dead, as are three other

people," the director said. "The only thing I care about is gathering as much information as possible to mitigate any deaths in similar situations." She looked at me expectantly.

"Was this the same type of shedim as the one who originally made Crackle?" I ticked items off on my fingers. "How specifically were the victims affected? How did the Eishei Kodesh find the demon to imprison her?"

"Exactly. We'll have to wait until Jasmine is cleared to be interviewed for that last point. Hopefully it won't be long because the Authority will want her transferred to Sector A."

I shivered at the mention of the maximum-security jail where people who colluded with demons or rogue vamps were sent. Its location was secret, as was its existence from the general public—and to Maccabees below a level two status. Yeah, achieving that goal had come with a hell of a shock with this new information.

Jasmine had been taken to the healers to treat her shock and injuries. She'd seen me as Cherry, and me as *me*, and I hadn't figured out what lie to spin to make her believe the first part hadn't happened.

I had to do something, however, in case one operative's deepest secret was a fair trade to make her life in Sector A more palatable.

"I'll follow up with her as soon as possible," I said.

"You're not pursuing this."

I fell back in my chair in disbelief. "You can't seriously think I wouldn't!"

My mother's voice softened. "You've been through a lot tonight, Aviva. You need to go home, rest, and then have a session with Sarah."

It was standard procedure for Maccabees to see our top psychologist and be cleared for duty after a traumatic event, but I wasn't going to be sidelined. Not on this. The drug bust had spiraled so far out of my control and resulted in so much death and panic that I had to do something. If I walked away now, I'd always have nightmares about today. But if I could put an end to this, then maybe I'd be able to sleep properly again.

Maybe.

"Don't take me off this. I need answers. Need closure," I amended. "See what Sarah says after our session tomorrow, but if she's good with me continuing, then don't take this away from me."

"All right. Provided Sarah signs off, you can work with Cécile to close this case. Shedim are the Spook Squad's jurisdiction, and we'll wrap up the case faster with two of you on it."

The Québécois vampire was the senior member of Vancouver's Spook Squad, and yes, this should go to her, but I was raw and flayed from tonight's shitstorm, and I wanted to work with someone I was close to. Not someone my mother was foisting on me as a babysitter.

"Can I have Sachie?" I fiddled with the hem of my shirt, trying to keep a brave face and not sound like I was begging, but I didn't have it in me to act tough right now. I wanted my best friend by my side. "Please," I said quietly.

She finally nodded. "Meantime, I'll have Louis type up what you've told me. When you have the other answers, you can complete the report."

All in all, that wasn't one of our more fractious interactions. I'd gotten my partner of choice, and I hadn't come clean about Cherry's appearance.

I made it as far as the door before Michael spoke again.

"Don't overtax yourself." There was the tiniest pause before "overtax."

Any bystander would hear a show of concern from a leader for her team member or a mother for her child, but I was fluent in every tiny flicker of Michael's gaze, each minuscule stress of a syllable, and every weighty hesitation.

"I won't." I nodded, playing it like I took her words at face value, even though inside I was seething, a lifetime of her teachings playing on repeat in my head. *Don't expose your shedim side.*

Don't expose me.

I'd seen how far she'd go to make sure Cherry's existence was never revealed.

My mother had stolen Sire's Spark, a magic artifact rumored to possess powerful healing abilities, from a Trad gallery hosting an exhibit including debunked supernatural items. All the items had been found and returned, save for that one, which was currently hidden in my mother's safe. Though not for much longer.

The more insidious ability I suspected the crystal capable of? Sussing out half shedim, placing us at the mercy of those who sought to use us—or kill us. Had she taken it out of fear, or perhaps a desire to protect me? Maybe, but it was hard to reconcile either of those motivations with how quickly and insistently she'd ordered me not to investigate who was truly behind the deaths of some murdered half shedim. Or, in her own words, "No one cares about infernals!"

I tamped down a mean little smile as I left the room. We'd see just who cared about infernals by the time I was through.

Chapter 4

Seven hours of sleep later, I was refreshed, fed, and had scored rock-star parking at Granville Island. The popular tourist destination was a foodie's paradise with a public market selling everything from fresh fish at the docks, to baked goods, produce, and artisanal olive oil. It also hosted a few small live performance venues, was home to outdoor concerts in the summer, and was a haven for artists.

The streetlamps blinked on, and I beeped my fob, checking that the locks had descended. My replacement vehicle (after a vampire had blown up my deteriorating but beloved college sedan a couple months ago) was a basic secondhand hatchback, but it had heated seats. If things didn't work out rooming with Sachie, I'd live in my car.

I picked up my pace to complete my errand before the store closed. Many of the small retailers' doors were adorned with festive wreaths, and sparkly lights were strung through the branches of the trees on the island. It was all very pretty and I didn't begrudge the Christmas decorations, but it seemed like holiday mania kicked in earlier every year. It was only the beginning of December and I'd been hearing Christmas music for weeks at my local supermarket.

Not to mention there was already holiday-themed tat for sale everywhere, but when it came to buying Hanukkah candles, the one and only thing required for my celebrations, I had to go to a special store. Sure, it was my favorite bagel place with fantastic rugelach, but that wasn't the point.

Sometimes at this time of year I felt invisible. I already battled those emotions in regards to my half-shedim side, so having the Jewish part of my identity struggle with that really sucked. Some days, it was all just too much.

I ducked into a small business selling crystals and tarot cards. The sound of flowing water playing off the docked iPhone was soothing and the incense burning in the corner lessened some of the tension in my shoulders.

Crystals of every shape and size adorned tasteful displays. Some of the larger ones were locked away in cases, along with jewelry made by the artist in residence.

"Can I help you?" A bespectacled young woman in an ankle-length poncho approached me with a smile.

"Hi. I'm here to pick up an order. It's under Aviva Fleischer."

"Oh yes." She pushed her glasses up her nose. "It's in the back. Let me grab it."

"Thanks." I was browsing a display case of adorable tiny owl statues with crystal eyes when the bell jingled over the store.

I glanced over my shoulder at the newcomer out of habit, but the man was beelining for the other employee with a hesitant smile on his face, his phone held up. *Bet he's shopping for a romantic partner.*

"I'm looking for a bracelet for my wife's gift," he said.

I snorted softly and moved on to the next display case.

"I've got your order." The woman helping me held up a small box.

I joined her at the counter, bouncing on my heels while she cut through the tape and opened the box. I picked the item up. "It's perfect."

According to legend, Sire's Spark, a rough octagonal crystal about the size of a man's palm, belonged to Abraham Ben Haim, a Yellow Flame and one of the world's most powerful healers, who lived in a shtetl in Poland in the late 1700s.

Supposedly, he'd infused the crystal with his blood, giving the artifact its pinkish hue—and its alleged magic properties. The crystal's powers were based on the element of connection, or as the sage himself said, "Blood calls to blood."

The same phrase that Roman Whittaker, former operative, infernal killer, and dead vamp, had uttered about someone finding me.

This octagonal crystal I held was a dead ringer for Sire's Spark from its shape to its weight and soft pink color. The only thing it was missing?

Magic.

The other customer approached the till where I was paying for my purchase. He cleared his throat and held up a bracelet. "Can I get your opinion? Is it too much?"

The piece was comprised of four beaded strands, each with a raw chunky purple crystal charm.

"It's bold," I said.

His face fell.

Damn it. That hadn't come out as diplomatic as I'd intended.

"I'm guessing your wife has browsed this store before, right?" Off his nod, I smiled. "And that purple is her favorite color?"

He blinked at me. "Are you a cop?"

I held up my hand with the Maccabee ring.

The man grinned at me. "Nice. I'm with the VPD."

"Then trust your gut, dude," I teased.

"Dead bodies, great instincts. This?" He poked one of the beads carefully. "Not so much."

The store bell jingled.

"Got the coffees, Hank," a familiar man's voice said. "You done?"

I froze for a split second, then making sure the box with the crystal was sealed up tight, I put my credit card away, and took the bag with my purchases.

Hank, the cop with the bracelet, waved Detective Olivier Desmond over. "Can we poach a Maccabee?" he joked.

"Aviva?" Olivier's wide-eyed blink was followed by a frown.

"Good to see you again." I resisted the urge to check whether I'd grimaced, because he'd narrowed his eyes at my greeting.

"I thought you didn't have any interest in crystals." Look at that. His Nova Scotian accent with its New Yorker/Irish flavor got stronger when he was suspicious.

I almost laughed at his pointed remark, except this was no laughing matter.

When Trad cops were given the investigation into the missing gallery artifacts, I'd gone to Olivier and told him that I suspected Sire's Spark really did have magic, in which case, finding it was within Maccabee purview.

My simple hope of finding the crystal without infringing on the Trad cops' rights became anything but. I ended up concealing an informant's involvement in the murder of the thief, who bore the same name as a young man on her crew. Rukhsana Gill hadn't killed the thief, but she had murdered a collector who'd attacked her after *he* killed the guy, believing she had the missing artifacts.

Olivier had made the connection between Rukhsana and me, and that I was hiding something. His intelligence was one of the reasons I'd dated him a couple of times. His lean muscular build from all his surfing that showed off his gunmetal suit with a model's perfection didn't hurt either. Usually, I'd have added the twinkle in his green eyes that popped against his black skin to that list, but he currently looked as steamed as the coffee that Hank was sipping.

"I'm picking up a gift for a friend." I pulled out the dangly earrings I'd added to my purchase as a cover for why I'd been in the store. "Trusting my gut that she'll like the set."

Hank chuckled. "You'll be fine."

Olivier's frown deepened. *Don't like my chumminess with your buddy? Tough.* "Those don't look like Rambolette's style," he said. "Not enough sharp edges."

Suppressing my unholy glee at misinterpreting his frown, I raised an eyebrow. "Who said they were for Sachie? But nice to know she made an impression when you met her, what, two months ago?"

Olivier opened his mouth. Shut it. Glared at Hank for smirking at him. Then his expression softened. "Hank, get Danielle the bracelet with the bright blue crystals."

Hank poked at the bracelet. "But purple is her favorite color."

"And blue will match Nico's eyes. Dani will be able to carry around a memento of the baby when she's at work and missing him."

Hank clapped his friend on the shoulder. "She'll go apeshit for that. Good call, buddy."

It was more than a good call. It was an incredibly thoughtful and insightful suggestion. One made by the kind of friend who noticed even the smallest details in your life.

I dropped the earrings back in the bag. "I've got to get going, but happy holidays to you both." Olivier celebrated Christmas, but I didn't want to presume with Hank.

"You too," Hank said, already at the display case pointing out the other bracelet to the employee.

Olivier scrubbed a hand over his close-cropped, afro-textured hair, shifting his weight from side to side. "Happy Hanukkah, Aviva," he said with an awkward smile.

My answering one was a bit too wide and a bit too insistent. "Likewise! You doing anything fun to celebrate the holidays?"

Olivier shrugged, inching toward me to let a group of teenage patrons with more hair colors than a Kool-Aid variety pack pass by him.

I scooted back, bumping into a display and hastily righting it at the same time Olivier reached out to help. We bashed knuckles.

"Same old," he said, shaking out his hand. "I haul the decorations out of my mom's storage. I like seeing the old things."

I nodded. This was somewhere between pulling teeth and strangers anxiously trying to avoid each other on a dance floor, but at least we weren't actively at each other's throats. Maybe someday we could even be friends again.

"Yeah," I said. "I like seeing the old things too. Take care, Olivier."

I walked back to my car, my heart pounding from the encounter. The fake crystal was safe, but my exhilaration wasn't just for my narrow escape. The ship had sailed on Olivier and me, but he was still a great catch. And I couldn't wait to help a certain someone reel him in.

LESS THAN AN HOUR LATER, all my fond matchmaking thoughts were forgotten in the face of the crime in progress at Maccabee HQ.

This thief was skilled, deadly, and, given her gleaming eyes, more than willing to hurt me.

But I was holding my own and protecting what was mine. And Michael implied I wasn't up to remaining on this case? Please. I'd gotten Sarah's permission, but even without our psychologist's sign-off, I'd be able to neutralize this threat.

I stepped sideways, hiding the last double chocolate chip cookie from my attacker, and brandished the espresso holder full of fresh grounds. "Stand down or I *will* throw them," I growled. "People will hear those precious little kitten sneezes of yours and your rep as the person with the most knives and fewest misses will be shot."

Sachie Saito, willowy warrior and my lifelong best friend, jabbed her pen at me, planted in a fighting stance that even dynamite couldn't shift. She'd been growing out her pixie cut, yet remarkably, the flippy bits in the back and new candy-pink color detracted from her menace not one whit. "You wouldn't dare."

"Try me."

Sach danced forward on the balls of her feet. "Hand over my elevenses, Fleischer."

"First off, It's 6PM. Second—" I flinched at the glint of metal, spilling grounds onto the toe of my heeled boots. "Jesus! Where did those nail scissors come from?"

Sachie smirked, her two weapons held aloft like she was wielding dual swords.

Gemma Huang, a level two operative with a mastery of white flame magic and bitchery, forward-lunged her way into the kitchen, one deep knee bend after the other. A vision in moisture-wicking workout gear, with a light sheen of sweat on her toned bare arms, and her dark hair in a slick high ponytail, she grabbed a water from the fridge and lunged back out.

Fascinated, Sach and I tracked her progress through the doorway. Gemma lunged past workstations, a comfy chair, and one of the bookcases. During the day, this huge open space on the third floor was flooded with natural light, but was now illuminated by a combination of street-lights and the moon glowing outside the windows.

"Her intensity is off the charts," Sachie said.

"I bet she's leveling up hard to get Marv to take her under his wing as his permanent junior now that Victoria was promoted to level three."

"She's got stiff competition from Joe."

The overhead lights were dimmed to a soft warmth and the few operatives at work were plugged into their laptops with headphones on. None of them raised an eyebrow at Gemma's excessive behavior.

Shaking coffee grounds off my boot, I shoved the espresso basket into the machine and nodded at the cookie. "Well, that broke the mood. Help yourself."

Sach dropped her weapons on the counter. She reached past me, broke off a piece of the cookie, and popped it in her mouth. "Mmmmm."

I hit the button for a double espresso, raising my voice to speak over the hum of the machine. "But seriously, where were you hiding those scissors and how did I not see you pull them out?"

"Hanging with vamps on the regular is incredibly instructive." Sach twirled the nail scissors expertly before sheathing them in a hidden holster.

"Not for the rest of us humans."

Sach shrugged. "That's a meatsack problem."

"You do remember you're one too, right?"

She tucked the pen behind her ear. "I'm meatsack plus. Meatsack enhanced?"

"You and Darsh haven't come up with a catchy name yet, have you?"

"No, but we're working on a signature dance move."

Of course they were. My fond smile turned mischievous. "I ran into Olivier today."

"Yeah?" She broke off another piece of cookie. "How's Point Break?" Her indifferent tone wasn't fooling anyone. Okay, correction. It would fool ninety-nine percent of the population, but I'd been her best friend since first grade. The two of them were on mutual nickname usage; there'd been mutually assessing glances.

Sachie's stance on romance had always been "find the right person and love will be easy." She had an active dating life, but I feared my best friend equated easygoing partners with easy for her to walk away from or easy for her to keep at a distance.

"He looked good," I said. "There's still some weirdness over what happened with the stolen artifacts but I'd like to be friends with him again. If we all grabbed a coffee, would you be down to come make things less awkward?"

"Bricks have been thrown through windows with more subtlety."

I grinned. "Maccabee is derived from the word for 'hammer.' I'm just living up to the name."

"I was going to ask how you were holding up after the bust," she said grumpily, "but now I care fifty percent less."

Heh. That wasn't a no.

Still, I couldn't answer her question without remembering Edward and all the horrific injuries, and any amusement vanished. "This morning I'd have answered with 'By my fingertips' but I'm up to a firm handhold."

"Progress."

"Exactly." I added the double shot of espresso to the mug containing my frothed and heated milk and brought it halfway to my mouth. "Maccabees can't be everywhere, I get that, and sometimes we have to rely on Trad cops for our intel, like with this drug lab. They can spot vamps, but most don't realize demons exist."

She picked up a yellow file folder she'd brought with her off the counter. "To be fair, even Maccabees might have missed the shedim's presence. It was imprisoned in a windowless basement. They wouldn't have had eyes on it."

"I know." I slung my laptop bag over my shoulder, grabbed the plate with my share of the cookie along with my coffee mug, and we left the kitchen area. "We prepped for a takedown. Between hiking at night in winter, apprehending four Eishei Kodesh criminals, and securing the drug lab, there were plenty of variables to account for."

The heat from one of the overhead vents ruffled one of the brightly colored cardboard dreidels hanging from the ceiling. Maccabees had taken their name from the heroes of the Hanukkah miracle, honoring them and the flame that formed the basis of our Eishei Kodesh magic.

Despite the fact that not all operatives were Jewish nowadays, Hanukkah was our Christmas and the Super Bowl rolled into one. It went beyond hanging ornaments. One of my favorite aspects was the dreidels of all sizes placed throughout HQ in anticipation of the first night tomorrow, along with mesh bags of gold coins—shitty chocolates in shiny wrappings that I secretly loved—for anyone playing a round or two of the spinning top game.

One of the operatives setting out the gold gelt now was explaining the rules to some level ones and how signups for the competitive dreidel tournaments were already full.

There'd even been menorah-making classes, with people's attempts adorning their desks. My favorite was the one that Monique, a level three, had fashioned out of blue and white LEGO complete with translucent LEGO flames for when she "lit" it. Some Maccabees, not even all Jewish ones, brought menorahs in from home so they could light them at sundown for the eight days, but the big lighting ceremony would be held at our fancy staff party tomorrow.

We walked past fat gel letters spelling out "Happy Hanukkah" on the wall next to the elevators, matching the ones stuck to the windows, and I got a little verklempt.

It mattered that I had this refuge and that it was a big deal to all Maccabees, regardless of the individual operatives' religions or lack thereof. For these eight days, we all came together to celebrate the Festival of Lights during the darkest time of the year.

My happiness slipped as I picked up the thread of my thoughts about the drug bust. "Curve balls were to be expected, but a shedim-sized one that moved freely despite appearances to the contrary, and whose secretions induced extreme self-maiming? Oh, and let's not forget that its compulsions were passed on secondhand. I've seen some shit during my career, Sach, but this?" I shook my head and exhaled.

Sachie pressed the down call button. "One thing at a time."

Good advice, but when everything had a code-red urgency to it, it was easier said than done.

Chapter 5

I polished off my cookie during the descent to the Spook Squad's digs, carrying my empty dish past sturdy, brightly colored, oversized couches and chairs. The furniture was grouped under multicolored silk lanterns hand-painted with delicate flowers, which infused it with a jaunty air.

The Hanukkah decorations extended to this part of the building as well, though with no windows in the basement of the former garment factory, they'd forgone the gel letters for a large Happy Hanukkah banner.

There was one downside to the space. With no natural light—and no sense of day or night—hanging out here made me feel like I was in a Vegas casino where time was irrelevant. Sunshine wouldn't have hurt the three vamps who Sach worked with, since they'd all been Eishei Kodesh in life and could withstand the sun's rays to varying degrees, but any Trad vamp suspects who made it this far would be fried in their cells if exposed.

My chest twisted as I passed Bentley, the large unicorn stuffie riding a stumpy palm tree in a fancy Italian tile planter, who currently had a bag of chocolate gold coins hanging off his horn. Bentley was the squad's unofficial mascot and the beneficiary of a mint green hat, knitted and bestowed with great care by my ex, Ezra Cardoso.

Did running the Copper Hell leave Ezra any time to unwind with his favorite pastime? The unwanted image of him thrusting into me, his hands gripping my hips, from our last encounter two months ago, rose unbidden.

I tasted blood. Wincing, I freed my bottom lip from my teeth and licked the wound, quickly looking around to confirm none of the vamps were present. They'd smell even the faintest hint of that copper tang, and while they were trained to control their urges, it was still a crappy thing to bleed in front of them.

I followed Sach into one of the conference rooms. Ezra could do whatever he pleased with his free time. I slammed the empty plate onto the table.

Sach opened the file folder and reviewed the notes she'd made on her copy of my report.

I logged into the Maccabee database. "It would make life so much easier if shedim could be categorized by a species and type instead of being mostly evil randos."

My partner opened a browser on her phone. "Which demon do you want to research?"

"I'll take Bratwurst."

We didn't get much more about the original Crackle demon than it had an anteater's snout and green fur, whereas mine didn't have any nose at all and looked like a sausage with sloth digits.

"There's a note on the file, added after operatives tracked and killed the original shedim who produced Crackle," Sachie said. "It ingested a lichen species specific to the Queen Charlotte Islands in northern British Columbia, which, when combined with a demon enzyme, was presumed responsible for the euphoria-inducing secretion." She looked up from her screen. "Your shedim was

46

outside Revelstoke in the southeast corner of the province. Is that lichen found there?"

I typed in the query. "No."

"What if it ate a different kind of lichen and that variable in the enzymatic process accounts for why people were hurting themselves instead of going after a demonic rush?" she said.

"Could be." I clicked through a few more results. "Get this. Scientists in 2007 discovered thirteen tree-dwelling species of lichen specific to the Incomappleux Valley, right by the lab. The area is an inland rainforest and the only temperate rainforest in the world to grow four to six hundred kilometers from the ocean."

"I had no idea," Sach said, now crowding me from the next seat to read over my shoulder. "It's also the only rainforest in existence to derive most of its moisture from snow."

"There was no lack of that," I muttered. My thighs still ached from our snowshoeing trek. "Okay. The Eishei Kodesh were manufacturing the synthetic version, but at some point, they teamed up with the shedim to produce organic Crackle, assuming her secretion would have the same effect as the other demon's."

"The trouble was," Sachie said, twirling a dry-erase marker between her fingers, "that she'd eaten a different type of lichen, and her secretions produced a different effect. You're ruling out the vics being psychically compelled?"

"Yes, because I wasn't affected." Even as Cherry, I would have felt the compulsion, regardless of whether I could resist it. "That means it was a physical transmission. So how, specifically, did it occur? It wasn't direct physical contact, so blood? Sweat?" I flashed back to the jail cell, leaning back in my chair with my hands folded across my stomach. "You know how asparagus makes pee stinky

47

whereas beets can turn urine red but don't make it smell? Maybe what she'd eaten had a different effect on her urine? There was a chamber pot full of pee with the shedim."

Sach wrinkled her nose. "Edward didn't touch her chamber pot though. And Francesca and Paul didn't touch the shedim— Ew! You're telling me that all these people died because no one in that drug op washed their hands?"

"Not enough to combat the effects." I shuddered. "That answers the first couple of questions. First off, this wasn't the same type of shedim, though lichen plus a demon enzyme produces the secretion. Next, the effects are transmitted through directly handling the urine or touching someone else who came in contact with it."

"That leaves how the Eishei Kodesh got hold of the shedim." Sachie shook her head. "Sector A. Damn. I've heard their rehabilitation program to cleanse people's minds of demon existence is even worse than the prison itself."

The very mention of Sector A made me physically ill. Eishei Kodesh who knowingly colluded with shedim or rogue vamps were automatically sent there, regardless of the crime they were convicted of in the justice system. They were just quietly transferred when their trial ended and never released.

As determined as I was to reach level three and make an indelible difference in this world as a force for good and change people's attitudes about half shedim, I lived with a constant low-level anxiety that if the Maccabees didn't kill me outright for having infiltrated their ranks, they'd shove me in Sector A and I'd never see the light of day again.

"I doubt Jasmine and her crew called Bratwurst forth from the demon realm," I said, "but even if the shedim was already on earth, did they strike a deal or bind her?"

"Binding demons is almost impossible." Sach stood up

48

and cracked her back. "It's hardly a stretch that she willingly joined forces. She must not have expected to be locked up. But how did they find a demon with their exact needs?"

"Is there some demon matchmaker out there, hooking shedim up with humans to go forth and be evil together?"

Sach grinned. "He sits at an old computer with these grainy profile photos, entering answers from questionnaires like: magic ability, preferred geographic location of match, and favorite dictator in history."

"His office is in the back of a hair salon. One of those places with faded glamor shots from forty years ago in the windows that never seems to have any customers but still stays open."

Sach held up crossed fingers. "Now I really want to find this guy."

"Me too. Something to ask Jasmine when I interview her." I drummed my fingers on the table. "We've got two different demons who both eat lichen to spread their evil, and both use Crackle as a delivery mechanism. There's one other thing." I paused. "The shedim killed herself."

"That's weird," Sachie said, returning to her seat. "It wasn't in the report."

"Michael didn't think it was relevant," I said snippily.

"Is it? So long as she's dead."

I shook my head. "I don't like it. The shedim was wounded, down for the count. But instead of some last-ditch attack, she kills herself."

"A fuck-you?"

"Or pride, I guess, but right before she died, the shedim proclaimed she wasn't going back. Maccabees don't arrest demons, so what was she hoping to avoid?"

"You sure you heard her properly? You were concussed."

"I heard her," I said in a frustrated growl. It was bad

49

enough my best friend was dismissing my concerns but coming on the heels of Michael insisting it didn't matter, that my insights and observations were of no relevance here, it was hard to keep my cool.

"Hey." Sach touched my shoulder. "You lived through a horrible, senseless situation. It's normal to be looking for a way for it to make sense, but some overwrought demon declaration may not be it. Maybe you aren't remembering it correctly."

I brushed her hand off me with a sharp jerk.

"You were injured and in the middle of a battle," she said. "Or she was confused. I mean, she was so weak she hadn't bothered to escape while she was in the cage. She could have been worried you were going to put her back in it and keep starving her."

"I can't stop thinking about it."

"Like a compulsion?" Sach tried to check my temperature with the back of her hand to my forehead. "Could you have gotten the tiniest drop of her urine on you and it's tearing you apart psychologically, instead of physically? Do you want to go back to Sarah or a healer?"

"Absolutely not." Any doubts about my mental acuity and I'd be sidelined. "You're probably right that the suicide was born of starvation and confusion." I checked my notes, moving on. "The lab setup was suitable for manufacturing small batches of synthetic Crackle in a small distribution chain, but they brought a shedim in. That implies bigger plans, more dangerous ones."

Sachie whistled. "You thinking they're working for one of the vamp mobs?"

Vampires had long ago folded most human Mafias into their own organizations.

"That might explain how they were matched with this demon. Vamps know about shedim. Who controls Revelstoke?"

My friend snorted. "No one that I've heard of. Unless we have a secret snowshoeing vampire Mafia on our hands."

"Which means Jasmine's crew could have reached out to any mob, anywhere."

Sachie spun a tiny white dreidel on the table, grimacing when it landed on the Hebrew letter "shin," which would have required her to pony up a coin for the pot. "Let's divvy up vamp mobs by territory, crosschecking for any drug busts involving shedim."

"We can start in the last ten years and go from there."

It was a good plan, but hours later, after many more cups of coffee, a questionable package of beef jerky, and a late-night hailstorm, we were no closer to answers. We'd taken a number of dance breaks, however, a practice implemented by Darsh on our last case to shake off brain fog.

"I wish Jasmine would wake up," Sachie said. "She might have something to contribute on the subject."

That made one of us, because I was relieved the Eishei Kodesh woman remained in shock and under guard, unable to mention Cherry Bomb's presence at the lab. Right now, Edward's death and all the injuries were attributed to Bratwurst, but if it came out that there was another shedim, even a half-human one present? A shudder ran through me.

It was thanks to me that Paul, Francesca, and Jasmine were rescued, but even so the director—my own mother—disapproved of Cherry's suspected appearance in this case, and that was merely in regards to how I'd kept *myself* safe. Others would conflate Cherry with the injuries. I wasn't about to muddy the role I'd played with unfair allegations, speculation—or worse.

What could I say? Shedim self-preservation instincts were outstanding.

"Hopefully Jasmine will become conscious soon," I agreed. I think I sounded believable. I spun one of the dreidels, which landed on "gimmel." Winner takes all. "We need a different way to investigate. Just because we haven't busted anyone and don't have any official reports doesn't mean the vamps aren't a part of this."

Sach stretched her neck. "If only we knew someone with crazy hacking abilities who could dive into channels we can't access? Someone who is also a Maccabee and could be authorized to work with us?"

I laughed, the thought of Michael's and Darsh's heads-exploding reactions to this idea filling me with delight.

The director might be the one person who wanted Ezra to stay far from Vancouver more than I did, and her feelings about the Prime extended to his vampire best friend. To be fair, Silas was lovely, the personification of Southern charm, but for Michael, he was guilty by association. As for Darsh? His utter indifference to any mention of Silas these past two months made Sach's reaction to Olivier seem embarrassingly eager.

I smirked. "If only."

Sach and I agreed that our best chance at having Michael sign off on Silas working with us was to wait until tomorrow to ask her. She was always in a great mood on the day of the Hanukkah party, and the fact that she'd be distracted with everything she had to attend to didn't hurt either.

We cornered Michael's assistant, Louis, bright and early Tuesday morning.

I stood there, stone-faced with my arms crossed, while Sachie convinced him to let us speak to the director.

Louis played guard dog against everyone wanting a moment of Michael's precious time, but he was most aggressive about it with me. He knew what case we were investigating and given what had happened, he should have ushered us right in, instead of acting like Michael's speech for the Hanukkah party was of paramount importance. Half the operatives would be hammered by the time she gave it, and honestly, she gave some variation on the same one every year. She was a good speaker, but only the Maccababies hung off every word.

I didn't thank him when he finally relented. I didn't strangle him by his stupid skinny tie either, so I was still the bigger person.

Michael jabbed her index finger at her monitor. "There are only so many ways to describe light vanquishing darkness. Give me some good news to inspire me."

We filled Michael in on everything: the lichen, how the self-mutilation compulsion had been transmitted via urine, and that this was a copycat demon.

"That's all we need." Michael pressed down the silver foil on a dented edge of the menorah on her desk. "Other demons with those abilities connecting with humans to manufacture various drugs."

I'd made that menorah out of modeling clay when I was seven years old, painstakingly covering each holder in aluminum foil, and putting a glittery six-pointed gold star on the raised back. My mother inexplicably trotted it out every single year, setting it among the neatly stacked folders on her desk in a place of pride.

I swallowed through my thick throat. It had been a long time since I'd received that same delighted smile as when I presented her with that gift.

She definitely wasn't going to don it once we asked her to approve Silas. Hence the reason for Sach's and my heated rock, paper, scissors battle earlier to determine who'd be stuck as the designated speaker.

Michael adored Sachie, so I doubted she'd suffer the fate common to messengers.

"Speaking of manufacturing," Sachie said, "Aviva and I have come up with another aspect of this case that we believe should be investigated."

Michael motioned impatiently for us to get on with it, her focus half on her speech.

"We want to rule out the involvement of vamp mobs," I said. "It might be how Jasmine and the shedim were paired up and factor into proposed distribution plans."

"That's fair. You have my permission. Any available vamp operatives can help."

"Not just the local Mafias," Sachie said. "But the larger players globally."

"Like Natán Cardoso's?" Michael raised her eyebrow. "Something you want to tell me, Aviva?"

My hands clenched into fists. With great weariness of soul and incredible self-control, I unclenched them. "No," I said pleasantly. "I haven't spoken to Ezra since he left the Maccabees and I'd certainly never keep dangerous intel like that from you."

But also, how dare she jump to that conclusion?

"This is honestly a general theory we both think is worth pursuing," I said.

"All right, but you want something. What is it?"

I nervously licked my lips, my heart pounding in my ears.

That was my heart, right? And not the fake Sire's Spark stuffed deep in my purse in my locker downstairs that I swear was beating like something out of a story by Poe. I was positive Michael could hear it and had cottoned on to what I had planned for later.

Sachie shot me a weird look.

I stopped listening for a steady thumping shivering up from the floorboards.

"Uh…" Sach glanced at me for help, but I'd earned my silence when I won our game. Thank you, years of friendship, for my savvy psychological insights that my friend would throw scissors. Though given all the blades hidden on her person, it wasn't all that insightful.

Michael crossed her arms. "Spit it out, Operative Saito."

"Allow Silas to dig into it with us."

Michael laughed bitterly. "Are the two of you trying to kill me?"

"He isn't part of the Copper Hell," I said.

"No," Michael said, "he's just best friends with Natán's son, a Prime who wormed his way into the Maccabees to play spy, then went scorched earth with years of dangerous secrets in his possession to align himself with a shedim."

"The Maccabees haven't taken action against Ezra, so they're at least neutral about his decision." I said this with certainty, but it was a total fishing expedition.

She rooted around in her desk drawer for something, didn't find it, and shut the drawer harder than necessary. "They can't take action against someone who doesn't leave the Copper Hell."

I flinched. "You mean the plan *is* to kill him?"

Even Sachie gasped.

Darsh had thought it a possibility, but when Ezra was left alone all this time, I'd relaxed. Michael's pronouncement now made all those fears come rushing back.

"The Authority is waiting to see what Ezra does when he leaves the yacht," Michael said. "If his business doesn't interfere or harm ours in any way, there won't be an issue. However, if he forces their hand…" She fiddled with the menorah I'd made. "Well, there's no point speculating before then."

I gripped the armrests.

"Silas is still a Maccabee," Sachie said, "and he has

55

skills and connections we need. Ones our local vampire operatives don't."

Michael pressed her lips so tightly together they were nothing more than a white slash of disapproval.

"Michael," I said evenly, focusing on something I could control, "the reason you're sitting in this director's chair is because you rooted out unthinkable corruption in our organization, a group dedicated to fighting evil. You trusted your gut about that belief and amassed the proof you needed."

"Proof I wished had given me the opposite outcome," Michael said.

"Still," I said, "once the idea was in your head, you of all people couldn't ignore it. No matter how unthinkable it was. If the bigger vamp mobs are seeking out demon secretions to produce drugs, this will have terrible consequences, which is why we can't ignore it. You've always told me how hard it was to fight corruption alone. We need Silas."

"Hopefully we'll find the proof to rule it out," Sachie added.

Michael exhaled slowly and deeply. "Fine."

My gut uncramped. A bit. Part of what made Michael such a great leader was her ability to accept and act on new information without a lot of bluster or denial, but I hadn't expected her to green-light Silas this quickly.

"He's working out of the Tokyo chapter," I said. "And if it helps, he hates Natán."

"You're still in touch with Silas," she said flatly. "How lovely. And you want *me* to arrange the transfer with Director Abe. Are there any other Hanukkah miracles you'd like me to manifest?"

"Nope." Sachie grinned at her. "Thank you, Michael."

"Uh-huh. Go away and let me finish my speech."

We'd gotten Michael's approval to bring Silas here. If

vamp mobs were using shedim, that would be a whole other can of worms, but one that the Maccabees would throw all their resources behind.

As for Ezra? Hopefully he'd stay walled up at the Copper Hell. Out of sight, out of mind.

I left my mother muttering metaphors about vanquishing darkness, wondering what this year's speech would sound like.

Chapter 6

Sachie and I phoned Silas from our conference room downstairs in the Spook Squad. I put my cell on speaker while Sach shut the door. None of the other vamps were around yet, and the rooms were soundproofed against their super hearing, but they were so damn stealthy, and this contact was need to know only.

By which I meant Darsh would need to know only when Silas was about to walk through the door, in order to ensure our maximum entertainment at their reunion.

"Are you calling to beg off our next Scrabble game?" Silas teased in his slow, thick Southern drawl. "I'm mighty touched by your thoughtfulness, and I could be convinced if you'd like to be saved from further shame."

The vamp had invited Sach and me into a series of online Scrabble games with him after Ezra decamped for the Copper Hell. We never discussed the elephant in the room, our conversations a mix of trash talk and getting to know each other better, but this was his way of making sure I was okay.

"Not all of us read the dictionary for fun, you weirdo," Sachie snarked, though she was smiling.

"That's why I win," he said smugly.

"Just you wait," I threatened darkly.

"I'll hold my breath." He chuckled. "Seriously, though, what did y'all need?"

We filled him in on the Crackle case and our concerns over mob involvement.

A text notification popped up on my screen.

Sachie ground her teeth as I hurriedly dismissed the message to deal with after the call.

"Yikes," Silas said. "Yeah, if any of the Mafias are pursuing this, we need to shut them down fast. I'll hop on a plane as soon as Director Abe approves my transfer. Meantime, I'll poke around and see what I find. Sound good?"

I'd rather he just teleported here now—which wasn't a thing—but I couldn't demand he drop everything, the director's approval be damned. "That's perfect, thanks so much."

Sachie added that she was looking forward to seeing him again and we disconnected. She crossed her arms and glared at me. "A text, huh?"

"It's Hanukkah tonight." I quickly answered the message. "Obviously, they were going to send their greetings."

When Sach achieved her longtime goal of joining the Spook Squad, she'd had a very explosive and rare fight with her parents. Ben and Reina never wanted their daughter to be a Maccabee in the first place, going so far as to try to bribe her with a condo if she'd pick a less dangerous career path. My friend stuck to her guns. She still got the condo.

There'd been zero arguments during that era, and Ben and Reina had even gotten to the point of celebrating Sachie's accomplishments.

Not this one though. The three of them hadn't spoken for two months.

"It wasn't just holiday greetings. Mom asked about your injuries. That implies regular contact." Sach, in typical fashion, refused to discuss her feelings, though I could tell how much it bothered her. Their distance was like a splinter constantly lodged under her skin, but she wouldn't let me help get it out.

"I spent as much time at your place growing up as mine," I said. "My regular contact with them is not news. I love your parents and I'm not cutting them out of my life. This isn't some playground fight, Sach, where I pick sides. It's not a divorce either. Give them time to come to terms with their only child fighting vamps and shedim on the regular."

"Oh, you've picked your side."

I threw my hands up. "You're being as stubborn as they are. All of you are miserable. Maybe if you actually talked to them about the kinds of cases—"

Aaand she was gone, stomping through the main room back to the elevator.

I waited a few moments before going to grab my stuff from my locker. Other than a skeleton staff of level one operatives to handle any crises, everyone else was knocking off early to get ready for tonight's party. Dusk fell around 4:30PM, which was when the lighting ceremony would be held.

Sach had likely gone home to change. Slinging my purse with the fake Sire's Spark over my jacket, I used the excuse of giving her space to undertake part two of my plan for this artifact.

Michael would be at the hotel, inspecting the ballroom. She'd rented a room for her hair and makeup artists to get her ready for the party like always, which meant her condo was empty.

I still had a bullshit excuse ready about why I'd dropped by in case she was there, but it wasn't necessary. I didn't bother turning on the lights in her foyer. The curtains were open and besides, I'd followed this exact path into her study many times in the past couple months.

Some might call it obsession with the crystal; I called it double-checking a potentially dangerous artifact was locked away until I verified its exact function.

I opened the safe. The real Sire's Spark sat there undisturbed since the last time I'd come to visit—I mean, check on it. I sliced open the tape on the box containing my dummy artifact and dumped the fake into my palm.

Was stealing Sire's Spark from Michael really the best course of action? I'd spent countless hours since I'd come up with this plan talking myself in to and out of it.

Michael had a heavy-duty wall safe mounted behind a lovely painting of the Icelandic sky, whereas mine was smaller and bolted to the floor in my closet, hidden under a jumble of purses.

My gut insisted that having possession of the real artifact was best for me, but what if I wasn't the only one affected by it?

Roman Whittaker had admitted to killing those half shedim to make vamps untouchable. The undead were already immortal and super enhanced. This need for more was just greedy.

The missing blood was key to that, likely if used with a power word in a dark magic ritual. Was Sire's Spark also part of that ritual or was its "blood calls to blood" properties a way to detect other infernals?

I didn't have the whereabouts of the half-shedim blood or any idea what the power word was, but I did have this crystal. The problem was, if it *could* be used to amplify vampire abilities, then was it wise to remove it from Michael's safe?

As far as I knew, Trad cops weren't looking for this sole artifact still missing from the gallery theft, but the fact remained that at least one person had wanted it badly enough to kill for it. Rukhsana had taken care of the man who'd murdered the thief, but if this crystal did further vampire invincibility, others were looking for it.

I hefted the false crystal I'd purchased from the store on Granville Island, my eyes narrowed. Both my mother and I lived in secure towers with top-notch electronic security systems and magic wards, thanks to mezuzahs on our personal condos.

Those prayer scrolls wrapped in a decorative case were affixed to the doorways of Jewish homes because they were powerful prayer spells to keep the forces of evil at bay. The ones that Maccabees had access to were even stronger. After all, they'd kept Delacroix from accessing my place via a bathroom portal. Though they didn't keep him from speaking to me through the portal. I made a note to look into upgrades.

Maccabees could drag demons across those wards—though it hurt the fiends—but they couldn't get in of their own volition. Luckily, half shedim had no problem crossing. A point in our favor that our humanity trumped any inherent evil.

However, if the wards barred the way of that powerful shedim, they'd keep the real Sire's Spark safe. My condo was secure. Decision made (yet again), I swapped the real crystal for the fake one, locked up, and left.

Sachie wasn't around when I got home. Too bad. I'd wanted our spat over with before the party. My desire to protect her relationship with her parents—a dynamic so opposite to anything I'd ever had that I used it as a blueprint for any kids in my future—didn't give me leave to push Sachie back into speaking to Ben and Reina.

I unzipped my boots and slid them off, then hung my coat in our small front closet. Sach had to work through this as much as her parents did.

Meantime, I'd apologize and support her.

I flicked on my bedroom light, casting a soft glow over dreamy blue walls that matched the tumble of wildflowers on my duvet cover. I allowed myself only a single longing glance at the splash of crimson on my white pillowcase.

It wasn't the blood of my enemies. Oh, if only. It would be much less complicated that way. No, the carefully folded bundle was the soft-as-angel-wings sweater that Ezra had knitted for me, gifting me with it right before he left for the Copper Hell. It was freshly laundered, smelling of the "soft linen" scent I'd used to scrub all traces of Ezra's cardamom, cloves, and bergamot cologne that mingled with the fresh, cool whisper of a summer breeze that always lingered on his skin.

If I slept in it once or three times a week, it was only because my room got cold at night. I stilled. Was Ezra cold at night or did the newly minted Lord of the Copper Hell have his pick of bodies to keep him warm?

I slammed my purse on my high gloss dresser. It wasn't the sweater's fault that my ex was a lying liar, spouting all that bullshit about laying siege and getting me back. Mi cielo, my ass.

Ezra was persona non grata in my life, and I gave as good as I got. Actually, everyone at Vancouver HQ treated him that way, and honestly? Given the rampant gossip and interest when my chapter learned Ezra was an operative, the total lack of speculation about his absence now was curious.

It was almost as if everyone else had gotten a very sternly worded memo ordering them on pain of death to forget he ever existed. (Not that they had. I'd checked with my friend, Dr. Malika Ayad, the Maccabee coroner. No magic forget-him spell either. That, at least, would have been useful.)

Only Ezra's fans, his Ezracurriculars, were speculating on his decreased media presence with theories of him going off-grid for a mob hit to him shacking up with—insert hot famous woman—at a secluded love nest. It would have been amusing, a joke to share with Ezra, had he bothered to be in touch.

But no, my ex had made his choice, and even if he'd reached out, I'd have politely declined further contact. I was a Maccabee. I had career goals, none of which would be furthered by my association with the co-owner of one of the most notorious and untrackable gambling hubs of the modern and, I guess, Victorian eras, the Copper Hell.

I snatched my hand away, ceasing my stroking of the sweater, and went into the bathroom to pee, though first I checked my reflection to see if my good hair day was still going strong.

It was, but I jerked back because the glass in the mirror was melting like one of Dalí's clocks. To a normal person, the red and purple portal pulsing behind the runny surface of the glass would have been terrifying. To me, it was still terrifying, but this, at least, was a familiar horror.

I glared at it. "Not now."

"Refusing an invitation before it's even been issued?" Delacroix's disembodied voice said. There was the sound of the shedim taking a deep drag on a cigarette. "Where have your manners gone, girl detective?"

I definitely required a portal allowing one hundred percent less demon communication.

The mezuzah was protecting me and this portal wasn't the black mesh one that led to the Copper Hell. It led to Flaming Flapjacks.

Sadly, the destination was not what made my heart drop into my feet. Or, maybe it was. Maybe if it *did* lead to the Hell but had been issued by a supposedly deadly vampire who'd grown some balls, I'd feel just fine with its presence.

"I have to be somewhere," I said curtly.

"Somewhere more paramount than breakfast? It's the most important meal of the day."

"It's the middle of the afternoon here."

"Brimstone Breakfast Club doesn't adhere to Pacific Standard Time, girlie. My statement stands." Delacroix snapped his fingers. "Move it."

"Delighted as I am that you want to reconnect—"

"As you should be."

"Tonight is the first night of Hanukkah." I attempted to touch up my blush, but the runny mirror made it challenging to find my cheekbones. "Dusk is in less than an hour and I need to get ready and across town for a lighting ceremony. Rain check."

"Rain check?" He sounded gobsmacked. Even the portal rippled as though in shock at my refusal.

"Yes." I nodded firmly, though I wasn't sure he could see me. I grimaced. Given he kept opening the portal in my bathroom, he better not have been able to see me. I certainly didn't see beyond the red and purple magic, so fingers crossed, I was safe from prying eyes. "I'm not missing that ceremony for you or anyone else. Skip past the threats and accept it."

The portal expanded threateningly to encompass one entire wall.

"Rain check," I insisted over the thundering of my heart.

There was a low growl and then the portal winked out.

I didn't have time to worry about why demon daddy had initiated contact with me again, because I really was on a tight deadline. After I destressed my bladder and washed my hands, I dressed and touched up my makeup, pleased that my hair continued to look fabulous with dark juicy curls.

I was sitting on the tufted bench at the foot of my bed, fastening the clasp of a dark green choker to complement my silky dress in the same color when I saw the beaded earrings I'd purchased sitting on my side table. They were totally unsuitable for this ensemble, but it kicked me into gear to switch necessary items for tonight from my regular purse to my clutch.

My last item of business was to lock the real Sire's Spark up nice and tight.

Artifact in hand, I padded across the plush carpet, knelt down in front of my open closet door, knocking aside purses, and unlocked the safe.

Sire's Spark didn't feel any different than the bogus crystal I'd left at Michael's place. There wasn't a handy thrum of magic coursing through it. Had I accidentally brought the fake version home? No. I'd paid attention to which was which. Except, now that the thought was in my head, I couldn't squelch that tiny niggle of doubt.

There was one way to check, because if the real crystal was powerful, it had to be activated.

I traced a finger over one of the octagonal edges.

Do it.

I shook away Cherry's encouragement. She couldn't compel me to do anything, it was more like when I stood at the top of the high diving board, looking down at how far the water seemed with my toes poking off the edge of the board. My breath would be harsh in my ears and most of me wanted to turn around and walk safely down to ground level, but damn, that water was shimmery, and the rush of air and cool splash would feel so good. Yet, I'd still stand there until something in me said jump. And I did.

That said, while yes, Sire's Spark's magic should be tested, I'd do it under highly controlled circumstances and certainly not when I was headed for a party full of operatives to—

I flinched, gaping at the dot of blood on my lightly throbbing finger courtesy of my shedim claw. My pulse fluttered madly in my throat. *Cherry, you asshole!*

My inner demon gave me the equivalent of a bored hair flip. *I'm saving us both the bullshit.*

It would be so much easier if Cherry Bomb, the Brimstone Baroness, was really a separate entity inside me and I could blame any untoward or reckless actions on her, but as I'd explained to my mother on more than one occasion, I wasn't her mindless puppet. Since we were one and the same, I had free will and self-control where my darling inner voice was concerned. She could say jump, but ultimately I was the one choosing to leap.

Case in point: *I absolutely did not have to* press the drop of blood against Sire's Spark and see if it activated. I chose to, because after all this time obsessing about how dangerous it was, I had to know firsthand.

Nothing happened. Part of me had wished I'd get some cool new power, but I didn't feel any different than usual. I couldn't crush the crystal in my fist and I didn't hear anything through the wall I shared with our neighbor. There wasn't even a faint hum or vibration off the artifact.

My blood hadn't activated it after all. Was it just a pretty paperweight and this situation was like the demon suicide? Was I convinced there was something to obsess over, when this was another non-starter?

The alarm I'd set on my phone sounded and I hastily locked the (probably real) crystal up.

I took a cab across town to the botanical gardens since Uber wanted ridiculous amounts of money at this time of day. The lush oasis in the heart of Vancouver was criss-crossed by paths that wound along multiple lakes and tiny waterfalls, over small bridges, through meditation gardens, and past thousands of varieties of plant life from around the world.

My favorite place bar none had always been the hedge maze. Michael would sit on one of the benches overlooking the entrances and exits, her face turned up to the sun, while I ran in and out to my heart's content.

The taxi pulled up to Garden Hall, a huge, stunning building designed to mimic the petals of a British Columbia orchid with a central atrium as its heart. The single-story structure felt spun of glass with a swoopy living green roof, the entire space blending into the surrounding landscape.

I paid the cabbie, transfixed by the fairylike glow of the hall.

"Have fun in there," the driver said.

"Thanks. I will."

For all the serenity out here, the inside was a mad crush. Tasteful classical music provided by a quartet in some unseen corner was almost drowned out by all the operatives catching up with friends and colleagues. Though the feeling of being inside a flower was emphasized by the soaring wooden ceiling slats that undulated high overhead.

I plucked a glass of prosecco off a tray held by a gloved server in a crisp white shirt and black pants and pushed my way into the dolled-up crowd, headed for the dais, which held a large menorah on a tall base. I wanted a front row seat to the lighting of the first night's candle.

Every year, Michael chose one operative to do the honor. I hadn't been picked yet, but that was okay. It would happen one day. Sachie had done it a couple of years back and it was adorable how nervous my stoic, unflappable friend had been. She'd practiced the first night prayers for a solid week, even though she'd sung them with Michael and me at our house on many a Hanukkah, the same way I spent Christmas with her family.

Nasir was the lucky recipient this year. According to Darsh, his Spook Squad colleague had taken the decision with the same excitable enthusiasm that he greeted everything with. Anyone convinced vamps were uniformly world-weary or constantly menacing would be pleasantly surprised by Nasir.

My progress was slow going, but since it was to exchange greetings with operatives I hadn't seen in a while, I was happy to hang out and eat every single delicious appetizer offered to me. There'd be a full buffet laid out for us later, but it was best to warm up my belly.

Besides, Michael would announce when it was time to light the candles.

After a particularly hilarious conversation with a few of my colleagues about a recent IT snafu, this feeling of hope swelled up inside me that I could come clean about Cherry and still enjoy this easy camaraderie.

My set-in-stone plan had been to become a level three and then spend at least another decade making a name for myself as a force for good. Then, and only then, I'd planned to reassess the timeline for revealing Cherry. Having a plan was supposed to comfort me and act as a beacon to guide me through tough moments. Instead, I just felt more lost than ever.

Acceptance for my half-shedim self felt so far off, I couldn't even imagine it.

We'd gathered to celebrate the miracle of light, but what if, instead of seeking some steady flame of acceptance, it was the tiny pinpricks of friendship that would eventually blaze up in support?

Was tonight the night I struck that first match of trust and told Sachie what I was? A smile blossomed over my face. Yeah. I think it was.

I was chatting with Malika about her daughter's soccer scholarship when Michael called for our attention. Spying a familiar candy-pink head, I excused myself and slipped through a gap to join Sachie in front of the dais.

I nudged her. "About before? I'm really sorry. I had no business butting in."

She nudged me back, resplendent in a black tux complete with bowtie. "Considering you're my parents' non-biological alternative girl child, it's okay. I'll talk to them soon. Ish. Probably."

She needed time. I didn't. Her conflict with her parents pressed home that I could stand to be more open about my own situation. I'd hate to die and not know if my most important people still thought I was important back if I was a half shedim.

I grinned into my glass of prosecco. I'd be speaking with Sach about a long overdue subject when we got home later.

"Hey, pipe down," a male voice grumbled from my other side. "Some of us care about the reverence of this moment."

"Mason!" I hugged him.

The retired Vietnamese Canadian forensics expert allowed it for three whole seconds. I was totally one of his favorite human beings. After his memory was wiped on the case involving the staked Prime, Mason had walked away from his career. Happily, he had no regrets and was living it up in retirement, but it was still great to see him now.

We caught up while Michael and Nasir conferred at

the menorah. She handed Nasir the lighter and clapped her hands to quiet the crowd. When that didn't work, she put two fingers in her mouth and let out an ear-splitting whistle.

The silence was immediate.

Michael smiled innocently at us.

Nasir lit the shamash candle, the one in the middle position, whose holder was raised slightly higher than the rest. Shamash, which translated from the Hebrew as "helper," was used each night to light the rest of the candles in the hanukkiah. That's exactly what Nasir did now, touching its small flame to the wick of the single candle in the rightmost position.

While Hanukkah candles were placed from right to left (same as Hebrew was written), they were lit from left to right. It was irrelevant for the first night though.

Nasir sang the prayers in a charmingly off-key voice, grinning the entire time. He placed the shamash back in its elevated spot, where it would naturally burn out, just like the regular candles.

There was a moment of silence after he finished, then the entire room broke out into a loud roar of "Happy Hanukkah" and much cheek kissing.

Nasir got a lot of back slaps and high fives when he stepped off the dais.

Michael indulged everyone for a few moments, then she held up her hand. This time, we fell quiet without the whistle. Her speech was very nice. Sure, it mentioned light and darkness blah blah blah, but it was mostly about all of us coming together with a higher purpose, how important we were to this fight, and how grateful she was for each and every one of us.

More than a few people surreptitiously wiped tears out of their eyes.

Best of all, it was short.

She raised her champagne flute. "Chag sameach to us all. Now eat, drink, and be merry!"

"Chag sameach," we all echoed back.

After the horror of the other night, I, for one, was ready to wrap myself in all the light and laughter possible. Time to party.

Chapter 7

I was texting Happy Hanukkah to Ezra's cousin, Orly, when someone jabbed me in the small of my back, almost causing me to spill my—third? fourth?—glass of prosecco. I looked up at the culprit, expecting a drunken smile and apology.

Instead, I found myself on the receiving end of two glaring brownish-gold eyes and a ferocious scowl.

"You invited him here?" Darsh poked me in the chest.

I rubbed my boob. "Sach!"

My bestie grinned tipsily at me from behind the vamp. "It's a party. I shared the good news." She held up her highball glass. "L'chaim!"

Orly returned my holiday greetings, adding that she'd binged the crime drama I recommended. She texted a recommendation for a new show to watch next.

We'd met on the murdered infernals case that brought Ezra back into my life. I'd mistaken her for his romantic partner, but though she was the person he loved most in the world, she was a sister to him. She was also a wealthy, gorgeous, multilingual economist. It would have been easy to hate her, but Orly was funny, kind, and a pure joy to spend time with. Sach, Darsh, and I were happily getting to know her better.

"Well?" Darsh huffed. "Silas?"

I shoved my glass at him to hold while I put my phone back in my clutch. Then I tucked the purse under my arm and took my drink back. "I thought you didn't care if you ever saw him again."

"He made me text him."

I faked a gasp, my hand flying to my mouth. "That monster."

"I don't like texting. Or phone calls." No, Darsh preferred in-person communication where he could read body language and more fully assess for threats. Not that texting Silas back was a threat.

It was a tactical maneuver.

I'd really hoped that once the investigation that had brought Silas into our lives had wrapped up, that he and Darsh would go their separate ways. Darsh was a hell of a mensch, but the guy was also a hit-and-run repeat offender and Silas wasn't built like that.

"You could have used your words and said no," Sachie pointed out.

"Silas is so..." Darsh grimaced. "Upbeat and relentlessly personable. Ignoring him or just not engaging at the same level felt like kicking a puppy."

"What's your point?" I sipped my prosecco to tamp down any frustration. Silas was a grown-up—and the size of a mountain range, but he was so sweet. While we'd met only a couple of months ago, he triggered my protective instincts, even against one of my best friends.

"My point?" Darsh swiveled from side to side as if seeking affirmation from bystanders that I was clearly an idiot.

Sachie shrugged.

Darsh narrowed his eyes. "My point is that I engaged in certain behaviors—"

"Texting," Sach said. "Mild flirting. Not even sexting yet. We'd know, since you do love to dish."

"*Certain behaviors*," Darsh continued through clenched teeth, "believing we'd eventually meet up somewhere neutral for a one-time encounter and get any attraction out of our systems before I would return—"

"Flee," Sachie said in a cough.

I nudged her with a "quit provoking him" glower.

A red haze descended over Darsh's eyes for a second before he wrangled himself back into control. "I would *return* to my own territory many, many miles away from his."

Where he'd ghost Silas.

I sucked back more booze. Ever since Darsh had told me about losing his brother, and the visible grief I witnessed him still battling decades later, his insane inability to engage further with any romantic potentials once the deed was done made sense.

Romantic feelings obviously weren't the same as fraternal love, but they still involved being vulnerable.

Darsh could happily pursue a guy for weeks, but any intimacy after the physical act made his walls slam into place and cartoon puffs of smoke trail in his wake as he bolted. His heartbreak had never fully healed, preventing him from using that muscle anymore.

Especially since he didn't need it to breathe. One side of my mouth kicked up.

He jabbed his finger at me. "You've screwed every-thing up by inviting Silas onto my home turf and turning all the fine groundwork I laid into a hangman's noose."

"A bit dramatic, don't you think?" I placed my empty glass on a high bistro table. "Silas is our friend, not one of your disposable boy toys. Act responsibly."

"Avi's right." Sachie nodded. "No sneaking out and blocking his number. Silas deserves better. Or don't sleep with him at all."

"Yes." I pointed at Sach. "That last bit."

"I don't sneak," Darsh said haughtily. "I leave them better than I found them."

I snorted.

Sach pressed a hand to her heart. "Parting is such sweet sorrow," she proclaimed theatrically.

I screwed up my face. "Is it though?"

"But now this Silas situation will be messy and dramatic." Darsh flung his hair off his shoulders. "I hate that."

"You live for drama," I countered.

"Not when it's mine," he hissed. He spun sharply on his heel and stalked off.

Darsh was one hundred and fifty percent there for Sachie and me, but our friendship had never required him making himself vulnerable. In fact, he'd always been quite tight-lipped with personal details. (Except sexual conquests. Those didn't count. Enough said.)

Until he told us about Patrin. That had been a huge step, but Sach and I had built up trust with Darsh over a couple of years and no one else, not even Silas, held a spot in that delicate inner circle.

Sach propped her elbow on my shoulder, an irritating habit of my taller bestie. "Darsh likes Silas."

I shrugged off her arm. "Are you that surprised? Silas impressed the honky-tonk out of Darsh when we worked that infernal case together."

"Yeah," Sachie admitted, "but it's more than that. They're texting! That's huge for Darsh."

"It's going to be so messy." I sighed.

"We'll help the big idiot through it," Sach said.

"Which one? Darsh, or Silas for engaging when he should clearly know better?"

"Yes." Sach saluted me with her glass and headed off in the same direction as Darsh.

I snagged another flute of prosecco from a passing server's tray, but stilled with it halfway to my mouth, holding out my hand against the rush of nausea that slapped me upside the face. Sweat beaded my temples as I lurched to the closest bar and poured myself a glass of water.

I was the worst about remembering to hydrate. Sadly, two glasses later, my symptoms had only grown worse. I was burning up from inside and had to squint because everything was too bright. Too saturated.

Things looked exactly as they did when I entered Babel, the vampire megacity. I tapped my heel against the polished floor to assure myself that I hadn't somehow transported to another realm, but that wasn't it. I gripped the bar top, attempting to burn the booze out of my system. While this was one of my shedim abilities, sometimes I liked being tipsy and enjoying the same energy as everyone else. This, however, was a little too much. I concentrated on removing the buzz like I normally did.

To my abject horror and embarrassment, it didn't work.

Blotting my forehead, I made my way toward the corridor with the restrooms. Maybe some cold water on my face would fix this.

Excitement from Cherry spiked through me so hard that I swayed.

"Jesus, Fleischer," Gemma said with a sneer. This was one of the few times the operative was just standing there like a normal person, elegant in a cream sheath dress and pearls, instead of exercising or stretching. "Pace yourself."

I opened my mouth to give her a snarky retort when the next spike of excitement made me slam my hand against the wall for balance.

"What are you, mommy's little rager? Get a grip." Gemma rolled her eyes and walked away. All compassion, that one.

Still, I was relieved she was gone, because Cherry Bomb got this enthusiastic only in the presence of grave danger, usually shedim-based. Had a demon targeted a room full of Maccabees? Was there a glamored staff member?

Had Delacroix come back for me?

I tottered down the hallway toward the bathroom door. Good thing it was in the direction that Cherry pressed me to go, because I was pulled down the corridor to the restrooms as if by a giant hook.

I slid into my blue synesthete vision, my queasiness worsening at being in my regular sight and my Eishei Kodesh one at the same time. Despite my vow to the contrary, I couldn't stop myself from illuminating weaknesses in every Maccabee I passed. I issued silent apologies for violating their privacy, but I couldn't seize control of my magic. Though after I spied a navy swath in one operative's testicles, I dropped my eyes to the carpet.

This was another reason I didn't illuminate my colleagues. I didn't want to know that they had a medical issue requiring attention, because there was nothing I could do about it. People did not appreciate me walking up to them and saying "Get a mammogram," no matter how much I tried to ease into the message. Ask me how I knew.

There was another door right before the restrooms, and I entered the smaller room before I fully processed what I was doing, blinking at the woman in the bright red coat with her back to me.

Thanks to my synesthete vision and shedim magic, the shifting blue shadows swimming in the back of her head in her hindbrain (the primal part responsible for survival, drive, and instinct) were clear as day. They marked her as a fellow half demon.

This was it. This was what Sire's Spark had been leading me toward. I sucked in a breath, the magic pull that had drawn me here now stilled.

The woman turned around.

"Maud?" I rubbed my eyes. My synesthete vision subsided, but my nausea got so bad, I pressed a hand over my mouth, swallowing hard on the taste of bile. "Why aren't you in Hong Kong?"

After Maud Liu, professional poker player and all-around champion in snark, was arrested for kidnapping Calista and going after Delacroix, the two of us came up with a story about how another vamp had compelled her. It had taken some time, but Maud had been cleared and allowed to leave Vancouver a few weeks ago for home.

I had yet to admit we were related, but I was positive that she suspected. We hadn't kept in touch since I'd snuck out to the airport to say goodbye to her, even though I'd intended to reach out, and I was glad, if confused to see her now.

"I was just coming to find you." Her English had a British lilt common to some Hong Kongers I'd met in Vancouver, but her voice was unusually strained. Normally, she was a glamorous woman, but she wore leggings, and even her natural afro looked deflated. "Who did you tell about me being a half shedim?" she hissed, her eyes wild.

At the words "half shedim" my body vibrated like a tuning fork, and the blue of my synesthete vision flared so brightly it blinded me for a second.

"N-no one." I curled my fingernails into my palms. Oh, shit. Sire's Spark. What a way to confirm that its magic sussed out other half demons.

"Well, someone knows." She pulled her phone out of her pocket and waved it at me. "I'm being blackmailed."

Because being a half shedim was the ultimate dirty laundry.

I pressed my hands against my cheeks. I was burning up. "Show me the correspondence."

It took every ounce of concentration to force my synesthete vision away and read the texts from the blocked number, because the walls were closing in.

"What's wrong with you?" Maud said. "You're sweating like crazy! Are you drunk?"

"Stomach flu," I mumbled. I pulled at the V-neck of my dress to get air into my lungs. "You've never told anyone else what you are?"

Her scathing look should have incinerated me. "What do you think? You're the only living human who knows."

True, and that was because I'd seen her shedim form, not because I'd detected anything amiss. This, right here, was Sire's Spark's doing.

Blood calls to blood. Mine must have activated the magic in Sire's Spark, which infused into me and made me an infernal detector with my blood seeking out hers.

I shivered and wiped my brow again. "Delacroix knows, but he wouldn't bother with blackmail. Not for cash anyway. How much do they want?"

"Ten thousand dollars."

"That's a weird amount." I wobbled over to a stack of chairs and pulled one free, crashing onto it with zero grace. "Do you have that kind of cash?"

"It's only ten grand." She paused. "Canadian."

"Simmer down. Our cash may look like Monopoly money, but ten k isn't exactly chump change for most people." I frowned. "Though it is low for blackmail."

"Who cares about the amount?" She shook my shoulders. "Sober up already and help me!"

The world swung in a nauseating blur.

I knocked her arms off me. "Why does everyone think I'm drunk?"

I simply activated a powerful magic crystal with my blood. Now, I'm some spawn detector, the sister I always wanted makes me feel like puking, and knowing Gemma, she's gleefully dishing about what a sloppy drunk I am.

I'm not sure which part of that horrified me most.

Bing! Bing! We've definitely got a winner for most disturbing aspect, Fleischer. Remember that first bit where you used your blood on a supernatural artifact, blithely confident that you wouldn't end up the same cautionary tale as every single other idiot in myth and legend?

Yeah, well, I figured I'd feel the crystal power up when I did that. That *it* would be the means of detection, not that it would turn me into a tool. However, I'd used my blood on Sire's Spark and detected Maud. Anyone in possession of the crystal wouldn't need actual half shedim to find more of us, just our blood. Say to fuel a dark magic ritual to achieve vamp invincibility?

I bolted up, barely even gagging. Ooh, look at that, I'd acclimatized to the nausea. "This isn't about cash. Your blackmailer has another agenda."

Maud slapped her forehead, her eyes comically wide. "NO. WAY." She snapped her fingers in front of my face. "Could you bring smart Aviva back, please? Because I just spent nine hours on a plane to consult with her before the handover and—"

"First." I shot her the finger. "And second, why is the handover here when you live in Hong Kong?"

"The texts started before I left. They may not have realized I'd gone back home."

"Who besides the Maccabees knew you were here in Vancouver?" I said.

"Some other poker players."

"You entered a tournament while you were under investigation?!"

"Of course not," she said with a toss of her hair. "I played some friendly games against local high rollers." She sneered those last two words.

"Sorry they didn't meet your standards," I fired back. "You should have been keeping a low profile."

"It was a very stressful time." Maud straightened her collar with a sharp tug. "Poker is how I stay calm."

"Exactly. It *was* stressful. What if the tiniest hint of your shedim nature was revealed?"

"Don't insult me. I've built my career projecting nothing other than a blank mask." Her tone was waspish, but she plucked nervously at the sleeve of her coat.

Great. "You should know the worst-case scenario," I said. "I had a case a while back where half shedim were murdered in a ritual killing. Your blackmailer wants your blood and they'll do anything to get it."

Maud swayed slightly, a greenish cast to her cheeks. "Let's avoid that, shall we?"

"When is the meet?"

"It was supposed to be tomorrow night, but they've moved it up. It's in ninety minutes."

"Wow, working with you is never easy, is it?" I blotted the back of my neck. "Any other impossible tasks you need me to do besides catching your blackmailer in record time? Perhaps I could catch a falling star and put it in my pocket?"

A fractious response was already brewing on Maud's lips, I could tell, but we didn't have time to snipe at each other in the bathroom.

"I'm sorry. Rough night on my part." I took a deep breath, relieved that my skin no longer felt like the inside of Satan's ass crack. "We'll catch your blackmailer, but I need to tell Sachie and Darsh."

I'd been trying to curb my impulses to tackle everything on my own. I'd told Sachie when I started searching for the missing half shedim blood and later fessed up to Darsh about my search as well. It would be smart to loop them in now. Besides, the more sympathetic they were to the plight of half shedim, the easier it'd be to break my news to them.

"Forget it." Maud grimaced. "I was just cleared of any wrongdoing. The last thing I need is other Maccabees finding out I'm an infernal and reopening my case."

"What do you think happens when I catch this perp?" I said. "If they're human, I arrest them. That requires you pressing charges."

"Can't you just make them go away?" She swept her hand through the air.

"No," I said, fixing her with a steely glare. "Because I'm not a hitman."

Of course not, Cherry agreed. *Which is why we'll only rough the bastard up a bit.*

I took it under advisement.

Chapter 8

The effects from Sire's Spark had almost worn off, thank fuck. I'd half feared they were permanent, so I was decidedly cheerful.

"You know a hitman though." Maud waved her phone at me. "I don't have the Crimson Prince's number, but you must."

So much for my good mood. "That's not—no—did you miss the part where I was in debt to him? We weren't drinking buddies."

Besides, one did not just ask the assassin one may have pined over to kill someone after they'd sided with one's estranged parent in a misguided attempt to keep one safe. I'm certain that any etiquette books written on the topic would be clear on that point.

"Please." She scoffed. "That was all an act to get you into the Copper Hell."

I crossed my arms. "When did you figure that out?"

"Calm down. You were very believable at the time." That didn't sound patronizing or anything.

"Believable enough that you didn't see me coming," I said. "And the answer is still no. Ezra and I concluded our business. Over. Done. Fini." I brushed my hands together. "Nor do I condone assassinating humans," I added.

After a pause.

The important part was that I clarified my moral stance and Maud understood that my refusal came from my ethics, not because I never intended to speak to my ex again. "If Ezra was the only reason why you came to me—"

She sighed. "It's not. You're the only one I trust."

I got a mushy warmth in my chest. Maud came to me, not as an operative, but because she trusted me.

Yeah, dummy, she knows you're her sister. In my head, Cherry Bomb shot me puppy-dog eyes. *Tell her.*

It never occurred to me that wanting to have a sibling or close friend who was a half shedim wasn't just a human Aviva desire. My demon side craved the connection as well.

After we catch the blackmailer, I assured Cherry.

"I won't tell Sach and Darsh you're a half shedim," I said to Maud, "just that someone is blackmailing you to that effect. You're a public person in a competitive field and the mere rumor of that could ruin your life. Or make you a target. People's prejudices work in our favor here." I patted her shoulder. "I'll get you safely out of this, but I can't do it on my own."

"Because you're drunk," Maud said. But there was no heat in her words, and she mustered up a faint smile.

"Because it could be dangerous, and I trust those two with my life."

"All right," she said. "Hit me with your brilliance."

Maud left shortly after I outlined my plan. After checking that the coast was clear, I escorted her to the exit in the venue's bustling kitchen, watching until she'd disappeared into the shadows in the vast gardens.

Striding past sous-chefs chopping veggies at warp

speed, stirring boiling pots, and plating hors d'oeuvres, I returned along the service hallway and through the door to the rest of the venue.

Sach and I almost bumped into each other just inside the atrium.

"Just the person I—"

She grabbed my arm. "Silas was arrested by Maccabees in Tokyo."

"*What?!* What the fuck is wrong with everyone tonight?"

My friend frantically motioned for me to lower my voice.

The party was in full swing, and no one paid us any attention. Still, I cranked down the volume on my incredulity. "On what charge?"

"Corruption. Using his position to benefit the vampire Mafias."

"That is trumped-up bullshit," I said in a hard voice, my fists clenched at my sides.

"I know. They're trying to get to the Crimson Prince through him." Sachie raked her hands through her hair, her expression tight with frustration. "Michael wandered past me on her phone, mentioning Silas, so I followed to hear what was up."

"And?"

"She took the call in one of the rooms for privacy, but conveniently left the door open."

Typical Michael tactics. Plausible deniability. I motioned for Sachie to get to the important part.

"I don't know what proof Director Abe gave Michael, but he was asking about our involvement," Sach said. "Michael said none of her agents were corrupt, and given how she'd built her career on rooting that out, was he implying she'd gotten stupid or just plain lazy? Either way, she'd be happy to come to Tokyo and discuss it, because she took her reputation very seriously."

I'm not going to Sector A. I'm not going to Sector A. I surreptitiously wiped my sweaty palms on the sides of my dress. "What about the investigation?"

"As far as I can gather, Silas manipulated us into bringing him on this case to control the flow of information and get any insider intel to take back to the vamps. The Authority wants the investigation terminated."

"She's not doing it, is she?" I said urgently.

"Please. She very frostily reminded Director Abe that we had a copycat demon responsible for multiple deaths, including that of a Maccabee." Sach dropped into a bang-on impression of my mother. "'I tasked the pair with learning everything possible about this shedim, including whether vampire mobs are now pairing with demons to produce deadly drugs. However, if you wish to tell Edward's family that his murder isn't worth investigating, Yuto, I'll give you his wife's number.'"

Go Mom.

Some of the tension ebbed from my shoulders. Michael hadn't allowed Sach to hear the call because she was pissed off, but because she didn't want to blindside us with her necessary next step of detaining us for questioning.

We'd have the freedom to continue our investigation, but to discover what brought those charges about, we'd have to maintain an image that was beyond reproach.

What a pain in the ass.

"I take it you got out of there before she finished the call," I said.

"Obviously," Sachie said. "Since I'm not detained."

I checked the time on my phone. An hour and twenty minutes until Maud's meeting with her blackmailer. "How long do you think we can push showing ourselves?"

"Not longer than tomorrow afternoon, and we'd be using one hell of a party hangover excuse. Still, that's enough time to break Silas out. He might be currently in a cell, but they seem pretty determined to make these charges stick, and when they do, they'll stake him."

Vamps, even ones who were operatives, didn't make it to Sector A.

I rose onto tiptoe looking for my mother. "Then he has to be free before Michael pulls us in to formally question us."

She was to our right, so Sach and I went left, taking a roundabout route to the main exit.

Sachie veered us out of the path of a venue employee balancing eight dirty plates. "Those stupid questioning sessions can last hours."

I shook away the offer of another prosecco from the server who stepped into our escape path, though it took all my willpower to not swing by the latkes bar to load up on my way out. I'd been looking forward to those all day. "How will we free Silas? It'll take too long to fly to Tokyo, and even if we get there before anything...bad happens, it's not like we can waltz in and unlock his cell. Not as the unlucky duo who were his last contacts."

"A compromised twosome? That sounds juicy."

I screamed, jumping at Darsh's sudden appearance.

"Don't worry." He slung an arm over our shoulders. "I forgive you for inviting the puppy to town."

Mitigating Darsh's reaction to the other vamp's imprisonment was crucial. It wasn't simply because it was Silas in danger: Darsh despised injustice for anyone.

A couple years back, a Trad couple who owned the local dry cleaners in Darsh's hood asked him if he had any leads on apartments. They were being evicted by the land-lord, who intended to move his daughter into the apartment.

This was perfectly legal, but our city's rental market was low on inventory. The couple wasn't sure that the daughter part was true, or whether the landlord intended to boot them and get more rent from the next poor sap.

Darsh took it upon himself to learn the truth. It took a few months, but he procured photographic evidence that the new tenant wasn't the daughter, instigated a lawsuit against the landlord under a breach of tenancy law, and got them a cash settlement.

It was really nice of him, other than the fact that he threw himself into learning rental law and staking the place out to the point of calling in sick and stepping on the toes of the Trad cops to make things right for this family. He ended up on thin ice with Michael, and given how much leeway she tended to allow Darsh, that was saying something.

Silas's predicament was so much worse. Darsh would freak out if we told him, but standing here at this critical juncture, where I should have lied my way out of this conversation, my mind blanked.

"It's our upstairs neighbors," Sachie said. "Their shower leaked into ours during sex stuff. Just got the call and have to get home." She stepped out of Darsh's hold.

He reeled her back in. "Your mastery of your heart rate is better when you lie now, but not quite there yet. What's going on?"

"We need to get out of here," I insisted, scanning for Michael.

"I'll help, then you'll talk." He sagged between us like he was drunk. "Gap in the crowd. Two o'clock. Gets you directly to the exit."

We "supported" him through the sliding doors onto the sidewalk in front of the venue, where Sachie filled him in on Silas.

Darsh punched a lamppost, denting it.

"We're going to break him out," I said. Maybe Darsh could handle this after all. He was mad, for sure, but he wasn't flying off the handle as much as I'd thought. "Obviously. We're not just going to let this happen."

"Silas will fight you," Darsh snapped. "For all that he's the size of a small pyramid, he has the street smarts of a plastic bag. I bet he's sitting peacefully in a cell trusting that justice will prevail."

"His street smarts are fine," I said, "and I like that he believes in justice, not violence."

Darsh's shoulders slumped. He scrubbed a hand over his face. "So do I, puiul meu."

I blinked at that admission.

"But not when it's a false hope that will get him killed," he said.

"That's why we need someone who can get to Japan faster than any of us," Sachie said. "Someone who might have leverage on the Maccabees from all their own intel gathering for our organization." She fidgeted with her phone, her gaze downcast, then grimaced. "I'm the last person to encourage you to reach out, but we need him."

I threw my head back and screamed, startling an owl in a nearby tree, who hooted loudly back. In the last two months, I'd resisted one drunken, and roughly forty-seven stone-cold sober impulses to call Ezra. He was the one who left. Again. He could contact me.

Besides, I got what I wanted from him and even received a lovely parting gift in the form of my sweater.

I checked the time again. An hour and ten minutes before the meet-up with Maud. I couldn't abandon either my sister or Silas. I swore again.

Sachie peered at me. "Is that a yes?"

"How's this? You call him and I won't throw your phone into traffic."

"Good enough."

I turned to Darsh. "Can you go back in and cover for us? Distract Michael."

"Say I saw you go thataway when you went thisaway?" Darsh mustered up a ghost of a smile. "The band doesn't get to stay together for this gig?"

"No," I said gently, "because the lead singer is liable to trash the venue. Besides, you know Ezra, he's a solo act."

Darsh swore under his breath.

"Ezra will do anything to secure Silas's release," Sachie said. "That's his best friend."

Her words were for Darsh, who reluctantly nodded, but they hit me in the gut, because my idiot ex had an overdeveloped sense of responsibility for the people he cared about. Partnering up with Delacroix to secure my safety was dangerous enough, but at least my demon daddy was getting something out of the deal.

Michael had insisted the Authority was determining their next action depending on what Ezra did, but apparently their patience was limited. By imprisoning Silas, they'd ensured Ezra had no choice. They'd played a hand that allowed them to pounce. There'd be no mercy.

The Maccabees were gunning for Ezra, and we were asking him to willingly step into the line of fire.

"Tell me the second anything changes," Darsh said. "For better or worse." When we promised, he staggered back inside.

Sachie and I left the botanical garden and hit the deserted grounds of the high school across the street to call Ezra, but the oh-so-busy Prime didn't answer. Not Sach's call or her 911 text.

My cell rang and my heart skipped a beat, but it was Michael. I showed Sach the screen, letting the call go to voice mail. It was happening already. I hadn't expected Michael to have to reach out to us until at least after the party. Not a good sign.

She powered down her own cell for when Michael inevitably tried her next. "Avi?"

"I know." I took a deep breath and called Ezra, so my number showed up on his screen.

Except he rang me first. "If Sachie is going to 911 me, tell her to keep her damn phone on," he growled.

Unable to tell if his terseness stemmed from concern or annoyance, I tightened my grip on the phone. *No, I'm not bleeding out in an emergency, thanks so much for asking about my well-being.* I steeled my shoulders. This was about Silas, not me.

From the way Ezra cursed me out after I told him about Silas's arrest, had I been in another explosion, my ex would have stepped over me this time and gone about his day.

"What are you really after?" Ezra said.

"Stopping any other fuck-ups like that bust," I said, putting him on speaker.

Was he sitting in Calista's former office, staring out at the vast expanse of sea? The megayacht housing the Copper Hell wasn't trackable, but both times I'd been on it, it had been night. I looked up at the sky. Were we looking at the same stars?

I stomped any wistful nonsense to dust.

"Investigating the various Mafias in light of that shouldn't have landed Silas in hot water," Ezra said. "Did you tell him anything else?"

"No, but if we had, it's not like any of his devices are tracked or monitored," I said. "Silas wouldn't let anyone get the jump on him."

Sach held up a fist. "Paranoia for the win."

Ezra chuckled. "Right? Hi, Sachie. Sorry you had to hear Aviva and me sniping at each other."

"Better than other stuff I've overheard the two of you engaged in," she said sweetly.

How big was Ezra's bed on the yacht? King-size or—

"Silas's search into vamp mobs triggered some kind of alarm," I said tightly. "Making you as much to blame for this as we are, Cardoso."

"Do tell," he said in a cold voice.

"The Maccabees seized on the perfect excuse to use Silas to get to you. You know, his best friend who defected to play with demons."

"The Maccabees and I are in a détente."

Détente, my ass.

"Drop the snarky face, Aviva," Ezra said.

"This isn't a video call," I snapped. "I'm the picture of professionalism right now, you presumptuous jerk. And you're either naïve or willfully deluded about your status with the Maccabees."

"The Authority is pretending I don't exist so long as I don't cause trouble," he said. "Which I haven't."

"Right," I said. "I'm sure you've been a model of good behavior."

His dark laugh shivered through me.

I wrapped my free arm around myself because my nipples were hard. It was cold. I didn't have a jacket.

Sach shoved my shoulder. "Get your head in the game," she hissed. "Prioritize rescuing Silas."

"Besides, I might not be their prey, but bait," Ezra said, giving no indication he'd heard that. "Imprisoning Silas wouldn't get any mob boss's attention, but I'm the Crimson Prince and the son of another former operative with far too much power, who'd be forced to respond. This one play accomplishes a lot." Was that honestly admiration in his voice?

I was rendered speechless, my mouth hanging open, shaking my head like it would knock sense into him.

"Can you get Silas out or not?" Sachie said to Ezra.

"Yes."

My screen showed an hour until go time. There was enough time to get to the blackmail location and Ezra would rescue Silas. I could hang up.

"You can't leave the yacht and go yourself," I blurted out. "It's too dangerous."

Ezra paused before answering, "I'll keep myself safe." He said it carefully, like my words were a trap, instead of concern, however reluctant, for his continued well-being.

He shouldn't have to keep himself safe while freeing his best friend. That was the trouble with Ezra, his first instinct wasn't ever to have someone watch his six.

My relationship with my ex was either a twisted mess or a non-entity, but either way, fears of Maccabee retaliation against him woke me up nights. He'd killed the only other Prime in existence when he was supposed to be rescuing her. It was at Delacroix's command, but Ezra refused to say he was forced into doing it, and the Maccabees refused to see that he'd done them a favor by taking Calista off the gameboard, since her vengeance for being kidnapped wouldn't have been pretty.

All of which made my worries about the idiot's continued existence very real, even though he'd betrayed my trust by joining Team Demon and assuming I wanted his protection instead of discussing it with me.

It wasn't just my position he'd jeopardized with the Maccabees either. By going rogue on our last case and murdering Calista, he'd undermined Darsh's leadership and even Sach had been thrown under the bus politically. Other Maccabees had avoided her to an extent that hadn't happened since her desire to work with the Spook Squad had first become public.

Ezra had a lot to answer for, and the thought of him mostly inspired a low-simmering rage in me these days, but however misguided his actions, how would he ever get it through his thick skull that he didn't always have to ride

94

to the rescue by himself, given Sachie and I had asked him to do exactly that?

"I'm coming with you," I said.

"It's too dangerous," he retorted.

"No, it's too dangerous for you to do this solo. If the Authority gets their hands on you, you'll vanish without a trace or they'll make up some story about you succumbing to madness and taking your own life. Like they did with Calista."

"Calista was at an advanced age where that lie was believable. It isn't with me," he said.

I actually shook the phone. It was a poor substitute for his neck. If he wouldn't take care of himself, I'd appeal to reason. "You being caught doesn't help Silas."

There was a pause. "Silas," Ezra said. "Right. Well, I need a few hours to put some things into place and—"

"We don't know how long Silas has already been sitting in that cell, but they won't hold him there much longer," Sachie said. "Maybe half a day tops."

"I'm well aware of the danger my best friend is in, Sachie," Ezra said coldly.

"Sorry."

"We have one chance to get him out." He'd softened his tone. "Rushing will do more harm than good."

"You're right." She took a deep breath. "We need to be smart about this."

"Silas is still an operative," Ezra assured us. "If they are waiting for me to show up, then that's precisely what keeps him safe from being staked. That said, I don't want him languishing in some cell. Both of you meet me here at the Copper Hell in three hours."

"I might be a bit late," I said.

Sach raised an eyebrow.

"So sorry," Ezra said with a silkiness Darsh would

approve of, "I didn't realize your social calendar was so full tonight."

I had to help Maud, and I'd have said as much, but he didn't need to make it sound like I was complaining about missing my favorite television show for this. "I've got an assignation I just can't miss."

He laughed. It wasn't dark or sensual. It was stupid and annoying. "Be at the Copper Hell in three hours. On the dot."

So much for any home turf advantage at our reunion.

My ex, my demon daddy, a dangerous clientele, and my weapon-happy bestie all on the same seafaring vessel sought after by the most lethal police force in the world. Fantastic.

"Give us your word we'll have safe passage," I said. "That includes keeping Sach and me from any Delacroix encounters."

"I would never let either of you be harmed." Ezra's voice had softened, like he was hurt.

That didn't mean he wasn't also playing some other game. Prime Playboy, Crimson Prince, Lord of the Copper Hell, friend, ex—many things could be true at the same time with Ezra. "Your word," I repeated.

"I give you my word neither of you will be harmed. But Aviva? Don't be late and make me come looking for you."

"How high-handed of you, Count von Cardoso. I'd say Delacroix's imperiousness was rubbing off on you, but I suspect that's a big reason why he brought you on as partner in the first place."

"Don't forget my good looks and incredible charm."

"Not ringing any bells," I said, and hung up.

Sach flagged down a passing taxi with its light on. "Let's get home, get changed, and make a just-in-case game plan."

Michael had left three more messages that I had no desire to listen to.

Now totally sober, I powered down my phone. "I really do have something else to take care of. That wasn't just me pissing Ezra off. We need to get home, grab my car, and go somewhere before the Hell." I opened the back door to the cab. "Up for stopping a little blackmail first?"

Sachie grinned—a two-dimple smile. "Always."

Chapter 9

"Dante forgot to include this level of Hell." Sachie scrunched up her nose, a razor's edge to her voice, like she'd just tasted something sour.

We stared out my car window at the venue down the block in a suburban retail area. A hefty tip for the cabbie, the world's fastest clothing change back at the condo, and me driving like a Formula 1 driver—or like my best friend —had gotten us here with seven minutes to spare.

A faded sign proclaimed the building where the handover was to occur "Lollipop Lane Play Palace."

"That right there is why I'm never having kids." My friend jabbed a finger at the front of the Play Palace, where garish faces of leering children were painted against a field of planted lollipops. If that wasn't bad enough, the largest lollipop boasted "multiple candy-land themed attractions!" like it was a plus.

The levels of awful awaiting us inside were too much for my brain to compute. All I could stutter out was "Why?"

"It's a demon invention to destroy a parent's soul?" Sach shrugged. "Fuck if I know."

"Why choose this place for the handover?" I pulled up the website on my phone. "Let's see, two-story climbing structure, toddler area, ball pit—"

Sachie shuddered. "I watched a news report about ball pits. Percolating stews of fecal matter. They intend to push Maud in. This isn't about blackmail. It's straight-up murder."

I flicked through the photo gallery. "The danger zone is that central climbing structure. Look." I shared the screen. "First there's the section with those punching bag–looking things to bounce between, then it's a rope ladder with netting on both sides blocking you in."

"It's a kill chute." Sach grimaced. "What kind of sicko thought that was suitable for children?"

"I'm going to say someone who just wanted kids to have a fun experience and isn't always looking for the dark side?"

"Naïve fools," she scoffed. "But it's wrong that they're making Maud do the drop inside. It should have been somewhere in the open where they could watch her leave the envelope and go. They haven't even specified where to place the cash."

At a noise outside the car, I peered in the side mirror but it was just a raccoon. I checked the time. "Maud should be here any minute."

"I understand why she came to you," Sachie said, "given you saved her from Delacroix, but is she actually an infernal?" My friend was a dark shadow in the seat next to me so I couldn't see her expression, but she didn't sound disgusted. Mystified, but not horrified.

"Of course she isn't."

"I'll admit she doesn't fit the profile, but you only have her word for that."

"What profile?" I turned toward my best friend and partner, my gut in knots, and my dream of this evening ending with Sachie hugging me in Cherry Bomb form exploding into smithereens. "The humanitarians who were ritually slaughtered? That thirteen-year-old boy?"

Sach flapped a hand. "Of the six murder victims, four were good people. Maybe five. We didn't have enough information about one of them to build a profile. They were outliers though. The final one was a gang member with a rap sheet. A criminal like all other infernals we hear about."

"Infernals are a minuscule part of the world's population, and they stay hidden for their own safety. How would you hear about ones that are just like you and me?" My stomach clenched tighter as I waited for her answer.

"I guess," Sach admitted, "but Maud is a poker player. She lies for a living." That was rich, coming from someone who hid weapons on herself for a living.

"Bluffing isn't lying, nor is it illegal," I retorted through gritted teeth. "It's a basic tactic in that game."

"Yeah, but she's world-champion good at it." Sachie unbuckled her seat belt. "On the other hand, I wouldn't think an infernal could fall victim to a vamp's schemes and be compelled to go after Delacroix. Though it makes sense why the vamp chose her. Use a demon to kill a demon."

That was the exact rationale Maud and I hoped people would give should they find out about her, but hearing those prejudices said so matter-of-factly still grated.

I snapped my seat belt open. "Speculating about someone being an infernal could cause them a lot of harm."

"That's true, but if she *is* one, shouldn't we know that?"

"Why?"

"I dunno, Avi." She threw her hands up. "We make

vamps register so we can track them, maybe we should do the same with infernals."

I gaped at her, shaking my head like that could rewind time and suck those words out of my brain. "You want half shedim tracked?" I grabbed my purse off the middle console and rooted inside for a mint or some gum. Anything to wash away the metallic taste in my mouth. "Darsh is one of your best friends. Do you tell him you're glad that vampires must be registered?"

"I'm not glad about it, but that practice isn't going away. So, isn't it fair that people with a half-demon side be registered? Not all vamps are bad. *All* shedim are. And yes, with some infernals, their humanity wins out, but what about all the others? Just because we haven't heard about them doesn't mean they're not out there being evil. They might just be smart enough not to get caught."

I shoved three pieces of gum in my mouth, chewing with a tight jaw. Ever since Sachie had learned the murder victims were half shedim, she'd differentiated the "good infernals," the ones deserving justice, from the others. "How would you prove whether a person is an infernal or not? Torture that reveal out of them? Because historically that's how it goes."

Sachie pulled down the visor to look in the mirror while she smoothed her hair. "Ever since that murder case, you've been all in on the side of infernals."

"I'm all in on the side of people in general and half shedim are people."

"They're also demons." Sach spread her hands wide.

Our fingers were close enough to brush together. A flicker of understanding fluttered in my chest, reminding me of the countless nights we'd spent discussing the intricacies of good versus evil. Sach had always been driven by an unwavering sense of justice, her convictions carved into her very core.

Same as mine.

Funny, that our black-and-white views on right and wrong weren't the same all-encompassing circle, but a Venn diagram with infernals in the center.

I gripped the door handle, scared that if I reached out, Sachie would just keep getting farther and farther away, those final millimeters a vast chasm that we could never breach.

A rap on the window made me jump.

Maud stood outside the car, her shoulders hunched. She was dressed in a nondescript black jacket, with her hair tucked under a fleece cap.

I popped the lock and Maud scrambled into the back seat.

"Here." She held out her red coat to Sach, along with a matching hat. My friend put on the coat while Maud leaned forward between the seats. "You really think this will work? I'm Chinese and you're Japanese."

Sachie snorted, carefully hiding her short pink hair under the hat before affixing an earpiece to her left ear. "You think a blackmailer has racial sensitivity? We're roughly the same height and build. We're Asian. We're female. It'll work. Besides, anyone who looked into you is prepped for yellow flame magic. You know, the lie you fed everyone to keep your real blue flame abilities hidden." She shot me a pointed look.

"Because Maud's particular fire sight talents are so rare, it would have made her a target," I said. "Either way, they won't anticipate a trained operative with orange flame magic."

"Surprising bad guys is such fun." Sachie held out her hand for the manila envelope with the cash. Given there was ten thousand Canadian in there, it wasn't as thick as I expected.

"Sach?" I touched my own earpiece to turn it on.

She stilled, halfway out of the car.

"Be careful."

"Always." With that, she headed down the block to the Play Palace, keeping to the shadows.

Maud gnawed on a cuticle. "Now what?"

"Watch."

Between the car and the parking lot in front of the building, Sachie's entire posture changed. She hunched her shoulders up to her ears, darting nervous glances around every few seconds and practically white-knuckling the manila envelope. When she reached the glass front doors of the play center, she swore under her breath in Japanese. She whispered but I heard her loud and clear through the earpiece.

"Report," I said.

"It's like a paint store threw up in there," she whined. "They won't need to punch me in the head to disorient me, just make me stare at that carpet for ten seconds." She sighed. "Lots of hiding places to ambush a victim, but there's a pirate ship just past the entrance that you should be able to get to undetected." She gave another sigh that was really more of a growl and wrenched the door open.

"I'm going in as backup," I explained to Maud. "Stay put."

She didn't listen, insisting as she ran behind me that she was a million times safer sticking by my side.

I tugged on the door, the glass now opaque. "Fuck!" I kicked it but it didn't even crack.

"Over there." Maud sprinted off.

"Sach, check in," I said steadily.

"Hello?" she tremulously called out.

Good. She was unharmed.

By the time Maud returned, I'd picked the lock and was stashing the tiny tool kit inside my jacket pocket. I rolled the shopping cart she'd brought with her to one side. "Was I supposed to use this to smash the door down?"

"I didn't know what else to do."

"It's not your job to figure that out. It was to, what was it again?" I snapped my fingers. "Stay in the car. But if you won't do that, then quit talking." I opened the door to the Play Palace.

"Old MacDonald Had a Farm" as sung by a cheerful midlevel marketer and a chorus of sugared-up preschoolers blasted out from the main room into the reception area. It was reminiscent of the musical torture the US Army used to flush out a military leader in the late '80s.

Yet that annoying tactic fell a distant second to the massive scythe embedded in the wall behind the check-in desk, the rope securing it to an overhead pipe pulled taut.

I pried Maud's fingers off my shoulder. "It was designed to scare, not kill," I whispered. "See? It's well above head height. You sure you won't wait in the car?"

She shook her head, the expressionless mask that had won her world titles snapping into place.

"Stay behind me and stay close." I unsheathed a dagger from my thigh holder and crept toward the pirate ship.

Honestly, it was more like I bounced forward. Silas was still locked up and in danger, and I was about to not only see Ezra for the first time in two months, but possibly destroy my career with the Maccabees by being a party to Silas's rescue. However, I stood by my belief that Ezra shouldn't do this alone. Plus, Sach and I bore some responsibility for our roles, albeit unwitting ones.

I was eager to burn off all the angry energy bouncing around inside me with a chase, or better still, a brutal fight.

Cherry cast her vote.

The emergency lights and light pollution coming through the back glass wall provided the only illumination to navigate by, leaving the room shrouded in shadows. Given the three different carpet patterns, slides painted in every single color, and plastic plant life and animal statues in tacky shades not existing in nature, all I could say was God help anyone who saw it properly lit up. Two seconds of visual exposure now left my head throbbing and my shoulders tight.

I ushered Maud into one of the low arched entrances on the pirate ship, ducking under a lion who inexplicably sat with his feet dangling over the side. They hadn't even given him an eyepatch or a hat or a pegleg. Aesthetically and thematically, this place was shit.

I crouched in the belly of the ship, sticking to the shadows while tracking Sach through one of the low arches.

She stood in the center of the room in front of the main climbing structure, turning in a slow circle, the envelope held up. "You can have the money. I'm no infernal. Please don't destroy my career."

A plastic cannon swiveled toward her, firing plastic balls with a series of tha-wumps.

Sach threw herself sideways, missing most of the volley, but she whacked her knee on the way down.

I strained against the urge to rush to my partner's rescue, because I had to let her attacker show themselves. Even Cherry held herself in check.

Other than Maud's muted gasp from behind me, all was still for a second. Well, all except for a dance remix of "Baby Shark." New level of Hell unlocked.

Suddenly, two vamps built like brick shithouses rose silently from the ball pit, dislodging showers of colorful plastic.

Disguise discarded, Sachie ran to meet them with a deranged grin.

I sighed and shoved Maud deeper into the shadows in the belly of the ship. "Stay here," I ordered, and jumped into the fray.

Sachie had unleashed her orange magic on the ball pit duo, but two more flung themselves from tunnels on the second level of the climbing structure to box me in.

I rushed the closest one, slicing his side with a dagger.

He hissed, then just stood there, staring at his injury in confusion.

I narrowed my eyes. Where was the follow-up? For that matter, how had Sachie already dispatched the bigger of her two opponents?

My other attacker raced forward—a sprint, not a blur, allowing me to step out of his path. Poor baby couldn't stop and correct his course, and he crashed into a plastic slide with a grunt.

I lunged and swiped my blade at the bloodsucker that I'd already cut.

He dodged it with all the grace of a baby calf getting to its feet for the first time, confirming my suspicions.

I grabbed his arm, stabbed him, and danced away.

What second-rate blackmailer sent Nippers—newbie vamps—as muscle? This crew was so recently turned, they were still finding their footing. And the dude who was bleeding had warm skin.

The vamps hadn't even shown up hungry, which would have compensated for their lack of coordination.

I spun at a loud crack, finding Sachie rubbing her jaw, murder in her eyes.

"You said she'd change," one of them said, flexing his hand.

Oh shit. I whipped my gaze up. A half dozen mounted

security cameras with steady red recording lights were trained on us.

My inattention cost me. A blinding pain shot through my head, my vision doubling, then tripling. I spat on the ground, tasting blood, then dropped into a crouch, my blade at the ready.

Bleeding Vamp ran at me. It was almost comical how he tried to turn his unsteady lumber into lethal speed. Except for the part that there was still an enormous undead fiend bearing down on me and if he grabbed me, he'd snap me like a twig.

I held my ground, ignoring my brain screaming at me to run. The second he launched himself off the ground to tackle me from above, I also jumped, shoving my knife upward into his gut.

His body crashed down, pinning me for a second.

Luckily, I also had a stake at the ready. I plunged it into his heart, and he disintegrated in a shower of ash. I wiped my sleeve across my mouth and leapt to my feet.

A quick glance showed that Sachie had killed her two vamps and taken on my other opponent, which was nice of her. I owed her a poutine for that. Their fight raged over the playground equipment. Having slides, ropes, and tunnels to contend with, though, did not turn this battle into some cool feat of choreography.

She waited for him to catch up, slowly and precisely turning him into shriveled-up jerky with her orange flame magic.

"Stop toying with him," I called over my shoulder, jogging toward a door marked "Employees Only." Hopefully I'd find the security system there to erase the video footage.

"He needs to learn to put some effort in it." Stake in hand, Sach beckoned the vamp forward like Morpheus in *The Matrix*.

Maud screamed.

I reversed course, sprinting for her and skidding around a carousel made for toddlers.

A fifth vampire had her by the throat, squeezing the air out of her while slamming her back against the wall.

Her eyes glowed toxic green.

My pulse spiked. I ran at him, skidding at the last minute along the ground to slice his Achilles.

Howling, he crashed to one knee, dropping Maud. He was short, skinny, and without his enhanced strength, wouldn't have been much of an opponent.

Sachie was still occupied with her vamp, so that meant rescuing Maud was on me. And I'd damn well better act fast, because she was sucking in a deep breath, shaking and fighting for control.

"Snap out of it," I ordered, though I patted her shoulder. "The staff room. Find the video footage." I pushed her away. "And get yourself under control."

Maud shot me a hurt look, but protecting her—from Sachie and from whomever was recording us—was more important than having her like me.

I shook off the sting in my chest. "Go!"

She ran.

I spun sharply at a noise behind me, caught the vamp by his arm, and used his momentum against him to throw him to the carpet. "You're undead. You don't need to breathe."

He started to get up, but I kicked his bleeding Achilles tendon with my pointy-toed boot, and he fell back with a howl. "Bitch." His ears, which stuck out unfortunately far from his head, and his crooked nose were familiar.

"I know you." I snapped my fingers. "Zaven Barsamian. You were part of the crew doing those home invasions in Brentwood a few years ago. Did your time and figured your best path forward was to be turned, did you? Why did you think Maud was an infernal?"

He shrugged. "You hear things."

I stomped on his hand, dropped to my knees before he could recover, and slammed the blade through his palm, pinning him to the ground. "Yeah? From who? I love a good game of telephone."

"You have no idea who you're messing with." Zaven tore free with a snarl and grabbed my hair, freezing when I pressed my stake against his pec.

"This looks fun." Sachie stood over us, twirling her own stake.

"Highlight of my day." I dug the tip into Zaven's chest, tearing his Henley. "Let go."

His grip on my scalp tightened and I winced.

Sachie waved her weapon at him. "I'd do as she says. Her hair takes forever to grow back, and she gets very cranky. Ask her about the incident with the gum."

I tried to lower my heart rate, but at this close range, Zaven had the advantage. He could easily rip the weapons from my grasp and break my neck.

My only hope was the way he warily looked between his still-healing Achilles, and Sach and me.

He tossed me off him and scooted back.

I rubbed my tailbone. "Who hired you?"

"Who turned you?" Sachie said.

I pointed at her. "One and the same? We can easily find out who changed you, then we'll tell them you ratted them out about this job."

Zaven laughed. "Good luck with that."

"Not the same person." Sach scratched her chin. "Thanks for confirming that."

His face fell.

"Was this a test?" I said. Zaven chose to be turned; he

wanted power. "A job interview for one of the local vamp mobs?"

A muscle ticked in his jaw. "Nobody's fucking testing me and I'm not some goon for hire. It was *my* plan. Got it?"

"Criminal mastermind. Check," I said sarcastically.

"My. Fucking. Plan." Zaven wasn't scared and taking the fall for someone. He was furious that I didn't believe him.

I narrowed my eyes. This wasn't a test; it was a tactical move designed to impress. But who? Before I could figure out how to send Sachie away and question Zaven more freely, I was knocked sideways. I blinked, but Zaven hadn't moved.

No, I'd been hip-checked by Maud, who was wielding an industrial stapler that she clocked Zaven in the head with. "I'M. NOT. AN. INFERNAL! You fucking vampire!" Her fury lent weight to our lie that she'd been compelled by a different vamp when she kidnapped Calista and tried to kill Delacroix.

Zaven clutched his bleeding head with a dazed expression.

Wow. Those staplers were sturdy. Sachie was already eyeing it in possibility.

"Focus," I murmured.

She pulled Maud away mid-swing, but my sister tore free and snatched Sachie's stake, shoving it into the convenient "X marks the spot" tear I'd made in Zaven's shirt.

Contrary to film and television, it wasn't easy to jam a piece of pointy wood through muscle and ribs. Vamp magic made them more susceptible, but most people still couldn't pull it off, which was good, because human vigilantes going around getting themselves killed would be a disaster.

Zaven flung Maud across the room and pushed unsteadily to his feet.

Sachie kicked him in the backs of the knees, then knocked him to the carpet via a heel strike to the nuts.

Zaven curled up, moaning.

This was pointless and I was tired. The most likely angle was that Zaven did this to impress someone in the local vamp mob, in which case, I could investigate those ties on my own. I'd done what I could for Maud, and with the clock ticking, it was time to prioritize Silas.

I crouched down, stake at the ready.

"No. Wait." Zaven reached into his pocket.

I jammed the stake into his chest before he could pull out another weapon.

Zaven gasped and something fluttered from his hand.

I picked up the photo he'd dropped, shaking it to dislodge his ashy remains. A petite blonde woman held a laughing toddler up to the camera. He had a family? He'd gotten this woman pregnant when he was human because turned vamps couldn't impregnate anyone and besides, this kid had been around longer than Zaven had been a vampire.

I wiped a smudge of ash off the woman's face. It wasn't like a criminal vamp would be winning any father-of-the-year awards.

No? If he was the one calling the shots, then he'd arranged this spot as the location for the exchange. How would someone like him know about the Play Palace otherwise? I rubbed my fist against my forehead.

Zaven's partner would spend months darting glances at the door, praying today was the day he came home. His son would wonder why his dad abandoned them. Would it send him down the same path that led Zaven to his death?

Was it worse if I'd stolen their hope for their happy

future as a family or turned it into a lie that sustained them?

"What's that?" Sachie said.

I crumpled the photo in my hand. "Nothing."

Chapter 10

Breaking into the Jolly Hellhound in the middle of the night when we couldn't contact anyone to open the pub for us to access the portal wasn't résumé-appropriate, but we weren't going to lose sleep over it either.

Sach eased the door open, and I sprinted for the alarm system, describing it to my longtime informant Rukhsana Gill over the phone.

While I hadn't seen her since she'd been attacked over the mistaken belief that she'd stolen Sire's Spark, she'd reached out after finding new digs. The young Frenchwoman didn't just run a small crew at a chop shop, she was plugged into all levels of society here in town and had loads of intel at her fingertips.

Much like someone else I knew and probably why the two of them had hit it off.

Rukhsana yawned and had me read the model number of the alarm system.

"Ten seconds." Sach was behind the bar with a countdown app, searching for the button to open the portal door.

We couldn't be certain how long we had before the

alarm was triggered but we'd erred on the conservative side.

I punched in the manufacturer's reset code that Rukhsana rattled off, muttering at it to hurry up. The light on the pad went from red to green a split second before the timer on Sach's phone beeped, and I heaved a sigh of relief. "Thanks, Rukhsana."

"No problem, chère. I'll send you an encrypted text with my new account details for payment."

I winced. We'd graduated to encrypted? That level of security was for sure going to be folded into what she charged me. "Understood."

"We're good to go," Sachie said.

We jogged into the back room where the portal to the Copper Hell was located. The space was private but basic: four small tables, each with a beat-up lampshade overhead, a clanky baseboard heater, and a metal door that opened to the portal.

"Ready?" Sachie said.

Not even a bit. I wanted to catch my breath and have a second to decompress from the blackmail attempt. We'd cleaned up the Play Palace, double-checked that all the footage was erased, and verified the security system had no internet connection.

Sach had driven my car to the Jolly Hellhound like a speed demon (which, as far as I was aware, was not a thing), with Maud in the back, holding the manila envelope with all the cash and explaining why she was anxious to get back to Hong Kong.

It turns out being a world champion poker player involved a lot more than showing up to kill it at a tournament and then fuck off to some glamorous location to enjoy the winnings. Maud spent hours using specialized software to review every losing hand she played and checking for leaks so she could learn from her mistakes. She constantly analyzed every step of her play, and that of her opponents. Mad respect to my sister; her dedication and training made her the Tiger Woods of poker.

Even Sachie was blown away by the work Maud put into her craft, which hopefully would win my best friend over should she ever learn the truth about my sister.

Once we reached the pub, I gave Maud my keys to drive herself to the airport. The valet parking charges would be a bitch, but I'd get my keys and car back later today.

Hating this rushed goodbye, I'd promised to touch base with her soon. It wasn't just about keeping her updated, the two of us needed to have an overdue talk about who we really were to each other.

The attackers were dead, no footage had been live streamed, and we had a solid clue. I should have been enjoying this win, not feeling cold and hollow.

I motioned at the metal door. "Go for it."

The first time I'd gone through the portal into the Copper Hell, some presence had unravelled me, cutting off my awareness of Cherry while simultaneously forcing my shedim body front and center. The second time, there were no issues with the portal, but I'd faced Delacroix's true form—a giant serpent—and honestly, had been allowed to leave only because it amused him to keep me alive.

Ezra hadn't ordered us to glamor or take off our Maccabee rings, but I still tensed when Sach said "See you on the other side" and stepped into the mesh net of magic light woven across the open doorway.

Hopefully, this time, we'd both make it out.

I waited for a minute in case she bounced right out like on her last attempt, then followed her.

There was no sentience in the portal, no danger at all.

From one step to the next I went from the pub to the small foyer on the yacht.

Was that first time dangerous only because I was glamored or was the portal no longer policed? Its settings and alarm system had been keyed to Calista's awareness, and perhaps Ezra didn't bother, but I highly doubted it. He had some way of tracking every single visitor to the Copper Hell.

Our trouble-free entry through the portal was at His Highness's pleasure.

Wait. Where was Sachie?

I looked into the main room, but not seeing her, spun back around to the portal.

She staggered out, looking wan. "Warn a girl next time."

"About what?" I examined her for injury—just with my naked eye, not my magic—but she appeared unharmed.

"It was like something surged toward me when I stepped through. It pinned me in place and I swear it scanned me down to the marrow of my bones." She rubbed her arms. "I wasn't sure it was going to let me go," she admitted quietly.

"Ezra," I snarled. "He changed up the security settings."

Delacroix's demon magic formed the basis of the security on the portal, but it was keyed to the Prime in charge.

A Prime who'd let me waltz right through.

"Leave it," Sachie said. "I'd increase security if I were in his shoes too." She shook herself off.

Anyone not familiar with my friend would only see a bored expression when she left the foyer, but I pegged the entranced glimmer in her eyes for the tables hosting everything from poker to board games to mah-jongg, and the slight quirk of her lips at the outlandish attire of a group cheering on a heated game of dreidel.

My heart swelled. It was either incredibly sweet, if somewhat weird, or very sad that Ezra had included dreidel among the offerings at the Hell. Depending on whether he was doing it out of nostalgia or because he'd never had anyone to play it with him.

Sachie clocked each and every Li'l Hellion—my nickname for the vamp staff—her fingers flexing as she took in the bruiser at the far end of the room guarding the velvet rope that blocked the circular staircase to the next floor where the high rollers played.

Cherry Bomb conducted the same thorough study of the Hell, noting there wasn't a trace of any of the damage from my last visit. Thankfully, she didn't bombard me with excited spikes of adrenaline at the danger lurking in every corner.

My little demoness is growing up. That earned me a growl.

The yacht was so smooth that aside from the faint hum of the engines vibrating up through the floor, there was no sense of being in the middle of the ocean. And while the honey-colored lights spread across the ceiling warmed the room, they also made the darkness outside the evenly spaced narrow windows more pronounced. It was impossible to delineate where the night sky ended and the inky waters began, the view through the glass similar to gazing into the vastness of space.

The roulette wheel clacked, chips riffled against the felt, and patrons conversed in dozens of languages, not all of them native to earth.

I sunk into my blue flame synesthete vision to determine exactly what percentage was human, but my magic barely illuminated anyone's weaknesses. There were either far fewer humans than expected, or some of them were using an expensive and difficult-to-obtain device that shielded them from all magic psychological attacks.

No matter what the clientele wore or how badly some were glamored, as if they were AI-generated mishaps—hello, man with four ears—Sachie and I stood out like sore thumbs, so it didn't surprise me that within seconds of our appearance, two Li'l Hellions were moving in.

Their stares were flatter than the gunmetal gray of their uniforms or their thin-lipped expressions.

I wasn't concerned with them, all my attention snagged on a new addition to this floor: a wrought iron balcony set dead center along one of the rippling brushed-steel walls that wrapped around the huge circular room. It was created for kings to preside over their kingdoms. Except this ruler couldn't even be bothered to spare a glance for the little people.

Yeah, well, looks were deceiving. I'd have bet both kidneys that despite Ezra's focus on the cards he laid out on a table—and the pair of Li'l Hellions speaking with him, one of whom was consulting a tablet as they spoke—he could describe in precise detail what everyone was doing.

And that Sach and I had arrived.

I tried not to take his lack of so much as a wave personally. Also, for all his bitching about me being on time, why was he just sitting there calmly handling business matters that couldn't be as important as Silas?

"Touch me again and I'm taking the hand back with me as a souvenir. I have an extensive collection and I love expanding it," Sachie said with a pleasant and threatening smile. "Cardoso's expecting us."

The male vamp who'd grabbed her elbow tapped his earpiece, asking for clarification about our presence.

Sach pointed at his female colleague, specifically the Copper Hell logo of a fat flame bound diagonally by a thin copper band that was embroidered over her heart. "X marks the spot. Handy."

The vamp bared her fangs.

The one other time I'd been here with Ezra, I had to pretend I was in his debt, cowering in his presence. With this visit, Ezra sniped about our meeting time, still hadn't deigned to look our way, and now he made us stand here like peons?

"They're cleared," the male vamp said. "Informants."

We'd been upgraded from hapless cops to corrupt Maccabees handing over intel. Sensible, but shitty.

I pushed through the undead duo and stomped toward the cage elevator under Count von Cardoso's balcony.

The vamps followed.

I stopped clear of the closed bronze gate and raised an impatient eyebrow at the female Hellion. "You first."

She shared a look with her male colleague, and at his nod, raised her wrist, revealing a small tattoo of the Copper Hell logo, which she pressed against the gate's handle.

It slid open.

"What would have happened if I touched the handle before you'd done that?" I said, unable to help my curiosity.

"You'd have been portaled directly into the yacht's propellers. Then we'd invite everyone to watch the fish feed." She eyed me in disappointment.

Sach, her hands in her pockets, breezed right past her. "Hey, Avi, think we could talk to strata about upping their security protocols?"

I stepped into the car behind my friend. "With Bill heading up council? He'd bitch about the pink mist attracting pigeons."

"He's such a killjoy."

The Hellion slid the gate shut, whereupon the doors silently closed, and the elevator began its ascent.

Sach looked at the inlaid mother-of-pearl design on the ceiling that matched the pattern on the floor. "Fancy."

"The balcony wasn't here last time. I guess Calista didn't feel the need to play Eva Perón."

Sach snickered. "I'd pay good money to see Cardoso stand up there and belt his woes."

I winced. "Do you not remember his singing voice? I'll take the propellers, thanks."

The elevator chimed that we'd arrived, and I stepped out with a hard exhale.

It wasn't any quieter up here, but it was slightly warmer, and the air around the balcony was tinged light green, encasing it like a bubble. That detail hadn't been visible from down below.

"The magic in the cursed watch the House acquired was corrupted," the male vamp with the tablet said. "Delacroix wants you to let the Iron Hand Mafia know that their forfeit has not been paid and must be settled up at once. With interest."

Ezra, in his throne-like chair, moved the ten of diamonds to its corresponding jack in his Solitaire game. The top two buttons of his crisp white shirt were undone, exposing a triangle of brown skin, and his suit was as black as his cloud of curls, but his eyes were dulled by fatigue, a muted silvery-blue, the ocean on an overcast day.

"That can wait," the female vamp said insistently. "Ezra has to rectify the issue with the gin supplier first. She refuses to listen to reason about delivery dates."

Ezra tapped the remaining deck in his hand against the wood, a muscle ticking in his jaw. The gold edging on one of his onyx cuff links caught the light.

I followed the line of his sleeve up to his biceps.

120

My ex had tattooed his desire for me on his skin. Was his indifference now some kind of payback for my goodbye fuck? Had he let the tattoo heal, the letters vanishing one by one until there was no trace of that desire at all?

I turned away, too tired and fried to deal with him.

The two vamps began arguing over first rights to Ezra. It would have been funny if I wasn't massively stressed, worried, and exhausted from saving Maud.

"I'll handle all of it," he said brusquely. "Now leave me."

I put on my game face as the vamps left via the elevator.

Ezra flipped a card over. "You're late."

"We're two minutes early." I crossed my arms against the urge to run a hand over his jaw, because Ezra had shaved off the close-cropped beard and mustache that had given him a piratical air. "Is Silas okay? Any updates?"

His clean-shaven look should have mitigated his predatory aura, but it drew the eye to his sharp cheekbones, the set of his strong chin, and his lush mouth that did nothing to soften the impression that he was king of every jungle.

"For you, two minutes early *is* late." Ezra's phone beeped and he slid it out of his pocket. "But he's as okay as he can be. Locked up, which means nulling magic, and that isn't pleasant even for a vampire, but he's otherwise unharmed." Ezra checked the screen. "Perfect. The final piece is in play. We can go." He played the ten of hearts on his Solitaire game, then ambled toward the double doors off the balcony.

Grumbling, I moved to follow His Majesty, with Sachie close behind, when a ripple in the atmosphere made me pull up short.

Ezra spun around, his arm shooting out to grab the spiky shedim emerging out of thin air by the throat. Blood dripped to the floor, my ex now bleeding from a fat thorny protrusion piercing his palm.

But Ezra just smiled coldly at the demon. "That all you've got?"

Spikes blew off the demon with the sound of champagne corks popping, but none of them tore through Ezra's suit. Instead, they bounced harmlessly to the ground.

I narrowed my eyes at the fabric. Huh.

Ezra leaned in and tsked his attacker. "I told you, Zamoric, you'd have one shot at me, so make it count."

Zamoric replied in an angry, albeit strangled voice, in some demon language, but he barely got out three words before Ezra tore the top of his skull off, plucked out the shedim's brain, and crushed it under one heel.

I swallowed. Well. He certainly hadn't done that when we were dating.

He dropkicked the corpse off the balcony like errant trash, plucked the thorn from his palm, and tossed it over the railing as well.

I grabbed his injured hand, which had ballooned up. "Are you poisoned? Is there an antidote?" I looked around frantically.

He tugged his hand away. "It was just a drop. My healing magic will take care of it in about fifteen minutes."

How regular an occurrence was shit like this that Ezra took poisoning in stride? Once again, I could have shaken him for putting himself in this position.

"Your suit is armor," Sach said. She lowered the blade she'd pulled after the shedim appeared. "Is that the new trend or did you see this coming?"

Ezra shrugged. "Never a dull moment at the Copper Hell. But that's neither here nor there. We need to focus on Silas."

"That shedim came out of nowhere." Sachie

122

narrowed her eyes. "You can't ward this area against unwanted visitors? Don't you control the security systems?"

Ezra jerked his chin down at the demon's body, which was being given a wide berth. And not being cleaned up by any Hellion. "Sometimes an example is more instructive than any ward."

All the better to dissuade future attackers. In strength, sensory perception, and predatory instincts, Ezra was top of the heap. But he couldn't stay there forever.

I understood why he couldn't show weakness; that didn't mean I had to like it.

Sachie sat down on the throne chair. "Actually, I think I like the view from here. You two go ahead and I'll hold down the fort." She frowned. "Hold down the gambling megayacht? What's the right expression for that?"

Ezra cocked his head like he didn't understand. "You don't need to do that. It's fully automated to run even if I'm not physically present."

She heaved a sigh. "I'm making sure that you don't have an unpleasant surprise when you return, probably exhausted from freeing our friend. Silas would be heartbroken if you got assassinated right away." She took out a knife and casually began to sharpen it on a whetstone she'd pulled from somewhere. "Besides, I'll have a grand old time greeting them."

"Say thank you to the woman with the bloodlust," I said, "and let's go."

Sach's offer was genuine, and it was best to not walk into any trouble when we returned, but it was also a smart move on her part to take advantage of this situation to further our own agenda here at the Hell.

There was a little divot between Ezra's brows when he thanked her, then he opened a portal and stepped through.

"Stay sharp," Sachie said.

"Stay safe," I replied, and followed Ezra.

The portal exited into a minuscule storage closet lined with boxes of booze. I strode out the already opened door, finding myself in the tiniest bar I'd ever seen, with barely enough room for a single counter and six bar stools.

The bartender didn't pay me any attention beyond a bored glance and a step sideways to let me pass, but I froze because the sole customer wasn't there for drinks and the cozy atmosphere.

Director Yuto Abe, head of Maccabee Tokyo HQ, had come to greet us.

Chapter 11

Director Abe snorted softly—and Ezra was nowhere to be seen.

Thinking fast about what could have happened, I traced a hand over the man's shoulder. It was a slenderer frame, not Ezra's brawny physique.

I experienced a brief, exquisite moment of panic at this monster of a social faux pas. Michael was going to lose it when Director Abe told her I'd felt him up. I wasn't sure how I'd ever live that down.

Then a familiar voice said: "Got a thing for older men?"

"You're the worst," I growled at my glamored, highly-awful-for-not-giving-me-a-heads-up ex.

Chuckling, Ezra held the door open for me.

The strip of night sky visible above somewhat ramshackle bars was clear and the air was crisp. Neon lights from dozens of signs flickered and danced across the pavement and the bustling narrow street pulsed with a life of its own. It had been around 5AM Vancouver time when we left the Hell so was about 9PM here.

I swerved around a couple chatting animatedly in

Japanese, darting glances into the windows of each tiny bar like I was opening the windows of a nativity calendar. One was dominated by an opulent chandelier, another boasted dozens of Troll dolls on shelves. There was kitschy folk art, wallpaper made from faded band posters, and one place, barely bigger than a closet, was adorned with plastic hangers. "Where are we?"

Inside one open door was a set of stairs leading to a bar on the second floor that were so steep, they qualified for ladderhood.

"Golden Gai district in Shinjuku. A former black market. It used to be a hub for the Tokyo subculture and underground arts scene. It's also nice and close to Maccabee HQ."

Lost to the charm of this area, I'd momentarily forgotten Ezra's appearance as Director Abe. The disguise was unnerving, and a sober reminder of exactly what we were up against, but combined with the sense of untold mysteries hiding behind each door, it all left me breathless with anticipation. "How did you instaglamor?"

Ezra turned the corner onto another narrow road, deftly avoiding a man riding a bike that was hooked to a cart loaded with softly clanking boxes.

I picked up my pace to match his stride, catching a small vial that was a quarter full of murky liquid that he tossed over to me. "What's this?"

"A certain kind of shedim sweat mixed with corn syrup. Disgusting but effective." He pulled out his phone, quickly scrolling through until he held up a photo of a Japanese woman. "Drink it and focus on this photo. Himari Yui is a level three operative here in Tokyo."

I shuddered down the concoction, which tasted like ball sweat with a sugary chaser. Icy prickles stung me from within, freezing me in my tracks with a full-body shiver.

"For fuck's sake!" I sniffled, swiping a hand at my streaming eyes.

Ezra handed me a pressed linen handkerchief. "You're her spitting image."

I dabbed at my eyes, loudly blew my nose, and then stuffed the hankie in my pocket to wash before returning. My hands appeared—and felt—smaller, as did my feet in their glamored, polished black lace-ups.

Ezra offered to show me my face with his camera, but I declined, not wanting any further sense of disorientation on this foreign mission. Putting the phone away, he turned another corner and pointed to a tower a couple of blocks away. "Tokyo HQ."

I hurried after him. "You've ensured we won't run into either the director or Operative Yui?"

"But of course."

"How?"

His answering smile was a blade that I never wanted to see on the real Director Abe's face. "I know many things. Including some very hidden peccadillos of Operative Yui's." He pulled a mock sad face. "They've just come to light, resulting in Director Abe's presence on scene at an illegal gambling house to clean up a rather unfortunate mess." He snickered. "I hope he brought gloves."

What exactly—I shook my head. Better not to know. "You're going to just stroll in as the director and have him release Silas? No one will buy that."

"Of course they won't. But they will buy that my trusted operative with a very public hatred of vampires and excellent aim has been brought in to subdue Silas enough to get him into a Maccabee transport van."

"An execution vehicle, you mean. Being an operative has kept Silas alive this long, but vamps don't even get the option of life in Sector A." I kicked a rock against a building. "Poor Silas. It's a shitty trick to pull on him. I know this ruse will save his life and we have to sell it, but I don't like the idea of him being scared he's about to die."

"I like it less than you do, but it's that or he really dies." He paused. "Then we do."

I held up a fist that trembled only slightly. "Sector A for me, boyo."

Ezra chucked me under the chin. "I like your optimism." His expression turned serious. "There's no such thing as an infallible plan, and Sector A is a definite risk for you. You don't have to come."

The mere mention of that prison made my knees weak, but I wasn't going to abandon Silas. Or Ezra. My ex and I were still going to have a serious talk about his behavior over the past couple months, but that was for later. Besides, Ezra was the house at the Copper Hell. He'd have made sure the odds were in his favor no matter what game he played.

"I'm in it to win it," I said, jogging through the crosswalk and craning my head up at the slender tower. It was merely glass and steel with nary a hostile vibe emanating off it. In fact, the light streaming through the windows was a welcoming beacon in the night, and I even spied letters spelling out "Happy Hanukkah" in English and Japanese on some of the glass panes.

I notched my chin up, shoulders back, and marched through the motion-controlled front doors into the airy lobby.

Ezra headed straight for the employee door behind the reception desk.

My breath caught when the young man working there spoke to Ezra in Japanese, but he simply nodded and produced a security pass to buzz himself into the inner sanctum.

I didn't speak until we were in the elevators heading down into the basement. "Glamors, security passes," I murmured. "Someone was busy. And lucky that whatever the receptionist said was a yes or no question."

One side of Ezra's—Director Abe's—mouth quirked up.

We stepped out of the elevator to a half dozen guards stationed outside the metal door of Silas's cell.

One of them started speaking to Ezra in rapid-fire Japanese. Our luck had run out.

I inched my fingers toward the knife I had stashed in a wrist sheath under my sleeve that Sachie had pressed upon me before we broke into the Jolly Hellhound. *Sector A* pulsed against my brain like a death knell.

Ezra answered back. In calm and thoughtful Japanese. No hesitation.

The guard inclined his head and I swallowed my gasp. Ezra had trotted out his French before, which was impressive and sexy, but not that much of a stretch given the similarities to his native Spanish. Mastering Japanese well enough to fool everyone into believing he was Director Abe and send three of the operatives sprinting off to do his bidding, however?

Butterflies fluttered in my stomach.

Had he picked this up in the past six years? Learning Japanese at this level would have taken a long time and quite the dedication to his lessons.

How many hours that I'd blithely assumed he'd spent partying around the world or playing assassin for his father had been spent studying? Knitting, Japanese, Ezra was like a lantern where all I'd initially seen was a narrow beam of light, but where he kept sliding aside shutters to reveal more of his brilliance.

"Transport," Ezra murmured in English for my ears only.

I stared blankly at him.

He shot me a "get it together" look.

One of the remaining guards opened Silas's cell and Ezra marched inside, with me on his heels.

My heart sank.

It wasn't enough that Silas's magic had flatlined into the same dull ache that I felt under my skin, both his wrists were manacled to the wall with heavy iron cuffs, there were bruised smudges under his eyes, and he'd gnawed his bottom lip raw.

Shit! Nulling magic. I darted a glance at Ezra, then relaxed. Our demon magic glamors remained intact.

When he saw Director Abe, Silas's face lit up with a wary hope. "Yuto. Good. I'd like to go through the individual charges and…" Silas trailed off at the sight of me, or rather, Operative Yui. "So that's how it is," he said softly in his Southern drawl. "No presumed innocence for vamps, huh, Himari?" He rested his head back against the wall. "You're still Maccabees and I do hereby demand my due process."

Had Darsh been here, he would have lost his shit at Silas expecting any form of justice, and even I wanted to rail at him to fight back with fists, not words.

Unable to understand Japanese and unfamiliar with my environment, I was more keenly attuned to everyone's body language, homing in on any little twitch with the gaze of a predator.

"We're going to unlock the manacles and you will come with us." Ezra spoke English in his director impersonation without a trace of an accent. It was lower than Ezra's normal voice but must have been accurate because none of the guards blinked. "You will wear nulling cuffs. Fighting is pointless."

"I'm not about to confirm your opinion of me as a monster," Silas said. "And for the record, neither is Ezra."

My ex's lips thinned. "This isn't about Cardoso."

Silas laughed without a trace of humor. "Tell yourself whatever'll help you sleep at night, Yuto. The Authority wants him and they're happy to throw away the life of an operative who's served them faithfully to lure him out."

The operative who unlocked Silas and put the new cuffs on him was gentle, apologizing quietly in English. He must have been one of the people Silas had worked with here.

Silas clapped his shoulder with a sad smile and the man stepped back, his head hung in shame.

The other two operatives had no qualms about viciously prodding Silas into the elevator, shooting me looks as if seeking Himari's approval for their roughness.

I kept my face a blank mask, since I couldn't exactly praise them in Japanese. In my head though? I hurled obscenities. Silas was an operative, same as them, but just because he was a vampire, law and order could be dispensed with. None of his good work over the years mattered.

Is this what awaited me when everyone found out I was an infernal? Would I be the one whose years of hard work keeping humanity safe suddenly became irrelevant?

I dug my nails into my palms to keep from reacting. The thing is, even if I had the abilities to fully embody my role, I was relieved to be relegated to a prop and that the Authority would never be able to prove that I'd been a part of this.

There were people out there who'd prioritize their personal convictions that justice be served over their personal well-being and part of me was ashamed I wasn't more like them, but my pragmatic side knew that standing up against this travesty as Aviva would be a noble sacrifice on my part and not much else.

Moral lines were tricky, shifting bastards, but mine were solid. Should this operation go sideways, I'd fight tooth and nail to save all of us, but for now, I remained silent, my instincts on high alert.

Ezra headed around to the front of the transport van with one of the cruel operatives acting as our driver, while Silas and I climbed into the back of the panel van onto opposite benches. He was chained to a ring in the floor, but I had my doubts about whether that could truly hold him. Regardless, he didn't make a move as we were locked in from outside.

"Sure wish I could see the sky one last time," he said, then he lapsed into silence.

Unsure of what the driver could hear, I couldn't answer Silas or assure him all would be well.

We traveled for almost an hour in stop-and-go city traffic before the van came to a stop.

Nothing happened for a few minutes, then the doors were flung open and the keys to Silas's chains tossed inside. I unlocked him and we climbed out into the middle of a run-down industrial area with the lights of Tokyo blazing in the distance.

Silas stared up at the sky as if memorizing it, but I was glued to the sight of the operative crumpled on the ground next to the van.

"Is he dead?"

At the sound of my normal voice, Silas whipped his head to me.

"Sadly, no," Ezra said drolly in his regular voice. He pulled out another vial, drank half the contents, handed it to me, and shoved Silas in the shoulder. "Pendejo. Next time you're being transported to your death, don't just comply."

His glamor fell away, as did mine within seconds of drinking this second liquid. It tasted like bitter almonds so that was a step up.

"I wouldn't have let it go that far," Silas said, "but first I had to pursue avenues that kept my morals intact."

"Your morals are going to be the death of me," Ezra muttered. "I should have walked the other way when I found you trying to rescue that lame tiger and getting your hand practically torn off for your troubles."

Silas rescued tigers? How sweet was that.

"Says the guy who got teary when we visited Javan at the sanctuary in Malawai," Silas said cheekily.

"There was a five-hundred-pound beast bearing down on me," Ezra said, opening a portal. "They were tears of terror."

"Right. Hugs and ear scratches are primal fear responses when it comes to big cats."

I gaped at them. Ezra got to *hug* tigers? I wanted to hug a tiger.

My eyes slid sideways to my ex.

"You going to keep busting my balls, chamo, or get the hell out of here before this one wakes up?" Ezra prodded the unconscious operative.

"I'm going. I'm going." Silas patted my shoulder. "Thanks for coming to save me, Avi."

"Sorry for getting you in that mess in the first place," I said.

"Not your fault." He walked into the mesh portal.

"You get thanked, and I get grief. What a friendship," Ezra grumbled.

"You think that's grief?" I flashed him a hard smile. "Strap in, Cardoso, because you and I have a lot to discuss."

"Wonderful." He heaved a dramatic sigh then winked at me. "But we had fun, right? Partners in crime."

My answering grin was fifty percent me, fifty percent Cherry Bomb. "Crazy fun."

Chapter 12

We entered the balcony on the Hell and Sachie dropped the six of hearts she'd been about to place on top of the house of cards she'd built. "What happened?"

"Silas is safe," Ezra said. "I portaled him to a guest room to have a shower, change, and get his bearings before we reconvene." He reclaimed his throne-like chair and frowned at the structure now occupying most of the small table on the balcony. "I wasn't finished with my game of Solitaire."

"Yeah, you were," Sachie said. "You had two moves, tops. I spared you the humiliation of losing."

I raised an eyebrow at Sachie, but she shook her head. Our plan had not advanced while I'd been gone.

Ezra waved his hand through the tower, collapsing the structure before deftly sweeping the cards up to shuffle them.

"Are you just going to ignore us while we wait for Silas?" I said. "Rude."

"He needs to press his dominance to prove his ego wasn't hurt when you fucked him and fucked off," Sachie said, deliberately goading him.

I flinched. It was true that I had shared those details with my best friend and that Ezra likely expected it, but it felt tawdry having them flung out like that, especially after our adventure in Tokyo.

"I'm pretty certain I was the one who left first," Ezra said mildly. "Again."

Had I been looking at my ex instead of at a woman in an orange ball gown down on the casino floor trying to untangle one of those metal ring puzzles that magicians used, would I have seen the bland expression that went with his tone, or did Sachie's comment produce the barest flash of anger? Or hurt?

Regardless, Sach and I had agreed she'd handle things and I was fine with that, because I wasn't going to rile Ezra up until we were alone.

Cherry cracked an eye open.

Not like that, I chided.

She huffed quietly in my head.

The double doors connecting the balcony to some other room opened, but Silas hadn't joined us.

I gritted my teeth.

"A woman who isn't a fan of the illustrious Ezra Cardoso?" Delacroix said. His voice, while gravelly, had a mellifluous beauty, much like the swell of a stormy wave. One best seen from afar. He wore his favorite wool fisherman's sweater and there was a starfish stuck in his windswept salt-and-pepper hair like he'd set it there while looking for something else and then forgotten about both items. "Today is truly an auspicious day."

"Funny," Ezra muttered.

Aw. Trouble in paradise, kitten? Then I remembered Ezra's fatigue when we'd first arrived, not to mention the shedim who attacked him, and tamped down my smirk. Was our partners-in-crime escapade the first time he had someone fighting alongside him versus fighting against him since he'd become Lord of the Copper Hell? At least he'd have Silas with him now, but it had been weeks of Ezra navigating this fragile power balance by himself.

"Who are you?" Sachie demanded.

Delacroix blinked. "What?"

"Sorry," she said. "What. Is. Your. Name?" She spoke each word slowly and loudly, the way some people did with her.

I bit the inside of my cheek so I didn't laugh.

Ezra guffawed.

The demon looked from his partner to mine, his brow slightly furrowed like he wasn't sure if he was being pranked. "Delacroix," he snarled.

"The shedim." Sach snapped her fingers at him. "Make yourself useful and get me a drink."

His mouth fell open.

This truly was an auspicious day.

Also, my bestie was my forever hero.

Delacroix scritched his stubble with a nicotine-stained finger. "Drinks are only free for players."

Sachie laughed. "Like I'm going to play any game here. Basic tenet of gambling. The house always wins."

The demon gave an unrepentant grin. "You're awfully quiet, girl detective," he said to me. "Nothing to say to Cardoso at your big reunion? Don't want to do your little song and dance and slash out at each other?"

"Yeah, they're the worst for that." Sach waved a hand at me. "Get it out of your system so I don't have to hear you bitch about him later. Just make it short so we can conclude our business and get back to work."

"Fuck off," I said and turned back to the balcony railing.

Sach wasn't being a bitch. I simply hadn't given her the signal that I'd found our plant on the gaming hall floor, so she was buying me time.

This bird's-eye view made my task of watching the door to the portal foyer a lot easier.

Sach and I had reconsidered involving Darsh, phoning him on our drive to the Play Palace. We hadn't changed our stance on him coming for the jailbreak part, but since he was excellent at extracting information, his job was to discreetly suss out from the patrons at the Copper Hell whether vamp mobs were using shedim secretions to manufacture drugs, or if someone was matchmaking demons with humans.

It made sense that Ezra was keyed to everyone's comings and goings like Calista had been, though apparently, he'd tightened things up. In the event that Ezra was around when Darsh entered through the portal, Sach was supposed to keep Ezra distracted enough to allow our friend through undetected.

I crossed my fingers. Whether the old guard or the new, the Powers That Be at the Copper Hell did not take kindly to Maccabees poking around.

Sachie was committed to her assignment, currently laying into Ezra for going rogue on our last case and killing the vampire we were supposed to rescue. "Enjoy betraying the team, did you?"

Delacroix chuckled, so she tore into him as well for ordering the hit in the first place.

I gripped the railing, my pulse skyrocketing at the thought that my father would commence destroying my best friend, but he laughed harder. Fucking perverse shedim.

Where was Darsh? He hadn't been able to tell us what disguise he'd rustled up, but since we couldn't risk any magic glamor being stripped off him when he went through the portal, he'd promised to use a physical costume.

Had Sach missed his entrance, and he was already here doing recon?

I discounted the portly man by a mah-jongg table as too short and the guy with red eyes engrossed in a checkers game as too obvious.

"I'm not standing around," Sachie said. "I'm going to get that drink." She paused. "Unless you've got a problem with that?"

With my back turned, I couldn't tell if she was speaking to the shedim or the Prime, but my focus was on the floor.

Darsh's last visit to the Hell had resulted in physical injury, and we'd pressed upon him that he didn't have to help us, but he'd blithely dismissed our concerns, saying it would be fun to go in right under Ezra's nose and play spy.

Delacroix was busy gushing over Sachie's moxie. Well, as much as the evil spawn gushed, which was to offer her a tour of the Hell.

Ezra chimed in to bitch about this not being a social call.

A slender woman with a demure fall of blond hair and a smart gray silk dress strode out of the foyer into the casino.

I leaned forward, cataloguing her stance—and her height. At almost six feet, she was tall to begin with, yet she wore the extra inches in her stilettos in confidence.

She studied the games laid out before her, tapping one French-manicured nail against her leather clutch, then took the final chair in a game of bridge, nodding coolly at the other female vamp opponents.

Game on.

"You're not going off with Delacroix, Sach," I said, turning away from the railing and fiddling with the back of one earring. "He'll mess with you. That's what he does."

Sach caught the signal. Her eyes twinkled.

"Ooh," Delacroix mocked. "The girl detective is profiling me."

"Hardly a challenge," I said. "Ezra, go get Silas."

"By all means," Ezra said, crossing his arms, "let me dance to your tune like a trained monkey."

That wasn't what I meant, but I wasn't about to apologize to Ezra in front of Delacroix so I leaned into it and pressed my hands to my heart. "Is it my birthday?"

"Hilarious," Ezra said drolly. "I have a few questions for you first." Did he now? He waved Delacroix off. "Go away."

The shedim sucked on his cigarette. "You were the worst business decision I ever made."

Ezra gave a crooked grin. His amusement in these situations was more infuriating than Sach's. And that was saying something. "Then kill me."

He and Delacroix exchanged a long, tense look. Great. One more mystery to add to the list where my ex was concerned. I didn't particularly love him having secrets with my demon daddy, even if neither was aware of that relationship.

Nor did I approve of Ezra taunting the shedim to do to him what Delacroix had done to Calista.

The demon snorted and looked away first.

"Not today?" Ezra shrugged. His initial encounter with Delacroix ended with my ex imprisoned in watery bindings and agreeing to kill Calista. Now the shedim was the first to cave? What did Ezra have on him? "Ah well," he said. "Give us twenty minutes, then you can return Sachie unharmed."

"Delighted to have your permission," Delacroix snapped.

"And I'm standing right here," Sachie added in the same tone of voice. "You're such a dick." A stake appeared in her hand. "Please give me a reason to come after you."

"Enjoying the scarf I made you?" Ezra said.

"Love it. But I don't need another one, which means you're expendable." She pointed the sharp end of the weapon at him. "Remember that," she said, and followed Delacroix into the elevator.

"You got a scarf?" the shedim said with an annoyed frown.

Ezra waited a moment after the doors closed. "They're bonded against me now. He won't touch her."

I blinked. "That was all an act?"

"Everything here is an act, Aviva," he said wearily.

I dug my nails into my palms. He had Silas now.

"Also," he said, "I wanted alone time."

I waved at everyone down on the casino floor. "I do not think that means what you think it means."

Below on the gaming floor, the woman in gray calmly played bridge and chatted with her tablemates.

Ezra pointed at the light green tinge to the air encasing the balcony. "This area is soundproof, but let's keep away from prying eyes." He rose with a fluid elegance, gathered up his deck of cards, and sauntered to the double doors off the balcony.

I followed him into his private lair with only a small falter in my step. But a metric ton of curiosity.

Two brown leather sofas flanked a wide coffee table. Behind one couch stood a bookcase bolted to the charcoal-colored wall, its neatly ordered titles tucked safely behind glass. Moonlight streamed in through the picture windows looking out over the ocean, sending cool beams over wooden planks worn shiny with age, while logs stacked carefully in the small fireplace tempted with promises of cheerful flames and soothing crackling.

It smelled like Ezra, along with a not unpleasant clove-scented tinge of cigar smoke.

"Private enough?" He flicked off the overhead light, leaving only a floor lamp behind one of the sofas to provide illumination.

The masculine space could have come off as heavy and dark, but it was livened up by personal touches: a beautifully crafted chess table whose pieces were in mid-play, an antique wine and bar cabinet, and a rich water-color of a couple's erotic embrace, which hung dead center over the mantel.

Ezra dropped onto the sofa and tossed the deck of cards on the coffee table. "I could do anything to you and no one would be the wiser. No one would hear you scream."

A vein in my forehead throbbed at his cat-who-ate-the-canary smile. "Back at you."

His smile widened and his hand drifted to one of the buttons on his shirt. "You want to make me scream?"

"In your dreams." I scoffed.

"Often, mi cielo."

My heart skipped a beat. Memories of our past flooded my brain, and for a moment, I was transported back to a time when we were happy. When he'd whisper that endear-ment in my ear as we lay tangled in the early morning light. Part of me yearned to be his sky once more, but not like this. Not when it was only unleashed to knock me off-balance.

I shifted my weight, seeking center. "If you had normal intentions toward me, you wouldn't have ghosted me for two months."

"I didn't mean to let it go that long." Ezra rubbed a hand over his head, his expression contrite. "I had to secure my position here first. I couldn't risk contacting you when it would have been seen as…" He shook his head.

An exploitable weakness?

"Will you sit down?" he said. When I didn't move, he motioned at the club chair across from him. "Please?"

This was my chance to press him for some long-awaited answers. I just hoped I didn't regret asking the questions.

Chapter 13

"There's always an agenda with you," I said, taking a seat, "and it never involves being transparent with me."

"That's not—"

"You didn't break up with me because of Cherry, and while I have some suspicions, I'm still not entirely sure of the reason." While I spoke, I ticked items off on my fingers. "You went to great lengths to be hired by Maccabees, but again, I have no clue why, nor have you ever cleared up why you were the one who absolutely had to investigate the murdered half shedim and drop back into my life. Then there's your partnership with my father, which once again, you swore wasn't all about me, though you also admitted that it's why Delacroix allowed me to walk away unharmed. Do you see the pattern here? You make decisions that involve me, either tangentially or directly, but when I press for answers, you shut me out."

Ezra stiffened. "It's not—I regret..." He pinched the bridge of his nose. "I've made the decisions I believed were necessary."

"No shit," I said, though without any heat. "But has it

ever occurred to you that if you can't share those reasons then that might be a warning sign?"

"Back at you."

"You're right. I've kept a lot of things from my friends and coworkers, but I did share everything with one person, knowing that relationship couldn't work without honesty and trust. And in the vein of more honesty, this back-and-forth with you is making me crazy. I trust you with my life and our connection at times is as strong as ever, and I love working together, being in sync like that."

It was terrifying being that open with him, handing him that power, but it was freeing too. And there was a not-small part of me that was curious to see what he did with it.

"But?" He leaned forward, his arms loosely braced on his knees, but his hands were twisted together and his eyes searched mine.

"Lay siege. That's how you see us."

"Give me a break, Aviva." He sliced his hand through the air. "You started those metaphors with wanting to conquer me, remember?"

"Fair," I said quietly. I rubbed my hand over the back of my neck. "I was trying to find some desperately needed agency where the two of us were concerned, and I went about it the wrong way. It was hurtful, and I'm sorry."

"The encounter had its moments." He shot me a wry grin. "Let me do better. Start us off with the romance you deserve."

"That wasn't a plea for hearts and flowers, Ezra. I *deserve* honesty. Even if you did answer all my questions *and* I was willing to get past our history, how do you see this working? I'm a Maccabee and you're in bed with a demon."

He raised an eyebrow. "Definitely not the one I want to be in bed with."

"Ezra."

"My partnership with Delacroix," he continued smoothly, "is a means to an end. Not a lifetime commitment."

"That's hardly reassuring given you're immortal." I spun the short stack of books on the coffee table around to look at their spines, but the titles were all in Spanish. "Will three hundred years be enough time to accomplish your top-secret agenda? Five hundred? You can come visit my grave when you're done."

"Don't be so sure. Half shedim have been known to live a couple hundred years."

I jerked, knocking the books. "What?"

Cherry Bomb came to the same sudden alertness as a cat who'd sniffed out a mouse. Except in her case, it was for much wanted answers about who she was.

Who *I* was.

The desire to know more flooded me so completely that I briefly closed my eyes against a surge of dizziness. I might outlive Sachie? My mom? By a lot? I rubbed a hand against my chest. Would I grow old and stay that way for decades or would my aging process go at a snail's pace? How would that factor into my plans for acceptance? Would it be one more nail against me?

"This is a fact?" I said.

"Humans might not know about infernals, but some demons do, and I'm now in the perfect position to learn everything." Ezra picked up the cards, cutting and re-cutting the deck. "I'd never get you anything as trite as flowers, Aviva." He flipped over a card.

It was the queen of hearts.

"Do you know why vampires were so successful in their campaign to be accepted by people?" he said, shuffling the card back into the deck.

"Human stupidity?"

Ezra wagged a finger at me, amusement dancing in his silvery-blue eyes. "So cynical. It's because we were transparent."

"About some things."

"Enough that we removed the fear of the unknown, gave humans the agency they so desperately crave." He split the deck in half. "I don't agree with all the restrictions people put in place against us, but overall, it worked in our favor. We have power, respect. Adoration even. You could too."

Yes, yes, and yes, Cherry whispered.

The cards thwapped softly against the table as he shuffled them. I usually found that rhythmic fluttering comforting, but it was drowned out by my pulse trumpeting in my ears. "What would it cost me?"

"Coño," he swore. "I'm not going to hold information about you hostage."

The room was still, save for the gentle sway of the curtains in the breeze of the open window. The only sound was the steady beat of my heart disturbing the awkward silence that had fallen.

Ezra twisted around to stare out the window, his face completely averted from mine, which was odd. Unless... Was the man who always wore a mask unable to conjure one up now?

I cleared my throat. "Should you check in on Silas?"

My ex draped an arm along the back of the sofa and impassively met my gaze, infuriatingly not doing as commanded. "Whatever hornet's nest you've kicked looking into this copycat demon is going to sting you, all of you, and sting hard."

Had he unearthed new information on this that he also wasn't sharing? *Maybe it's just concern.*

Even without my blue flame magic, which didn't work on vamps, I was trained to read people, but interpreting

146

Ezra was like watching a traffic light cycling through colors. And I couldn't tell anymore if the malfunction was on his end or mine.

I mimicked his nonchalant body language. "Is that an order to drop it?"

"It's merely advice."

"Which I didn't ask for."

"You didn't ask me to have your back either," he said. "You called and demanded I help free Silas. I won't get in your way, but you involved my best friend. You involved *me*, so you don't get to decide my involvement is done because you got what you wanted."

I ran my thumb against the edges of the cards. "This isn't like when I... When we..."

"Really," he said flatly.

I flung the top card at him. In my head it was a sharp-edged weapon that sliced into his throat. In actuality, the two of spades fluttered uselessly to the table. "The Maccabees were leaving you alone so long as you didn't leave this yacht, and I risked that, risked *you*, to have you save Silas."

"Disarming me with truth?" he murmured.

"I don't want you dead, Ezra. That's still a long way from wherever you see us."

He studied me for a long moment. "I'll go get Silas." He exited back onto the balcony, the hum of the elevator growing fainter.

I was sorely tempted to check if the frosted glass door next to the bookshelf led to Ezra's bedroom, but I didn't. With my luck, he'd scent it when he returned and get ideas that I was more into moving things along than I was. We'd had fun together saving Silas, but that didn't reset us to the same easy intimacy we had when we were younger.

I flipped through the cards until I found the queen of hearts, and pressed my thumbs over the red hearts so only

147

the double image of the queen was visible. Two queens. Two parts of me: human Aviva and Cherry Bomb, a baroness with aspirations of royalty.

Damn straight, she said proudly.

Still, both versions were unified on this one card. Face-up for the entire world to see.

The only person I'd ever relied on to reach my goal of universal acceptance for half shedim was me, so did I trust Ezra to obtain information on this?

I tapped the card against the table. Ezra claimed that he didn't dump me because of Cherry, despite it coming on the heels of my revelation. Nowadays I was mostly convinced he was truthful on that score, and I appreciated him satisfying my thirst for knowledge about my kind, but any relationship between us felt impossible, given his behavior and us being on very different sides now. Our chemistry was irrelevant if we weren't friends, and how could we be friends without honesty?

Sachie strolled in from the balcony, sipping a froufrou drink with chunks of pineapple speared on a fancy pink plastic sword next to a pink straw. "Nice digs."

I massaged a temple. I was such a hypocrite.

You said it, not me, Cherry said snidely.

Delacroix followed Sach, grinding his teeth and carrying a matching beverage, which he set in front of me.

I eyed the glass, more worried about whatever combination of booze produced the fumes wafting off it than any poison he might have added. "Thanks. Good tour?"

Sach placed her drink on the table and took the spot that Ezra had vacated. "It was okay. I like Vegas better."

Delacroix was going to need major dental surgery if he didn't stop grinding his teeth. He muttered something about work and vanished through the wall.

It was one thing not to ward up the balcony, which was in plain view of the gambling floor below, to let everyone see the futility of any attacks, but this was Ezra's private space.

No matter how quiet or stealthy I'd been, I'd never managed to make physical contact when he was sleeping without him waking up in time, but I was a human. Was Ezra condemned to a constant vigilance here? Even if it was just against Delacroix, that was more than enough. No wonder Ezra looked exhausted.

I clenched my fists. *He has Silas here now.*

Sachie leaned in. "This place is incredible," she whispered. "You have got to try the buffet."

"So people keep telling me."

Ezra and Silas returned, and Sach jumped up, peppering our friend with questions, but the vamp assured her he was fine. His hair was damp and he'd changed into clean clothes, but he still looked rumpled and beat-up.

A moment later the woman in gray stepped into the doorway from the balcony, her chin tipped up in defiance.

"Darsh." Ezra motioned my friend forward. "Glad you could join us."

Silas was transfixed.

"How'd you know?" Darsh popped a hip, planting his hand on the fall of silk.

"Don't insult me." Ezra laughed at Sachie and me. "The look on your faces."

"Glad we amuse you," I said.

He grinned. "Yes. I'm incredibly entertained by your secret plot to sneak Darsh in. You couldn't just ask, mi cielo?"

At his term of endearment for me, Sach made a strangled noise in her throat, but she relaxed at my clenched jaw.

Darsh snapped his fingers at Silas. "Close your mouth, Cowpoke. You're catching flies. I'm in a dress. What of it?"

"Adelaide Edwards, heiress and entrepreneur." Silas crossed his arms, flexing his biceps. "That alias of yours has had a hit on her since you tangled with the Fog City Mob in the '90s."

Darsh flicked his hair off his shoulder. "And?" he said in a deceptively mild voice.

Sachie stared at Silas, wide-eyed. "You snooped into Darsh's background?"

"He'll do better," I said. "Right, Silas? Don't curse him with the evil eye."

Darsh and I once spent an evening comparing Romani and Jewish cursing abilities, finally agreeing that both our people were skilled in those arts. Regardless, we'd just saved Silas. He wasn't being offed now by one pissed-off vamp.

Darsh sat next to Sachie and crossed his legs. "Next time you want to know something, Cowpoke, ask me. That is, if you don't get yourself executed first. How'd all that idealism work out for you?"

Silas smirked. "I'm here, aren't I?"

"Because the calvary rode to the rescue." Darsh glared at my ex. "And I have plenty to say about this being said calvary's fault in the first place."

"Ez wasn't at fault." Silas's words were infused with steel, and he held Darsh's eye in challenge.

The other vamp held up his hands. "All I'm saying is that you shouldn't have trusted justice to prevail in a world that trades heavily in power and very little in ideals. Vampires aren't jailed. Even operatives found guilty are staked. End of story."

"Except for one vampire in history to make it to the epilogue," Silas said. "Whatever you did to get on their radar, the Maccabees made you an operative and decades later, here you still are."

Darsh's left eye twitched. "I'm the glorious exception

to all things and should not be taken as a roadmap to survival. You, however"—he jabbed a finger a Silas— "could have easily resisted arrest."

"Through violence." Silas shook his head. "Hurting or killing people."

"Saving yourself," Darsh growled. "You're a fucking vampire, Silas."

"I didn't get to choose what I am." There was a stubborn set to Silas's chin. "But I can choose *who* I am. Which I have. Just like you're choosing to avoid giving me a straight answer right now about why you chose to resurrect Adelaide."

I feel you, buddy.

Darsh unfurled a Cheshire Cat smile. "Why do straight when twisted is so much more fun?" He eyed Silas up and down. "But if you must know, I've been careful to maintain Adelaide's reputation over the years, and with some of the wives of the Southbank Mob gathering here for the past couple of months, I chose to have her make a rare appearance."

My eyebrows shot into my hairline. With most people, Darsh would have ended that conversation with his "twisted" quip. Reassuring Silas, a man he allegedly wanted no complicated entanglements with, was not normal behavior.

I set that aside to ponder later and clapped my hands together to get us back on track. "Can we compare notes while we're all here? Darsh, did you learn anything?"

"Not particularly," Darsh said. "I dropped that I was looking to expand my business ventures, but no one knew of a way to pair shedim up with drug manufacturers, or any vamps already involved in that line of work."

"Silas?" I turned to him.

He shook his head. "My initial searches before I was arrested didn't bring anything up either."

151

"Because there's nothing to find." Ezra strolled over to the bar cabinet and grabbed some fancy glass bottles of water from a small fridge hidden cleverly inside the vintage piece. "Think of all the trouble and stress you could have saved us all if you'd only asked me first."

"Riiiiight," I said. "Because you're positively chatty on anything related to vamp Mafias. Oh, and also?" I jabbed a finger at him. "I had no reason to believe we were on speaking terms at the time."

"I told you—" He slammed the water bottles on the table, then shook his head, looking like he was pulling his anger back inside himself through a physical act of will. He turned to Silas. "Why didn't *you* just ask me straight up about it instead of getting yourself arrested?"

I got the strongest feeling that he was more upset with Silas than with me.

"It was a legit search in the wake of the drug bust," Silas said. "If you weren't bouncing from one place to the other trying—"

I leaned so far forward waiting for him to finish that sentence that I was in danger of toppling over.

Ezra coughed behind one hand. Very politely. Very insistently.

Silas uncapped a bottle of water. "Sorry. That was uncalled for. But no, none of my myriad searches bore fruit."

"It is what it is." Ezra sat down, closed his eyes for a second, his features pinched tight. "In regards to vamp mobs infusing drugs with demon magic, the idea's been floated many times before, but working with shedim is too unpredictable. Vamps generally don't trust demons enough to willingly partner with them, and imprisoning a demon puts a target on the jailer since others will attempt to gain possession of it."

"That makes sense." Sachie cracked open a bottle.

"Plus, you can't rely on magic to behave consistently when mixed with drugs. Even designer drugs using Eishei Kodesh magic are too hard to regulate. Sometimes they do nothing. It's financially unstable to invest in that."

Awesome. Silas was on the run, I'd inadvertently provided the Maccabees with an excuse to go after Ezra, and we had nothing to show for it. I stilled. My mother said the Authority was waiting to see what Ezra did when he left the yacht, and even Ezra said he was in a détente with them. So why did they feel the need to act and draw him out now?

Unless this wasn't about Ezra at all?

It was about me.

Chapter 14

More precisely, it was about the demon suicide I'd witnessed.

"Aviva?" Ezra prompted, his drink halfway to his mouth.

I picked up a bottle but toyed with the label instead of opening it. "I didn't kill the shedim. It ended its own life after saying it refused to go back somewhere."

Sachie sighed. "Not this again. We agreed—"

"It was a fuck-you, or I'm not remembering it right, but I am and it wasn't. I'm not stuck on this because I was hit with the demon secretion either, Sach. There's something wrong with this picture, and people keep dismissing me when I bring it up, but what else has the Maccabees so wound up that they arrested Silas? His vamp connections and hacker abilities that made him perfectly placed to unearth—"

"Are you hearing yourself?" Sachie spread her hands wide. "How paranoid you sound?"

Ezra swirled his drink. "That doesn't mean she's wrong."

She glared at him before turning to me. "Say you're

correct. The only people you told were Michael and me. That detail isn't in the initial report. You think she phoned someone and put all this in motion?"

"No."

"You think I did?"

I waved that preposterous idea away. "Of course not."

Sach lost the tension in her shoulders and leaned forward. "Then how would anyone else find out? Explain it to me, Avi, because all I'm hearing are conspiracy theories."

"The Maccabees aren't the bastions of nobility you'd like to believe," Ezra said.

"Neither is the guy who dipped to go party on a demon boat." She whirled on him. "I'd like to believe that I've spent the past few years risking my life and my relationship with my family for something *worth* believing in!" She raised her water bottle like she was about to wing it across the room and only the fact that it was glass had her lower it again.

I dropped my gaze to the carpet. Sachie's feelings were valid, but so were my instincts. I just wasn't sure how to reconcile the two without one of us feeling hurt. More hurt.

"Let's play this out," Silas said calmly. "If Aviva heard the shedim correctly, where didn't she want to go back to? Demons are worse than hissing cockroaches for staying alive when you plain don't want 'em to be. Why not at least try and escape?"

"She was weak," Sachie said. "She could come and go from her cage at will but didn't."

"That tracks." Silas nodded. "I buy her ending her life on her terms. Dead is dead, but she goes out with dignity."

"Unless dead isn't dead," Darsh said slowly. "What if Maccabees killing shedim sends them back to the demon realm but if they kill themselves, it's truly the end?"

I wrenched off the bottle cap with a sharp crack, churning through the horrific implications.

Shedim had haunted our world for centuries, wreaking havoc on innocent lives. We had dedicated ourselves to eradicating them, believing that each time we vanquished one, it was gone forever.

If we were essentially in a video game where demons had infinite lives, that would mean our attempts to rid the world of them weren't just pathetic.

They were useless.

The idea was terrifying, but it didn't mesh with other things I knew about demons. "When we kill shedim, they shrivel into a whorl of skin or crack apart, or die in one of a dozen other pretty definite not-coming-back-from-this ways."

I'd killed enough shedim to have my own data, though everyone except Ezra would assume I knew this from our lessons during Maccabee training. One day, I'd live as a proud, out half shedim, but until I changed people's minds about infernals, my fellow operatives wouldn't benefit from my firsthand knowledge.

I took a sip of water. "What they don't do is open a portal and get sucked through to the demon realm. Or regenerate."

"Well, they don't do either of those things in ways we can see," Darsh said, combing his nails through his blond wig, "but we don't see them come through from their realm to earth in the first place. We don't even know how that happens. Who's to say what else we're missing?"

Between Eishei Kodesh, vampires, and shedim, the latter was the group that Maccabees had the least information on. The general public wasn't aware of their existence, and we didn't have demon informants out there assisting us. Maccabee policy was to hunt and kill them, not have heart-to-hearts.

We didn't usually bring them in for questioning either. Imagine if they exerted their demonic influence in a chapter filled with dangerous, skilled operatives? Hard pass. Any demon encounter was painstakingly related back to HQ by the Maccabees involved, and that information added to the records to help mitigate future damage.

Maybe our vamp operatives had heard something? Cécile was only in her forties, but Nasir was close to seventy and Darsh was way older than that. How old, we weren't sure, but I'd bet he'd been around at least three hundred years.

"Has the squad discussed shedim deaths?" I said.

"No," Darsh said. "It was just the shedim's choice of words when you were about to kill her. 'Go back.' My mind supplied 'to where she came from.' Shedim have agendas. Missions, so to speak. Suppose they do end up back in the demon realm when we dispatch them. I doubt they're getting a 'better luck next time' speech."

"The demon realm is probably all kinds of suck ass—" I said.

"Flaming Flapjacks sounds okay," Sachie said with a shrug.

I startled, having expected her to keep fuming and remain silent, then squeezed the water bottle tightly. One dumb tour and she was buddy-buddy with Delacroix? A demon she *knew* had threatened and harmed me multiple times?

Including at that very restaurant? Flaming Flapjacks existed in some demon realm–lite place. It was still creepy and they served things best not examined too closely along with short stacks, but I wasn't forced against my will to bust out my full Cherry form.

A fact that had probably saved my life.

"The waffles looked good." I placed the water bottle on the table so I didn't smash it to vent my anger and frustration. "Everything you're saying makes sense, Darsh, but I really hope that's not the case. We already had to update Maccabee intel that staking doesn't kill Primes."

Maccabees clung to certain givens in our fight to keep humanity safe, the two most important being: Eishei Kodesh flame types presented in consistent, expected ways, and vampires were killed when staked.

Let's just say that after Darsh filed the case report with that new information about Primes, Michael had come out of a lot of unscheduled calls with the Authority looking grim and had shoved an extreme by-the-book adherence down our chapter's collective throat for weeks.

Sachie, Darsh, and I, as the ones who'd confirmed Primes' deviation from the norm, became those kids in the cafeteria looking for a table to sit at and just getting a lot of backs and cold shoulders. It had sucked and we were only just coming out of our freeze-out.

My friends' downcast expressions said the two of them remembered this all too clearly.

"This isn't the same," Silas said. "The more demon intel, the better."

"You sure?" I shook my head. "The sum total of all born vamps currently in existence is exactly one, so telling the Authority the truth about staking him shouldn't have been a big deal, but they all freaked out."

"It's a big deal to me," Ezra said blandly.

"Sorry." I backpedaled hard, because staking a Prime trapped them in their body, alive, aware, and incapacitated. "Of course it is."

"I'm just messing with you," he said.

I glared at him.

Ezra raised an eyebrow. "Too soon?"

Silas shook his head at his friend. "Continue, Aviva."

"Even the relatively few shedim here on earth are too many." I faced Sachie and Darsh. "You really want to be the bearer of bad news again? *This* bad news?" I crossed my legs and gave a breezy wave. "Hey, Authority Council, heads-up. You know the thousands of demons we've killed since our founding way back when? Well, they're not actually dead. They're chilling in the demon realm, regenerating from a sprout like Groot. It might take two thousand years or twenty minutes, but all those shedim we assumed were the same type? Nope. They're actually the same demon. Good luck."

"You're assuming they don't already know," Ezra said.

I groaned and buried my head in my hands. "A gift basket is not in our future."

A heavy silence settled as we contemplated their reaction.

I finally raised my head. "Is it horrible that part of me hopes we're correct?"

"It depends why," Silas said.

"You didn't see the victims at the lab. God, Edward…" I faltered at the memory of his bleak stare, pressing my hands against my eyelids. But those kinds of images were never so easily blocked out. "Shedim victims never truly get justice, but if we're sending the fiends back to be tortured, to be at the mercy of demonic creativity for inflicting pain, then part of me is all for it."

Darsh raised his hand, smiling brightly. "When you put it like that, so am I."

"You're the oldest one here," Ezra said. "How likely do you think this is?"

Darsh thought about it a moment, then shook his head. "My first instinct is that if Maccabees were simply sending shedim back to their home realm, the demons would rub it in our faces. What happens in the demon realm stays in the demon realm, and for all we know, they get a lovely vacation when they return. We have no proof they're tortured, and thus there's no reason not to tell us how ineffective we are should they return. So why haven't they?" Darsh twirled a lock of blond hair around his finger.

Silas tracked the hair twirl.

"That's my biggest stumbling block with this theory," Darsh said. "Shedim would absolutely use that to undermine our confidence in this fight against evil."

Silas nodded. "I concur. Regardless of whether the Authority Council knows or not, the demons wouldn't keep silent on that score."

Sachie tapped her finger against the pillbox compartment on her Maccabee ring. "Then it's exactly like I said in the first place. There's nothing nefarious to this suicide and the Authority isn't keeping any secret because there's nothing to hide. Our magic kills them. End of story."

Darsh and Silas wore the same "matter settled" expression as Sachie, but Ezra had a tiny crease between his brows.

Should I accept that I was reading too much into it and drop it? What if this theory was correct though? Did it change anything? Maccabees had spent hundreds of years finding the magic cocktail to get us even this far in the fight. If we had no way to kill shedim, then we were doing the best we could. Was that enough?

"Not being a Maccabee anymore, I have no skin in this game," Ezra said. Was it really that easy for him to walk away and change allegiances? Maybe, if his only allegiance had ever been to himself?

Everything here is an act. Ezra had risked his life to save Silas and would do the same for any one of us in this room. He let this fiction about his all-consuming self-serving motives stand because it was another mask he could hide behind to keep himself safe. Didn't he ever get really lonely always being someone other than himself? Even though I hid Cherry, I could at least always be me.

"But I think," Ezra continued, "that it's always better to have all the information."

"Once a spy," Darsh said dryly.

The corner of Ezra's mouth tugged up. "Aviva, it was your suspicion. Are you convinced otherwise, or do you want to keep digging into this until you're positive one way or the other?"

I stood up and walked to the window, looking out over the ocean. The magic in our rings let people aware of shedim sleep at night, knowing we had a means of fighting them.

Hope was a powerful motivator.

What was worse? If I found proof, spoke up, and stole other operatives' hope for a happy future where they made a difference, but allowed us to solve this problem? Or let their hope stand as a lie that sustained them?

At the end of the day, there might not be anything to find, just like Sachie kept insisting. I'd already gotten Silas arrested and the Maccabees had implicated Sachie and me as his pawns.

Why keep digging and get all of us into worse trouble?

I wiped a smudge off the glass with my sleeve, unable to get the image of Zaven's grinning son out of my head. Why extinguish anyone's hope?

"I'm convinced," I said. "Vamp mobs aren't working with shedim. I can put that into my report. The only end to tie up is how the Eishei Kodesh drug makers found the demon and I'll interview Jasmine for that answer."

"Silas can stay with me until this all dies down," Ezra said. "He can work on clearing his name from the safety of the Hell."

"'Safety of the Hell,'" Darsh said. "Is that an oxymoron like friendly fire?"

Sach snickered.

"What if we need to contact Silas?" I said.

"Already ahead of you, partner." Silas checked our phones for any bugs, then set up encrypted chats with Sachie and me.

Sachie yawned. "Now that everything's settled, which way out?"

Ezra pointed at the double doors, which now had mesh netting woven across their entrance. Have portal, will travel.

"Later, Cardoso." She strode through the portal.

Darsh strutted out after her, his hips swaying. He threw a single look back over his shoulder.

"One last glance for the road, Rapunzel?" Silas said.

Darsh slitted his eyes, huffed, and sashayed through the portal.

Ezra nudged Silas. "You're so fucked, chamo."

His bestie was adorably flushed, but he smirked at Ezra. "Because 'mi cielo' is a real puddle at your feet."

I barked a laugh, loving this teasing side of Silas.

He winked at me.

Still, my chest ached, and I hugged Silas like I could bundle him far from the devastation to come with Darsh. He hugged me back, albeit with a confused wrinkle in his brow.

Ezra escorted me to the portal. "What, after running around Tokyo illegally and heisting my best friend, I don't get a hug?" he said dryly.

I tossed my hair. "You've had enough excitement for one night."

As I walked away on his laughter, a strange mix of emotions flooded my heart. Our encounter had been tumultuous as always, yet I couldn't shake off the feeling that something momentous was about to happen.

Hopefully it was the kind that ended in public accolades, and not torture, unemployment, or further heartbreak, but I was nothing if not deeply cynical.

Chapter 15

Torture it was.

Good thing Sachie and I fortified ourselves with a hearty lunch at the Jolly Hellhound, because our interrogation back at Maccabee HQ turned out to be questioning by committee. Michael was joined by two Authority Council members via video call. Dr. Olsen was the specialist Michael had brought in to break Maud's story about being compelled to kidnap Calista. Thankfully, it passed muster.

I'd never met Dmitri Kozlov, the other council member joining us on the call.

Dr. Olsen took the meeting while walking along the shore of a brilliant blue lake, while Kozlov's austere office had a view of a gloomy river.

Our HR manager, Lars, rounded out the panel, clearing his sinuses with a series of wet snorts, honks, and snuffles for the entirety of this session in his office.

I talked them through the drug lab bust until I was hoarse, then Sachie and I fielded endless repetitive questions about our findings on the copycat demon and why we suspected vamp mob involvement.

"Operative Saito." Dmitri pushed his wire-frame glasses up his nose, revealing a hole in the elbow of his dad cardigan. "You've had an interesting trajectory with our organization."

Sachie gave a polite smile. "I'd say all trajectories with the Maccabees are interesting."

Dmitri chuckled. "That's true, but it's rare that Eishei Kodesh operatives choose to work exclusively with their vampire counterparts."

My stomach twisted and I darted a glance at Michael, willing her to step in as our director and shut this down.

She placidly watched the screen, but there was a coiled quality to her posture, like she was poised to strike.

"Is that a question or a statement?" Sachie said. "Because I don't have conclusive data to tell you whether or not that's true."

"It's a statement," he said. "What drew you to them?"

"The Maccabees were founded to fight vampires and shedim." She propped her ankle on her other knee, her hand creeping down to whatever weapon she had stashed in her boot.

I coughed—loudly and pointedly.

She dropped her hand. "It's the battle at the heart of our organization. I wanted in."

"It's unusual is all," Dr. Olsen said. The older woman's phone bobbed with each step, her face free of makeup and her hair in a messy bun.

"Enough, Lena. You too, Dmitri." My mother clicked her cheap ballpoint pen. The more she deemed a meeting total and utter BS, the lower the quality of her writing implements.

No one ever noticed that about her.

Today, Director Michael Hannah Fleischer had chosen plastic. "Stop browbeating my operatives," she said. "I approved Saito's request to work with our vampires, just like I approved the request to have Silas assist on this investigation. Do you plan to tell me that my actions were unusual as well?"

"Of course not." Dr. Olsen momentarily dipped out of the screen before righting the camera. "But speaking of Silas, whose idea was it to bring him into the investigation?"

"Mine," I said. "Just like I brought Sachie onto this case. I would have asked my colleagues on the lab bust, but one of my fellow members was dead, and my team leader and the other operative are still healing from shock and physical injuries at the hand of that shedim, so they weren't available."

"Don't take that tone with us, Operative," Dmitri said coldly.

"We've done everything by the book," I said.

"Bringing a vampire with hacking abilities—"

"Who works for the Maccabees," I retorted.

"Operative Fleischer," Michael chided. "Calm down."

I ground my teeth together. Her oh-so-rational tone of voice was thrusting me into warp-speed fury like I was fifteen again. It was okay for her to be angry with this bull-shit, but I had to sit here and play nice?

"Silas has known ties with a vampire Mafia," Dr. Olsen added.

I waved a hand around, my chest tight. It was taking all my willpower to keep Cherry from breaking out. "His friend's dad. That's known ties? Yikes. Sachie, what happened with that tax audit of your mom's? I wouldn't want my known ties with her to get me in trouble."

"Avi," Sach murmured. "They're not worth getting disciplined."

No, they weren't, but I couldn't stop myself. This entire trumped-up charge, this questioning, targeting Ezra —all of it was unfair.

I gripped the armrests, unable to slow the anger spewing out of me. "You had no issue with all these facts about Silas for decades. Same with Ezra's past when you brought him on and had him play spy for you for four years. Or when you gave him carte blanche to show up here in Vancouver and let us meet Silas in the first place."

"You mean when we placed your ex in your path?" If snakes could smile, they'd wear the one on Dmitri's face.

The loud gasp in the sudden silence wasn't mine. I checked. Twice.

"Did you use my chapter as bait?" Michael's voice dripped ice.

Sachie rested her hand on her ankle, her fingers twitching, and Lars finally reached for his tissue box—but just to blot his forehead.

The director's glacial tone only spurred my anger into the stratosphere. It wasn't a surprise that concern for her chapter superseded any for her only child, but damn.

Dr. Olsen gave Michael the same "don't be melodramatic" shake of the head that my mother had used on me throughout my life.

I was so numb that I couldn't even enjoy seeing her on the receiving end of it.

"If his position with the Maccabees had become untenable," Michael said, "then you should have spoken to me directly, instead of playing games."

I waited for her to add something about not using her daughter, or even just not using her operatives, but nope, that was it.

"Questions had arisen about how Cardoso inveigled his way into the Maccabees," Dmitri said.

Fair. I wondered about that myself.

"And he was getting harder to control," Dr. Olsen said.

I turned my snort into a cough. What about Ezra

suggested he was easy to control at any point in time? His biddable manner? His easygoing acquiescence?

He acquiesced to you easily enough when you wanted to get naked, Cherry reminisced fondly.

I thumped my fist against my chest to clear my cough.

"We expected you'd be displeased with the carte blanche he was given on that case," Dr. Olsen said to Michael. "You'd want him gone as quickly as possible. We were hoping that you'd find something we could use, since expelling him without a serious charge was not possible, given his connections."

Didn't want him marshalling any vamp Mafia buddies in retaliation? Good call.

"Instead, Michael, you allowed him to work a second investigation," Dmitri said.

"Because a Prime was abducted," she replied. "His insights were valuable."

"Indeed. So valuable that he walked away with all of them," Dmitri sneered.

Michael stiffened.

"Cardoso somehow perverted justice and freed Silas," Dmitri said.

Sach's eyes widened. "Silas is free?"

I looked down at the table to hide my smirk.

Dmitri sat back, his arms crossed, and his knobby elbow poking out of the hole in the fabric. "What about your relationships with both vampires, Operative Fleischer?" he said, not missing a beat. "Were you part of this jailbreak?"

"No," I said evenly. "This is the first I've heard of it." I frowned. "Are you saying someone waltzed into a Maccabee jail and sprung him? Do you have footage of any suspects?"

A muscle ticked in Dmitri's jaw. "The footage isn't usable."

Because it showed the chapter director and a top operative escorting Silas out with help from other operatives? Yeah, I bet it wasn't usable.

Silas faced an impossible battle to clear his name, and if they charged me with collusion, my career, *my life* was fucked. *Sector A. Sector A. Sector A.* The name of the prison thudded in my head like footsteps leading to the gallows.

"That's a very serious charge," Michael said. "If you have proof, then show it."

Dmitri waved his hand like hard evidence when someone's life was on the line was of no importance.

"That's what I thought," my mother said.

Lars sniffled three times in rapid, nervous succession. "Can we conclude that Operatives Saito and Fleischer were not manipulated or compelled by Silas, and they both acted in good faith?"

Dr. Olsen calmly agreed, though Dmitri conceded the point with a reluctant nod, looking like he'd stepped in dog shit.

I unclenched my hands, which I'd been painfully twisting in my lap. "What about the charges against Silas?"

My answer was corporate speak for "Mind your own business."

I was permitted to interview Jasmine, my orders clear: learn how she found the shedim. If there was a middleman involved (they didn't use the term "matchmaker," but in my head, the song from *Fiddler on the Roof* played on a loop), find out who it was. The Authority would put other people on it to track that middleman down.

"Any Eishei Kodesh who is guilty of colluding with shedim must be rounded up and sent to Sector A. And if another shedim or a vampire is involved, they will be killed." Dmitri removed his glasses. "I trust you can handle one simple interview to get that information and enable the Maccabees to prevail in this fight against evil." He folded his glasses and set them on his desk.

It took everything in me not to stare at the unnaturally sharp jut of his elbow. "You can count on me."

"Good, because I'll be frank."

Like he'd been holding back so far. Inwardly, I sighed. End this stupid interrogation already.

"I don't like your personal relationships with people in positions to severely undermine our organization," Dmitri said. "Get answers, wrap this case up, and don't give me any reason to doubt your loyalty."

Sachie and I were dismissed.

I stepped into the hallway with my fists clenched and my jaw tight, almost vibrating at the strain of keeping Cherry under wraps instead of busting her out, going back in, and vowing to make them all pay.

"Fuck them," Sachie said.

This case had been a nightmare from the moment I strapped on those stupid snowshoes. Now they were threatening me with doubts about my loyalty? After I'd spent my entire career going above and beyond to dedicate myself to the cause and the Maccabees?

We walked down the hall to the elevators.

"Let's grab dinner," she said. "We'll be a bit late lighting the Hanukkah candles tonight, but it's still within acceptable leeway."

I smiled faintly and did my best to shake off churning emotions. There were plenty of years when we couldn't light the candles at dusk because of work, so we agreed that keeping humanity safe was "acceptable leeway" for our lateness.

The temptation to hang out with my best friend and salvage this horrible day was overwhelming, but there was one more awful task I had to undertake.

"I want to get Zaven's address and check his place out.

Would you wait for me to light the candles? I won't be long."

She stepped into the car. "You sure that's wise? Maybe let this drop for a while?"

"I have to go in before anyone realizes he's missing and destroys any valuable evidence. It's not ideal, but…" I sighed.

Sach had suggested last night that given only vampires were involved in the blackmail attempt against Maud, and none of them were going to file a complaint, that we treat this as an off-the-books job, meaning no paperwork.

I'd gratefully agreed because there'd be no official record of any suspicion about my sister. The downside about no paperwork, though, was that Zaven's family wouldn't get any answers. When operatives staked vamps, next of kin were notified, but his death wasn't recorded.

I owed it to his family to look them in the eye, even if I wasn't about to admit my role in their tragedy. Or that they didn't yet know there was any tragedy at all. I could call it furthering my investigation into who'd hired Maud, and it was. But it was also penance.

I hit the elevator button. "It won't raise any red flags to get the last-known address of a man on record as Eishei Kodesh."

Sach drove me to his place, and even offered to grab some takeout for me. "You didn't have to take all the blame for bringing Silas on," she said. "It was my idea."

"You wouldn't have been on the case if it wasn't for me." I stared bleary-eyed out the window.

"Still." She pulled up to the curb at an apartment building close to the abandoned laundromat that housed the rift into the Brink, smack dab in vamp territory.

Surprisingly, this was a sought-after neighborhood. Vamp mobs who owned the areas around urban rifts were savvy enough to pump a lot of money back into those neighborhoods to keep them safe and desirable areas. It was smart on a lot of levels: having regular people live there meant that anyone shady or too official looking (Maccabees and Trad cops) would stand out.

"You sure you want to go in on your own?" she said.

"Yeah. They won't hurt a Maccabee who's just asking questions." Should any vamp discover we were covering up those deaths, it could go very differently. I got out of the car and waved her off.

A human father and his tween daughter breezed past on bikes.

Since the vamps had eyes everywhere, I didn't bother hiding my Maccabee ring with gloves that would be perfectly suitable in this weather.

The female vampire sitting on the stoop of Zaven's apartment building pulled her earbuds out. Being December, it was already dark in the late afternoon, so I couldn't tell if she'd been Trad or Eishei Kodesh in life. She stood up, fangs visible.

Unconcerned, I pushed past her. "Yeah, you're very scary. Run along and report back to your emo overlord."

I wrenched the door open and stomped up the stairs to Zaven's place on the second floor.

His wife, Carine, served me sweet tea, helped her son, Davit, build a tower of blocks, and answered my "routine questions" about how long her husband had been a vampire, all with the same serene demeanor, while I tried not to squirm uncomfortably.

Zaven hadn't registered his vamp status with the Maccabees. That wasn't unusual, especially when the newbie in question had a rap sheet when human, but it was the perfect excuse for my presence. If he wouldn't answer the questions on the form, then his family had to.

Carine didn't know who'd turned him, just that it happened right after he got out of prison.

Davit thrust a red block in my face with a chubby hand and a grubby smile. He couldn't have been more than a couple of years old, having been born while Zaven was locked up. A conjugal visit baby.

I wasn't great with kids at the best of times, and sitting here in their small but cozy living room, pretending like his father wasn't dead, and oh yeah, that I'd killed him, did not make for the best of times. I overcompensated hard, doing some freaky dance with the block on my head that made the toddler cry.

I dropped the toy to the carpet. "It can't have been easy, having your husband become a bloodsucker."

Carine flinched, just a bit, but that crack in her easy-going disposition spoke volumes. "Zaven does his best for us."

Her husband was a criminal who'd done hard time. That wasn't my definition of doing his best for his family, but I simply smiled politely and nodded.

"I checked the conditions of Zaven's parole," I said. "It doesn't prohibit him from working for a vampire employer, but I require a name to follow up and make sure his job is all aboveboard." Come on, lady. Get me a connection to one of the local vamp Mafias.

Carine bounced Davit on her lap to soothe him. "He hasn't found a job yet. I've been supporting us. I'm a nurse."

"Are you?" My smile turned to a grimace. She was out there taking care of people and I'd killed her husband.

"Zaven is on daddy duty when I work." She rubbed her nose against her son's. "Isn't he, sweet baby?"

I swallowed down the sour taste of vomit. "Can I use your bathroom?"

Luckily, Carine didn't realize she was pointing a monster down the hall to the second door on the left.

I locked myself in and splashed water on my face with

shaking hands. I'd widowed a lovely nurse and thrust her baby into the arms of a succession of shadier and shadier babysitters.

Get hold of yourself, Cherry growled in my head. *You are losing your shit.*

I pinched my cheeks hard to get some color back into my pale cheeks and let the sharp bite smarten me up. Suppose Zaven kept Carine in the dark about his vamp acquaintances and his plans to impress one of their ilk—for her safety. I'd looked up his record. He wasn't affiliated with any vamps prior to his incarceration and wouldn't have come into contact with any there. But something made him decide to not only get turned but go after Maud. Could someone he met in prison have pointed him to Maud?

I stepped back into the hallway.

Carine was running the tap in the kitchen, singing to Davit.

I hurried into her bedroom, quickly searching through nightstand drawers and running a hand between the mattress and the box spring. It was clean enough under the bed to have a picnic and I didn't find anything in my frantic search of the pockets of Zaven's clothing in the closet.

I returned to the living room as Carine exited the kitchen.

"Are you okay? You were in there awhile."

"Yes. Thanks. One last question. To your knowledge, is Zaven in contact with any of his former cellmates?"

Carine frowned. "That's not a parole violation, is it?"

"As long as they aren't up to anything illegal." I picked up the registration papers that I'd brought with me. "It's my experience that vampires who don't register aren't going to answer questions about who turned them. And we really need that information for our records. You've got a lot on your plate with your job and a small child, and I don't want to cause more problems for you. Now, I can hang around and wait for Zaven, but if he still refuses to cooperate?" I shook my head sadly. "This becomes an official mark against him and he'll end up back in prison. But if you can provide me with the names of any friends of his from during his incarceration and they lead me to the vampire who turned Zaven, well, that vamp becomes the one in violation. We'll charge him as a rogue and your husband will be off the hook."

I wasn't lying. Not entirely. Technically, vampires were supposed to provide notarized consent forms when they turned someone. Otherwise they'd be charged as rogues and staked, but actually enforcing that, especially if the newly turned vampire refused to give them up, was next to impossible. Still, in that event, Zaven would be off the hook—were he actually around to be off the hook, that was.

I mentally crossed my fingers that Carine didn't invite me to wait around for her husband to get home and answer it himself.

"His bunkmate was Jimmy Tucco," Carine said. "A Red Flame, I think. But Zaven mostly mentioned another man, Darby Connor. He's a White Flame." She peered at me anxiously. "Does that help?"

"Yes. Thank you." Cellmates could be found via internal prison records, which, given I wasn't officially investigating anything, I couldn't access. Getting the name of a friend, though, was better.

Davit entered the room doing that weird zombie lurch common to small children. His mom had taken his sweater off, revealing his shirt with the logo of a vamp soccer team.

The same logo Ezra had on his shirt that night we'd slept together and he'd decamped for the Hell that had prompted me to look up the team. My heart stuttered. Oh, please no. I pointed at the logo. "Is Zaven a fan of the Bloodhounds?"

Carine laughed. "You have no idea. Davit's room is full of their memorabilia. My husband never cared much about anything besides hockey, but I guess they watched a lot of soccer in prison, because he became obsessed with the team. Goes on about stats. Knows everything about the owner too. He promised Davit he'd take him to a game soon and they'd get to meet all the players."

"That's nice." I gathered my jacket and purse, hoping Carine didn't see my shaking hands. "Thanks so much for your help."

For the life of me, I have no idea what Carine said as I was leaving, because my blood was rushing in my ears. The second the door closed behind me and I was back in the building hallway, I sagged against the wall.

The Babel Bloodhounds had been a mediocre team until a new owner infused a ton of cash into them and raised them to vamp superstars.

Natán Cardoso. The ultimate vampire for Zaven to impress.

Chapter 16

Had Natán hired Zaven to go after Maud? No, Zaven was very insistent about that being his plan. It had been a boast. He wanted Natán to know he'd found an infernal.

I spent the ride home in a blur of jumbled thoughts.

When Roman Whittaker, a British vamp operative, and serial killer of half shedim, was brought back to London HQ, he was murdered in his cell. Director Booker Harrison, the head of that chapter, covered that fact up. Roman would have been staked anyway, since he'd confessed to the murders, but the undetected access to him in that secured cell was what made Ezra and me suspect a Maccabee's involvement in killing infernals.

Someone with knowledge of Maccabee vamp cells, arrest procedures, and the ability to dodge all security protocols—both magic and tech-based—had silenced Roman.

I'd spent the past two months chasing any whisper to substantiate our suspicions, but concluded that while a powerful figure was involved, it wasn't anyone from my organization.

Natán Cardoso fit the parameters. He was a former

level three Maccabee, knew our procedures inside and out, and I had no doubt he could bypass any security protocols. It also made total sense that a dangerous undead Mafia head would be interested in vampire invincibility.

If I didn't still feel sick to my stomach that the Authority Council was focused on Ezra, I'd have laughed, because they should have been targeting an entirely different Cardoso.

How long would it be before Natán came for me? Or was it too late?

Was I already in his sights?

When I got home, I lit the second night Hanukkah candles with a quarter of my usual enthusiasm, then I stood by the microwave reheating the risotto Sachie had bought for me, staring into space.

How was I supposed to broach this with Ezra? Asking him if his dad was tangled up in killing infernals would be far worse than when I'd asked if Primes left bodies when staked.

"Earth to Avi." Sach leaned back against the kitchen counter.

I shook my head to clear it and removed the steaming plate from the microwave.

"Bets on whether Darsh and Silas have slept together yet?" She waggled her eyebrows.

"We'd have heard from Darsh if that were the case. Besides, Silas wouldn't go down that fast."

"Phrasing." Sachie snickered. She sat down across from me, elbow on the dining room table and head in hand. "Want to tell me what you found at Zaven's place?"

Well, his wife sang off-key but with laughter in her voice, and his little boy liked carrot sticks and the moment that towers fell over and he could stomp among the blocks like he was Godzilla.

"Zaven blackmailed Maud to impress Natán Cardoso."

Sachie whistled. "You sure?"

"Very strongly positive. Walk through it with me?"

She nodded.

"Starting from the top," I said. "Six half shedim are murdered in ritualistic killings. Their eyes and hearts are cut out and they're exsanguinated."

"No sign of the organs or blood in the vamp black market," Sachie said.

"Right. However, the killers use a very rare and expensive drug called Claret to speed up the blood loss. Our main suspects are a British vamp operative called Roman Whittaker and Dr. Athena Metaxas."

"Their motive being that they were using infernal blood to inoculate humans from being turned." Sachie reached for my fork. "Are you going to eat that, or…"

I pulled my plate closer and took a bite. "When we captured Roman, he confessed to killing Metaxas. She was his link to Claret." She was also how Roman found the infernals, being one herself. I didn't have that ability, but different shedim magic for different half shedim and all that. "Roman twisted her hatred of vampires into a belief that she was doing good in the world," I said. "But the inoculation was a lie. Darsh posited that vamps wanted the infernals' blood to perform dark magic, which Roman basically confirmed. He was after vampire invincibility."

Sachie plucked an apple out of the fruit bowl on the table. "How does that lead to Natán specifically, versus any one of a hundred vampires?"

"Roman was murdered in his cell at British HQ."

"That points to a Maccabee with clearance."

"I investigated and ruled it out."

"Why didn't you tell me you were looking into that angle?"

"Plausible deniability and lack of hard evidence."

"I don't need protecting." She shook her half-eaten apple at me. "Yes, Natán was a Maccabee and could have gotten to Roman. He'd also have a fast track to procuring Claret."

"Right? Suppose he has the missing infernal blood. That brings us to Sire's Spark."

Sachie swallowed her next bite. "Natán wasn't involved in the original theft from the gallery, but he could have stolen it afterward. He could have even arranged for the other artifacts to go back to the cops as a red herring."

I nodded, though that had been my mother, not Natán. Either he didn't know about the artifact, or he was still looking for it. I very resolutely did not look toward my bedroom.

"That gives us murdered infernals, their missing blood with magic properties, and an allegedly powerful artifact." Sachie placed the apple core on a napkin. "I'm going to ask you a question. I'll ask it once and then never again because I believe that you'll answer honestly. Did you know Maud was an infernal when you arrested her and then lie to Darsh and me? Plausible deniability?"

I'd wondered when my reckoning for all the lies I'd told Sachie would come. And whether it would be a relief.

I chewed my risotto like it was delicious and not a lump of cardboard in my mouth. The shittiest part of having done exactly what Sachie was asking?

It was the fact that I hadn't lost a second's worth of sleep over telling them this fib. I'd drawn a line in the sand that night. Okay, it was more of a circle, with Maccabees, including my mother and my best friends, on the outside, and me and my sister within.

Being an infernal was an identity-level secret that would change how Maud was perceived by the world. All her accomplishments, the fact she was smart, and funny, or any little personality quirks, they'd be eclipsed by the prevalent belief that all shedim were evil, which trumped any humanity.

Sachie didn't understand that, or it didn't matter to her, because she wasn't a half shedim. She didn't live her life on guard, terrified she'd slip and reveal this core self-truth.

So, no, I would never out Maud.

"She's not an infernal," I said.

"Okay." Sach gathered up her apple core. "Promise me you'll speak to Ezra immediately about his father and not confront Natán directly."

"Ezra isn't his father's keeper," I said hotly. He wasn't even involved with the Kosher Nostra anymore, not that that was mine to share, even with Sach.

"Chill, Avi." She spoke as she headed for the kitchen with her dishes. "I'll happily point out Ezra's many crimes, but this isn't one of them. I worked that infernals case with him. He was upset and angry."

"I won't confront Natán. I can't promise a timeline on the rest."

"Fair enough." There was the sound of the compost bucket lid opening.

Tell her. Cherry's desire pulsed in my head.

Sachie had opened a door. All I had to do was step through and unburden myself with the secret that had weighed me down my entire life. That relief was almost overwhelming.

I owed her the truth.

Except Sachie didn't want truth; she wanted hope.

My best friend had risked her relationship with her family for her belief in our organization and the work she did keeping humanity safe. When I floated my demon realm theory, I'd dented her faith—her hope—that what she did was important enough to pay the price with her parents, and that the Maccabees were on the right side of the line between good and evil.

Because of me, she'd been forced into that Authority interrogation, and taken a hit to her career.

I couldn't work up the courage to deal the worst betrayal of all: having hidden something of this magnitude from her over decades of friendship, living together, and working together.

She might eventually accept Cherry, but she'd never forgive *me*.

I cleaned up my dirty dishes, feeling like our friendship had shifted slightly out of alignment, because I'd severely fucked up. Like I could see and hear Sach perfectly, but it was through a membrane-thin barrier of my making.

The Hanukkah candles snuffed out, leaving nothing but a faint smudge of smoke.

I was ready to call it a day. At 8:30PM. Screw it. My eyelids were gummy and I was scraped raw. I was an adult. I could go to bed whenever I damn well pleased.

My closet door was slightly ajar and some of the purses on the floor had fallen out. I tossed them back inside, covering up the safe like I was bricking Sire's Spark up.

It's not like the crystal was whispering to me or sending shivers up my spine. I didn't have any scary dreams about having used it and any side effects had worn off that same night. I was still twitchy this close to it, though, because it had turned me into a bloodhound for infernals.

That alone was reason enough for Michael to have liberated it and hidden it in her safe, but whoever blackmailed Maud found her without the artifact's help.

I pitched my clothes into my hamper. Now I had a potential connection between Zaven and Natán. Sire's Spark detected my kind, but was that all it did or was it also a factor in vampire invincibility? I had to determine which it was, which meant speaking to Ezra sooner rather than later.

I froze, my arms jammed into the sleeves of the crimson sweater and my head inside the fabric, realizing I'd instinctively sought it out after a stressful day. Given what I faced, the smart move would be to clothe myself in impersonal synthetic, not this silken cloud whose every stitch was a reminder of the time and care that Ezra had poured into it. I shoved my head through the neck hole and folded the cuffs with their sparkly accents back.

It was just a sweater, not some Trojan Horse worming its way past my defenses. I crawled under the covers, my phone in hand. I'd never complimented Ezra on his successful last-minute rescue, though did I want to deal with the inevitable cocky retort?

I placed my phone on the bedside table. He was probably busy hanging out with Silas.

Unless he was being swarmed by Hellions or fending off attacks.

I grabbed the phone and texted: *Where did you learn Japanese?*

His response was instant. Almost like he'd been waiting—or hoping—to hear from me. *My father was a firm believer in the importance of knowing different languages.*

Oh. That was actually a nice fact about his dad. I was about to text as much when he sent another message.

I wanted to learn Italian to impress girls, but he spoke that already so it wasn't a good use of my education.

If I hadn't already hated Natán, this would have done it. Everything about Ezra's upbringing had been a calculated move to further his dad's power base. I tapped my thumb against the side of my phone. This was the perfect opening to launch into what I'd learned about Natán and Zaven.

Me: *Spanish wasn't seductive enough? Greedy of you, Cardoso.*

It may shock you to learn that my teen years were unfortunate in the appearance department. I needed all the help I could get.

Pics or it didn't happen. My fingers flew over the keyboard.

All evidence was destroyed.

Coward. I watched the screen intently for his reply.

He sent back a photo of a toad with a mullet.

Oof, I typed, snickering. *That is unfortunate.*

Do you ever wear the sweater I made you?

The question caught me off guard. My first instinct was to lie, but once upon a time Ezra had been one of my best friends and I missed that more than I craved our chemistry. Plus, this text exchange had been fun and I was tired of everything between us being either combative or mission related.

We needed a chance to just be us.

I sent back a photo of me mugging at the camera, but with the covers at my waist so he could clearly see the sweater I wore to bed. *I love it.*

Thank you. Sweet dreams, Aviva.

Sweet dreams, Ezra.

Chapter 17

Jasmine's room at the Maccabee rehab clinic had a view of the mountains, state-of-the-art equipment to bolster any magic healing treatments, and two steely-eyed operatives on guard outside her door.

The elderly Eishei Kodesh leader of the drug ring looked fragile under her pile of heated blankets, her left wrist manacled to the bed rail with a magic-nulling handcuff. The side of her head with her missing ear was bandaged, but there was no bruising or other visible injury and her vacant stare wasn't due to pain medication.

She wasn't responding to treatment and Monica, the Maccabee healer in charge of her case, feared her trauma was too severe. Thankfully, that wasn't the case for Francesca and Paul, though even they were healing slowly.

I'd come up empty searching for anyone matching shedim with humans, and now my interviewee was almost comatose. Had Dmitri set me up to fail?

Monica showed me the call button in case I required assistance and left me with the patient.

"Jasmine? I'm Aviva Fleisher. I'm the operative who

got you out that night." I leaned forward, directly into her field of vision.

Her gaze paused on me for a fraction of a second before slipping off, but she didn't flinch or scream in horror that I was a demon. The only sound was her slow breathing against the percussive beeps of her heart monitor.

I prayed that her brain was so scrambled that the sight of my Cherry form had blended together with her memory of Bratwurst Demon into a single nightmarish fever dream. I pulled a chair close to the bed and sat down. "How did you find the shedim, Jasmine?"

She made a soft croaking sound.

"Take all the time you need. You're safe now and getting the best care possible."

A tear leaked out of one eye. Was she thinking that getting well would only speed up her inevitable path to incarceration?

Well, it's not like the metal cuff on her wrist was the latest in Parisian accessories.

I draped my forearms on my thighs. "You can have a lawyer present if you like, however, this is just a friendly visit asking for your assistance. Who connected you with the demon?"

Jasmine's lips moved.

I cocked my head, trying to catch what she said. "Again, please?"

She made the faintest sound.

I gripped the sides of the chair against the urge to clap my hands over my ears because she was humming, and the sound thrust me back to the horror of the drug lab. The sterile room wavered, overlaid with my memory of blood and mangled bodies, while the scent of lemons washed over me.

I fought to keep my breath steady and banish the all-too-real memory. "Jasmine, you're guilty of colluding with a demon and there's a special prison for criminals like you." Sector A was the only outcome. "If there's anything you can tell me about the shedim you were producing drugs with, that would work in your favor. Get you some special privileges to make your life easier there." My lie was so smooth, it would have fooled the magic to detect them.

Her hummed melody was annoying but familiar, some golden oldie heard in dentists' offices or supermarkets. It grew stronger and steadier, almost like a fuck-you. Weirdly, that eased the tension in my shoulders. This, at least, was familiar territory. She was a suspect; this was her way of refusing to cooperate.

Unfortunately, it didn't matter how I phrased my questions, all she did was hum.

Jasmine hadn't looked at me this entire time, staring out the window like she was an empty house. I wished the owners had locked this one up before they left and not left a window open with the radio on, because it was creepy as hell.

The song she hummed was slow, dreamy, and now burned into my brain like the worst earworm. I recalled it had a lot of falsetto in it, even though I didn't remember the title or any of the lyrics.

My questioning grew louder and more insistent. I needed the answer as to how she teamed up with the shedim for my report and I needed it now.

The door to the room opened and Monica strode in. "You need to stop. Her vitals are soaring."

"I'm authorized to be here," I said.

Monica lifted Jasmine's uncuffed wrist and checked her pulse. "No, you were permitted to ask my patient questions at *my* discretion. You've lost my goodwill and now it's time to go."

I stood up, ready to argue, but Monica called out for the other two operatives to come escort me out. I saved the "fuuuuuck" building into a scream at the back of my throat for when I was in my car and could add slamming my hand against the wheel for good measure.

I couldn't put this pointless interview in my report. Dmitri would seize on the excuse to discipline me. Did Sector A have visiting hours?

That earworm melody stuck in my head didn't help my mood. The song swam around in my brain, defying my attempts to overwrite it with better music. Well, there was one answer I could get. I pulled up an app on my phone for recognizing songs, which I only had because this one café near work played great music and I was always asking the barista what the song was. She finally suggested I get this app.

I felt really stupid sitting in my car humming the same snippet of melody at my phone and doing it so poorly that the app didn't produce any results, but it was driving me nuts to have a song stuck in my head that I couldn't identify.

A car pulled up next to me, the driver gesturing to ask whether I was leaving.

I threw my phone on the passenger seat, started my engine, and pulled out. Six soft hits on an AM station later, I was yawning like a fiend, but that song hadn't played. I pulled into a spot in the parking garage at work and cut the engine.

Right as the notes in my head came out of my speakers.

I wrenched the engine back on, stabbing at the buttons on the stereo screen to get to the title and band. It was "Unchained Melody" by the Righteous Brothers.

I listened to the rest of the lyrics, wondering why Jasmine infected my brain with this love song. Was it personal to her? Did it bring back a nostalgic memory from a long-lost romance? I winced. That last high note really hit the back molars.

Fifteen minutes later, I stared at the email in my inbox from Dmitri, not wanting to open it because he'd see I'd read it and hadn't yet filed my final report. He didn't want piecemeal information, but I had to buy myself time to get him all the answers he desired.

While I let a plan percolate in the back of my brain, I did a Google search on Jimmy Tucco and Darby Connor, the two Eishei Kodesh whom Zaven met in prison. I used my phone's data plan instead of going through Maccabee Wi-Fi so my queries weren't tracked.

Jimmy was still serving time for assault. One photo of him showed his gang tat from a group with a virulent and very public hatred of vampires. They blamed vamps for muscling in on what used to be human mobs and their clashes were bloody. I didn't find anything that pointed to a connection with Maud or knowledge of demon existence.

I opened the first search result on Darby Connor, expecting more of the same, and froze.

Before Dermot "Darby" Connor went to prison for embezzlement, he'd been an up-and-coming poker player on the Vegas circuit.

I fired a text off to Maud that I needed to speak to her, but the message remained unread, even though she was back in Hong Kong. Faced with both her silence and my unfinished report, I did what the situation called for: got a bag of chips from the staff kitchen and procrastinated at my workstation.

A photo of a naked man with a flabby ass being chased by two grossed-out looking Hellions popped up on my phone. Ezra had captioned it, *Another day in Hell.*

Grimacing, I opened our text chain and fired back four vomiting emojis.

It was a forfeit. Ezra punctuated it with not one, not two, but three laughing crying emojis.

He forfeit his clothes? That didn't seem like an acceptable wager at the Hell.

He forfeit his wealth. It turns out his designer suit was all he had. They're trying to catch him but he's like a slippery pig. How's your workday?

We Maccabees only engage in serious endeavors, Cardoso. I sent him a photo of me eating chips.

Well, I won't distract you further from those weighty pursuits. Get it? Chips? Weighty?

I pressed my lips together, holding in a laugh. I'd missed his nerdy side. *GROAN.*

He didn't reply but the exchange had cheered me up. While I finished my snack, I perused some search results about "Unchained Melody." Apparently, it was used in an infamous sexy pottery scene in the movie *Ghost.* That sounded vaguely familiar.

"'Released in 1965.'" Gemma stood at my shoulder, doing biceps curls with a water bottle. She wrinkled her nose. "Old people music do it for you?"

I slammed my laptop shut. "Creeping on colleagues do it for you? Back the fuck out of my personal space."

"I'm not speaking to you by choice. Marv sent me. You're our new team bitch."

"I'm finishing up a case."

"Michael said that wouldn't take up all your time. We need help and she told Marv you were available." Gemma snapped her fingers at me. "Those papers won't file themselves."

Marv may have been the level three lead on this fraud case, but Gemma took it upon herself to model how to debase me for the rest of the team.

Case in point, me now painstakingly taping together a document that she'd instructed me to shred, then denied, claiming it was of vital importance and how could I be so stupid.

Outwardly, I let it all bounce off me, complying with a smile and a can-do attitude, while internally, I ground my teeth and imagined ways to slowly eviscerate her. It gave me something to do besides obsess over how the Eishei Kodesh drug makers and Bratwurst Demon found each other.

Gemma made a snarky comment about me leaving at five on the dot, but I'd put in a full shift and doing another photocopy run was not overtime worthy.

Maud checked in, saying she'd just woken up and could talk later.

I texted Silas but didn't receive a reply that my request was a go until I was back home making dinner. After reading his precise instructions with a sigh, I scarfed down my pasta and salad, and tightly closed all the curtains. However, it took a while to find a slotted screwdriver. I searched the toolbox in the closet, under Sachie's mattress, and in all the kitchen drawers before finding one in her medicine cabinet sitting in a cup with her toothbrush.

Taking it with a grimace, I headed for our front door to lever the mezuzah off the right door post. Was my plan worth removing the magic ward? Especially when it was in order to allow a portal made of demon magic from the Copper Hell into my apartment? What if Delacroix crashed the party? Unlike vampires, shedim did not require an invitation to enter someone's home, hence the ward to keep them out.

Mezuzahs were supposed to be permanently affixed with a rabbi's blessing. Once I took this down, I couldn't just stick it back up. I'd have to call the security company to come set a new ward. I didn't mind paying for that, even though these special heavy-duty versions of the wards did not come cheap, but our home would be vulnerable until then, and this wasn't just my decision to make.

I phoned Sach at work, explaining about Jasmine's condition, what I wanted to do in the wake of that and why. She agreed that Delacroix likely wouldn't hurt me until after I'd joined him for Brimstone Breakfast Club, the risk of some random demon showing up was slight, and gave her permission.

I worked the mezuzah free, just in time for a rift with black magic mesh strung across it to open next to my sofa.

Silas stood in its mouth. "You need to invite me in."

"Please come in."

He stepped through, looking out at the impressive water view while he toed off his shoes.

Mezuzah in hand, I waited for the portal to close, but it just hung there.

Ezra walked into view. The cut of his suit was as severe as his jawline and the steeliness in his eyes. He'd slicked his curls off his forehead, contributing to his ruthless demeanor. "Going to invite me over too?"

This wasn't the vampire I'd been enjoying a renewed text friendship with; it was a warrior.

Mezuzahs didn't keep out vampires, and the myth about them needing to be invited into homes was true. But Ezra had been invited in way back when and there was no way to rescind that invitation.

I planted my feet wide, goaded into battle mode myself. "You already know you can come and go as you please. I can't stop you."

He flinched and I wished I could take the words back. "Much as you wish you could," he said.

"You dumped me, Ezra. Yeah, I wanted to rescind all your rights to this place. I also wished flaming hemorrhoids on you. Did those ever kick in?" I peered at him hopefully.

"Charming," he said dryly.

"I wasn't kidding. About either."

"I'm not forcing my way into your home."

Maybe if he'd behaved like his text self version, I'd have let him in.

Excising his presence from my home after our breakup had almost cost me my sanity. It *had* cost me a lovely bedding set after repeated washings removed his scent but not the memories of what we'd gotten up to on it. So maybe not.

"Thank you for bringing Silas," I said.

"Once again, you've asked me to put myself out," he said. "It's not easy to open portals this way. Harder still to keep it from Delacroix."

I stormed over to him, any guilt at not inviting him in gone. "Is that a threat?"

Ezra shook his head sadly. "Why is that always your first instinct with me? No, Aviva. It's not a threat. It's just a fact. You claim to love those. Yet you keep expecting me to help you, which I do, every time, even when you don't explain why. You won't even give me a fucking inch, but that fact is of no importance to you."

I opened my mouth, but Ezra and the portal vanished.

"It's not of no importance," I muttered to the empty air.

"Instead of spouting obscure double negatives to the wall, care to tell me why I'm here?" My poor sofa creaked under Silas's bulk. "I'm all for a clandestine rendezvous when the Jolly Hellhound and the entrance to your condo tower are probably being monitored," he said, "but what was so urgent that I had to come tonight?"

I perched on the edge of a plush chair. "See, the

reason I asked you here is, well..." I rubbed my hand over the back of my neck. "I want you to hypnotize me."

Silas slung his arm along the back of the sofa. "I'm not quite old enough to compel you, but even if I was, why in heaven's name would you want that? To do what?"

"I don't want you to compel me. Our chapter had a vamp operative a few years back around your age. He couldn't compel either, but he had this one case where a witness was willing to give us their account, except their trauma locked them out of their memories to it. Regular hypnotherapy didn't work, yet he was able to touch their skull and funnel his magic into them enough to relax them and guide them through the incident." I hugged a cushion to my chest. "I was hoping you could do something similar for me, with details I don't consciously remember because they didn't seem important during the lab bust. I'm under the gun to get answers and wrap up this investigation."

Silas glanced at the spot where the portal had been. "Why me?"

"I trust you."

He laughed darkly and I shivered at the menacing sound coming out of this preternaturally polite man. "Oh, sweetheart," he said, "that right there's the last thing you should do."

Chapter 18

Cherry raised her head and I let my shedim magic dance under my skin, clocking all the hidey holes in the room with weapons.

Cherry wasn't visible, but it was as if Silas sensed something dangerous about me because he blinked and raised his hands. "No, I didn't mean... I wouldn't ever deliberately hurt you."

"Obviously, since you wouldn't even hurt the people who'd imprisoned you. You're one of the kindest people I've met."

He rubbed a hand across his jaw. "I have to work at it."

"You and me both."

"It's not the same. You don't live to be an almost two-hundred-year-old vampire without some serious stains on your soul." He tapped his head. "There's a lot of dark shit in here. You don't want to be giving me leave to root around in your head, in case it gets too tempting to leave you different from how I found you." He gave me a wry smile. "Darsh might be a better bet. None of us are saints, but he's a little more honest with what he is."

"Darsh isn't knee-deep in this, and I'd like to keep it that way."

"Sorry, Avi." Silas placed both his hands on his thighs like he was about to stand up. "I'm not comfortable with this."

Ironically, the more he warned me off trusting him, the more I did. However, I'd respect his boundaries. "It's okay," I said, motioning for him to stay put. "I'm sorry for asking and putting you in that position. It was a long shot anyway."

"But one you felt was important enough to attempt this." Silas pursed his lips, his eyes narrowed. "There's got to be a way."

"I can't go to an Eishei Kodesh hypnotherapist because the Authority has eyes on me until I wrap up this case," I said, frustration lacing my voice.

"Mm. I imagine they'd interpret you talking to any shrink, especially while you're on an active investigation, as a sign of weakness. A nice old one-way ticket to mental health leave."

"Given the interrogation I just had with them, 'on leave' would be the best-case scenario."

Silas scratched his fingers through the dark reddish stubble along his jaw. Vampires couldn't grow their hair, but stubble was somehow a go. So weird. "There's always Ezra."

My pulse spiked. "He's a Prime vampire but he's too young to have any sway over my head or emotions. Isn't he?"

"He is," Silas said gently. "But if you were blood bonded, you could give him access to your memory to walk through it with an objective eye at a deep and clear level."

I laughed, my mirth ending in an abrupt snort.

"Feeding off Ezra to heal was intense enough. I'm not bonding myself to him. Nuh-uh. No way. Nope."

Silas raised an eyebrow. "Me thinks the woman doth protest too much."

I shifted uncomfortably in my seat, trying to shake off the unsettling idea that he'd planted in my mind. Blood bonding with a vampire was a serious commitment, one that went far beyond just sharing memories. The ritual was an intimate connection that would join us on a primal, ancient level together forever. Our magic would strengthen each other when close, but weaken us when apart. Ezra was a Prime while I was primarily human with limited shedim magic. It would never be an equal dynamic.

The idea of being blood bonded to Ezra, of giving him even more power over me, was terrifying. But at the same time, there was a part of me that couldn't deny that lure, no matter how dangerous it was.

And if Silas was right, it could get me much-needed answers.

Taking a deep breath, I met Silas's piercing gaze head-on. "I'm sure," I said firmly, trying to convince myself as much as him. "I'll find another way to deal with this without sacrificing my autonomy."

"Then I've got one last suggestion. It won't unlock any details that aren't already at the forefront of your consciousness, but maybe it'll remind you of something you noticed that night and simply forgot. I can guide you, ask questions you might not think to ask yourself, with the help of this." He dug into his pocket and pulled out a pipe.

I looked at the pipe and back at Silas, lost. "You want me to vape?"

"Cannabis. Not that gross-flavored smoke shit. I use it to relax and focus, but if you've never done it or it affects you adversely, then don't take it." He grinned at my surprised expression. "You didn't peg me for the type, did you?"

"Not even a little bit, and that's what I get for making assumptions." I plucked the pipe from his fingers, examining its sleek design. "I enjoy smoking up occasionally, but I've only done it socially, never to accomplish something."

I was fifteen the first time I smoked weed. Sach and I had plans to try it at a party we'd been invited to, but I had to test its effects on Cherry by myself before I smoked it in public with my friend. Luckily, it chilled the Baroness right out. Cherry hummed contentedly while I sprawled on my bed in a patch of sunlight, bobbing my head to a Beastie Boys' album, and feeling any tension in my chest unwind with each breath.

I handed Silas back the pipe, unsure of which buttons to press. "Light us up, Jeeves," I said in my snootiest British accent.

Once the vape was at temperature, I took a deep drag, savoring the sweet taste on my lips. The smoke curled upward, dancing in glow of the floor lamp before disappearing into the air. No sense of impending doom or anxiety gnawed at me. It was just me, Silas, and the soft haze of weed hanging in the air.

"Ready?" Silas lay on my sofa, his feet hanging over the edge.

"Ready." I draped myself sideways over my chair, getting comfortable, and closed my eyes.

Silas took me through the snowshoe trek in the forest that night, guiding me through to when I first saw the barn.

"The snow fell off the tree with a whispery sound," I said. "The pine needle branches quivered for a moment and even the snow wanted to get somewhere warmer."

197

"If you take a deep breath, what do you smell back in the forest?"

I inhaled. "Lemon."

There was a rustle of clothing and the sound of my fridge opening. A moment later Silas pressed something cool into my hands. "Sniff it. Let the scent connect you to the memory."

I pressed the lemon to my nose, letting Silas take me step by step through that night, and falling into an almost trancelike state. I relived every sensory memory, but with enough awareness for one very important edit.

I made no mention of Cherry, sticking with the story I'd given Michael about my gloves keeping me from making physical contact with any of the afflicted or the shedim herself.

Thirty years of practice keeping my secret intact under any situation sure came in handy now.

Silas kept his voice gentle and nonjudgmental, giving me space when I hesitated, until finally, I had the key to Bratwurst Demon's cage in my hand.

"She contorted her body and slipped free before I could unlock it."

"Then she was never truly imprisoned," Silas said. "You think the Eishei Kodesh were aware of that?"

Every inch of that cage was clear as day in my mind. "I'd say no, because the bars were made of iron, not steel. They were intended to weaken her and help prevent any escape. And the door had a lock on it. A heavy one." I drummed my fingers on the top of the chair. "That was the thing she was most dismissive of."

"How so?"

I carefully cast my mind back to get her wording correct because I'd had so much doubt thrown on what I'd heard that it was imperative I remember it correctly. "She said, 'Stupid humans thought this would hold me.' She was referring to the lock, not the iron bars."

"Was there anything unusual about the lock?" Silas said.

My frown deepened. Other than the shedim squeezed it into a twisted lump like it was Silly Putty? "I didn't think to check it. Why?"

"It could have been warded."

"If that's the case?" I sat up and opened my eyes, rubbing my spine from where the armrest had been digging into it. This was a solid lead. "It'll be with the rest of the evidence in lockup, so I can use it to find the Eishei Kodesh who bespelled it. See if that gets us anywhere."

While I pursued that, Silas would plumb the depths of the dark web for anyone advertising the service of matching shedim eager to do evil, with humans eager for the same.

"Can I ask you a question?" I said.

"Shoot."

"After all that went down…" I plucked at a loose thread on my sofa cushion. "Do you even want to be a Maccabee anymore?"

Silas reached for his shoes and slid one on. "I don't know. I devoted the past fifty years of my life to them, and they threw me under the bus like none of that service mattered. Like *I* didn't matter."

Silas, Sachie, me, all of us were struggling with our relationship to the Maccabees. This case had hammered home like nothing else that my organization dealt in absolutes. That we were all expendable in the face of its grand mission.

So why was I enduring brutal training and giving two hundred percent to every assignment? Why was I so stuck on the idea that being the perfect Maccabee was my only hope of acceptance?

Silas tied up his laces. "I could have joined one of the vamp Mafias. Hell, my life would have been easier, but I didn't want that path because..." He double knotted the lace.

The mesh net portal to the Copper Hell opened and Silas stood up and hugged me. "I've got your back." He adopted a casual pose that was painful in its awkwardness. "Hey, does Darsh have any hobbies?"

Well, he worked hard and played hard. Both were full-time pursuits that left no room for hobbies. Now would be the perfect opportunity to gently steer Silas away from Darsh, but I couldn't bring myself to do it.

Silas wasn't stupid. He knew what Darsh was like, and if he wanted to pursue him, then it wasn't my place to shit on that.

Darsh's heart was damaged, true, but if he could get past that, he'd be an amazing partner for someone. Especially someone steady and kind like Silas who'd ground him.

I just wasn't sure Darsh *could* get past it.

I shrugged lightly. "No hobbies that I know of."

Ezra clapped Silas's shoulder as his friend passed by him in the portal, then yawned. The worn-out T-shirt he'd changed into clung to his muscular frame, emphasizing the contours of his chest and arms. As he ran a hand through his messy hair, a faint smile tugged at the corners of his lips, revealing a hint of that famous Cardoso charm. "I'd ask what new developments you two found, but I'm not sure my heart could take it."

I wasn't sure my heart could take the pang of nostalgia as I took in the sight of this man I'd once loved, looking tired and deliciously rumpled. "Do you want to hang out?"

Ezra flared his nostrils. "Because you're high and horny? Pass."

I clasped my hands behind my back so I didn't press my palms to my flushed cheeks, and instantly burned all the THC out of my system with my shedim magic. "That's not it at all," I lied, shame spearing my chest at how I'd have so easily used him given half a chance. "I want to speak to you."

He motioned at my living room. "Ask nicely."

I opened my mouth, working silent words through a thick throat.

"I don't know why I bother," he muttered and turned away.

The portal began to close.

Memories flooded back to me: stolen kisses in the darkness, whispered endearments, but also so much laughter and endless conversations about both the weight of the world and the most trivial of topics. I'd missed all of it.

"Come in, Ezra." I paused, but the portal continued to shrink. "Please."

It stopped, no larger across than a basketball, and hung there not reversing course. I bowed my head, feeling I'd grasped for something important just a moment too late.

The portal vibrated, then opened back up.

As Ezra crossed its threshold into my apartment, a shiver ran down my spine. The decision had been made. I'd invited him in, knowing full well the danger that lay ahead.

His musky cologne wrapped around me, his presence suffusing my condo with a weight that threatened to shake the concrete foundation.

Adrenaline raced through my veins. Too bad I couldn't tell if it was because I'd made the best decision or the worst one.

Ezra didn't move, looking around him as if he stood on a tiny safe island in a sea of lava.

I was the host. I should put my guest at ease. "Any more naked butts?"

He snorted, the tension leaving his body. "Thankfully, no."

"Don't feel the need to share should it happen again."

He struck a theatrical pose, one hand to his forehead. "I'm a delicate flower, Aviva. I can't process that trauma on my own."

"You're something all right."

He winked at me and took a seat at the dining room table, though he folded his hands on top like he was in a legal deposition. "What did you want to discuss?"

"Maud Liu was being blackmailed."

"Why?"

I sat down across from him, my hands also folded. "For being an infernal."

Ezra huffed a wry laugh. "Your other plans last night. Suddenly, it all makes sense. Tell me, did you include that she's a half shedim in your report or is it another secret you're keeping?"

"It doesn't matter whether Maud actually is one, only that she's accused of it." I wasn't fooling him.

"Why is this my concern? Unless you think I'm responsible?" He had a deadly glint in his eyes. Had anyone else looked at me that way, I'd already have bolted, leaving nothing but dust in my wake like a cartoon character.

But Ezra didn't look that way because he intended to hurt me.

"Don't be absurd," I said. "I think the blackmailer did it to get your dad's attention."

He raised an eyebrow. "Capturing an infernal would hardly get my father's attention."

There was no love lost between Ezra and his father, just a business transaction where both maintained the fiction that Ezra was still the Crimson Prince. However, he didn't have to dismiss my theory out of hand.

"Why not?" I said. "A half shedim could be useful to a vamp mobster."

"What would an infernal do for him that a full shedim couldn't? Natán is the rare vampire unafraid to partner with demons." Like father like son. "Plus, he can buy off any Eishei Kodesh or Trad he wants to. Top government officials, leading thinkers, it doesn't matter, my father can bribe or blackmail them. An infernal in and of themself has no currency to him."

"Their blood does." I explained how I'd discounted any Maccabee as Roman Whittaker's killer, talking Ezra through Maud's blackmailer having been turned, Zaven's insistence on taking credit for the plan, and his obsession with the soccer team Natán owned. How he'd told his son they'd go to a game soon and get to meet all the players.

Ezra's expression became more and more incredulous. "How high are you?"

"Perfectly sober," I said through clenched teeth. "Natán could have murdered Roman in that Maccabee cell, and if he's after vamp invincibility, he has a motive for killing infernals."

Ezra scraped at some dried melted wax on the menorah in the center of the table. "Trust me, I'd be first in line to find my father guilty, but I've looked and looked and found nothing to substantiate that claim for him. Or for any of the Mafia heads. Lots of run-of-the-mill power plays, but that's it."

"Zaven believed this enough to blackmail Maud and get proof of her changing on camera. It bears looking into your dad one more time."

"All right, Aviva." Ezra stood up, the portal opening by the sofa. "I'll see what I can find."

I followed him. "I want to remain involved until I determine that Maud is safe."

"She is," he said. "You killed Zaven before he had time to contact Natán."

I made a face at Ezra because I hadn't mentioned killing Maud's blackmailer.

He smirked. "I know you. You protect the people you care about."

Just like you do. "Then you understand why I want to be part of the investigation until I'm satisfied your father is off the hook for the missing infernal blood."

"You don't want to meet him." Ezra headed for the portal. "Trust me."

"That was true until now, but with my training and my blue flame magic, I could illuminate his weaknesses when you question him, interpret that data and extrapolate whether he's lying or not."

Ezra spun around with the swiftness of a cobra about to strike. "You want to do this in Babel?! No fucking way."

"I would be glamored—"

"Cherry isn't a glamor. She's a bull's-eye."

"Not as Cherry. As someone else. A vamp or—"

A muscle ticked in his jaw. "You aren't getting near my father, because you'd end up handing him information he could use against you later."

"I'm not a total rookie," I shot back. "Why do you persist in acting like I am?"

"Because even with all my experience spying and acting a role," he roared, "I'm terrified of slipping up and doing the exact same thing."

I shook my head, my brow wrinkled. "Giving your dad something to use against me?"

Ezra's expression tightened in pain before it smoothed out to a cold, inscrutable mask. "Not my father, Aviva. Yours."

Chapter 19

Ezra vanished through the portal before my shock wore off.

I stumbled to the sofa, fighting past my icy panic that Delacroix was waiting to ambush me with the information about me being his daughter. *Think logically about how Ezra found out.*

He must have seen Delacroix's demon form and put two and two together from our shared toxic green eyes, frosted scales, and those crimson spikes around demon daddy's neck that matched Cherry's hair.

Is that why Ezra asked if I'd kept Maud's status a secret from the Maccabees? I'd shared my wish of having grown up with a sibling with him when we were together. Obviously, I'd protect my sister—especially one with the same secret as me.

I grabbed my phone off the coffee table, but I knew Ezra wouldn't answer if I reached out. Fine, he could have his little mic-drop moment, however, we were revisiting this. Besides, there was only one person I was in the mood to speak to.

"Aviva?" Maud's worried face filled the screen. "Is

everything okay?"

"Where are you? It's very loud."

She held the screen up for a moment, revealing a large food court that was bustling with people. "One of the hawker centers," she said. "I had a craving for roast duck. Hang on." She shouldered through the crowd until the sound of conversation was replaced by traffic. "Okay. Did you find out why the blackmailer was...you know. Am I going to be targeted again?"

"Tell me about Darby Connor."

"Never heard of him," she said.

"I see your bluff and call."

"That's not how it—" She shook her head. "I don't know him."

"Bullshit. You said no one other than me knew what you were, but Darby Connor was friends with your blackmailer. They met in prison. This is not a coincidence. You came to me, Maud, so you don't get to withhold important details now."

"Darby..." She slowly lowered herself onto the bench, her movements stiff and heavy, and tightened her fingers around the edges of the seat, her nails digging into the wood as if seeking some sort of anchor. "He was my boyfriend. We broke up before his arrest."

"You told him. You lied to me."

"I didn't lie. I said no other living human knew. He OD'd after he got out. A couple months ago." Her expression twisted. "He told that vampire about me? Did he tell anyone else?" She looked over her shoulder.

"No." I squelched any uncertainty about that fact, infusing my voice with steel. "You're safe."

"Safe?" She laughed bitterly. "He swore he'd never say anything." The look in her eyes was a mix of shock, hurt, and betrayal.

One I'd seen in the mirror more than once. It was a

shitty way to learn about knowing who to trust, but I'd come out the other side stronger and smarter.

"I appreciate that you need time to grieve," I said, "but you've got to move on with your life."

"I wish I'd never gone down this road. Never told Darby, never gone after Delacroix." She paused. "He came to see me, you know."

I straightened up from my slouched position. "Did he hurt you?"

"No. He took me for breakfast at this demon pancake house." She shook her head, but chuckled. "We played poker."

A tinge of jealousy shot through my chest, a tendril of resentment creeping into my mind. I shook it off, annoyed with myself. The last thing I wanted was for Delacroix to know I was his daughter, nor did I have any desire to endure the Brimstone Breakfast Club again.

If he took Maud, all the better. I was no longer a person of interest to him. He'd leave me alone.

"Does that bother you?" she said.

"Who said it did?"

Maud peered at me intently, then her brown eyes clouded and she shrugged. "My mistake."

In my head, Cherry sighed.

"I'd rather Delacroix leave us both alone," I said. "But if he contacts you again, or bothers you in any way, tell me." I paused, intending to simply say bye and end the call, but that wasn't the sentiment pulsing inside my skull or the words rising in my throat, demanding to be let out.

"You're awfully concerned about me," Maud said. "That's not my experience with Maccabees."

I dug my nails into my palm.

Cherry kept silent, waves of longing rolling off her. I snorted softly. Rolling off *me*. If I couldn't tell Maud, what hope did I have of showing my true self to anyone else?

I let out a deep breath. "I hear it's an older sister's job to look out for her reckless younger sibling."

Maud didn't react for a moment, and my stomach twisted with the fear I'd gotten this all wrong. That she *didn't* suspect I was her sister and I'd just outed myself as a half shedim.

Then she smiled, wide and bright. "Yeah, well, I hear it's a younger sister's job to annoy the shit out of her older sibling."

"Try it."

We grinned stupidly at each other.

"We should get roast duck together sometime. I know a good spot," she said. "Later, sis."

"Bye, munchkin."

Natán didn't know about Maud, and no one would be coming after her. My sister was free to annoy me for the next fifty years. Or longer.

I fell asleep with a smile on my face.

I slept so well, in fact, that I missed my alarm on Friday morning, racing around like a chicken with its head cut off to get out the door in time. While I was walking across the parking garage, I called the security company about resetting the mezuzah ward.

An employee explained they were fully booked today, and since tonight was Shabbat, and they didn't work on Saturday nights after Shabbat was over, they couldn't get to me until Sunday afternoon.

I made the appointment—agreeing to emergency pricing—and even got to work by 9:10AM. With Sachie on night shift, she'd been asleep when I headed out, but I'd left her a note about the progress of resetting the ward.

Gemma confronted me the second I entered the conference room that Marv's team had commandeered. "Must be nice to waltz in whenever and know Mommy will protect you."

Marv wasn't around, and two of the operatives ignored her, but one woman, Alison, snickered. She was tight with Gemma.

Normally, I'd clap back, but Gemma wasn't doing lunges or tricep curls or climbing a wall like a lizard, as per usual. She sat in a chair, surrounded by paperwork, her normally chic nails bitten to the quick. The strain of jockeying to be Marv's mentee was wearing on her.

I didn't have the heart to grind her down that much more. Though the second that position had been determined, she was fair game.

Marv rushed in, waving his hands, enthusiastically explaining about a break they'd had in the case. Apparently, our suspect had been working with a rogue vamp.

"Let's Sector A the bastard!" Marv high-fived one of the operatives.

Alison leaned over to her friend. "I heard those anti-magic collars prisoners have to wear drive them mad."

"I'd take insanity over some of the experiments they do on them," a male operative replied.

"Or Arcane Rot," Alison said. She shuddered. "Gemma, can you imagine a dark energy seeping into you, twisting and warping you down to the marrow of your bones?"

I swallowed down the taste of bile. Here it came, Gemma's razor-sharp description of all the gross torture that she no doubt delighted sending criminals to. Wonderful. My stomach started aching.

"That's truly horrible and actually kind of unethical," Gemma said. "I wouldn't wish that on my worst enemy."

"Yeah, right," I said.

"What's that supposed to mean?" she said.

The entire team, including Marv, looked at me curiously and a little excitedly like they were pumped for some Aviva/Gemma cage match.

I should have dropped it, kept things professional, but with Sector A hanging over my head and the endless needling I'd taken from Gemma over the years, I'd had it. "It means," I said evenly, "I figured the suffering at Sector A would be right up your alley."

Since Marv was present, I didn't add that she was an A1 bitch who enjoyed other people's suffering.

Gemma crossed her arms. "I don't punch down."

"The people in Sector A deserve it," one teammate piped up. "They colluded with shedim or rogue vamps."

"They deserve a regulated prison," Gemma corrected. "Not some secret facility with such a lack of transparency that all we have are rumors and speculation and where every sentence is for life." She glared at me. "Quit staring."

Marv set me to work after that and things got crazy, so I didn't have time to apologize for misjudging her—only on this one specific point.

Sadly, I didn't have time for a break and the next step of my plan either until mid-afternoon.

After wolfing down my sandwich, I headed to lockup, requesting to see the evidence from the drug lab bust. I was directed to a large locked room where the lab equipment was boxed next to personal effects.

I sighed. There went any time to decompress from this morning's hectic pace. I scanned the labels on the boxes, quickly sorting through the most promising ones until I found the twisted gold padlock that had been broken off Bratwurst's cage.

I slipped it into an evidence bag to take with me for a wardmaker to examine and was doing one last rummage through some banker's boxes when a glint of metal caught my eye. There was a second lock.

This one was silver, with two sets of initials carved inside a heart. D.L. + R.R. Neither set fit Jasmine Bakshi, but that didn't mean it wasn't hers. Or that it wasn't warded, since I couldn't detect those.

I held it up to the light, opening one eye and then the other, but when I didn't have any "aha!" revelations, I placed it in another evidence bag, and signed out both locks.

The good thing about being run off my feet for the rest of the afternoon, even for the most menial tasks, was that time flew by. I announced I was leaving at 4PM on the dot.

Gemma tightly pressed her lips together, clearly wanting to make some bitchy comment about me leaving early, but any Maccabee not engaged in vital work had leave to get home in time to light the Hanukkah candles. A sweet perk of the job. Those who couldn't leave but wanted to participate in the prayers and ritual could use one of the menorahs the Maccabees kept on hand.

As photocopying didn't qualify as vital, I traipsed out of there with a breezy "Have a nice weekend."

I hummed my way through the first few blocks of my drive home, groaned when I realized it was "Unchained Melody," and hit the button on my car stereo to blast some Joan Jett.

Much better.

Sachie wasn't home when I arrived, so I lit the candles by myself, letting the prayer and the sound of the struck match ease a deep well of tension. I wasn't religious, but Hanukkah was my favorite holiday. Michael and I had always made a big deal of all eight nights, inviting friends over to celebrate, and even when it was just us, we sang songs and played endless rounds of dreidel.

My mother and I hadn't celebrated together in years, but I felt more connected to her when I lit these candles than at most other times. Maybe that's why I did it.

I allowed myself a few moments to watch the dancing

flames playing over the colorful wax before heading out to the wardmaker. I didn't love leaving open flames unattended, but there was plenty of aluminum foil under the menorah to catch and snuff out a fallen candle or stray spark.

Wards, Inc. wasn't the most original name for the discreet office located in a small complex just off Main Street, but its owner, Noa Borstein, was an in-demand Eishei Kodesh who created wards for not only the magic community, but Trad government buildings and private companies.

She didn't use mezuzahs—only rabbis could set those —and she couldn't ward against shedim, if she was even aware of their existence. Her wards neutralized human-based magic threats and were also used to shore up security. For example, placed on a lock to make whatever it secured impregnable.

I buzzed in and stated my name and business into the speaker.

The door unlocked with a soft click, and I stepped inside.

Wards, Inc. was a cross between a high-tech lab and an art studio. Interactive displays mounted on the walls showcased intricate magical diagrams while LED lights embedded in the ceiling bathed the space in a tasteful glow.

The centerpiece of the room was a large drafting table covered in tracing paper with complicated designs for wards. It also housed state-of-the-art equipment with touch-sensitive screens. I couldn't guess their functions, but I also wouldn't randomly stick fingers in front of one lest I trigger some laser.

My mouth fell open with a whispered "Whoa."

A woman gave a throaty chuckle. "It is rather 'whoa.'" With her sleek coral linen tunic, loose pants, and sharply cut bob, she reflected the artsy–hi tech dichotomy of her office. "What can I do for you, Operative Fleischer?"

I pulled the twisted gold lock out of the evidence bag and placed it on the reception counter. "Is there a ward on this?"

Noa lowered a jeweler's loupe that she wore on a strap around her head. She peered through the loupe, closing one bright green–eyeshadowed lid to see better. "Nice work, but it's not one of mine." She prodded the broken hinge and tsked. "Breaking this open doesn't affect the ward, but the lock mechanism won't function anymore."

"How do you break a ward?" I replaced the gold lock in its evidence bag.

"You don't. Only the wardmaker can undo their work."

"What about this one? Is it warded as well?" I placed the silver lock with the initials on the counter.

Noa examined it for several minutes, swinging the open hinge back and forth, and flipping it over and back. "There's no magic on this one. It's just a lock." She ran a finger over the initials. "What do they call them? Love locks?"

I took it back with a rush of disappointment. "I think so. Can you tell who warded the gold lock? I need to find out who they sold this particular one to."

She pushed the loupe back into her hair. "I'm fairly certain I recognize whose work this is, but these particular ward and lock combinations are very popular items. Good for storage lockers and such. I don't keep detailed records of those transactions and there's no reason to think that he would either."

"Could you check with him? Please? It's important."

"Sure. Give me a moment." She disappeared through a door into the back.

I played a few games of Solitaire on my phone while I waited.

"I got the invoice for the ward and lock." Noa returned to the counter, paper in hand.

A fax? Who used those anymore?

I scanned the receipt that had been sent over. No name on the invoice, cash transaction. Who carried cash anymore? Oh, right, criminals.

The only useful details were that the ward and lock had been sold two weeks before the bust, in Kamloops, the largest town close to the drug lab.

I folded the fax and placed it in my purse. "Thank you."

Afterward, I sat in my car, slotting these pieces into place. This cemented the theory that the Eishei Kodesh gang found the shedim and not vice versa, since they'd prepared for her stay with a cage and this warded lock.

The two-week time frame was interesting. Had they bought the lock with time to spare before she showed up or was it a last-minute thing?

There wasn't any information about how long it took the shedim to produce enough urine for one batch of Crackle, and Jasmine, in her current condition, couldn't shed any light on that.

The Maccabees who'd rounded up the evidence once our team was headed back to Vancouver had destroyed the drug. Given the bloodshed that would occur had any other organic batches been distributed, we'd have heard about it, but thankfully, there were no reports to that end. We'd prevented a horrible disaster.

I still had to solve how Jasmine's crew had gotten hold of Bratwurst though. Even if summoning and binding a demon was possible—and according to Sachie, the chances were slim to none—Jasmine's lot didn't strike me as the type to have that knowledge.

That left my hypothesis about a third party with the ability to procure not just any demon, but one who was weak enough that it could be manhandled into a jail cell cage and had the right enzyme for the drug.

I messaged Silas regarding any possible matchmakers. He'd hit a lot of dead ends but had one tenuous lead to follow up on and would get back to me in the morning.

My stomach growled. It was almost 8PM and the Jolly Hellhound was a short drive away. Say what you will about the establishment being a front for the Copper Hell, it still did an excellent burger. After a day like today, it was exactly what the doctor ordered.

Sachie took me up on my offer to meet there. She was just leaving the gym and starving so it was perfect timing.

As soon as the door to the pub swung open, the inviting scent of beer, crispy fries, and sizzling grilled meat wafted through the air. The dimly lit interior was filled with the buzz of conversation and clinking glasses, a haven for those seeking solace and camaraderie. Local sports leagues' flags were mounted around the pub, the air conditioning making them flutter like pirate flags in the ocean breeze.

I snagged a booth, tracing a finger over the grooves in the worn wooden table while I perused the specials on the chalkboard behind the bar. Nothing swayed me from my burger goal, and while I accepted the menu I was given, I ordered only an IPA on tap, waiting until Sach had arrived to get my food.

A group of men walked in and the air sharpened. Dressed in casual clothing, they weren't particularly muscular, and the ones who weren't joking around with each other were focused on their phones, yet there was no mistaking what they were.

Vampires.

Chapter 20

The cheerful chatter and clinking of glasses faded into an eerie silence. My heart hammered. I'd seen vamp patrons here before—was this particular crowd simply unaccustomed to them?

The vampires, who'd been so jovial a second ago, stilled.

A glass shattered.

The largest of the bloodsuckers growled, his fangs descending.

I rose, ready to intervene, but the hostess was already crossing the pub, chastising the busboy who'd dropped a glass, and motioning to the vamps with a bored expression that washed any tension away.

Reality snapped back, conversations once more bright, and the vibe easy.

My gaze lingered on the vampires for a moment longer.

Had one of them turned Zaven? Probably not, but it got me wondering about the blackmailer, which led to questions about Natán Cardoso. For such a larger-than-life figure, I knew very little about the man.

I opened a browser and fell down a rabbit hole. Unfortunately, there was little new to learn, other than his age (sixty-two), and the account of how he grew a small vampire mob into one of the strongest global players. A Mafia he dubbed the Kosher Nostra after the nickname given to Jewish mobs in Prohibition-era United States.

Unsettled, I set my phone down. Natán had wealth, power, and was immortal. What could he possibly add to that arsenal that would make him more invincible and untouchable?

Other than Ezra?

Ezra hadn't found evidence of any vampires pursuing that invincibility, but Roman Whittaker had no reason to lie about the real reason infernals were murdered.

I sipped my beer. Once upon a time, Natán had been a Maccabee operative whose job had gone so wrong that a vengeful vampire turned him and his pregnant wife. Did that speak to motive? For Natán and Eva, observant Jews, this was a fate worse than death, and to make matters worse, she was pregnant with Ezra.

There weren't many articles about the day she walked into the scorching midday sun in Caracas; fewer still about her life. Ezra had given me glimpses of his mother, but he was five when she died, and everything he said was clouded with nostalgia and loss.

After some digging, I came across a single article written in Spanish about Eva. Google Translate turned reading it into a linguistic puzzle, but I got the gist. Eva had been a successful level three operative before she became a vamp. Both she and her husband attempted to remain with the organization, but about a year before her suicide, she'd left the Maccabees to open a crisis center to help other vampires who were struggling. By all accounts, this had given her renewed purpose and peace.

Could she have succumbed to the darkness of her

trauma? Of course. She'd suffered horribly. However, she'd been interviewed for this article a couple of weeks before she died. It wasn't merely this crisis center that provided her with a reason to live. There was another reason, one that brought a joyous expression to her face in one of the photographs: her young son, Ezra.

There were newly turned vampires, even ones who'd consented to this, who couldn't handle the loss of their humanity, but Eva had hung in for five years already. She had the crisis center and Ezra, and she'd been a religious Jew. Maybe she'd lost that faith, but the prohibition against suicide would be ingrained in her.

Why, after all that time, had she been overwhelmed by despair?

A primal surge of electric energy coursed through me, the jolt of having finally found that single thread that could pull apart an entire complicated knot.

Something was terribly off about Eva's suicide, and I was going to find out what.

I'm sorry I dumped knowing about Delacroix on you like that. Ezra's text almost made me knock over my drink, coming on the heels of me looking into his mom.

Me: *It's okay. You were bound to make the connection. I just haven't fully processed it yet, you know? It's one thing for him not to recognize me, but he's tried to kill me more than once.*

Dots appeared and disappeared. I waited for the undoubtedly sympathetic response.

I'm glad you got Michael's looks.

Oh my God. *Wow.*

"You stealing my burger joint, Fleischer?" Olivier stood next to my table, arms crossed, but his green eyes twinkled. "Because I take theft very seriously."

I grinned, relieved to hear the teasing note in his voice, instead of the suspicious one I'd become all too familiar with, and spread my hands wide. "I don't see your name stamped anywhere on the place, Detective Olivier Desmond."

"Are you here alone?" he said. "Want company?"

"I'd love company." I waited until he'd slid into the booth to add, "Sachie should be here any moment."

He froze, tried to slide back out, got caught on his coat, and swore.

I laughed. "You're welcome to join us."

Olivier narrowed his green eyes. "I feel like I'm being set up."

I blinked my lashes at him. "I have only the purest of intentions."

"Uh-huh." Grumbling, he shrugged out of his peacoat, his biceps flexing and shifting.

A complicated relationship with my ex did not preclude me enjoying the current view, until Sachie entered, her cheeks pink from the cold and her hair damp from showering at the gym.

I waved her over, delighted that Olivier was out of her sightline.

"Were you waiting long?" She did a double take when she came up to the booth. "Point Break? What are you doing here?" She shot me the same suspicious glare that Olivier had.

I scooted over on the padded bench to make room for my friend. "Olivier and I ran into each other here." I checked the appetizer list, but nothing appealed to me. Just a burger then.

I teased Olivier about ordering a lobster roll as his East Coast comfort food.

"I'm a proud Nova Scotian," he said. "Mock my lobster at your peril."

Ezra sent me a poorly photoshopped image of my head on a serpent's body. *Alternate universe Aviva is also cute, even with her father's looks instead of her mother's.*

Don't quit your day job to photoshop with the youth, Cardoso. Also, keep it up and I won't entertain you with tales of the dinner I'm having with Sachie and the cop I want to set her up with.

Once we'd placed our orders, the conversation turned to shop talk. It started with familiar bitching about all the bureaucracy and then swapping funny stories of previous cases, but when our food arrived, the conversation shifted to whether the Trad and Maccabee forces should be merged: a hotly contested topic.

"Eishei Kodesh make up a fraction of the world's population," I said, "and there's a lot of anti-magic sentiment out there. I think there's a world where we do work together, but we're a long way off."

"To be fair," Sachie said, cutting her massive piece of schnitzel, "that prejudice goes both ways. Lots of operatives see Trad cops as inferior."

Has she stabbed you yet for trying to matchmake her? Ezra texted. *Inquiring minds want to know.*

Olivier regarded her over the rim of his pint glass. "You're the first Maccabee I've ever heard admit that."

"We're magic," Sach said dryly, "not saints."

I'm a matchmaking wonder, I texted back. *The children are playing nicely.*

Olivier took a long pull of his drink. "You're working with vamps now, aren't you?"

Sachie tensed. "What of it?" she said warily.

Whoops. Spoke too soon. Usually, I'd consider it rude to be texting, but neither Sachie nor Olivier were paying any attention to me. And that was a good sign.

"Police forces struggle with profiling," he said, "which in turn undermines prioritizing ethical conduct and fairness in dealing with both victims and the accused." He scooped up some coleslaw that had fallen out of his lobster roll. "Having magic adds a layer of complexity, would you agree?"

"Sure."

"But at the end of the day, we're all human. We have a justice system in place. One that vampires aren't given access to. Once their guilt is determined, they're executed. And if it turns out at some point that they were falsely accused, it's too late. One strike and you're dead is a hell of a systemic bias."

"Vampires aren't a marginalized community," she said. "They're apex predators. And incarceration doesn't work with them. You can't sentence immortal beings to twenty years and expect any kind of rehabilitation, and we don't have a practical way to lock them up for life. Not that that would work either. Our current flawed system is the best we've got. That said, the operatives in the Vancouver Spook Squad do an incredibly thorough job to determine guilt before carrying out punishment, precisely because they're vampires. Other chapters where humans alone run the Spook Squad are not as vigorous." Her voice was thick with disgust.

Olivier forked up some coleslaw. "You struggle to reconcile what's fundamentally vigilantism with ethical conduct, don't you?" He asked the question without any judgment in his voice, his expression open and curious.

Ezra: *You can't leave me hanging like that. Update?*

I answered his inquiry with *High-stakes ethics discussion happening here.*

Yawn.

"I struggle with it every day." Sachie buttered a roll. "Which is exactly why I wanted to join that squad. It's important to face it and choose to stay on the right side of a moral line with every new case and not mindlessly kill. I'm doing this as much for myself as anything, but how will we foster understanding and a better community for everyone if cops stay in their own little bubbles? That includes both working with and policing vampires."

He nodded. "I've been saying that for years about Trads and Maccabees working together, but I never put vamps into the equation. Even ones who are colleagues. I pride myself on my inclusive mindset, but it seems I've got some blinders to work on removing."

"Admitting that puts you ahead of a lot of Maccabees," Sachie said.

Me to Ezra: *Ooh. Points to Olivier for being open-minded.*

Ezra: *Wait. Olivier? The guy you were with at the pub when I ran into you that time?*

"You've given me a lot to think about," Olivier said.

"I appreciate you keeping an open mind, especially about my work on the Spook Squad. A lot of people don't." Sachie cut through her last piece of schnitzel with a bit too much force and the knife scraped against the plate.

I flinched—not from the sound, but because this was a sore spot for her. She'd taken a lot of flak from other operatives and now her relationship with her own parents was strained. Whatever my frustrations with Sachie about her lack of acceptance for half shedim, her desire to do the right thing was sincere and I was tired of seeing her judged for it.

Ezra: *Aviva?*

I didn't reply, worried about Sach.

She had allowed very few romantic relationships to progress past a casual status. I'd always suspected it had a lot to do with her desire to work on the Spook Squad. Her partners—regardless of their gender—either protested the danger of working with and policing vampires, thought she was misguided, or accused her as doing it for the thrill. Yes, my best friend was bloodthirsty, but she wasn't hungry for senseless violence. She enjoyed fighting, but if there was a different, better system in place, she'd embrace that wholeheartedly.

"A lot of people could stand to listen more and talk less," Olivier said.

One corner of Sach's lips quirked up. "Get out there and give them pointers already, Olivier."

Me to Ezra: *VICTORY IS MINE! She just used his first name instead of calling him Point Break.*

Ezra: *Him being Olivier who you were on a date with.*

Me: *It wasn't a date.*

Ezra: *Good.*

Me: *That time.*

Ezra: *Aviva.*

I grinned, practically hearing the growl, and quickly typed, *I am literally setting them up. Focus on the point: I am the best matchmaker ever.*

Thanks to my previous talks with Olivier on our failed dates, I pegged him as someone with an experience-based understanding of Sachie's career, as well as the self-confidence and kindness she deserved in a match.

Olivier was chill enough to meet Sach's low-maintenance relationship requirements while being intelligent enough, with enough of an edge, to keep her interest longer than most. That surfer rode the waves of life's ups and downs with equanimity, but water had hidden depths and undertows. A nice guy who'd challenge her sounded like her perfect partner.

"I do want to take on more teaching and community outreach," he said.

"Really?" Sachie took a sip of her Coke, wriggled her nose, and sneezed. It was a gentle, nay, almost dainty "choo" followed by a tinkly squeak.

Olivier gaped at her, his lobster roll halfway to his mouth. Then he got a wicked glint in his eyes with a matching evil grin and set his sandwich down. "Rambo-lette, that was the most adorable sound I've ever heard. Are you made of cotton candy and unicorns?"

Me: *OLIVIER IS ABOUT TO DIE!*

Ezra sent back a gif of someone playing the world's smallest violin.

"Try barbed wire and spite." Sachie toyed with the cuff of her sleeve, her answering grin edged with violence. "What's inside *you?*"

Oh fuck. She was totally wearing wrist sheaths.

I smacked her hand.

She narrowed her eyes at me.

"You had a mosquito."

She left the weapon sheathed, but her glower was still out in full force.

"Okay, but seriously." Olivier didn't bother hiding his chuckle. "What happens when you're fighting a vamp and you sneeze like that? Do they explode into stardust under the force of all that cuteness?"

I stared at Olivier in fascination, revising my previous assessment of him as a man who carefully and thoughtfully evaluated every situation for risk, then followed the smartest course of action. I shoved some fries in my mouth. At least his demise would be entertaining.

My phone buzzed. *Is he still alive?*

Sach slammed her now-drained glass on the table and pinned Olivier in her stare. "If this is your lame way of saying you want to fight me, you'll have to do better than that."

Olivier furrowed his brow.

Me: *Alive for the moment. Olivier is super obtuse and hasn't figured out that she can want to fuck him and kill him at the same time.*

Ezra: *Ah. Foreplay.*

Me: *Right? Where are those stellar cop instincts that fast-tracked his career?*

I swallowed my mouthful of savory meat and melted cheese. This awkward silence demanded my assistance.

"Sach has been boxing for years. I've seen her drop a dude with fifty pounds more muscle."

She mimed a left hook. "Well-placed liver shot," she said modestly.

Olivier leaned forward, a spark of intrigue in his gaze. "Where do you train?"

"Gore Street Gym."

"Steve's place? The one on the second floor?" Olivier whistled. "That's hardcore."

"Works for me." She helped herself to a few of my fries, having polished off her schnitzel.

I drew the line at her squirting ketchup on my plate. "These fries are perfection without it. Gum up your own dish."

She rolled her eyes but obeyed. "Where do you train?"

Olivier named a popular fitness chain. "I use it mostly for interval training to keep in shape for surfing. They have some private boxing instructors in-house, but I've been looking for a place to step up my fighting game."

Sachie nodded.

When there was zero follow-up past that, I kicked her under the table.

A familiar surge of heat from one ticked-off Orange Flame seared my insides.

"Avi, are you all right?" Olivier said. "Your cheeks are really flushed."

"Acid reflux." I dabbed at the sweat on my brow. "Great burger, but oof."

Sachie slid a sideways glance at me, daring me to out her for using her magic on me. Or threatening to do more of the same but worse. I couldn't always tell the difference, and choosing wrong was detrimental to my well-being.

Throwing caution to the wind, I kicked her under the table again. Harder.

"Fine," she snapped. "If you're free on Tuesday, I could show you around the gym after work."

Olivier wiped his mouth with his napkin. "No worries," he said coolly. "I can go on my own."

This was the trouble with having sexual partners and romantic interests make the first move. Sachie wasn't used to putting herself out there.

I sent Ezra another text. *She tried to ask him. It sounded like a declaration of war. #hopeless*

Ezra: *Come on, padawan.*

I laughed and Sachie looked at me. "Cat meme," I said lamely. "It had a pancake on its head."

She dragged a fry through the ketchup. "I'd like to show you around the gym, Olivier." She added a smile for good effect, but it had too many teeth, and he flinched.

"We can spar," she said viciously.

"Okay." His equanimity was restored.

Weirdos.

Me: *Bow down to the matchmaking queen.*

Ezra: *They're going on a date? Where exactly would that be? A knife convention? A dark alley?*

Me: *The gym obviously. Where she can beat him up.*

Ezra: *Isn't that what I said?*

Dinner wrapped up soon after that. Olivier treated us, which was very nice of him, and Sachie excused herself to use the restroom.

"Is this going to be weird?" Olivier said.

"Because we tried to date or because you suspected me of stealing Sire's Spark?"

"Yes? Either? Both?"

"We're good, Olivier. Honestly. I think you and Sach would be great together, but no pressure. As for us, I just hope we're friends again."

"No worries about that," he said.

Sach and I drove our own cars home. I braced myself

227

for an attack when I stepped through the front door, but all she did was shake her head. "You're an asshole and you're lucky I love you."

"You're welcome." I ruffled her hair, earning a sharp hand slap.

"Who were you texting? Darsh?"

"Ezra." I shrugged off her piercing stare. "We're becoming friends again."

"Uh-huh." She turned back on her way to her bedroom. "Did you get your final report in?"

"Not yet," I said. "I've got a couple things to follow up on." Finding whomever connected Jasmine with Bratwurst, not to mention convincing Ezra to let me be present when he questioned Natán to determine his father's complicity in the missing infernal blood. Or ordering their murders in the first place.

But that was a problem for tomorrow me.

I woke up the next morning to a text from Silas with an address for Express Recruitment, an employment agency in southeast Vancouver, so I checked out the website. Its owner, Chandra Nichols, matched the name Silas had sent. The company seemed legit, but it was also a good cover story for people seeking special employees. Ms. Nichols was a smart woman.

Since the agency was open only in the afternoon on Saturdays, I did some grocery shopping and had lunch before driving over. I was practically at my car when my phone buzzed with a notification from Ezra.

Expecting it to be another message either praising me or teasing me, I opened it immediately. Short and to the point, it was anything but.

My father killed Roman.

Chapter 21

I tore out of the garage, left my car in a lot near the Jolly Hellhound, and barked at the bartender to open the door in the back room

Last night, everything had been great here. The atmosphere was friendly, I'd been hanging out with Sachie and Olivier, and having fun texting Ezra. Now, I stormed past tables like I was going to war and bolted through the portal, ready to physically attack any Hellion who got in my way.

Skidding to a stop, I blinked to let my eyes adjust to the dark and silence until I'd gotten my bearings enough to see that I'd been brought through the portal to his inner sanctum instead of the foyer on the main floor.

It appeared as though a bomb had exploded in Ezra's living room. The furniture, once arranged with care, lay shattered and overturned. His sofa was torn open in a snarl of untwisted metal springs and straw-colored stuffing, while the coffee table was splintered into jagged shards, scattered across the floor like broken bones. A curtain fluttered on its damaged rod like a flag waving surrender.

Deep gouges were carved into the walls, and the ceiling light was reduced to wires dangling precariously over glass embedded in the carpet.

The overcast night sky did fuck all to relieve the oppressive gloom in here.

"Ezra?" I called softly.

"In here." He sounded so raw that I didn't hesitate to enter his bedroom.

He sat on the floor with his back against a woebegone mattress leaning against the wall. His legs were splayed out, his shoulders were slumped, and his hair streamed back from the wind blowing in through the massive hole where the window once was, while the whitecaps of the waves churned and thrashed, mirroring the storm brewing in his eyes.

I kicked away part of the metal bedframe and lowered myself next to him. "Disrupting your environment as a commentary on the absurdity of striving for perfection. Nice." I nodded. "If the gaming hell gig doesn't work out, you've got a promising future as a performance artist."

Ezra sighed, the sound shuddering out of him like his sadness was too vast to physically contain, and laid his head on my shoulder. "I'm so tired, Avi."

"Because you keep fighting, Zee."

"Now there's a name I haven't heard in a while." He gave the ghost of a laugh. "From A to Zee."

Hearing the phrase I used to jokingly say before giving him a smacking smooch made me smile wistfully.

We sat there together, the waves rocking the boat like a cradle.

The combination of that rhythm, the smell of the ocean, and leaning against Ezra lulled me into a drowsy stupor. "Did he admit to killing Roman?" I murmured.

"Natán Cardoso does not admit to anything," Ezra scoffed. "If he was looking at a banana and you asked if it was yellow, he'd find a way to make you feel small for questioning him in the first place."

"How can you be certain he did it?" I brushed away a carved chess piece that had rolled into my leg.

"I got Remy drunk after we spoke."

I frowned, trying to place the name, then chuckled. We'd met Remy in the Crypt. The weaselly vamp had been ordered to attack Ezra and, instead, had ended up bonding with him like a puppy with its new owner. "Remy had dirt on your father?"

"Hell no." Ezra pulled at rug fibers like they were weeds. "He asked how my night out with Alastair in London was."

"Wait." I pressed my fingers to my temples like I was summoning a thought, hoping to earn a ghost of a smile from Ezra. I didn't. "This imaginary hang out happened while Roman was murdered?"

"The night before," Ezra said. "Alastair was spotted in London by a mutual acquaintance who mentioned it to Remy. He questioned Alastair about why he was in Europe instead of in Babel overseeing the inventory of one of Natán's clubs."

"Alastair fed him that lie."

"He didn't expect me to ever be in touch with Remy." Ezra let the gathered fibers fall free. "Alastair, on the other hand, would have dirt on my father."

"Or do his dirty work," I said.

"That too. I still haven't found anything to connect my father with the murders of those half shedim or the missing blood, but I swear, if he's behind it…" His voice cracked. "I'm so sorry, Aviva."

I found his hand and twined our fingers together. "Don't start comparing the sins of our fathers, because I'm pretty certain I've got that one wrapped up."

"So competitive," he chided.

I shook my head. "Teasing aside, I hate that my suspicions about your dad were right. That's brutal."

"And yet, not one of the worst things he's done." He looked around the detritus of his room. "Sorry to make you witness my temper tantrum. I should clean this up."

"You don't have to make light of this, and you don't have to apologize for being upset."

"Then how about for being more like him than I want to be?"

"Stop it. Even if he's a monster, you are not his clone." I clasped my free hand over our intertwined ones.

"My mother always said el que la hace, la paga, what goes around comes around, but I don't think there's anything evil Natán could incite, that would be his undoing." His shoulders slumped, his head bowed low in defeat.

I carefully set a broken light bulb on the top of an overturned chair next to us so no one stepped on it. "Forget Natán. Tell me about your mother."

Ezra leaned away from me, his expression wary. Though he didn't remove his hand from mine. "My mother? I lost her when I was little. There's not much beyond random anecdotes to tell."

"I don't believe that. I bet that even though Natán raised you, Eva had a far greater influence on the man you are today." I licked my lips nervously. "I looked her up because I was curious about her. Was that okay?"

He nodded slowly. "Yeah. Other than Orly and my aunt, I don't have anyone to talk about her with."

"It was impressive how even after being struck by such tragedy when she was changed, she turned it around into a way to help others."

"That was her to a T," he said.

I worried my bottom lip between my teeth. "Hard to

believe she ended it five years after the fact, when she sounded so hopeful about her life and loved you so much."

"She wasn't murdered, if that's what you're thinking. Well, not directly. I watched her walk into the sun."

My hand flew to my mouth. "You were there?"

"Yeah. I was playing in the shade of the porch."

Imagine witnessing your mother become dust in front of you, not even turning back to say goodbye. I shuddered. "Did something happen? Did someone show up?"

He roughly scrubbed a hand over his face. "I've gone over that day a million times, but I was so young. I don't think anyone else was home except me. One thing I do remember, though, is that she'd been fighting with my father a lot in the days before she died."

"Is that why you joined the Maccabees? You were hoping to find something since your parents were former operatives?"

He put his head back on my shoulder and leaned against me. "I wanted all the intel they had of the incident that ended with my parents turned into vampires. Once I was working for them, I got the official unredacted report, but everything corroborated what I already knew. My father killed a vampire in self-defence on a mission and her lover took revenge by turning two religious Jews."

"Okay, but explain something to me. You were raised to be the Crimson Prince, right?"

"Yes, Avi. I didn't dream of being an assassin when I was little. It was just a given. After I finished my MBA, I was expected to join the family business."

"But you delayed going back to school when we were together. If you didn't dump me because of Cherry Bomb, then why did you leave? It was tied to your mom, wasn't it?"

"It was, but I haven't been totally honest about learning you were a half shedim."

233

I stiffened and tried to pull my hand away, but he tightened his grip.

"Hear me out. Please. The reason I was in Vancouver in the first place, that kayak trip? It was because I discovered that right before Mamá died, she received a phone call. The number had come from inside Maccabee HQ in Caracas."

"Their old chapter," I said.

He nodded. "Whatever she learned was so unbearable that she killed herself in front of her child. Combined with whatever my parents had been fighting about, well, Natán was culpable for her death in some way." He picked the broken light bulb up off the chair. "After we lost Mamá, he'd sit night after night with this one tiny photo of her, until he burned it a few months after her funeral. Then we moved to Babel, and suddenly there was a much larger copy of that photo framed over the fireplace like some damned shrine that he could tour people past." He winged the bulb at the wall.

I resolutely didn't flinch.

"After I learned about the phone call," he said, "my curiosity about why she'd done it turned into an obsession. I reasoned that the Maccabees could help me solve this and I fled Babel trying to figure out how to make that happen."

"Then you met me. Why didn't you just tell me about all this?"

He laughed. "I was trying to impress you, not scare you away with all my baggage."

I elbowed him. "You wouldn't have—"

"Do you remember that barbecue you took me to?"

I blinked at his abrupt change of subject. "What barbecue?"

"Some Maccababies you'd been novices with were

there. We'd been hanging out in the shade, and you were finishing up a popsicle, intending to introduce me to all your friends, but they iced you out for bringing a vampire. You came home and cried."

I had a dim memory of the popsicle, and sitting and laughing with Ezra, so happy and proud to be with him, but not the rest. "I don't remember that."

"I do," he said darkly. "I wanted to make you smile, not be the reason for your tears."

I stared up at the ceiling. All this time, I'd had an almost fairy tale–like recollection of our time together until the fateful night of our breakup.

Had it been easier to frame our being together in a purely positive light because it allowed me to paint him as the villain for ending the most perfect relationship ever, instead of acknowledging there were other, very real reasons we might not have made it?

"Graduating to full Maccabee status meant the world to you," he said, "and I couldn't tell you that I planned to use them to learn the truth. You'd be waiting for me to ask you to help me, force you to choose who you were loyal to. And maybe part of me was scared that if I stayed, I'd do just that."

"So, me telling you about Cherry was just an excuse for you to do what you were always going to do? Leave?" There was no familiar flare of anger.

I, too, was tired of fighting.

Plus, for the first time ever, Ezra was being totally honest with me.

"I was happier with you than I'd ever been." His sweet smile was reminiscent of the one he'd train on me back when we were together. "Mamá was dead, and knowing why wouldn't bring her back. I'd convinced myself to stay, and I was ready to tell you everything about who I was, and hope you'd still want me." His expression darkened. "Then my father showed up in Vancouver."

"I didn't know that."

"I'd never stuck around in one place for anyone before and Natán got curious. Never a good thing."

"Natán never learned I was an infernal, he found out you were dating a Maccabee."

"Not just any Maccabee. The daughter of his old friend. What a perfect way to ingratiate himself with you, then use you." Ezra smiled bitterly. "Like father like son."

"It's not the same."

He shrugged. "I used the timing of your revelation about Cherry as an excuse. Better to hurt you over being a half shedim than drag you into something much worse. I told myself that I had to do this for my mother. Go back to Natán and play nice until I had a way to uncover the truth of her death. Believe it or not, I also did it for Michael."

"Why?"

"She was one of the few people from my parents' operative life who stayed friends with them. She remained close with Mamá and I was grateful for that. I couldn't give my father ammunition to hurt her. Either of you."

"You did hurt me though," I said gently.

"It was the lesser of many evils at that point." He shook his head. "That's not entirely true. I was so obsessed with knowing what had happened to my mother, that I justified hurting you. I can't take that back, but I've regretted it every single day since then and…" He searched my face. "How do you feel about dinner?"

"Do I finally get to try the buffet?"

He shot me an exasperated look.

"Oh, you meant you buy me dinner, like a date?" I shifted uneasily. "Look, you had a shock and I'm totally here for you—"

"But I don't want a pity date," he mocked in a terrible impression of me. "You're feeling vulnerable and that's making you nostalgic. Our sex is still off the charts, but—" He made a "blah blah blah" motion with his hand.

"You forgot the part where if you really wanted me back you had six years to reach out," I said.

"I was too busy lying to myself about being better off without you."

I slammed a hand on the ground. "You fuck up or play games and then drop these truths that are supposed to disarm me and make it all better. It doesn't work that way."

Ezra sagged back against the mattress. "You're right."

My chest filled with an achy hollow feeling at how easily he agreed.

"I've forced you into going along with my decisions," he said. "If we're going to have a shot, then it has to be as a meeting of equals." He opened his hand, freeing me.

My fingers looked so fragile resting on his palm.

"If I've blown it," he said, "I'll spend the rest of my life regretting that, but I'll accept your decision and I'll always be there for you. But if I can prove I'm a man worth giving a second chance to, then let me do that. Please."

Ezra had given me honesty.

I looked around the wreckage of the room, born of the wreckage of Ezra's life. Except unlike the furniture to be trashed, maybe he'd had to break in order to heal stronger than ever. Embrace the art of damage and fuse those pieces back together with gold into a new, no less beautiful piece.

Just like I had.

That was all well and good, but I still didn't see how to bridge the divide between me being a Maccabee and him running the Copper Hell.

Ezra watched me patiently, not pressing for an answer.

All I had to do was stand up and he'd let me go. That ship would sail into the horizon, never to be seen again. It would be that easy, a small shape fading into nothing, and we'd be done.

Chapter 22

I folded my hand over his. "Then what happened?"

He stared down at them. "Is that a yes to dinner?"

"It's not a no."

He smiled impishly at me.

"Tell me the rest of the story." A particularly strong gust blew in through the window and I shivered.

Ezra grabbed one of the blankets that had fallen when he overturned the mattress and carefully tucked it around me before holding my hand again. "I became the Crimson Prince. About a year later, I found out my father had ordered a hit on one of the Authority Council."

"Secretary Pederson?" The one who'd authorized his carte blanche on our murdered half shedim case.

"Got it in one. I flushed out when the attempt was to occur, then I showed up and killed the assassin."

"If Natán attempted to kill a Maccabee before..." I searched for a kind way to put this.

"Why was I so stunned that he'd killed Roman? My father never learned I'd outmanoeuvred him. I'd have known," he added bitterly. "But I stupidly thought that with Pederson alerted to this attempt, he'd back off the Maccabees for good."

"Was that why you joined us?"

He clamped his lips together and looked away, but a moment later he gave a resigned nod. "Partially. It was pretty easy after that to convince Pederson that I'd be an asset to the organization. In exchange, I was given clearance on everything relating to my parents. But our deal was to be kept secret so no one found out how vulnerable she'd been."

"You didn't just spy for us. You killed for us. Humans too."

"They were evil pieces of shit, but yes. I told you I had."

"I didn't believe you. You spied, you assassinated for two different organizations, and you made yourself into a very public figure so that no one, on either side, could take you out without you being missed."

"I don't want your pity," he said sharply.

"It's not pity," I said. "You were hiding in plain sight. You think I don't understand what that feels like?"

He was silent, but he squeezed my hand.

"When did you actually stop being Natán's enforcer?" I asked.

"About a year ago."

"And when you had nothing left to learn from the Maccabees, you jumped ship. Literally. You came here where you had different sources of intel to ply."

He looped a finger around a strand of my hair and gently tugged. "That, and I hoped that leaving would keep you and Silas safe from any blowback from my actions."

"Yeah, well, the Maccabees are every bit as ruthless as the mob."

"You want to talk about it?" he asked quietly.

240

"Silas's arrest wasn't enough for you?" I shook my head and released his hand. "I should get back."

I reluctantly stood up. Even with all the wreckage strewn around us and all the truths that had come out, this interlude had been an oddly cozy bubble that I was loath to leave.

Ezra walked me to the portal that he'd opened in his living room.

"Not making me come and go through the portal downstairs like the rest of the chumps?" I teased.

"Exclusive status for esteemed matchmakers only." He gallantly moved the chess table he'd knocked over out of my way. "Marvel at your good fortune."

I laughed.

We stopped in front of the portal in a weirdly formal tableau, like a boy from the 1950s walking his date to her front door.

"I realize you want to question Natán," he said, "but he won't give anything up. We'll have to figure something else out, but…" His lips turned down.

"You need time to grieve him being part of all this. Part of something else horrible, besides whatever happened with your mom. I get it."

"Yeah," he said softly. "You do. About dinner? May I please take you out?"

I planted my hands on my hips and gave an aggrieved sigh. "Fiiiine. It must be mockingly pricey and feature a wide array of award-winning desserts."

"Challenge accepted," he said.

"I'll have dinner with you but that's all I'm promising."

"Understood." He lowered his lids halfway. "May I kiss you?"

My heart hammered in my throat. He'd laid himself bare to me. The truth wasn't pretty, but it had been freely given. I could kiss him, I could *have* him any way I wanted him, yet I preferred to wait. I liked being friends again, texting and joking like we had when things were easy. I wanted that to feel more solid before we complicated things with romantic intentions. If that was even in the cards for us.

"We'll see if you rock the dessert challenge," I teased.

He pumped his fist in the air. "I'm totally getting that kiss."

"You're impossible," I groused.

He brushed a hand across my cheek. "I'll contact you about the reservation, but in the meantime, be careful out there."

"You too, Zee."

His face lit up like my use of that old nickname was better than any birthday present he'd received. Jeez. I hadn't seen other children in Babel. Had Ezra ever had birthday parties with friends? I shook off the melancholy thought and, with a small wave, left the Copper Hell.

I may or may not have worn a dopey smile all the way over to Express Recruitment to question the matchmaker who'd paired Jasmine up with Bratwurst. Though I put on my best game face once I entered the office from the building's second-floor corridor.

Heh. This matchmaker versus matchmaker battle began now.

The bell jangled and a man with terrible posture and an obnoxiously green tie looked up from the reception desk. "Can I help you?"

Beyond him was a single main room with three desks, two printers, multiple filing cabinets, plus an office with a glass wall, and another door that presumably led to a back area or restroom.

"Hi." I held up my gloved hand in a half wave. "Is Chandra Nichols in?"

"Sure." He hit a button on his phone to let her know there was someone here to see her.

A moment later, an older woman with a bright smile and hard eyes stepped out of the office and walked briskly toward me. "I'm Chandra."

"Elyse Samuels." Should Chandra check, Elyse had served time for drug trafficking and superficially resembled me. "My friend Jasmine Bakshi recommended you."

Chandra's smile didn't flicker, nor did she look at her coworker. Either he was in on it, or she was one cool lady. Probably the latter, considering her side hustle. "How is Jasmine?" she said.

Majorly fucked. But props to me for calling that relationship correctly. "She had to take a leave from the business and asked me to step in."

She extended a hand toward her office. "Let's discuss your particular needs."

Only one of the desks was staffed, the female employee going over some career testing results with a client.

I didn't bother taking off my second-best pair of gloves or coat when I got into Chandra's office. All the better to hide my Maccabee ring, though I did slide into my synesthete vision in preparation for questioning her.

Chandra shut her office door and settled herself in her leather desk chair. "What are you hoping I can do for you?"

Not a single vital sign presented as in distress.

"We require a replacement employee," I said.

"That's a shame." She straightened one of the three piles of papers on her desk and set the large stapler she'd been using on top of the middle one. "However, Jasmine was on the waiting list for a qualified worker for some time. Individuals with those special skills don't just pop up on a regular basis."

I filed that interesting tidbit away.

Nothing about this conversation made Chandra nervous, nor did she get any particular thrill out of it. Her heartbeat remained steady, she didn't sweat, and I didn't detect any brain activity suggesting she was attempting to lie or stall.

I leaned forward insistently. "There's got to be something you can do. I have vendors with expectations. I'm willing to pay to jump the line."

"That won't help."

"Then I'll find someone else who's capable of getting what I need."

While Chandra's body language didn't change, a swath of blue shot across her brain and pulsed along her ribs.

Pissed you off, did I? Good. Now we were getting somewhere. There were subtle differences in the physiologies of anger and fear, one being that had Chandra been scared, she would have been breathing much faster. Fear also showed as a pulsing blue dot in the stomach, whereas Chandra's was clear.

"Good luck finding someone else who offers my particular service," Chandra said icily.

I stood up. "I'll ask my vendors to connect me with one."

"In which case, you'll have to tell them you can't make quota." She brushed away a slug's trail of dirt that had fallen from a ceramic planter onto her desk. "And the type of people you're in business with aren't big on giving extensions."

"They also aren't big on defective product," I sneered. "The so-called skilled employee you gave Jasmine was incapable of doing their job."

Her expression remained impassive, but while her

fingers tightened on her pen, she still didn't present any signs of fear in my synesthete vision.

"You have a choice," I said in a hard voice. "You can go down with me." I ticked the items off on my fingers. "Get me an actual skilled employee asap, or direct me to the person who actually found the shedim, since we both know you're just a middleman." I paused. "And middlemen do not do well in Sector A."

My guess that she'd know about that prison landed.

Chandra set down her pen, her eyes colder than a penguin's feet, and slowly stood up.

Suddenly, blue spiked through her so hot and bright that I was blinded.

Glass shattered with a sharp snap.

I dove to the floor.

Chandra collapsed, crumpling like a rag doll. A crimson ribbon streamed from the single bullet hole in her head.

I scrambled behind her desk and pushed it over a split second before bullets slammed into the thick wood. Splinters arced into the air.

An assassin trumped any concerns of being outed.

I swallowed past the panic making my limbs heavy and my blood run in icy sluggishness, and reached for Cherry. For the first time ever, I slipped her on like a favorite sweater, dissolving any mental barrier between us. It was as if a river of crimson and toxic green stardust shot into the marrow of my bones, its heat fueling me. I tossed off my coat, praying my armored scales protected me from guns.

The glass from the shot-out window crunching underfoot was my sole heads-up that the assassin had stepped into the room, since I was behind the desk, blocked from view. I mentally mapped the rest of the office, cataloguing all the furniture and any potential weapon. I grabbed the stapler first, but it was disappointingly light despite its size. The ceramic planter had a much nicer heft.

I popped up and hurled it.

It flew into the man who'd raised his arm with catlike instincts to block his face, knocking his baseball cap askew.

A shower of soil cascaded down his front and the planter hit the carpet, a jagged chunk breaking free.

I charged the man, my head into his gut, and bowled him over.

His gun and aviator glasses went flying. At the sight of my shedim self, his eyes widened, and he shoved me off him.

I grabbed the broken planter and swung, shattering his nose. My attacker howled and I inhaled, the tantalizing scent of hot copper filling my nostrils. The metallic aroma encompassed a world of emotions and sensations, but most of all, it made me feel brilliantly alive.

I slammed the planter into him again.

Snarling, he grabbed it and tossed it away, smashing his other fist into my kidneys.

I laughed, barely feeling it. The frosted edges of my scales darkened, and my short horns pulsed. Catching his fist, I jammed the fleshy part of his palm down onto one of the tips.

He screamed, the cry ending in a squeaky little croak when I viciously tore my horn free.

The air along his neck shimmered. The veins in his throat thickened, curling under his red flesh like gnarled tree roots, while the fist I still held now showed two more fingers than was polite.

I dropped his hand like I'd been burned.

His eyes were two red slits, and his mouth was a snarl of jagged teeth set in a pointy red face made of raised scarred points like a malevolent pincushion.

Shadows erupted from the man, flexing against me

with the sharpness of a cat's claws. Thin ribbons of inky corrosiveness drilled into me through my scales.

I screamed, bound in darkness and pain. My nerve endings were on fire, my blood boiling inside my veins, but I latched on to my determination to survive before I was swept under the rapids of my agony.

My pain flowed away from me into part of a unified dreamy wash to the world where Chandra's dead body, the carpet crushed under my knees, and my desire to destroy this demon—all were swells in a stormy ocean.

I erupted into a flurry of fists, teeth, and horns. I bit, punched, and stabbed any part of him I could find.

His shadows finally fell away, the darkness, burning pain, and my bloodlust clearing enough to see he lay bruised, bloodied, and unconscious.

Another swell to drift away.

A door slammed in the hallway outside the agency office. I flinched and swung toward the noise with a glare before catching myself with the stern reminder that other people being happy and untouched by this death and violence was a good thing.

The shedim had come in using a human glamor. Hard to say whether he'd locked the door, and it was a miracle that no one heard the gunfire, even with the silencer, but still. It was time to leave.

Chest heaving, I wiped his blood from my gloves onto his sweater and retrieved Maud's Maccabee ring from my jacket pocket. I raked a clinical eye over the demon, determining the base of his throat where his skin was markedly thicker as his kill spot.

Next, I swiped a finger clockwise over the five tiny gemstones embedded in the ring to activate the magic cocktail and determine if my guess was correct. Sure enough, a white circle flared brilliantly in time with the blue gemstone.

Next up was the red gemstone's time to shine. It blazed a thin stream of magic into the kill spot for a few seconds.

The shedim's entire body deflated. The orange stone glowed next, sucking all the heat out of the shedim. His spiky facial protrusions twisted and snapped like pretzels while the demon's body rolled up like a Swiss log cake.

I sat back on my calves against a rush of disappointment when the white gem went to town on the demon's emotions. The shedim was still unconscious so there was no enjoying the broken, haunting dirge of his fear.

Cherry chuckled in my head.

Last, but not least, the yellow gem shone like the sun, extinguishing the shedim's powers with its cleansing magic.

The shedim curled tighter and tighter until there was nothing left of him and all five gems on my ring went dark.

It wasn't justice, it wasn't satisfying, and it certainly wasn't closure. The demon may have been vanquished, but the questions he left behind prevailed.

Chapter 23

There were no witnesses.

I shook my head sharply. *Survivors.*

Call them what you want, Cherry said, *but move your ass.*

Chandra hadn't reverted to a shedim form when she was murdered, so she was human. It didn't matter why she'd chosen to work for demons, any rewards she'd reaped were irrelevant now.

I grabbed the dead receptionist's long puffy coat from the coat stand in the break room, grateful that my own jacket was short and would be covered by this one, then I tucked my hair under the large hood and adjusted my gait to be more like a man's.

There was nothing I could do about my size, but hopefully any security cameras outside would mistake my two jackets for a man's bulk. No wonder the shedim hadn't even bothered with gloves to hide his fingerprints, if authorities caught him on any security camera, they'd be hunting a glamor. One that would never be used again.

I tossed the puffy coat into a dumpster in an alley a few blocks away, smoothed my once-more brown hair down with my fingers, and checked on my camera that none of the blood I'd gotten on my scales showed on my face. My bloodstained gloves went into my pocket to be burned later.

No one gave me a second glance on the walk back to my car.

Out of shock, self-preservation, or both, I stuck with the mandated program, and kept moving. I put on a talk radio program about the state of potholes in the Lower Mainland to keep me company for the drive. Every time my brain veered off that topic and onto dangerous ground, I simply turned the radio up.

By the time I got home, I was partially deaf, but I'd made it back undetected and in one piece.

The second I stepped into my bedroom, my emotional defenses shattered, the lie of their brittleness revealed. I screamed and hurled my car keys across the room. I was shaking, my fists tightly clenched. I'd been so blinded by my suspicions of Maccabees that I'd missed a lethal threat and, as a result, failed to spot any danger to Chandra or those around her. The female employee and her client must have gone before the assassin showed up, but the receptionist was still dead.

Some poor soul would come into work later, or worse, not until the day after tomorrow on Monday, and find those corpses. It made me sick to my stomach to be complicit in that.

After a very hot shower where I scrubbed my skin raw, I threw on sweats and sank onto my bed, narrowing my eyes at the ceiling, upon which I visualized a timeline.

Based on when the warded gold lock was purchased, roughly two weeks ago, Jasmine got word from Chandra that a shedim with the special skills of creating a secretion to take Crackle to another level was available.

I tabled the question of where Bratwurst came from for the moment. Jasmine had been waiting a while for a suitable demon. Hopefully all the transactions that Chandra facilitated involved long wait times and a scarcity of "employees."

Jasmine had a cage and a warded lock ready to imprison the shedim, who wasn't strong enough to get free.

Two weeks went by. The shedim got stronger, and the drug manufacturers produced that batch of Crackle we found. Then came the night of the bust. Handling the shedim's urine hadn't been an issue before, but that evening even drops of it on their skin had deadly consequences.

Either the Eishei Kodesh manufacturers got sloppy or the secretion was more potent than expected and hit them with the subtlety of a wrecking ball.

That shit show ended with the demon refusing to go back somewhere and killing herself.

I'd found two locks in evidence: one gold and warded, the other a silver love lock with no magic on it.

Finally, a male shedim silenced Chandra. A Maccabee showing up to question her didn't cause her assassination. I wasn't in there long enough for my attacker to be alerted and arrive with a glamor on and a gun at the ready.

This had already been in motion long before I'd entered that room. But what set it off?

The encroaching darkness outside broke into my thoughts. I hauled myself up off my bed and lit the Hanukkah candles, the dancing flames steadying my emotions enough to come up with my next step in this case.

Jasmine believed the gold lock would hold Bratwurst, so was there more to it than an Eishei Kodesh ward? Had the shedim at the employment agency murdered Chandra to cover up his involvement?

I threw my closet door open, tossing all my purses out

251

until the keypad on the safe was exposed. If using my blood on Sire's Spark led me to Maud the night of the Maccabee party, could it lead me to some discovery about the demon assassin?

Quickly punching in the code to the safe, I pulled out the crystal and carried it and the gold lock I'd retrieved from my purse into my bathroom.

I shut the door and sliced my finger on a claw. A single bead of blood dotted my skin, and while I was hit with a faint tinge of nausea, it was nothing like the night of the party when I'd sensed Maud.

That was strange, though, because there *was* still nausea. Shouldn't I have had an all-or-nothing reaction? I scanned the gold lock with my synesthete vision, but my magic didn't reveal a damn thing. Normally, that would make sense since I illuminated weaknesses only in humans, not inanimate objects, but something was affecting me.

Leaving the crystal on the bathroom counter for the moment, I opened my door, intending to put the lock back in the evidence bag while I searched for the culprit. The moment I left the bathroom—as soon as I passed by the mezuzah ward on the doorframe—I was drenched in sweat, shivering icy cold and fever hot at the same time.

I swallowed twice against the nausea that surged up my throat and grabbed my dresser for balance.

Time spun out under the insane idea that Sachie was a half shedim and her scent and personal possessions all over the apartment was making me want to claw off my own skin. I dismissed the impossibility and ridiculousness of it even as I lurched closer to my bedroom door.

I reached for the knob, but my body twisted, hunched and bent under the force of a dark abomination pulsing out toward me.

Even Cherry flinched away from it, whimpering softly

in my head like a scared dog curled in a ball, hoping not to be struck.

Through my blurred vision, I scanned every item within arm's reach. My perfume bottle or that lone unused tampon wasn't the culprit, but a corner of the evidence bag with the *silver* love lock poked out of my open purse on top of my dresser.

I shook the lock free of the clear bag and gasped. The initials engraved into the heart were almost obscured by indigo and black runes scarring every inch of it, which I instinctively knew had been created with shedim magic and their blood.

A thick black scorch mark—again caused by magic, not fire—ran diagonally through the heart.

My hands shook so violently that I couldn't unseal the bag. I finally punctured it with my claw and was blasted to my knees by a wave of pure evil.

Using the drawer handles to pull myself up, I flipped the bag over, not daring to touch the lock directly. A meaningless string of numbers and letters glowed on the bottom of the lock next to the keyhole.

Repeating them under my breath, I grabbed my phone and wobbled into the bathroom, where I slammed the door and collapsed into the bathtub. My heart was racing, thumping against my chest like it was trying to escape, buy a plane ticket, and get to a safer place far, far away.

Same, heart, same.

I fell back against the cold enamel, my phone falling into my lap, trying to survive the stormy swells threatening to pull me under. They were subsiding now that I was once more protected by the mezuzah ward for my bathroom but not fast enough.

An eternity later, I'd recovered enough to plug the characters on the bottom of the lock into a search bar:

84XR7WH8+RF. I blinked at the result. What the fuck was a plus code?

The answer was simple but it didn't clear anything up. Plus codes were based on latitude and longitude, providing an address for people or places who didn't have one. This allowed for deliveries or to help others find those locations.

Runes on a lock was one thing, but I couldn't think of a single reason for that location here in town to be magically etched into the metal—and with demon magic no less. Luckily, I had a car and could drive over there myself to check it out.

I brought Sire's Spark with me in case I needed to reactivate my demon-sensing abilities, though using it was on my to-do list somewhere below "be swarmed by fire ants." I also brought the silver lock, tossing it in my trunk. The effects of using my blood on Sire's Spark had worn off and the silver lock appeared normal once more, with no visible signs of the runes or scorch mark and no sense of a foul abomination. However, my abhorrence of it wasn't easily shaken off.

The plus code took me to the east side in Strathcona, a historically lower-class neighborhood with pockets of gentrification in the remodeled heritage homes and cute little restaurants that had sprung up.

I parked at the plus code's specific location: a long pedestrian overpass encased with chain-link fence. Walking its length of shadows between the streetlights, I found two other locks attached to the fence. One was another padlock with initials, and the second was a partially rusted bike lock.

Bleeding on Sire's Spark didn't reveal shedim magic on either of them. I returned to my car and leaned against the hood, staring at the overpass and running through the facts.

The silver love lock didn't have an Eishei Kodesh ward

on it, but the plus code etched in demon magic pointed to this location. Had it been hanging on this fence? Why? And why was it in Jasmine's possession? Or in Bratwurst Demon's, since I wouldn't make assumptions.

I rubbed my cold hands together, then proceeded to inform myself about love locks.

There was some contention over where the tradition of placing these engraved locks on bridges started from, but many attributed the origin to Ljubavi, over a century ago. A Serbian couple, Nada and Relja, were separated during WWI, and when Relja fell for another woman, Nada died of a broken heart.

I rolled my eyes.

When other Serbian women heard about this, instead of threatening any other cheating partners with a broom, they inscribed their own initials and that of their lovers on a padlock and atttached them to the railing of the bridge where Nada and Relja used to meet.

You know what story I hated studying most in school? *Romeo and Juliet.* Yes, they were dumb teens and their actions were understandable through the lens of hormone-driven questionable ideas, but generations of adults had turned this into the be-all and end-all love story.

Shame on them.

And shame on the people who'd conveniently forgotten the cheating and Nada's death and decided the takeaway was to fetishize padlocks.

Grasping at straws, I did another search on "Unchained Melody," the love song that Jasmine had hummed at me, a snippet in one result catching my eye.

"Unchained Melody" was written for a film about a man in prison contemplating whether to go on the run or wait out his sentence and return to his family.

One thing that I hated more than *Romeo and Juliet?* Coincidences.

What if this song *was* Jasmine's way of answering my question. Not the "who" of her connection to Bratwurst, but the bigger picture of "how"?

When Bratwurst said that she wasn't going back, I'd taken that to mean to the demon realm, but I'd been dissuaded from that line of thinking. However, take one silver lock with demon magic on it, a song about jail, and Chandra—infrastructure? This wasn't a coincidence.

It was a mindfuck of a hypothesis.

I walked around and around my car, but when I couldn't disabuse myself of this idea, I picked up my phone to call the only person I, ironically, trusted to work through this with me, because for all her bluster and anger, she'd keep an open mind.

I hit a button in my contacts. "Michael? We need to talk."

Chapter 24

"What was so urgent that you dragged me out of a perfectly warm living room?" My mother, wearing warm leather gloves, handed me a takeout cup, her other hand resting on the top of her open car door.

The wind picked up, blowing away a cloud to reveal a sliver of moonlight.

I shivered against the breeze skittering down my neck, clasped my freezing hands around the cup, and inhaled. "Hot chocolate?"

"You'll be up all night if you drink caffeine now," she said. "Besides, you always clamored for hot chocolate on cold nights. Remember when we'd ride the train at Stanley Park to see the holiday light displays? We always bought some right after."

Because my nose would be numb from the cold. I'd take that first hot sip, feeling my insides heat up, then blow like a dragon to see the white puffs get thinner and thinner under the warmth of the chocolate.

"I didn't realize you remembered that," I said.

"I remember more than you give me credit for," she said briskly. "So, what's the emergency?"

I pulled the silver lock out of my pocket and handed it to her.

"Okay." She flipped it over a couple of times. "And?"

"Hear me out before you say anything."

She sighed. "All right, but let's at least get in my car where it's warm."

Her Mercedes had heated seats, so I wasn't about to argue.

Once we were comfortably settled, Michael listened to my theory, her expression an unreadable mask. For all that my sister was the champion poker player, I suspected that my mother could outbluff her in a heartbeat.

My words filled up more and more of the car's interior, until I wondered if we'd both be crowded out by the enormity of it.

"The plus code led me to this overpass." I pointed out the window, then fell silent, waiting to see what she made of all the information.

Michael placed her takeout cup in one of the holders. "Was Silas your informant about the employment agency?"

I nodded.

"Would you have told me about Chandra's murder if it weren't for the demon magic on the lock?"

"The Authority wanted answers, not more dead bodies. Dmitri had a hard-on to crucify me for my personal connections, and Silas, a vampire charged with corruption, had pointed me to Chandra. I didn't report the murders because I didn't dare let any official body know I'd been there, even anonymously. I was too paranoid that my good deed would not go unpunished."

"That's a no, then. How did you see the magic on the silver lock?" Michael narrowed her eyes.

My stomach twisted and I swallowed a metallic tang, adrenaline making my mouth go dry.

She was going to blow a gasket when she heard my answer. I marked the time on her car's console: 8:39PM. The moment my relationship with my mother was destroyed for good.

I formulated a dozen lies on the spot. I was good at that. But on some level, hadn't I called Michael because I didn't want to use them?

I notched my chin up. "I used my blood in conjunction with Sire's Spark."

My mother's flinch was delightful. Then she gave an incredulous laugh. "You stole it out of my safe and replaced it with a dummy artifact." Her admiration was a million times more satisfying than her surprise.

But it was also infuriating. "How can you act all proud when me stealing it, hell, when my entire life all comes down to you forcing me to hide what I was?"

My mother scrubbed at an invisible speck of dirt on the leather cover of her steering wheel. "I trained you to keep yourself safe."

I took an extra-long swig of hot chocolate, hoping the flavor would overpower my bitterness that all those years of treating my shedim side like a dirty secret were nothing more than training to her. However, I hadn't come here tonight to fight with her about a thirty-year-long hurt.

"The night of the drug bust," I said, "Bratwurst Demon claimed she didn't want to go back. That means wherever it was, she'd been there before, and it was so terrible, she preferred death. At her own hands." I fiddled with the window lock but didn't press the button. "Is it possible that Maccabees can't kill shedim?"

"Possible? Yes, for Eishei Kodesh. I suspect vampires do destroy shedim. They must, otherwise the demons wouldn't even appear to die. Nothing would happen at all and yet it looks identical to when we do it." She tapped the pillbox on her Maccabee ring. "Vampires don't have these rings, so the magic cocktail must mimic what they're doing."

"Do you agree that shedim would brag about Maccabees' inability to kill them if we were sending them to the demon realm?" I said.

"Absolutely."

"Is it possible that our magic sends them to some kind of gulag demon prison?"

"Again, yes to possible. And yes, this explains why they aren't using our failings to demoralize us. The demons don't realize we don't kill them until they end up in that prison. And they don't usually get out."

"You jumped ahead to the next question," I said wryly.

"You're a bad influence," she said.

I bit back my snarky retort that that was my shedim side. "If I'd been correct about sending them to the demon realm," I said, "then I could buy that only a few Maccabees knew the truth." I'd left out my friends' involvement in that conversation. "But a prison system requires massive amounts of resources. Guards and an actual facility. The prison's got to be huge, if there's even just one."

"You're thinking of it like a human jail with cells and three square meals a day," Michael said. "This is a place that horrified a *demon*. It doesn't even have to be in our pocket of reality."

We both looked at the silver lock lying on the console between our seats.

"Come on, that's batshit insane," I said. "That padlock isn't a demon prison like some kind of TARDIS and bigger on the inside."

"Maybe it's gruesomely small," Michael said. "No light, no space, just the shedim contorted into it for all eternity. You said the runes were scorched. That would neutralize the shedim magic, just like opening a cell door, which is how the shedim at the drug lab was released. As for how she got in there in the first place and her refusal to 'go back' when you were about to use your ring? Our magic cocktail must send shedim directly to an empty lock. No vehicular transport, large facilities, or guards necessary. The demons then take these locks, hide them in plain sight, and track them with these plus codes."

"It would explain the shedim's contempt for the gold padlock," I said. "A basic lock, even a warded one, is nothing in comparison."

"Is this where you ask me whether Maccabees are keeping this a secret since we developed the magic in our rings to begin with?" Michael said dryly.

"Dr. Olsen and Dmitri Kozlov threatened me if I didn't explain how Jasmine found the shedim. And Kozlov is fanatical about what should happen to people who collude. Why do that if they were in on such a heinous secret?" I shook my head. "Besides, Trad cops don't hide the fact that they incarcerate criminals. Even if Maccabees don't actually kill shedim, we still shouldn't conceal that the best we can do is imprison them. That's an accepted part of law enforcement. We wouldn't tell the general public because they don't know about demons, but operatives could know the score without feeling disheartened. So why don't we?"

I lowered the temperature on the seat heater because my butt was starting to bake. "There's also Chandra's murder," I said. "She was killed by a demon, not an operative, and there's shedim magic all over this lock, not an Eishei Kodesh ward. All that leads me to believe that the magic cocktail in our rings was designed with the purest of intention—to kill demons, but somehow that magic was perverted."

"All sound reasons." Michael nodded. "In which case,

traces of demon magic should be present in our rings' magic."

"Does the Authority have a way to do that?"

"Not at present."

I was silent. Sire's Spark might work but that would mean bringing it to the Authority's attention. It would be easy enough to explain how we'd gotten it, but I didn't want anyone to possess the means to detect half shedim. I bit the inside of my cheek. Perhaps Michael was justified not promoting me to level three if I wasn't willing to do that right thing, no matter what the personal cost.

"Something you want to share?" she said.

I shook my head.

"Okay, then. I'll call another meeting with Dr. Olsen and Dmitri. We'll present your findings at that time, starting with the shedim's actions on the night of the drug bust and including this nameless informant of yours, but with one exception. Should anyone ask, Chandra told you about the shedim magic on the lock before she was killed."

Michael's certainty about sharing all this eased that one sliver of doubt deep in my core. "I didn't realize until right now how badly I needed to hear you say that Maccabees weren't complicit."

My mother gazed out the window. "We've made thousands of batches of that magic cocktail since it was first developed back in the 1600s," she said. "As a Yellow Flame, I was fascinated with the underlying magic that held the five magic color types together and allowed them to work in conjunction with each other. I did a lot of research on the subject back when I was a Maccababy, but I never got a satisfying answer. Later, when I became director and had a deeper clearance level, I revisited the topic."

I was enthralled almost as much by the idea of a

young Michael and her curiosity as this story. "What did you find?"

"Would you believe it's like a sourdough starter? Maybe more like a self-replicating virus. The team that initially created the cocktail created a foundational magic strain that we keep in a special regenerating vault. The cocktail is created at a single facility, with every batch using this strain as its basis. While the recipe is a highly guarded secret—"

"With eleven herbs and spices?"

Michael snorted. "There's no documentation on the underlying strain."

"Why not? We love records."

"Right after the very first batch of our magic cocktail was produced, shedim stormed the original facility."

"They destroyed everything?"

"Almost everything. A tiny batch of the foundational strain survived. Just enough to allow the self-replication. The records were gone. That didn't matter for the rest of the cocktail recipe, since the surviving members were able to reproduce it, but this foundational strain was so complex that its survival was hailed as a miracle on the scale of the Hanukkah flame."

"Why weren't we taught this story in training?"

My mother smiled wryly. "And admit that we allowed shedim to get the jump on us before we even had a chance to use this magic formula? That we almost lost it—and any fighting chance along with it? The story isn't a secret, but it's not widely repeated either."

"Point taken," I said. "So shedim attacked us, using it as a cover to bake their magic into that foundational vector and divert demons into these prisons. Do you think that without the corrupted magic, our rings would have worked as advertised?"

"I'm hoping their attack is proof that it would have."

She picked up the silver lock. "Demons aren't incarcerating their own without a reason. One that is not in humanity's favor."

"And Bratwurst got out. Or was let out." She'd been weak at first and I was grateful that it had taken time for her to reach full strength, because had we not been at the drug lab that night, who knows how pervasive the carnage might have been? "How many others have been set free to further some demon agenda?" I took the lock from her and sealed it up in the evidence bag again. "I'll gather any other evidence I can to support this discussion before the meeting."

Michael rested her head against her seat. "What do you think happens when people in the government and the military who've been briefed about shedim learn about all this? The ones who make sure we get money and resources to kill demons in addition to policing Eishei Kodesh?"

I swore softly. "If we're not killing shedim like we claim, what's to stop governments or the military from taking over and cutting us out?"

"Right now, Maccabees have power, respect, even adoration." Michael's echo of Ezra's words to me about vampires took on a mocking edge. "And those in the know will do anything to keep it that way. The Authority isn't complicit," she said, her voice thick with disgust, "but out of arrogance for our own infallibility, laziness, or just plain willful ignorance, we fell for the longest con in history, and I'm not sure they'll have the balls to face that."

We hadn't discussed our mother-daughter relationship, but for the first time, the director had treated me like an operative she respected, sharing insights and opinions with me. She'd found it hilarious that I stole Sire's Spark too.

For all I accused Michael of reducing me to one thing, perhaps I'd done the same, placing her into some narrow definition. Tonight, I'd seen a new side of my mother, one who found humor in surprising situations and who had geeky fascinations.

It would be easy to blame her for never showing me those sides of her, but I wasn't a child anymore. Perhaps I'd just never cared to look.

I said goodbye softly and got out of her car.

The Authority's decision to act on this new information would come down to how strong their faith in making a difference was. Whether their hope that we mattered in this fight and had to do whatever it took to stem the tide of evil would prevail, even at the expense of admitting mistakes or not looking heroic and powerful.

My hand went to my purse with Sire's Spark inside. Not handing the crystal over to the Authority to detect demon magic on the locks was the right decision because it could also be used to hunt people. Any half shedim who broke the law had to be given the opportunity to be tried and convicted within the justice system, same as any other person.

I started the engine, having mostly convinced myself, but as I pulled away from the pedestrian overpass, I glanced in my rearview mirror.

Michael had dropped her head in her hands. For the first time in my life, her larger-than-life essence was diminished. She looked fragile, struggling under the weight of her authority.

I almost hit the brakes.

However, she'd see comfort as pity and that was the last emotion she'd tolerate. Especially from me. The person who kept ripping the scales from her eyes.

But even with everything we discussed, I was stuck on a single thought as I drove away: my mother hadn't asked me to give Sire's Spark back.

Chapter 25

I didn't have the energy to do much on Sunday morning beyond wait for this meeting and see how the chips fell. It's not like I didn't have other items to pursue. There was still the matter of the missing infernal blood, what the dark magic ritual for vamp invincibility entailed, and whether Sire's Spark was more than an infernal detector, but exhaustion washed over me like a heavy blanket, weighing down my eyelids and tugging at every muscle in my body. I yearned for a quiet corner and a chance to recharge.

The important thing was that no one was coming after Maud. Her (late) ex-boyfriend's inability to keep his mouth shut had led Zaven (also deceased) to seize on this opportunity to impress his hero (sadly, not fully deceased).

Natán might have ordered the deaths of those other half shedim and be plotting vamp invincibility, but I couldn't determine that without Ezra, and thinking about phoning him made my fatigue deepen.

I hauled myself out of bed and rummaged through my dresser. Forget about lying around. A run would do me a world of good: the adrenaline surge propelling me forward, each breath a cleansing wave, and the cool breeze whispering through my hair carrying a sense of freedom and release. All that would exist from moment to moment was the pounding of my feet against the pavement and the steady beat of my heart.

And if I was lucky? There'd be a shedim to fight off in the forest or a dark alley, my own pot of gold at the end of the rainbow.

I returned an hour later, drenched in sweat with every muscle aching in the best possible way.

I'd even fought a butterfly demon with a tramp stamp of a human on her lower back. Great sense of humor; I still killed her.

Even better, Sachie and Darsh were in the kitchen slicing bagels and mixing up mimosas for brunch.

"Sachie has been filling me in on your encounters with the Authority," Darsh said. "What's the noun for a collection of douches?"

"A canoe," I said.

"Oh, right." Something had Darsh off his game.

I raised an eyebrow at the pitcher containing blood instead of orange juice that Darsh was stirring since he didn't usually consume more than a couple of glasses. "What's driving you to drink? Your latest case? Sexual frustration?"

He tossed the wooden spoon he'd been using in our sink. "Cease your blaspheming. I can charm anyone, under any circumstances."

Sachie thrust her hips forward and back. "Save a horse, ride a cowboy."

"Yeehaw!" I mimed twirling a lasso.

Darsh very pointedly grabbed the platter of bagels and walked over to the trash.

Sachie lunged for him. "Don't harm them. Those are sesame bagels! Not shitty onion ones."

He held them above his head. "Are you going to play

nice?"

"Yes," I said contritely and held out my hand. The second he handed the platter over, I galloped to the dining room table, complete with horse clomping sounds.

Sach howled in laughter.

A wet sponge hit me between the shoulder blades.

"Gross!" I pulled at the back of my shirt.

"That's an improvement over your general disgusting-ness," Darsh called. "Go shower."

"I'm going." I stopped as if a thought had just struck me. "Poor Silas. Stuck at the Copper Hell while he clears his name. We should invite him to brunch."

Was this the opposite of protecting Silas? Yes. But this car crash was going to happen sooner rather than later, and it was better to rip the bandage off. Mixed metaphors aside.

Sach poured herself a glass of regular mimosa. "Who's to say I already haven't?"

"Wh-what?" Wow. I didn't know Darsh could sputter.

"That was nice of you," I said.

Darsh crossed his arms. "You better have invited Ezra too."

"No need for that," I said. I didn't trust these two farther than I could throw them, especially not with the fragile new friendship taking root between Ezra and me. If they found out about our upcoming dinner? I shuddered.

"Of course I invited him." Sachie took a sip then smacked her lips. "He gets all sad and grumpy if his friends exclude him."

I threw up my hands. "You're not friends. He betrayed you. You tolerate him at best, remember?"

"He made me a scarf," Sachie said.

Darsh nodded. "I love my toque."

"You can't just let him worm his way back into our lives with knitwear!" I protested.

"I, for one, like our woolen worm," Darsh said. "Very *Dune*. Ride 'em, spice girl."

I groaned.

"In all seriousness," Darsh said, "he does tend to have our backs when it counts."

"Plus, he didn't have a good male role model growing up," Sachie said sadly.

"Then I'm calling Olivier," I said.

"Who's Olivier?" Darsh peered between us.

"A new gym buddy," Sachie said.

I snorted.

Darsh gave a slow smile à la the Grinch. "Like that, is it?"

"Go take your shower, Aviva," Sachie said forcefully. "Since Ezra will be here in..." She checked her phone. "Fifteen minutes. With Silas."

Darsh and I exchanged panicked looks. "Lend me your eyeliner and hair spray and I'll be the model of propriety," he said.

"Deal."

We bolted for my bathroom to hand over supplies.

When I returned to the living room, twenty minutes later, having showered and put together an outfit that looked like I wasn't trying to impress while making me look fantastic, only Silas had arrived.

"Hey, Avi," he said. "Ezra sends his regards. There was an issue at the Hell that he had to deal with."

I'd torn apart my closet and four drawers for "his regards"? My annoyance blew away pretty quickly, though, because I was here with my friends and he was stuck there, and I fired off a quick *You okay?* text.

I sat down next to Darsh, who'd zhuzhed himself up, and helped myself to double servings of lox and cream cheese for my bagel.

Just business as usual, Ezra texted back. *Thank you for checking. And for yesterday.*

Anytime.

Darsh poured Silas a mimosa. "Been keeping yourself busy, Cowpoke?"

I settled in, prepared for good food and a good show, courtesy of the flirting bound to come.

"Plenty of diversions at the Copper Hell, Rapunzel." Silas sipped his beverage. "Delacroix alone is a full-time job. Piece of work, that one. Ez set me up with new electronics, and the shedim keeps seeping water into the room to mark his territory. You know how many cables I've had to replace already?"

Darsh grunted in disgust. "You sat there and took his shit."

"No." Silas cracked his knuckles. "I told him in no uncertain terms to keep away from my stuff."

"I would have threatened to electrocute him," Darsh said primly. "Fried eel is delicious."

Silas grinned and shrugged.

I hurriedly examined him for injury. "And you're still standing?"

"I can be persuasive when I want to be. I may have strong ideals but I'm not a pushover."

Darsh jabbed a finger at him. "Where was that attitude when you were locked up?"

"I wanted to make my case, but my convictions didn't extend to dying for a corrupt allegation. I'd worked out a more physical plan of escape." He spread his hands wide. "The odds were against me while I was at Maccabee HQ, but I had a plan for when that van stopped."

I shivered. "Glad you realized it was us before that happened."

"What if they'd tried to stake you while you were still in the cell?" Sachie said.

"I would have gone down swinging," he said.

"You shouldn't have been in any position to go down," Darsh charged.

"Have a clear mental picture of my going-down position, do you?" Silas smirked at him and Darsh blushed.

I took a mental snapshot to capture this beautiful moment, but also, oh shit. That wasn't hit-and-run behavior. Darsh was a deer walking into traffic, caught in Silas's giant headlights.

Under the table, Sach knocked her ankle gently against mine, a look of concern on her face.

"Shut up," Darsh said to the room at large. "You know what I mean."

Silas nodded somberly. "I do, but honestly? I was in a state of shock that it was happening. Fifty years of service. I thought it would count for more. That I would—"

Darsh reached for Silas, then curled his hand in. "Yeah," he said softly. "I would have as well."

The two smiled shyly at each other.

This was not a hit-and-run, a casual attraction. It was… I wrinkled my brow. Something unexpected, something deeper and potentially far more dangerous. Alarm bells wailed in my head.

Silas cleared his throat. "Anyway, I'm safe now. And it's a good thing, otherwise I couldn't have met this one beauty."

Darsh tossed his hair. "Do tell."

Sachie waggled her eyebrows at me from over the rim of her glass.

I bit into my bagel with a smile. Good. They were flirting. That was nice safe ground not involving shy smiles and out-of-the-ordinary blushes.

"She's like a sculpture in motion," Silas said.

"She?" Darsh tightened his grip on the stem of his champagne flute.

Sachie gripped her quarter bagel, her wide-eyed expression silently urging me to do something, but I had no idea what. How did you stop a trainwreck?

Silas drew a wavy line in the air with his hand. "Kinetic. All curves. I could spend hours drinking in every facet of her, how she carries this sense of mystery and adventure."

Darsh's expression turned more and more crestfallen. He should have been making some innuendo-laden retort, not looking like someone forgot his birthday.

I set my bagel down on my plate. Silas wasn't cruel. He wouldn't outright taunt Darsh if he'd fallen for someone else, and without a doubt, the attraction was mutual, but the Southern vamp was so animated. His eyes were alight and his face was creased in a crooked grin as he described this mystery woman.

"Her O scale is perfection." Silas kissed his fingers, then laughed at our confused expressions. "It's a rare model train. Some poor fool lost it in a forfeit at the Hell and Ez is being a real gentleman and letting me have it. I've always been a big old train nerd. Riding them, collecting them."

Sachie sucked in a breath, and my stomach lurched. Darsh was going to eviscerate this sweet man for his hobby.

"Modern or prewar track?" Darsh said.

My bagel hit the plate, lox spilling off it.

"Prewar." Silas's hazel eyes heated up more than if Darsh had stripped naked and given him a lap dance. "You a collector?"

Darsh shook his head. "My brother was. I inherited his set."

Sachie and I had only recently learned Darsh even had a brother. His name, Patrin, and the fact his death was connected to the Copper Hell was the full extent of our knowledge.

"What pieces do you have?" Silas said.

Darsh unleashed a wicked grin. "How about an early Carette live steam train set?"

Trains? With that setup about "his pieces" that was where he went? I gaped at him.

Silas's fingers twitched. "What gauge?"

"I believe it's I gauge. Want to see it?" Darsh tossed off the invitation a little breathlessly and rushed.

Oh no.

"Really?" Silas lit up like Rockefeller Plaza over Christmas. "You're not messing with me?"

Darsh frowned. "Why would I mess with you? I don't kick puppies."

"Huh?" Silas shook his head. "I just expected you to mock me."

"I used to tease my brother about it." Darsh looked off, a weight to the slump of his shoulders. "I wish I hadn't. It's shitty to make fun of something that brings someone joy. Besides, it would be nice to see it do more than collect dust. And maybe you could tell me train shit," he mumbled.

Silas smiled. "Yes, Darsh. I could tell you train shit. Do you want to go now?"

"What about brunch?" I said.

Darsh stood up and grabbed his jacket. "It was lovely. Thank you, darlings." He kissed Sach and me on both cheeks then went ahead of Silas to the front door.

The other vamp leaned down to hug me.

"Hurt Darsh and we will find you," I murmured.

Silas pulled back in alarm and looked to Sachie for reassurance.

She narrowed her eyes, and ran a finger over a

serrated bread knife. "Don't make me use this." She raised her voice and smiled broadly. "Bring it in, big guy."

The enormous vamp gave her the quickest hug in the history of mankind, then bolted for the front door and shoved his feet into his shoes, nattering about snake-pull couplers, whatever those were, in a pitchy voice.

"Relax. We have time." Darsh placed his hand on Silas's arm and the other vamp jumped. That earned us a suspicious look, but we waved them off with smiles.

The second the door shut behind them, Sachie leaned back in her chair. "God, people's love lives are exhausting."

"Being a matchmaker is not for the faint of heart." I reconstructed my bagel. "We've done all we can. Now it's up to them to move forward in a mature fashion."

We looked at each other, then burst out laughing.

To prepare for the emotional devastation to come, we ate our body weight in bagels (plus fixings), drank two pitchers of mimosas (sans blood), and finished off the latest K-drama that we'd been sucked into, all while we waited for the rabbi to come and set a new mezuzah ward.

It was a great plan. The show was equal parts hilarious and adorable, the mini Reese's Peanut Butter Cups we'd graduated to were the perfect dessert, and hanging out with my best friend was the soul restorer I'd desperately needed.

The intercom buzzer sounded.

I spoke into the small phone connected to the intercom at the condo tower's front doors. "Come on up." I buzzed the rabbi in.

A black mesh portal opened in our living room and I jokingly chucked a peanut butter cup at it. "Rude to show up hours late after you've sent your regards, buddy."

"My regards? What are you going on about, girlie?"

Delacroix stepped through and grimaced at the handful of candy Sachie had just tossed in her mouth. "Stop eating that crap. We're going for pancakes. You too, Saito."

"Is that an order?" I said waspishly.

"Say no again, and find out."

Chapter 26

"We're full," my bestie said through bulging cheeks. Her fingertips twitched.

"Put your magic away," the demon said. "You'll just tire yourself." He'd combed his unruly salt-and-pepper hair and exchanged his wool fisherman's sweater for a loose unbleached linen shirt that reminded me less of pirate's clothing and more of the sails of a ghost ship.

Was this effort for me, for Sachie, or did he just like to dress up whenever he went to Brimstone Breakfast Club?

Whatever the reason, if he wanted us dead, it would have happened already.

"What do you want?" I said.

"I told you, pancakes. Or waffles. I actually prefer those."

There was a rap at our door.

The shedim raised an eyebrow. "I hope you didn't pay extra to get the rabbi out here to reset your ward on a weekend."

"You're spying on me, stalker?"

"I keep tabs and the last time I checked there was no ward. Ergo…"

I unclenched my fists. "If you do anything to hurt the rabbi—"

"You'll what?" He strode over to the sofa, picked up the bag with the peanut butter cups, and sniffed it.

The rabbi knocked again.

"Don't keep him waiting." The demon popped a candy in his mouth, a surprised look on his face. He helped himself to a second one.

Sach shot me a "get him the fuck out of here" look which I replied to with a "How? Have at it." one.

At the third knock, I took a deep breath, plastered a smile on my face, and opened the door. "Hello. Thank you for venturing out this fine winter's eve."

Points to the security company for employing female rabbis, but points deducted to Team Aviva for the perplexed look she shot me at my old-timey turn of phrase.

She set a metal case on the ground. "You did say it was an emergency."

"And time and a half for you." Delacroix smirked, but at my glare, moseyed over to the rabbi. "Will you be cleaning the post first?"

"That's right." She clicked the case open and extracted a small spray bottle of fluid and a soft cloth from her bag. "Seen this before, have you?"

"Once or twice." He popped a hip against the wall. "I'm fascinated by the ways we keep evil at bay. Though it doesn't protect from yetzer hara, the innate inclination to evil."

The rabbi smiled and sprayed fluid on the door post. "Lucky for us, we counter that with yetzer hatov."

Sachie insistently beckoned me over. "What if him being here while the ward is replaced means he's exempt from its effects?" she whispered.

"Fuck!"

277

The rabbi and the demon broke off their Talmudic musings to shoot me identical chastising looks.

"Sorry. Uh, question, Rabbi." That's where I stalled out, unable to find a subtle way to phrase it.

"What happens if you set a ward in the presence of a shedim?" Sachie said.

"Terrifying prospect." Delacroix nodded sagely, which failed to mask the unholy glee in his eyes. "Would the ward affect them? Or even set at all, given the presence of such malice? For as it says in Deuteronomy—"

"Forget Deuteronomy," I snapped. "What's your opinion, Rabbi?"

She squatted down to rummage in her case. "I assure you the ward would set. As for any shedim present, it's hard to say. They might be exempt. Then again." She pulled a cloth-wrapped item out of her bag. "The force of the ward's magic might kill them."

"From your lips to God's ears," I said cheerfully.

"Maybe a puny demon," Delacroix muttered.

"Excuse us a moment," I said.

The rabbi nodded, unwrapping the new mezuzah.

I grabbed Delacroix's arm and tugged him into the kitchen. "What is it going to take to get you out of here until this ward is reset?"

He flicked a finger painfully against my forehead. "Do you have a head injury? I've told you twice now. Come for breakfast."

I crossed my arms. "You'll leave and let us ward ourselves up, all in exchange for coming with you to the restaurant?"

"It's not like I don't know where to find you," he said. "Besides, if you don't get a new ward, Cardoso will be all put out, and he's an annoying bastard when he gets grumpy."

"Why this sudden invitation?"

"It's not sudden. I asked you before and you said rain check. It's a thank-you meal. If it wasn't for you, I would have killed my daughter when we met." He shrugged. "I find I like having a kid."

"Do you now?" I snarled. *Where were you the past thirty years?*

"Shedim are capable of feelings." He sniffed primly. "And it's fun to run the odds of our progeny causing chaos. Give them incentives to play a certain hand versus another."

"So much for feelings. This is pure mercenary evil."

"The two aren't mutually exclusive, girlie."

"Oh my God," I muttered.

"The rabbi is ready to set the ward," Sachie anxiously called from the living room.

"We'll meet you in the alley behind the condo in half an hour," I said.

"You better." A narrow portal back to the Hell spun open.

"Leave through the door," I hissed. "Like a normal person."

Luckily, he did.

Creating a new ward was a simple matter involving industrial glue and four sets of prayers. The entire thing took less than fifteen minutes, then the rabbi was gone, leaving me to trust we were once more protected.

Sachie grumbled about my no-weapons decree as she put on her shoes, though her curiosity about visiting the demon realm won out over her rational desire to be armed to the teeth.

I remained human in this part of the demon realm, versus flaunting my Cherry Bomb side in Babel, so I wasn't concerned about being outed.

The red and purple light portal that Delacroix opened to Flaming Flapjacks when we stepped into the alley deposited us in the parking lot outside the restaurant.

Sachie was uncharacteristically subdued as she got her first glimpse of the 1950s-style pancake house with its large curved windows, chrome accents, and pastel green awning. Nestled against jagged obsidian cliffs, it was framed under a sky that burned with the fiery hues of a dying sun, casting an eerie crimson glow over the landscape. Ashen clouds roiled and churned, casting long ominous shadows that stretched against the cracked earth.

I threw an arm over my face to protect myself from the hot, arid wind buffeting me, and led Sach toward the building.

There was a tinge of mania to the pancake in a chef's hat doing the cancan on the neon sign while the "S" in Flaming Flapjacks had yet to be repaired, still flickering and hissing.

I held the restaurant door open for Sachie, wondering what it would be like to come here looking as Cherry? Would the food taste better? Would I be accepted or still treated as the abomination that most halfies were to full shedim? Not that I was seeking to build community here, but still.

The fly hostess (both an accurate physical description and subjective opinion about her look) was nowhere to be seen.

Guessing that Delacroix was out on the veranda, I grabbed a couple of plastic laminate menus from the hostess podium.

Elvis belted out a bluesy number about one night of sin on the jukebox as I led Sach through the mostly empty restaurant.

A rhino shedim with bright blue eyeshadow behind horn-rimmed glasses drank from a white coffee mug smeared with her red lipstick, while her companion, a buff gym rat with two extra arms, poked at what I hoped was cottage cheese.

We passed the sign reading, "Bring Your Appetite; Leave Your Grudges!" which hung over the table where a shedim who was nothing more than a mini tornado with glowing green eyes, hoovered up some kind of mash on its plate.

Sachie's eyes were wide and she had this delighted crooked smile on her face—with both dimples on display. I hadn't seen that exact expression since our grade-three field trip to the fire station when we were allowed to go through the fire engine and flick on the siren.

Delacroix was seated out on the screened veranda, fans spinning lazily overhead. Once more the humidity was off the charts, though none of his old man buddies had joined him today.

I blotted sweat off my forehead and took a seat across from him.

Sachie sat down next to me.

He nodded at her. "Well? Better than Vegas?"

"I'll tell you after I try the food."

Our server was squat and toad-like but the coffee they brought was fresh and our food (waffles for Delacroix, blueberry pancakes for Sach and me) was outstanding. Even Sach pronounced them the best pancakes she'd ever had.

Delacroix gave a pleased smile, took a sip of piping-hot coffee, and leaned back in his chair, cradling his mug. "Admit it, the Copper Hell impressed you."

She shrugged, though a smile tugged at her lips.

"I built a damn fine place," Delacroix said. "It impresses everyone. Even my daughter, and it turns out girlie's a tough nut to impress."

Girlie? I choked on my mouthful of pancake.

"You have a daughter? I hope she took after her mother," Sachie said dryly.

I pounded back half a glass of water.

"Mostly," Delacroix said grumpily. But then he brightened. "She got good stuff from me though. Scales, those green eyes, crimson hair, horns."

Did he mean Maud or me?

I swallowed hard. It had to be me. Delacroix was a demon. He'd found out I was his half shedim daughter and was drawing out this bombshell of a reveal, right here, right now, in front of my best friend. Payback for not telling him myself.

I gripped my glass, terrified to look at Sachie and see the disgust and anger in her eyes when Delacroix finally spoke my name. I braced myself for her to jump to her feet and scream my betrayal to the heavens.

Sach furrowed her brow, looking at me oddly.

Delacroix drank some more coffee, his expression thoughtful. "I'm thinking of running some poker tournaments at the Hell. Putting her up against high rollers I know."

The vise around my chest loosened. Not me. My secret was safe.

"You mean Maud?" Sach could be deadpan but I'd never heard her so devoid of emotion. It was as if shock had broken the lever that dispelled feelings.

The demon nodded at me. "This one didn't tell you? Kid tried to kill me and this girlie here stepped in, blustering about arrests and justice."

"No," Sachie said faintly. "This one didn't tell me." She stood up, the scrape of her chair along the floorboards a whisper instead of a furious howl. "I'd like to go home now."

Delacroix opened a portal without a word of protest.

"I—Sach—" I waved my hands in entreaty, but she

stepped away from me and vanished. I whirled on the shedim. "Why fuck me over like that?"

Delacroix fished a cigarette out of his back pocket and popped it in his mouth. "Maud was walking around free. You pulled one over on the Maccabees and I was curious whether your friends were in on it."

"Bullshit," I spat. "That's not why you did this."

"Sure it is. Information is power. But, I'll concede that's not the only reason." He unearthed a book of matches, struck one against the cover, then lit up and took a deep drag. "I let you brush off my previous invitation to breakfast because you said rain check. You never got back to me to reschedule and I hate it when people don't keep their promises. I am, after all, a man of my word."

"I was busy. And you've got a lot of nerve lecturing me about promises. You're a shedim. Yours don't have any worth."

"On the contrary." Delacroix blew a smoke ring into my face, his eyes glittering. "I always keep mine."

My urge to painfully destroy him was so overpowering that it made my teeth throb.

"Someone tried to blackmail Maud," I said. "They wanted proof of her changing on camera."

He punched the table. "Who?"

"I killed them."

"You want a gold star?"

"No. Answers. Do you know of a dark magic ritual involving infernal blood and a power word?"

"No." Delacroix narrowed his eyes. "For what purpose?"

"Vampire invincibility."

His expression hardened. Water swelled up from the floorboards.

I pulled my feet up onto my chair.

"Maud's blackmailer," Delacroix said. "He was a vampire?"

I nodded. "He did this to impress Natán Cardoso."

The water vanished and the shedim's expression eased. "Just because the blackmailer believed it doesn't make it so. I've heard a lot of stories people tell themselves to keep their hope alive."

Was that all it was? A story with nothing behind it?

"And I've dealt with Cardoso Sr.," Delacroix said. "Messing with dark magic isn't his style. A thorough and meticulous obliteration of anyone who gets in his way, sure. But not that. Someone is telling tales." He tapped ash onto the table. "What else you got tying Cardoso to this power play?"

I filled him in about Roman Whittaker's murder at the London HQ jail cell. "I ruled out Maccabee involvement."

"Who told you that operative was murdered?"

"Ezra."

"Any other proof?"

I blinked. "Why would he lie about it?"

The demon laughed. "He lies like he breathes. Who's to say he didn't want you looking into Maccabees for his own purposes?" He exhaled another stream of cigarette smoke. "Or that he didn't kill that vamp himself?"

Ezra had been in London when it happened. But why…? I shook my head. "This wasn't Ezra. Stop fucking with me."

Delacroix had the audacity to grin. "Can't blame a guy for trying." He waved his hand at the still-open portal. "You've taken up enough of my time."

"One more—" I was blasted back through the portal into my living room. Brimstone Breakfast Club was over, but Sachie would be waiting. My true reckoning was about to begin.

Chapter 27

Sachie sat at the dining room table next to the platter with the lone bagel we hadn't polished off. The faint scent of smoked salmon lingered in the air, mixing with the heavy weight of disappointment.

"I said I'd ask once." She spoke softly, her voice carrying a hint of sadness. "And I'd believe you, because you'd answer honestly."

My heart sank as I sat down across from her. "I couldn't."

Sachie's brown eyes held a deep weariness. "No. You *wouldn't*." I opened my mouth, but she cut me off. "Don't spout that plausible deniability shit. You point-blank lied to my face." She shrugged, hurt etched into her tight expression. "After almost thirty years of friendship, do I need to prove myself to you? Show I can be trusted? I've been there for you through everything in your life. But when push came to shove, you chose an infernal over your best friend."

"I didn't choose her over you, but this also wasn't my life we were talking about. It wasn't my place to out Maud."

"Out her," Sachie scoffed. "It's not the same thing."

I tapped the menorah against the table—harder than necessary—to remove some loose bits of wax. "No, because half shedim aren't considered human and thus they don't deserve any right to self-determination. Do you hear how hypocritical you're being? A *shedim* told you about Maud, and instead of feeling compassion for her suffering while living with this terrifying secret her entire life, or angry at Delacroix for exposing her, you're mad at *me*?"

Sachie ripped the bagel in half, shredding it into smaller and smaller crumbs. "You're still investigating the missing infernal blood; you lied about Maud. What's with this crusade? Is this payback at the director for not making you a level three? Or just payback at your mom?"

I gaped at her. "My mom?"

"Yeah. You realized when those infernals were murdered that she's not pro-infernal. Hell, maybe you've always known that, and this was your way to get back at her. Just like you've always done when you were mad at her."

"Because my professional career is built on me acting like a petulant child?" I said icily. "Fuck you, Sachie. But so long as we're on the subject of parents, how are Ben and Reina? Because you're rocking that dynamic like a fully functioning adult."

"Fuck you right back. At least I never lied to them."

"That's not the only barometer that matters. Why are you so prejudiced against half shedim?"

"I spent years trying to get onto the Spook Squad to rid the world of bad vamps and *all* shedim. Three months ago, I didn't expect to ever meet an infernal because they were supposedly so rare. Now I'm tripping over them."

"Percentage-wise, they're still rare."

"You know what I mean. Can't you cut me some slack

that I'm trying to figure out what justice means where their kids are concerned?"

"It doesn't sound like you're figuring out anything. More like you've already tried and convicted them."

"I helped Maud, didn't I?"

"Because you thought she was fully human."

Sachie systematically shredded the bagel while I repeatedly poked the end of a butter knife into the pad of my finger, trying to figure out how to repair this conversation.

The two of us had always been so smug that our childhood friendship would survive, and we'd one day become those madcap old ladies who didn't give a shit how the world judged them so long as they had that unbreakable bond.

Yet, here we were.

Sach's parents didn't trust her to make smart decisions about her life, and I didn't trust her to give me unconditional acceptance. For years, Michael's conditioning kept me silent, then Ezra dumping me did. Even when I wanted to speak up and just confess, I ran up against some disparaging remark. Not always from Sachie, though certainly sometimes. But she never defended my kind either.

I set the knife down. "I don't know what you want me to say."

"I don't know either. But one thing for sure? Keep rushing to defend infernals and the Authority will find out. They're already gunning for you. You'll be expelled." She snapped her fingers. "Your dreams, done."

"Are *you* done? Does a lifetime of friendship stop counting because I support half shedim? Because I lied?"

"That time can't be erased." Sachie's voice was low and tinged with sadness. "But trust...trust is a fragile thing. You chose their side over ours."

I squeezed my eyes shut, a surge of pain coursing through me. This was the divide between us, an unbridge-able gap that kept us on opposite sides.

"We're still friends, but…" She exhaled slowly. "I assumed that it was the two of us above everything. Seems I was wrong."

I wanted to scream that half shedim were also part of "us," because *I* was part of us.

She headed for her bedroom.

Our friendship had felt unbreakable, a sturdy vine that could withstand any storm or attack, but now, it felt like a delicate flower being buffeted by a harsh wind.

It either had to take root more firmly or be pulled out and die.

Another couple steps and Sachie would close her door. I shoved away the self-protective instincts screaming at me to let her go.

"Wait." I let my eyes turn toxic green, waving my arms like that would get her to turn around.

At the buzz of a text, she pulled her phone out of her pocket, then gasped. "Dad's had a heart attack."

My eyes had returned to normal before I was halfway out of my chair. "How is he?"

"I don't know. Mom's at Emergency with him." She jogged past me. "I have to get there."

"Do you want me to come with you?"

"No, it's okay." She didn't look at me as she stuffed her feet into her motorcycle boots, then grabbed her keys and jacket.

"Will you hug your mom from me and tell her if she needs anything, I'm here?"

Sachie turned around and faced me, one hand on the doorknob. "Yeah. I'll do that."

I nodded. "Thanks. And if you need me…"

"I know," she said softly and left.

I cleaned up the apartment and started the dishwasher. Long after Sachie had left, I finally dashed the wetness from my eyes.

Outside, muted orange, pink, and purple peeked through the gray afternoon clouds like weeds jutting up through cracks in the sidewalk. I lit the Hanukkah candles as the sun slipped behind the horizon, singing the prayers in a subdued voice.

The pancakes I'd consumed earlier sat heavy in my stomach, so dinner was a no-go, and since I didn't want to mope around the apartment, I drove to work and ensconced myself in the library.

Vancouver HQ didn't have a grand, elegant library like those in the Tel Aviv, Madrid, or Seoul chapters. There was no roaring fireplace or rolling ladders along ceiling-high bookcases. Ours was barely the size of a small school cafeteria, but it contained a surprisingly diverse collection, and there was this one table by the window that during the day was warmed by sunlight filtered through the broad leaves of the hearty magnolia tree outside.

The sliver of moonlight that made its way past the tree and into the library this evening wasn't bright enough to see by, but it washed the table in a calming silvery glow.

Declining any assistance from Bai, the librarian busy reshelving books off a cart, I wandered through the aisles pulling titles even vaguely related to the idea of demon prisons.

I carried my first stack over to my favorite table and cracked the top cover, chasing promising index entries and random footnotes until my neck and shoulders hurt from being hunched over, but I didn't find anything.

After yet another jaunt to the kitchen on the third floor for a cup of coffee, I went for a different approach, and looked up the history of padlocks on my phone, astonished to discover that they'd been around since ancient Rome.

Interestingly, back in the 1600s, which was when the magic cocktail in our rings was developed, barrel padlocks were developed in Sweden decorated with punched or chiseled patterns.

Could these have been the precursors of the love locks? Supposed the initials on love locks contained tracking information for shedim to know who was in each cell? Like the name or type of shedim. Plus codes were an even more recent invention, so what did they do before either of those elements were around?

Were these seemingly random patterns stamped on metal as a way of keeping track of these prisons? With corresponding records of this information, first in pattern form and later plus codes, stored in the demon realm allowing them to find demon X in location Y?

I sipped from my mug—and swallowed air. I'd finished the coffee while I was going down that rabbit hole. I put the cup in the dishwasher and went back to the library. I had padlocks and a magic cocktail in existence at the same time, but I didn't find any evidence that locks were randomly chained to public property back in the 1600s. In which case, shedim needed somewhere to house these cells.

I dumped my books back on the cart. What if, instead of demons using the existing love lock story as a cover, they'd started it? A tingle of excitement unfurled in my gut. Love locks were a WWI story, set in Serbia, which… I did another search on my phone, then sat back with my mouth agape.

One of the major causes of WWI was the assassination of Archduke Franz Ferdinand in Serbia.

Most resources that operatives required were online, on secure servers, but those searches were logged. Unless I checked any physical books out, my topic of interest wouldn't hit anyone's radar, and I didn't want to give Dr. Olsen or Dmitri any heads-up about the findings I intended to present at our meeting.

However, this connection was too big to waste time fumbling around on my own. Plus, unless someone had been following my line of thought, my new avenue of inquiry wasn't linked to how Jasmine found Bratwurst Demon.

Taking my chances, I practically sprinted over to the librarian. "Bai, this is very specific, but do we have anything on suspected shedim properties in the Balkans around WWI?"

The Chinese Canadian woman reshelved a book on the psychology of sociopaths and raised her heavy eyebrows, making the small gold ring on her left brow twinkle as it caught the light. "Not that I know of, but let's see what we can find."

Bless all librarians and their insatiable curiosity.

An hour later we had a shortlist of three castles, all situated close to Sarajevo where the duke had been murdered. People were capable of great evil, but shedim lived to steer us into the darkness. Had the demon equivalent of a hardened mass murderer been let out back then to drive events to a world war? Perhaps at the behest of some government?

Was there a group of shedim profiting from our inability to kill them and selling demons off to the highest bidder? Was money even involved or was it just for the thrill of enabling evil in the world?

If I was correct, then this wasn't something the Authority could turn away from.

However, it required verification. No shedim would willingly give that information out, but lucky for me, I had one who might be willing to play for it. The trouble was whether the cost justified it, either via a lost forfeit or Delacroix's reaction to me broaching this topic in the first place.

Perhaps there was another way.

I GOT TO WARDS, Inc. five minutes before it opened on Monday morning, sitting in my parked car in the alley behind the store. Rhythmically drumming my fingers against the steering wheel, I counted the minutes down to 10AM with butterflies in my stomach.

Michael texted to say that the video call with Dr. Olsen and Dmitri was set for tomorrow morning. It wasn't the largest time frame to learn everything I could about shedim prisons, but the Serbian connection I'd made was promising, and besides, I excelled under pressure.

Sire's Spark was lined up on my dashboard next to a newly polished silver lock. Not that I deluded myself into thinking that the shinier the prison, the less staggeringly horrific my reaction to it, but it never hurt to look one's best.

Case in point my cognac-colored crushed-velvet wrap dress that I'd paired with my nicest wool coat and favorite leather boots. The ones with the two-inch heel and decorative gold buckle at the ankle.

At thirty seconds to ten, I stabbed my finger with my shedim claw.

At four seconds to ten, I took a deep breath and dabbed my blood on Sire's Spark.

At 10:13, I came to with a cough, the imprint of the steering wheel on my face, and scratches all over my body from attempting to not only escape the putridity choking me, but apparently, to also molt along the way.

I barely threw the car door open in time to puke onto

the concrete. Six breath mints later, I made it inside Wards, Inc. with the crystal and silver lock stowed in my purse.

Noa looked up from the drafting table and blinked at me. "Oh. Hello. Did you have another question about that ward?"

"No." I lurched toward the counter, half falling over it in support. Cold sweat ran between my shoulder blades.

Noa backed up a step, the interactive wall display behind her inducing starbursts in my vision. "Are you sick?"

I blotted my forehead with my sleeve. "I'm fine." Frustrated with how this magic always made me look like I was either super drunk or super ill, I fumbled my purse open and dumped the contents out.

The silver lock slid free though I tipped my purse upright before the crystal got loose. I didn't want to accidentally crack it. My keys fell to the floor and my wallet spilled old parking receipts all over the reception counter, but I found the lipstick I'd been hunting for weeks.

"Check again for any ward on this lock. Please." I'd hoped that rubbing my blood on the lock—with Sire's Spark's magic in it—would illuminate the shedim magic for the wardmaker.

However, Noa gave no indication she saw the runes or scorch mark, though she grimaced at the blood smear. When she announced her intention to perform tests on it with some of her high-tech equipment—two of which truly had lasers—I fled outside.

While I waited, I attempted to burn the artifact's magic out of my system. The symptoms subsided, but there were three floors between me and that silver lock, so it might just have been distance.

Noa texted me to return, but she hadn't found anything. "What were you hoping I'd discover?"

At least my proximity to the lock was tolerable to the point of getting it back in my purse without incident. "A ward tying it to a case I'm working on."

Once back inside my car, I pounded a fist against the steering wheel. Frustrating as it was that Noa was unable to help me and that my only other avenue was to take this to Delacroix, I was furious with these shedim-detecting abilities in the first place.

Sire's Spark was imbued with the blood and powerful healing magic of its creator. I studied the tiny scar from using my claw on my index finger. It was still there, even though I'd touched the crystal.

Experts had debunked the crystal's magic as a myth. I'd agree with them except for the whole demon-detector part. Was it simply the healing abilities that were the urban legend?

I sighed again over this visit being a bust, then stilled, thinking about Noa's equipment setup. She had powerful magic, but she used technology to help her create wards. Just like the medical profession did.

Abraham didn't have access to MRI machines or CAT scans or any one of a million ways allowing modern medicine to detect injury back in the 1700s when he created Sire's Spark.

I pulled the crystal out of my purse. Unless *this* was the technology?

Did I have this all wrong and it wasn't my infernal blood that triggered Sire's Spark, but my *human* blood? That meant *anyone* in possession of the crystal could suss out my kind. For the first time ever, I was grateful that Michael had stolen it.

It sucked that the artifact perceived shedim magic as a wound, but I counted my blessings that it hadn't tried to "heal" me.

I shifted my left hand to a claw and flexed my fingers. Not that I was broken.

But did my mother share that belief?

As soon as we got through the meeting with Dr. Olsen and Dmitri, Michael and I were having a long-overdue chat. She was a Yellow Flame, so if she felt like making amends for wanting to "heal" her only kid, she could help me find the missing infernal blood and get to the bottom of why those half shedim were murdered once and for all.

First up, however, was a visit with my other parent.

That's when Gemma texted with a scathing message about playing hooky.

Any modicum of respect I'd gained for her with her anti–Sector A beliefs crumbled. I typed and deleted *Shove it up your ass* three times before I simply replied that I was working my other case. Then I initiated a video call with Ezra.

"Miss me?" His voice dripped with a hint of mischief and his deep ebony suit drank in the ambient light, causing it to glow against his brown skin. The perfectly tailored fabric hugged every inch of his broad shoulders and defined biceps, contributing to his air of confidence and power.

Ezra stood with his back to the balcony, the phone angled enough to catch a glimpse of the busy gaming floor below.

"Just checking that my dessert needs will be fulfilled," I said.

"You'll get all the sugar you require, mi cielo," he purred.

I pressed my inner thighs together. Friendship was good, but this squirmy heat that shot through me wasn't nothing. "Work before fun. Can you get me into the Hell somewhere close to wherever Delacroix is? We need to talk, and I'd like the element of surprise."

295

"Whatever could you be making me complicit to now?"

"You want the long answer or—"

"Every last detail."

I jumped at the rap on my window.

A parking enforcement officer motioned for me to roll it down. "There's no parking in this alley." He raised his ticketing device to scan my license plate.

"There is for me." Telling Ezra to hold on, I placed my phone in my cupholder, and held up the emergency vehicle card from my dashboard, giving Maccabees the right to temporarily park anywhere. Some operatives abused the system, displaying it while they went to a hockey game or out to dinner, but I kept it professional and employed it only when a regular spot was not possible. Either because there wasn't one, or because I had to do something like bleed on a magic crystal to activate demon magic and required a spot free from prying eyes.

The man hit a button on his device.

HQ didn't reimburse us for parking tickets, and I resented paying for this job-related expense. I held up my Maccabee ring. "I appreciate you're just doing your job, but so am I. And I am authorized to park here on work-related business."

"You were on your phone. How do I know you weren't chatting with your boyfriend? I'm duty bound to write you up. You can contest it, though I appreciate that will be a hassle." He made a sad face.

In my head, Cherry flared her nostrils and cracked her knuckles.

Tempting.

I held my hand out for the ticket.

Asshole took his time issuing it. "Have a nice day," he said with false sincerity.

I rolled up my window to the sound of Ezra's laughter from the other side of the phone.

"Scale of mild twinge to Godzilla rampaging across the city, how badly did you want to rip him a new one?" Ezra said.

"You want to mock me or hear the reason for my visit?"

"Can't I do both?"

"You cannot," I said flatly.

He took his time deciding. "Tell me."

My hypothesis of shedim imprisoning their brethren sobered him up pretty quickly.

He swore in Spanish. "Please don't tell me you intend to play Delacroix for confirmation."

I pulled into the parkade in my condo tower. "Okay, I won't. Now open the portal and get me to my father."

Chapter 28

For a moment, I considered using Sire's Spark to see if it allowed me to illuminate Delacroix's weaknesses so I could read him and have an advantage in any game we played, but any potential side-effects weren't worth it.

I crossed through the mesh net portal onto the topmost deck of the yacht. Confused by the small, empty platform, I turned for the stairs when something rippled silver in the air. I stopped and slowly moved my eyes left.

There was a bubble-like structure up here, its silvery iridescence visible only in certain quirks of the light.

A slash appeared in the bubble, light from inside spilling onto the deck, and Delacroix exited, lighting a cigarette. The sea serpent lived in what appeared to be a giant water bubble. That tracked. "Can't a shedim have any peace around here?"

I strode toward him, but when I was in arm's reach, he flicked glowing ashes at me. I slapped a stray spark away. "A little respect for the flammable human?"

He dragged deeply, then ground the cigarette out under his boot. "Bother me again and I'll tear your throat out."

"Play a game with me. Answers for winning hands."

He stared at me, his head tilted, then nodded. "I choose it. And if you lose, you take your forfeits like a man."

"Or the gender-appropriate version, but sure."

He rolled up the sleeves of his thick waffle-knit pullover. "No running and crying to your boyfriend."

"What about me has ever given you the impression that I'm some damsel in distress? That said, I want the game and all its rules clarified before I agree to anything."

"Whatever," he grumbled, but motioned me inside.

I brushed past him into his lair and froze.

The showpiece of the round room was an enormous chandelier made of weathered bones that dripped wax from the many gnarled candles. The furniture was made of bones as well, all sharp, uneven angles.

I swallowed. "Did you taxidermy all those rat carcasses yourself?"

Stuffed rodents ran the circumference of the room on their own special shelf.

Delacroix guffawed. "Remember my friend Evander? Looks like a bat?"

"Yes?" I looked around for signs of his taxidermized corpse.

My father waved a hand.

The room rippled and settled back into place, revealing a cheery roaring fireplace, comfortable wingback chairs in sage green and earth brown, and stunning framed photos of underwater life adorning the walls.

"He put a glamor on my place," Delacroix said. "To discourage repeat visitors."

I examined a print of a salmon swimming past in water so crisp and clear that I shivered, feeling its bracing cold. The fish was just under the surface and the photographer had caught both its progress and the wisps of fog clinging to the dark outlines of pine trees on shore.

Another portrait showed a clownfish, its white and orange stripes popping against spindly pink coral, and the position of its fin suggested it was waving at the camera.

Every breathtaking shot full of character.

"You took these?" I said.

"If it makes you feel better, I ripped out their spines after and swallowed them whole," he snarked, his jaw and shoulders tensed.

He was hurt that I didn't believe him capable of it. Fair enough. I hadn't.

My disbelief didn't just stem from a demon having this talent, but that *my father* did. What other surprising truths would I learn if I got to know him, besides that he was a sea serpent who hated people, but loved the ocean enough to document it with creativity and humor? Did he feel about swimming in the sea the way I did about running through the woods? That the freedom of pushing my limits through nature made me feel gloriously alive?

"Don't worry," I said. "Your evil rep is intact. What game do you propose?"

He beckoned me to take a seat by the fire while he pulled a set of banged-up bronze scales out of a cupboard. The kind of scales held by Lady Justice, not shoved under a bathtub where it was too much trouble to dig them out to weigh yourself. "Demon quid pro quo."

I shrugged out of my wool coat. "I hate it already."

Delacroix dragged a side table between us and set the scales on them. "The game is straightforward. We each get three questions, taking turns to ask them. Lay one hand on each of the scales, then think of a forfeit and a question. If the scales determine that your wager is equal in weight to the importance of the question, it will balance and you may speak."

"And if it doesn't?" I set my purse on the floor by my feet.

"You don't get to ask your question."

"Be specific. What will it do to me? Does it take my forfeit then and there?"

"Yes, smarty pants, so it has to be something personal that you don't want to lose. Above all, make sure that your forfeit is equal in weight to your question and don't modify your question after it's gone to the scales."

"How do I know you'll answer honestly?"

"The scales will know," he said in a bored voice and stretched out a leg, rubbing his knee.

"How?"

"I didn't agree to twenty questions as a lead-up. You playing or not?"

Delacroix was a demon, but he had a code of honor. One only understood by him and containing two loop-holes for every iron-clad certainty, but existing nonetheless. The thing was, while Demon Daddy was passionate about underwater photography, his other interest lay in collecting information. He'd expect me to give something up in return, but if he asked about Cherry, did I dare answer?

Would refusing simply confirm any suspicion he might have? Would the magic in the scales harm me—or worse? Delacroix might not know about these demon prisons, but I couldn't think of anyone else who might have that intel, and I planned to be armed to the teeth with facts when I met with Dr. Olsen and Dmitri tomorrow.

If he wants to see us, let him, Cherry counseled. *It won't be the end of the world.*

"Who asks first?" I said.

"You can." He clanked the scales together, then sat back in his chair.

The contraption rattled, the scales bouncing on their

slender chains. A golden glow swam up from the base to encompass the entire thing.

"It's ready," Delacroix said. "Lay your hands upon it and think of your forfeit and question. Remember. Make them equal in weight."

"Yeah, yeah. I got it."

The second my hands touched the warm metal, Delacroix's chair magically spun around with its back to me.

Asking him to confirm whether the silver padlock was a demon prison was big but not wagering-my-life big.

"Hurry up," he groused, still facing away.

I'd never have come up with my forfeit if it hadn't been for his photographs. He'd shared something of himself with me and I wanted to return the gesture. I'd wager a memory. If the scales didn't balance, then I'd lose it forever, but my desire for Delacroix to see it was even stronger than the pang of loss that shot through me.

I forfeit the memory of putting on my Maccabee ring and saying the tikkun olam oath.

An image, like a hologram, of me at my Maccababy graduation appeared, with my ring poised to slide onto my finger.

I sucked in a breath.

"All good?" Delacroix said without a trace of concern.

"Peachy," I said, annoyed with myself for giving in to sentimentality with a demon and risking a cherished memory.

My question is, are shedim imprisoning other shedim in these lock prisons?

The image of a silver padlock appeared over my other hand.

I stiffened, bracing for the memory to be ripped from my brain.

A soft gong clanged, and the images disappeared.

Delacroix's chair turned back around. He looked disappointed. "Ask your question."

I pulled the silver lock out of my purse and placed it next to the scale. "Are shedim imprisoning other shedim in these lock prisons?"

Delacroix blinked at the padlock. Then his eyes narrowed, his gaze assessing. He flipped the lock bottom side up, changed one finger to a claw, and jammed it into the keyhole.

My father screamed, crimson spikes exploding out of his throat and blood tears streaming over the streaks of silver scales along one cheekbone. He yanked his finger out and threw the lock into the fire.

"No!" I jumped to my feet.

The blaze flickered wildly, shooting black sparks into the air. Its smoke carried the pungent aroma of charred metal, and each lick of flames sounded like a chorus of twisted voices singing in union.

The blaze roared up, then winked out, leaving the unmarred padlock sitting in the ashes.

Delacroix's breaths came in heavy rasps. He wiped the blood from his eyes.

"Is that a yes?" I said.

"Where did you get that?" he demanded.

I flicked a finger against the scales. "Your turn."

Water rose out of the floor, and I tensed but it didn't assault me. It coalesced into a mirror showing Sachie driving away from the hospital at her usual breakneck speed.

Worried, I studied her grim expression, but if her father had taken a turn for the worse, she wouldn't leave. She must be getting food.

The image widened to depict the rest of the street. Water suddenly shot out of a grate like a pipe had burst. It was a very familiar plume that reminded me of seawater.

Sach flinched and swerved, almost hitting the car in the lane next to her.

"Leave her alone," I said.

"Then answer when I tell you to. Where did you get that lock?"

"It was found on a drug lab bust."

"And?" The magic mirror showed water seeping up out of a manhole cover a couple of car lengths away from my friend.

Delacroix didn't use the scales when he asked the question, already abandoning the game.

Hating him with every atom in my body, I walked him through Bratwurst Demon killing herself after crying she wouldn't go back.

Sachie made it into the parking garage at HQ.

I pointed at the mirror. "She's safe now behind wards." Though if she'd left the hospital to go to work, there was either a massive emergency at HQ, which I'd have heard about, or she'd fought with her parents and bolted.

"I've still got *you*." Delacroix motioned for me to keep talking.

"Do you only keep promises when they're threats?" I smacked the brass scales, sending one side swinging. "Enough with the one-way flow of information. Play the game we *both* agreed to."

The watery mirror morphed into a tentacle.

Yelping, I sprinted for the door.

The tentacle knocked me onto my belly and wrapped me like a fly in a spider's silk, leaving me hovering face-up in mid-air.

I gasped, struggling to get free.

"Talk," he growled.

I hit my watery bindings a couple of times, trying to indicate I couldn't speak.

He loosened its hold a fraction of an inch. Barely enough for me to drag in a breath.

Under duress, I shared my concerns that Maccabees didn't kill demons, we only sent them back to the demon realm.

My father stood over me. "There's more to it than that. Keep going."

When I hesitated, he slammed me against the floor. The air was knocked from my lungs and tears streamed down my cheeks.

Cherry itched to be set free. Our scaley armour would protect us but revealing her to Delacroix when I was at his mercy would make this nightmare infinitely worse. She stood down.

Prompted by that fucking water tentacle tenderizing me, I told Delacroix everything: "Unchained Melody" and Chandra matchmaking demons with Eishei Kodesh. I relived Chandra's murder in precise gruesome detail, my one tiny victory that I kept Cherry out of the story and that Delacroix bought my explanation that Chandra had told me about the runes and scorch marks on the lock. If a demon accepted it, the Authority would as well.

By the time I got to plus codes and locks on the pedestrian overpass hiding prisons in plain sight, my left shoulder was broken. The blazing pain clawed at me, but it didn't come close to the hot rage that I choked on.

After explaining that love locks showed up after Archduke Franz Ferdinand's assassination in Serbia, I backtracked to the shedim attack on the Maccabee team who'd created the magic cocktail in our rings. My lungs burned from the taste of salt water.

Delacroix had no sympathy for the bout of coughing that plagued me from his repeated near-drowning attempts and snarled at me to keep talking.

The theory that shedim incorporated their magic into

the foundational strain we'd been using for the last few hundred years to send demons into their prisons was pulled out of me after two of my ribs and my left hand were shattered.

I finished my story in a whisper, feeling like a ship bashed by waves against large rocks, and swimming in and out of consciousness from pain.

"Is that everything?"

I nodded, curled on the floor, cradling my broken hand and biting the inside of my cheek hard enough to draw blood in order to remain lucid. Delacroix might have kept promises that worked in his favor, but he cared little for agreements to play games according to the rules he, himself, had set.

Sach had no idea how lucky she was to have Ben, a parent who didn't manipulate, menace, or maim his kid when he didn't get his way.

The door flew off its hinges, sailed across the room, and shattered against the wall.

Terrified, I flinched and curled tighter into a ball, despite the blaze of pain that racked my chest.

"I've got you now, Aviva." Ezra picked me up so gently off the floor that I didn't even feel it. "You ever block me from her again," he said in a low, deadly voice, "and I'll burn this fucking place down with you in it."

Delacroix didn't react to the threat. He stood by the fireplace, holding the silver lock to the light with an inscrutable expression on his face.

Don't kill the messenger, I thought, and lost consciousness.

Chapter 29

A hand stroked my forehead, someone speaking to me in a hushed voice. Though the words were too fuzzy for me to make out, whoever this was would protect me.

I tried to lean into their touch, but I was racked with another bout of coughing that pushed me back under the dark ocean of pain.

A muscular arm slid under my head to raise it and two blazing silvery-blue orbs filled my vision.

I fought hard to stay with that light.

"Aviva, sweetheart. Please." Ezra's voice cracked. "Give me your consent to heal you."

I must have nodded because a moment later his bleeding wrist was against my lips. The flavor of peppermint and rain on a hot day exploded in my mouth, adrenaline hitting me like a rollercoaster shooting out of the gate.

I greedily fed off him, the spark of warmth flaring into a blazing heat that coursed through my veins. It brought no pain, only an intoxicating comfort not unlike a hot chocolate after I'd been standing outside and freezing for hours. My muscles, tense from the shock of injury, began to relax, the strain seeping away as though swept out by an ebbing tide. Bones knit together and my strength returned, pulsing through me with each breath. The sharp edges of pain were softened, blurred into a hazy memory by Ezra's otherworldly magic.

Along with the physical healing came a dizzying elation that left me breathless. It was as though a veil had been lifted, allowing me to experience the world in its full vibrancy. The gold flecks in his duvet cover sparked like embers, his bedroom furniture possessed the rich walnut hue of a living forest, and the lap of the waves outside the repaired window crooned a lullaby.

Ezra's inner wrist was velvety soft, his hint of cologne the faint scent of a favorite memory, while the full, pungent flavor of his blood tasted better than a rare vintage merlot. His mattress under my butt was as soft as a cloud.

He finally pulled his wrist away with a shiver so imperceptible that without my heightened senses, I'd have missed it. There was a vulnerability in the way he watched me, a crack in the façade of imperiousness that always surrounded him, and through it, I sensed the deep-seated hunger pulsing beneath his skin like a heartbeat.

He ran his tongue over his fangs, his hand ghosting up the side of my neck until his finger rested on my rapidly stuttering pulse.

I held myself very still, feeling like a bunny in a wolf's grip, albeit a bunny with very conflicted feelings, because cresting on this high from his magic, I yearned to take that next irrevocable step and blood bond with him.

My lids fell shut and my lips parted on a sigh, an invitation which Ezra accepted, brushing his fangs along the side of my throat, his warm breath sending shivers along my skin.

"No. You really don't want this," he said in a rough voice.

"Part of me does." I pressed my throat closer to his fangs, wanting to feel their sharp tips pierce my skin. But he didn't oblige. I opened my eyes to find him frowning at my hand bunched in the sheets.

A hand covered in frosted green scales. I made a small sound of distress because I hadn't even realized I'd changed into Cherry's form. I pulled my knees into my chest and wrapped my arms around them. "How long have I looked like this?"

"It happened almost immediately once you started to feed."

It was bad enough that I hadn't noticed, but I'd felt his closeness as acutely as if I'd been naked. "Is that why you didn't want—"

"*No.*" He gently pressed his hand against my lips for a moment to stop my protest. "You're vulnerable and not thinking clearly and I almost took advantage of that." A flicker of pain crossed his features.

"Right," I said softly. The decision to blood bond should only be made under the most lucid and sober of mindsets. I was very sober now and grateful he'd had the presence of mind to stop things, but... I dropped my head, allowing my crimson hair to hide my face.

Ezra brushed the strands away.

I tried to pull back, but he placed his hand against my spine to keep me in place.

"You're beautiful like this," he said huskily. "Cherry Bomb, the Brimstone Baroness."

"It's still me," I said, feeling an insistent compulsion to state that, despite—or because of—the way his piercing gaze roamed over every inch of my shedim body.

"Ah, mi cielo," he said, "I'm always desperately aware

of you. It doesn't matter if you look human or shedim, I always know it's you, and I want all of—"

I lunged for him, knocking him back against the mattress as our mouths fused together.

Ezra cupped the back of my head, tangling our tongues together, and I twisted closer, positive there was a live wire between my mouth and the pool of molten desire deep in my core.

The air between us thickened.

He ran his hands over my body. I nearly came when he stroked my horns, but my scales seemed more numb to touch than my human skin. Good for defense, but at a cost.

Note to self: the initial rush of Ezra's healing magic induced heightened sensations in this form that were otherwise missing.

Also, I was basically only a humanoid shape right now. Some crucial features—like sensitive nipples—were missing.

Well, that sucked.

I sat up, holding a hand against his chest when he followed, and relaxed into my regular human body. The shifting wasn't great for my clothes, but they were basically ruined from my earlier attack. A cold sweat beaded my brow but I shoved those memories away, drawing strength from Ezra's steady presence against my palm. "You may proceed."

He grinned. "May I? How magnanimous of you."

"I'm a giver." I placed his hands on my breasts. "And you like these."

"True." He brushed his thumbs over my nipples and I jerked with a breathy exhale. "There's the sound," he said in a darkly seductive voice. Gripping me by the hips, he yanked me against his jeans—*oh, hello*—his mouth once more finding mine.

His stubble chafed my cheeks but I didn't care because even that light stinging rasp felt brilliant.

I shoved his shirt up to run my hands over the dusting of dark hair on his chest, letting my fingers roam lower along his sculpted powerful pecs and down his slim waist to his hard abs. I scraped my teeth against his neck, dizzy with the taste and feel of him.

Ezra unbuttoned my raggedy shirt, each pop of the button accompanied with murmurs of what I was doing to him, our rocking growing faster, more crazed. He suddenly stilled with a laugh, resting his forehead against mine. "It's not a race. You're always running to get to your destination, and you miss important and wonderful things along the way."

I snorted, waiting for him to elaborate on these afore-mentioned wonderful things that he would no doubt guide me to.

"Like those baby deer you would never have watched playing in the forest on that one hike because you wanted to run up the mountain. Luckily for you, I insisted we take our time, and thanks to me, you have a lovely memory of Bambi." His voice was serious, but his eyes were lit up with laughter.

I trailed my fingers along the outline of his hard cock through his denim and he hissed. "You're comparing this to deer?" I said. "Deer who, may I remind you, you followed off the trail, forcing me to rescue you with my superior guiding skills." I gripped his hips, trying to get him to move. "Given that, I'm probably the only one who should ever lead."

He slowly ground his hips against mine, earning a moan from me. "Oh, I can lead just fine, sweetheart. And my considerable experience—"

"You really want to trot that out now, Prime Playboy?"

"I'm just saying let's slow the hell down."

I was soaking wet, and my clit throbbed. "That's the stupidest idea ever."

He sat back, the sudden lack of his body heat as shocking as being thrown into a cold lake. "Oh, so it's okay for you to take a time-out to shift into something more pleasurable, but I can't get the same leeway?"

"Mine is pleasurable for both of us." I scrambled into his lap and rocked along his cock, my lids falling halfway closed.

"Aviva," he growled in warning.

I snickered.

Ezra laid me back against the mattress. "Are you going to play nice or fight me?"

I batted my lashes at him. "Which gets me the better outcome?"

He cocked his head, raking a slow gaze along my body. His silver-blue eyes darkened like the ocean's depths, his jet-black curls tousled and his lips kiss-swollen. "Which one has you naked faster?"

"You're so easy."

He dipped his head. "I've never claimed to be other than a simple man with simple needs."

I laughed, but before the sound had drifted away, he'd divested me of my sweater and bra. "Nice," I murmured.

"I have my uses."

I leaned back on my elbows against the mattress. "Big words, Cardoso. Put your money where your mouth is."

"I'd rather put my mouth where the money is," he said, and placed his lips on my breast.

I dug my hands into his hair and arched against him, my breathing ragged, while Ezra sucked and lightly rasped his teeth over my nipple.

"You're so easy," he mocked. But he made short work of my torn pants, tossing them into a corner, and kneeled between my open legs, so I allowed it. He licked my clit, pressing a finger inside me, all the while watching me with cocksure eyes.

My insides tightened. I felt like a firecracker whose fuse had been lit. "Zee?"

He looked up, his present and past selves blurring into this one perfect moment of us being exactly like we were the first time we made love.

I tenderly brushed a lock of hair out of his eyes. "I need you inside me. I don't care how fast this is. I just need to feel you."

He gave me this sweet crooked half grin. "Okay," he said simply. His clothes were off in a flash, condom in hand from the side table.

For a moment, I was sorely tempted to tell him to go bare. I hadn't been with anyone since our last time together and vamps didn't carry STIs, but as a Prime, Ezra could get me pregnant. I didn't want to worry about that. Not tonight.

I took the condom from him and rolled it over his cock.

His nostrils flared at my touch, then he stretched out over me, his weight braced on his elbows. "Aviva." He whispered my name like a prayer, a lock of hair falling into his eyes. "Do I still have to buy you dinner?"

"Eh." I shrugged. "Just leave a couple hundred on the bedside table."

He furrowed his brow. "Who carries cash these days?"

"Criminals." I slapped his ass. "Talking drives up the price, big guy."

"Shit. I better get moving." Ezra thrust inside me and my eyes fluttered closed, my arms tightening around his neck, and my hips rolling.

Fiery tongues of desire licked at me from within, and Ezra's kiss was as tempestuous as a whirlwind, but we kept our lovemaking slow.

"Tú eres mí mundo y me has conquistador," he said.

You are my world and you've conquered me. The tattoo he'd inked on himself after seeing me again. The words I'd recalled more times to count.

I traced my fingers over them, relieved and awed he'd not just gotten that tattoo about me but that he'd kept it after all. "Bite me, Zee," I moaned.

He jerked back, but his pupils had dilated. "I told you. You don't want—"

I grabbed his forearms. "Not a blood bond. I want you to bite me."

He dropped his gaze, shaking his head.

"I'm lucid." A bit breathy, but of sound mind. "I want this. From you." I laid my hand on his cheek. "Only you."

Blazing eyes snapped to mine, and his fangs descended. "You're certain?"

I tilted my head to bare my neck.

Ezra caressed my cheek, then lowered his mouth.

There was a flash of pain and I arced up under him with a gasp, but it vanished in an instant, replaced by a dizzying euphoria. I dug my nails into his arms, my breathing ragged. It wasn't like when I fed off him to heal because underneath this electric connection was a languid sweetness, a tenderness that was undoing me, along with a sense of his emotions flooding into me, his loneliness and longing mixing with my own desires.

He withdrew his fangs and pressed his lips to my skin. I turned his head and caught his mouth in a kiss.

Our bodies found their familiar rhythm, our love-making entwining us in a new intimacy. It wasn't fucking and it wasn't laying siege. The rightness of it should have sent me screaming or slamming my walls into place, but I rode the wave with a breathless joy and the hope that for this moment at least, I'd banished some of his loneliness.

A starburst of pleasure exploded inside me, and shuddering, I cried out Ezra's name.

He followed shortly thereafter, gentling his kiss to the softest brush of our lips. He rolled off me, but didn't move, lying there and holding my hand tight. "Any regrets?"

"None. You?"

"Hard to say. We should try it again ten or twenty more times so I can decide."

"In the interests of fact gathering." I grinned at him.

"Yes," he said somberly, nodding, "facts." He got up and walked naked to his ensuite bathroom.

I barely had enough energy after that magnificent orgasm to turn my head and enjoy the clench of his tight glutes, but I rose to the challenge.

He returned with a damp cloth and cleaned me up, examining my neck. "Anything still hurt?"

I'd forgotten all about my previous injuries. I stretched, the only ache in my body, a delicious one. "No. I had an excellent physician."

"I pride myself on my bedside manner."

"Use it a lot, do you?" I tossed the rumpled cover aside, but my claw got stuck in the material. I swore under my breath.

"Your jealousy brings out the green in your eyes," he said in a voice laced with amusement.

I smacked him with the pillow, his curls flying up and the cutest grimace on his face as he swatted it away.

Ezra caught my wrists and leaned in, kissing me with a thoroughness that left me mindwhacked. "No one else."

"Huh?" I placed my hand on my racing heart.

"I haven't been with anyone else. Not since I came back to Vancouver and saw you after all those years." He pulled his jeans on, then opened a drawer and tossed me a set of sweats.

I held the dove-gray top made of a butter-soft fabric against my body, then checked the tag to be sure. "You bought this in my size?"

"A just-in-case pair. You have a knack for almost getting yourself killed and ruining your clothing. Not necessarily in that order."

"Appreciate the forethought." I scrambled into the clothes. "Now you may feed me while you tell me every last thing you know about Delacroix."

"I, uh, actually haven't made a reservation yet." He popped his head through his shirt, his wide-eyed anxiety making me chuckle.

"This isn't *the* dinner, but you don't want to see me hangry."

"Horrors." He gave an exaggerated shiver, then he winked and phoned someone to bring up cheeseburgers and fries. At the last second, he added a slice of chocolate cake.

I crossed my arms. "I'm not sharing."

Ezra slid his phone into his pocket. "You will if you want more orgasms like that."

"Humph." Chin in the air, I padded out to his living room, which, like his bedroom, bore no trace of destruction from my last visit. He'd even replaced his torn sofa with an identical model.

Ezra sat down on one side, his legs splayed, while I snuggled up against the cushions on the other side, my feet in his lap. Positions we'd taken countless times when watching movies or hanging out and talking. Sure enough, he massaged the instep of my left foot.

"Delacroix," I said. "You know something about him that you're not telling me. Don't say you're not; I know you too well. Spill."

Ezra cast his eyes to the ceiling as though asking the heavens for guidance, then pressed his thumb into the ball of my foot. "You're Canadian. Can you parse out the French etymology?"

"De la croix. Of the cross? He doesn't strike me as very Christian."

"That is the origin of the meaning, but you're dealing with a demon. Take nothing at face value. What word is buried in that name?"

"La Croix? He's king of fizzy drinks?"

Ezra chuckled. "Partially."

"Roi? He's a *demon king*?" I'd been running my finger over the site of the puncture wound, but it was already healed. I tucked my arm behind my head.

"He was. Centuries ago. One of about a dozen."

"I knew my aspirations of royalty were valid." I flipped my hair. "Princess Aviva."

"Not exactly legitimate progeny, Princess."

"Don't care. Still want a tiara. So how did he get from His Majesty to this yacht?"

"A power struggle. Delacroix backed the wrong side and fled to earth, setting up a court with his followers. It bounced around different places until he and Calista formed the Copper Hell back in the 1800s."

"It's a secure territory and he retains power through information," I said.

Ezra pressed his thumbs into my arches and I sighed happily. "Plus, every time someone loses," he said, "be they human, vampire, or shedim, their physical and psychological anguish feeds him."

"Why did he need Calista? Or you?"

"Think of Delacroix's magic like a siren's song, luring the unsuspecting with promises of wealth and power or whatever their heart desires."

"The lure of the Hell." The lure for my mother the night I was conceived.

"Exactly. It brings patrons in and has them place

317

forfeits that no sane person would ever suggest. But it also ebbs and flows like the tides. Delacroix requires a stabilizer to keep his magic at peak potency, and for some reason, Primes are the only ones capable of that."

"That's why you taunt him to kill you and he won't."

Ezra shrugged. "That and it's fun."

I dug my knuckles into his side and he laughed and kissed them.

"Being hooked to his magic," he said, "makes me attuned to every single patron who passes through that door and where they are at any given moment. If they deviate from their expected course, or behavior, I take care of it. Security on top of necessity."

I tapped my finger against my lip. "Calista was old, even for a vampire, and she failed to detect her own abductor."

Ezra smiled blandly, his fangs peeking out. "She was faulty and required replacement."

"Which wouldn't have happened if he didn't have you waiting in the wings." I touched his arm. "Do you blame me? If I hadn't insisted on coming here in the first place, you would never have been placed in his path."

"Delacroix was very aware of me before that. He always has a plan B. And C. Much like someone else I know." Ezra switched his massage to my other foot. "It's not your fault, especially since I freely agreed to take this on in exchange for my own information gathering."

I sat up. "He knows about your mother?"

Ezra nodded.

"Explain something to me," I said. "Delacroix mostly holes up on this ship, but he makes frequent visits to Flaming Flapjacks, which is in the demon realm."

"It's like the foyer of the realm. Barely within the threshold."

"Regardless, he's still in the demon realm, technically

speaking. How is that even remotely safe for him? Isn't he supposed to be deposed? Don't the new overlords really dislike having exiled royalty just running around?"

"The current Powers That Be leave him alone because he's just an old demon eating pancakes with friends."

I rubbed my recently broken ribs. "He's got them totally snowed."

Our food arrived after that, along with a knowing nod and smile from the Hellion who'd brought it at the sight of me in Ezra's quarters. "You're the one he's been texting and laughing with," he said.

Ezra shooed the other vamp to the door. "Go away, Hector."

"No, tell me more, Hector!" I beckoned him in.

Hector's smile widened and he stepped forward, but at Ezra's throat clearing, spun around immediately and left.

While the juicy burger had the correct bun-to-meat ratio and the fries were my preferred level of crispness, the revelations about Delacroix screwed with my appetite. I still polished everything off, but with a subdued gusto. And I even willingly shared the cake.

I wiped my mouth off with a linen napkin. "I want to finish my talk with Delacroix. Will you come with me?"

"Of course. But do you want to light the candles first?"

"What?" I looked outside but the yacht sailed under a night's sky as always.

"It's dusk in Vancouver." Ezra opened his armoire and removed a delicate gold menorah already set with seven candles plus the shamash.

"You've been lighting the candles? On Vancouver time?"

"Mamá and I always lit them, and it was one of the few traditions my dad kept up after her death. As for the time." He carried the menorah to the coffee table, pushing aside our dishes to set it in the center. "I had to pick a time zone and I liked thinking of us lighting them together." He tightened his grip on the matches. "Although maybe I shouldn't give you any ideas about fire around me."

I kissed him and took the match.

We sang the prayer, connected by our shared history. Like the pasts of our people, there was darkness there, but tonight we stood strong, bathed in firelight.

The flame of hope burned bright within me, but alongside it flickered a yearning to get answers for my many questions.

I allowed myself a few more moments to enjoy this quiet respite, then I tugged on my shoes and followed Ezra to Delacroix's bubble abode.

The door was unlocked, my father sitting in his chair and running his finger over a bumpy dried starfish like it was a lucky talisman.

I dropped into the seat across from him.

Ezra took up position at my six and scooped up the silver lock that had been tossed on the table next to the brass scales. I was surprised Delacroix hadn't nuked the lock yet, but it had survived the fire and remained unmarked. Maybe the magic on it precluded it from harm.

"All the information flowing through this place," I said, "and you had no clue this was happening, did you?"

"Gloating is unsportsmanlike, girlie."

I made a big production of looking around. "I missed your motto adorning this place. What's Latin for 'honor among evil supernatural scum'?"

Delacroix wrapped his fingers around the starfish like it was a ninja star he was about to whip at me. "You want an answer to that? Put your hands on the brass scales."

"It was rhetorical, and you're the one who kiboshed playing that game. Use your powers of deduction and tell me this: were all the locks stored in one place before? Like near Sarajevo, right before WWI? Then demons were let out and sold to the highest bidder to plunge us into a world war?"

"Answer her already," Ezra said tiredly. "Neither of you have time for power plays."

"The shedim aren't being let out." Delacroix pulled a cigarette from behind his ear and jammed it in the corner of his mouth but didn't light it. "Not by my kind anyway. Why do you think that woman was murdered?"

Certain humans had learned about these locks and how to release the demons within. Except… "Wards can only be undone by their maker," I said, "and there's shedim magic on this. Some demons are absolutely involved in letting them out."

"One bad apple doesn't mean all of us are," Delacroix replied.

"No, that's literally what the saying means," I countered.

Ezra held the lock up to the light.

"If this isn't all a plot to contain demons until they can be most useful and make someone a lot of money," I said, "what's the point?"

"I comped you one answer," Delacroix said. "You want more, you play for them."

"I don't quid pro quo with cheaters." Frustrated, I rose out of my chair, but Ezra placed his hand on my shoulder.

"Imprisoning shedim in these cells is like dumping waste," he said, "then building a park over it, knowing that the toxicity will be leaching out for eternity." He handed me back the lock. "I feel it. It's faint because this prison cell is empty, but that's what it was."

"Shedim arranged for their kind to be imprisoned so they could move them around and spread their evil like weeds?" The revelations sent shivers down my spine.

Being close to the silver lock had almost immobilized me. It was only discernable thanks to the magic from Sire's Spark, but the lock also had that scorch mark on it. That cell was empty, and it had practically brought me to my knees. "These things are fucking batteries, powering up evil in the world?"

Ezra nodded. "Wars, genocide, ecological disasters in delicate geographic areas. Anything is possible."

A muscle ticked in my jaw. "And now they're disguised as love locks and placed all over the globe. Think about cities like Paris with bridges famous for those stupid things and all the unrest and violence that erupts there. No one would ever suspect something so sweet of being so heinous."

"Brilliant, right?" Delacroix said in an admiring tone. "The sheer cunning and calculated nature of their actions is astonishing. Usually, you put three shedim in a room and you get four opinions. But these buggers not only had the vision to come up with this, they possessed the tactical ability to use Maccabees in the process." He sucked on his unlit cigarette. "Shedim don't like being used and they aren't controllable, but contained in these prisons, they're both."

"Well, it's not going to happen for much longer," I snarled. "I'm telling the Authority everything."

Delacroix laughed so hard that tears streamed down his face. "Please do," he said when he could finally breathe. "Those shedim will hail you as their hero."

"We'll stop them."

The demon shot me a look of contempt and wiped his eyes. "How? You spent hundreds of years developing a magic formula based on a delivery system that we shedim corrupted, while you spent the past couple centuries believing you made a difference, like children believing in Santa Claus. But absolutely tell your bosses that not only is it back to the drawing board, you've been actively assisting some of the worst events in human history." Delacroix swiped his tongue over his fangs that had appeared. "The demoralization will be delicious. It will be the end of those annoying do-gooders."

"You're underestimating our determination to keep humanity safe," I said.

"Not at all," Delacroix replied. "But determination only gets you so far, girlie. Even if the Authority throws all its resources into creating a new foundational strain—" He smirked at my surprised blink. "Did you really think I didn't know the plans to storm the production center in 1600?" He shook his head at my foolishness. "How long will it take to get a new cocktail allowing the five types of magic to work in harmony?" the demon said. "What will that determination look like in ten years? Twenty? Despair will take root and you'll get sloppy. Make more and more costly mistakes as you get more desperate to win this fight. Eventually you'll make the one that tips it forever. The thing that destroys the barriers between our realms and lets us devour you."

"And what do you think happens to you in that scenario?" I said. "Right now, you have your little king-dom." I leaned into the word, savoring Delacroix's flinch and surprised glance at Ezra. "You may devour humanity, but shedim also eat their own. It might be these jailers, or it might be others who come through as the barriers get weaker, but they'll look to usurp all your hard-won power. They'll storm your gates and take this ship and that will be the end of you." I mimed scrubbing tears from my cheeks. "The king is dead. Long live the king."

Delacroix crushed his cigarette in his fist, tobacco and paper falling to the floor. "Let me guess," he sneered. "You have a helpful solution."

I'd worried about whether it was worse to steal someone's hope or turn it into the lie that sustained them. Except, I had it wrong on both accounts. Hope wasn't a savior and it wasn't sustenance. It was the weapon we wielded through the darkness of our fears.

"Work with the Authority to dismantle this operation, destroy any imprisoned shedim, and kill those responsible."

"I don't work with Maccabees," he spat. "Come after me, I'll pull up ship, and jettison any unwanted cargo." He looked pointedly at Ezra, who just laughed. "That includes your little friend Sachie, and any single person you've ever spoken to. Are we clear?"

I stood up. "I won't have to come after you, Delacroix. The others will and you know it. Maybe not now, but what will the situation look like in ten years? Twenty? Will you be making costly mistakes in an effort to not just win, but survive? And what about Maud?"

"What about her?" he said sharply.

"You've publicly recognized her as your daughter. You took her to Flaming Flapjacks. You like having a kid? Then do what it takes to keep her alive." I walked out the door without a second look back.

Unlike with Maud, Delacroix hadn't played poker with me. He'd tortured me. On more than one occasion.

I didn't need a father.

But I'd take the devil I knew as an ally.

Chapter 30

Had I been facing a cadre of hungry vamps or an Eishei Kodesh with a grudge in the morning, I'd have caved to Ezra's persuasive ways and spent Monday night with him. But I had to be at my sharpest to deal with Dr. Olsen and Dmitri, even via video call, and that wouldn't happen on no sleep.

"We'll sleep," Ezra insisted.

I leveled a flat stare at him.

"We'll nap soundly," he said.

Down on the Hell floor, beneath our balcony, a vamp overturned tables with a roar, having lost his fangs in a forfeit, and three drunk Eishei Kodesh came to blows over accusations of cheating.

Li'l Hellions swarmed the troublemakers.

"Play your cards right and we'll spend the night together after our dinner date," I said. "It'll give you something to look forward to." I pointed downstairs. "A little excitement in your otherwise dull life."

Someone knocked on the door to Ezra's suite.

"Do I get a goodbye bite?" I wasn't addicted to it, but I

wasn't addicted to sugar and there were times I polished off a party-sized bag of M&M's too.

He narrowed his eyes and growled at me. "You can have a goodbye kiss."

"Eh."

He hauled me into a kiss that left my breathing ragged and me clutching his shoulders to stay upright.

"You play dirty," I gasped.

He grinned and booped my nose. "Remember that. This dinner is happening soon and when it does, I want your answer about giving me another chance. I want all of you, Aviva, my friend, my partner, not just a lover."

I patted his cheek. "We've got two out of three, which is a much better standing than I'd have predicted for us a couple of months ago."

He caught my hand, nuzzling into my palm. "How do I get a clean sweep?"

Keep being this version of yourself.

"I told you," I said lightly, because the knocking had turned to pounding on his door, "that's dessert dependent."

He opened a portal to the alley behind my condo tower since my new mezuzah ward prevented him from opening one directly into my apartment. "Coño! I'm coming!" He had the cutest scowl.

I almost grabbed his hand and pulled him back into the bedroom. Instead, I allowed myself one more quick kiss, dashing through the portal with a laugh as he tried to grab me.

I want this. Laughter and easy kisses so freely given that you didn't have to commit them to memory were the best. But having our friendship back? That was even better.

Yes, our family dynamics were less than ideal and our emotional baggage couldn't be safely stowed in the overhead compartment, but after Ezra shared his fears that there was more to his mother's suicide, I understood him better.

He'd been raised with questions he couldn't ask by a man who viewed his son as a weapon. It didn't matter that Ezra was a Prime, because he'd still been a little boy, and he'd carried those wounds with him.

I hadn't been fair to him about him playing games, either, because every single time I needed him since we'd been reunited, he showed up. That mattered. Put all that together with our being older, wiser, and more cynical now, and this might just work. I hadn't fully committed to a "yes," but I felt optimistic about us. That was a good feeling.

Sachie wasn't home from the hospital yet. I texted, asking about her dad, and was pleasantly surprised that she replied—and that Delacroix hadn't drowned her. I was even happier to learn that Ben was doing okay, though when I asked her how she was doing with her parents, I got a terse *Strained*. I sent her back a huge hug.

After that, I got a good night's sleep and was at a café close to HQ bright and early the next morning for breakfast with Michael. She insisted on paying for our coffees and muffins (thank you, company card), and we settled into a table in the corner.

"Stick with the facts at this meeting," she said. "There's no point in being nervous because it'll waste important energy and put you off your game."

"That's not what I wanted to talk about." I ran a finger around the rim of my mug.

Michael took the news of the cells being evil portable batteries quite well. I mean, her face turned the bright shade of a ripe tomato, her eyes bulged out comically, her mouth hanging open in an exaggerated "O" shape, and her eyebrows merged with her hairline, but other than that? She was fairly composed.

Since she was keeping it together with aplomb—or in shock, I'd take either—I pressed her for another answer. "Why did you steal Sire's Spark?"

Michael finished chewing her blueberry muffin. "You want to do this now?"

I was about to put my career on the line handing information to two members of the Authority Council, whom I viewed as the enemy. My question wasn't about "want," it was about the need to know how much of a hostile entity I had to treat my mother. I already had one parent in that category; two felt excessive.

"Yes," I said evenly. "I do."

She briskly brushed her hands together, discharging crumbs. "I was aware of the *Supernatural: Debunked* exhibit for months. Maccabees were interested in whether the artifacts were magic, but I trusted the experts who verified they were inert. Their reputations were excellent."

This wasn't quite the direction I'd intended for this conversation, but I was curious to discover what else Michael had known. "What made you question whether Sire's Spark of all of them had magic? Was it because the artifacts were stolen?"

"It was because someone murdered Roman Whittaker in his cell."

I choked on my swig of coffee. "You knew?"

"Obviously. Booker told me right after it happened, but he asked me to keep it quiet." She frowned. "I wasn't aware you were told."

"Director Harrison shared it with Ezra, who was in London when it happened."

Michael pursed her lips and nodded. "I see. Well, the other artifacts stolen from the gallery exhibit were reputed to be evil in some regard. Sire's Spark was the only one that had great healing power. I understood someone wanting the other items, but why this one?"

"The others were a smoke screen?"

"Eat." She pushed my zucchini walnut muffin at me. "You can't take this meeting on an empty stomach. Let me back up. According to the legend, Abraham infused his powerful healing magic into the crystal, using it to achieve miracles, correct?"

"Yes."

"He was a top level healer. What did he need a crystal for? That's not how that magic works."

"Abraham used his powers to turn the crystal into an injury detector at a time before medical imaging and X-rays and stuff."

"Smart thinking," she said, "but your reasoning is faulty. As a powerful healer, Abraham *himself* would detect a broken bone or a tumor. And supposedly anyone could use this crystal and it healed them? Even a Trad?" She shook her head. "We Yellow Flames can infuse our magic into ointments and smaller medical-assistance devices, but you can't slap a crystal against your head and dissolve a brain aneurysm. It doesn't work that way. The experts were right. There was no Eishei Kodesh magic on this crystal, but a gut instinct made me take it and find out the truth behind the myth."

My eyes widened. "You stole evidence on a gut feeling?"

"Good thing I did too. Because I've figured it out." She patted my knee. "You helped."

"I'm not sure I want to be an accessory to this," I muttered.

"You told me you found Maud using your blood and the crystal."

"My human blood detected her half shedim side, perceiving it as an injury."

"Not quite." She raised her eyebrows at me.

329

I sighed, having no idea what she expected me to think.

In my head, Cherry flicked the inside of my skull.

"Oh shit," I said. "It's a shedim artifact. That blood detected Maud's *human* blood as the wound? Wait, then why didn't it make me sick immediately? And why was my reaction to the demon prison so horrible?"

"Blood calls to blood, Aviva. It's not seeking out a wound. It's demon magic illuminating demon magic, either in people or on items like the prison cells."

"That means only shedim or half shedim can activate it." I crumpled my napkin into a tight ball. The Authority couldn't use Sire's Spark and handing it over would have raised lethal questions about me. I'd dodged a bullet.

"That's correct. Sire's Spark wasn't a smoke screen for the other stolen artifacts, the legend of Abraham himself was the smoke screen. I doubt he knew anything about the crystal."

Great. I had my answers. Reasonable ones. I could use my remaining time before this meeting to ready myself to share the information about the shedim locks with the Authority. All righty. Going back to HQ now.

"So why steal Sire's Spark?" I repeated. "Or at least tell me what you'd done?"

She swirled the dregs of coffee in her cup. "Gee, maybe because you were so upset about the missing blood, I was worried you'd try and get your hands on it and do something stupid that would get you hurt? Magic artifacts are dangerous and unpredictable."

"It allowed me to detect the shedim magic on the padlock," I said sulkily, "so there's that."

"Let's see how this meeting goes before we take that win."

"That wasn't why though. You wanted to heal me. Admit it."

330

My mother flinched. "Is that what you thought?" She reached for my hands, but stopped herself before making contact, and dropped her hands into her lap. "You can't heal genetics."

One of my favorite cartoons as a kid was one where Bugs Bunny spoofed the *Barber of Seville* opera. He plays a barber and Elmer Fudd is his client. At one point, Bugs rubs hair tonic on Elmer's bald head and the man's face lights up in translucent delight as the hair grows higher and thicker. Then it blooms into flowers and his face falls. He looks destroyed.

As a kid, I found this hilarious.

At my mother's initial shock, I'd experienced that same spurt of hope, but with her matter-of-fact pronouncement about genetics, I understood the sorrow that swamped that deluded cartoon idiot.

"Genetics," I said tightly.

"I have never wanted to heal you." Her eye roll was worthy of the most melodramatic teenager.

"Then you just wanted me to hide. Do you have any idea how that made me feel?"

"I was keeping you safe. From the Authority. From Sector A. The world isn't ready—"

"You think any of that mattered to me when I was a kid? Not that you ever explained that. No, all you did was reinforce that I was flawed and broken. A dirty secret."

A woman rocking her baby back and forth in its stroller a couple of tables over glared at me.

"This is not the time or place, Aviva." Michael's face hardened into her professional mask.

I lowered my voice. "It never is. I'll grant you that the skills you taught me were valuable and I agree that the world isn't ready for me yet, but you're my mother."

"You expected some kind of preferential treatment?" She slashed her hand through the air like she was zeroing out the very idea. "I'm sorry, Aviva, but I've dedicated my life to rooting out corruption and I wasn't about to make an exception, even for—"

"Oh my God. Are you deliberately missing the point? Where was my validation that I was enough, Mom?"

She shook her head tightly and gathered up our napkins and cups. "What are you talking about? Of course I validated you. I bragged to everyone about how smart you were."

"You're not supposed to just love the easy parts of me." The alarm on my phone beeped. "Forget it. We should get back."

"Why is this the first I'm hearing about this?" she said.

I bit the inside of my cheek to stop the prickling sensation in my eyes—be it tears or Cherry about to let loose, this was not the right time. "Why couldn't you tell? My entire life I've felt like I was on thin ice with you. That my status as your kid was one long probation period and you still haven't made up your mind whether the appointment is permanent or not."

"I see." She stood up with a cool nod. "We should get back."

I spent the three-minute walk berating myself for hoping for a different outcome. Had I been asked about my relationships four months ago, I'd have said that Hell would freeze over before I ever spoke to Ezra again, but that things with my mom were as good as they could be, and Sachie and I were great.

Yet somehow, I'd opened the door to a reconciliation with my ex, my most important friendship was tattered, and I wasn't sure if my mother and I had torn away what little connection we had, doomed to a professional acquaintanceship.

Would she even have my back against the Authority or had our fight pushed her to a place where, as my mother *and* my director, any support she'd once shown was gone?

Kudos to a lifetime of Michael's training, though; I had my game face on before we stepped into the elevator at HQ—almost bumping into Darsh, who was getting off.

I indicated for Michael to go on ahead and tugged playfully on the lapels of Darsh's shirt. "How were the trains?"

"My visit with Silas was very nice." The way he said "nice" implied he was rolling it around in his mouth, probing for traps.

I scrunched up my face. "And by nice you mean…"

"I mean nice. As was the next time we hung out."

"Oh-ho." I chortled gleefully.

"Stop it, Aviva. And don't bug Silas either."

I blinked at the sharpness in his tone, but it gave me hope as well. This mattered, *Silas* mattered, and Darsh was treating it as such. Silas was as well or there wouldn't have been a next time. "I won't."

Darsh searched my face, nodded, then hugged me. "Now go up there and give 'em hell."

"As much as I can via a video call."

"Video? Uh, no, dear heart." He winced at the color draining from my face. "They got in earlier this morning."

"Fuck!" I sprinted for the stairwell, fear tightening its cold grip around my heart, and my palm leaving sweat marks on the banister. Darsh had to be wrong. Dr. Olsen and Dimitri wouldn't have flown in for this.

Would they?

Cherry made a scoffing sound in my head.

I stopped in front of the conference room door, gripping the handle but not opening the door. Normally the blinds were open to the bright room, but they'd been drawn tight. I swallowed.

These two Authority members had withheld this

switch to an in-person visit. Did they suspect what Michael had concluded about the corrupt shedim magic in our rings? Had these representatives of our organization that was thousands of years old come in person to kill the messenger and cover up any trace of vulnerability and complicity?

Had Michael known and not warned me?

I pushed open the door and entered the room, faced not with two members of the council, but all of them. Michael didn't look any happier with this development than I was. That was something, I guess.

Dr. Olsen and Dmitri Kozlov had flown in from Norway and Moscow respectively, joined by Secretary Pederson from Copenhagen, Zhengyu Lin from Taiwan, and Dilip Kumar from Delhi.

Their unreadable expressions were a shit greeting, and the weight of their presence was suffocating, but I straightened my back, steeling myself against whatever challenges they planned to throw my way.

They'd chosen the smaller room, which was a bit of a tight fit, but had nulling magic on it, ensuring I couldn't use my blue flame abilities to illuminate any weaknesses.

That's okay, I'd just resort to my training. Still, the sound of my chair scraping across the floor as I sat down sounded like a warning bell.

"Share your findings, Operative Fleischer," Dmitri said.

Once again, I started from the beginning with the drug bust. Dmitri barked questions at me, attempting to poke holes in my story, but I had nothing to lie about.

Dr. Olsen's gaze kept drifting out the window like she'd rather be outside. She might not be actively sympathetic to my case, but she wasn't hostile either.

Dilip, a man with an almost pelt-like amount of hair on his arms, asked the occasional question, but always after a glance at Dmitri. Got it. One yes man and not to be counted upon for support.

Zhengyu, a silver-haired gentleman in a Real Madrid jersey of all things, was the only one to nod at me to continue whenever I paused.

Dmitri glared and bristled, clad in a hole-free yet hideous brown cardigan, with heavy framed glasses to match.

Then there was Secretary Pederson, the woman Ezra had saved from an assassination attempt, and who'd given him carte blanche to investigate the murdered half shedim. She'd had enough fire in her at some point to attract Natán's ire, but you'd never know it to look at her now. She was a shell of a human being, her face gaunt and her gray hair long and unkempt.

Whether or not she'd known that her nephew was a half shedim before he was killed along with the others, she'd loved him a great deal, and was lost to that grief.

I powered through my tale to the locks being the battery packs o' evil and wrapped up my findings.

My mother set down the silver pen she'd been drumming against her notepad and picked up one of the ballpoints scattered around the table.

Dilip rapped on the table to get my attention. "Who's your source?"

"Chandra Nichols alerted me to the——"

"Right. The woman who was conveniently murdered," Dmitri said.

"Is a cold-blooded assassination considered convenient now?" I said. "I must have missed that change in policy."

"You know what he means." Dilip flapped a hairy hand at me.

I crossed my arms. "Apparently not."

Zhengyu cleared his throat. "Regarding your source

about the cells. It is unlikely that an Eishei Kodesh was privy to that level of intelligence."

"Clearly, it was Ezra Cardoso." Dmitri looked at Dilip.

I looked away so he didn't see me roll my eyes.

"If he was in possession of this intelligence while he was Maccabee," Dilip said as cued, "then a reprisal would be sanctioned."

"It wasn't Ezra," I said. "And I'm under no obligation to give my source up. Even to you. I won't ruin a valuable relationship because you don't want to accept what I'm telling you."

"You are a level two operative," Dilip said. "You'll do as we say."

"Which is what? Tattle so you can silence everyone and bury your heads in the sand again?" I held up my finger with the Maccabee ring like it was a guiding light and nodded at Dmitri. "What happened to prevailing in the fight against evil? Did it get too hard for you? Are you scared?"

He pushed his glasses up, an angry flush hitting his cheeks. "You're on thin ice, Operative."

I glanced at Michael. It's not like it was the first time.

"Fifteen years ago," I said, "some Eishei Kodesh hacked into the security system for our most notorious prison. Dangerous Eishei Kodesh escaped. You didn't hide that fact from your operatives. You were fully transparent, gathering the best of us to work on fixing the problem. It gave us agency, it empowered us. Why can't you do the same now? It doesn't matter that this involves demons and not people, the principle is the same."

Dr. Olsen pulled her attention away from the window. "You sound like you have a proposal."

"I do. While the Authority puts its experts to the problem of cleansing the corrupted foundational strain and how to make our magic cocktail feasible again, you remember that all is not lost. Vampires can kill shedim. Mobilize every single one we have in our organization and put them on this. Chandra and Jasmine both knew about these demon prisons. Other people will as well. Find operatives with the best skills for gathering this intel." I folded my hands on the table. "You know, like Silas?"

"And so it comes full circle." Dmitri raised an eyebrow, smugness washing over his cold features. "I warned you not to give me any reason to doubt your loyalty."

"I haven't. I uncovered a deadly flaw in our system, given you all the information to find a solution, and proposed a sound plan."

"If there even is a solution," he said. "You consort with one owner of the Copper Hell, who's to say you're not on the payroll? After all, you let Delacroix live when you rescued Maud Liu."

"He's a giant sea serpent demon," I protested. "I didn't have a shot at him and trying would have gotten me killed."

"Trying would have given you agency," Dmitri mocked. "Empowered you. Instead, you present a tale designed to crush us. Exactly what the shedim want."

I slammed my hands on the table, half rising out of my seat. "That is total bullshit. Are you even hearing your-self right now?"

"Let's take this to a vote." Dilip looked around at the rest of the Authority.

Finally pulling your head out of your ass? Good. Hopefully reason would prevail and they'd approve my proposal. I didn't have to be on the team, though I'd be an asset. They simply needed to act.

"All in favor of Operative Fleisher keeping her active status?" Dilip said.

"Are you kidding me?" My pulse spiked, a vise closing

around my chest. They were supposed to be considering my plan, not using me as a pawn in their political game.

Dr. Olsen and Zhengyu voted in favor, Dmitri and Dilip against.

"Birgitte?" Dr. Olsen gently nudged Secretary Pederson.

The other woman roused herself slowly like she was waking up. "I'm abstaining," she said faintly. "I don't have enough information on the matter."

"Abstaining in the event of a tie counts as a negative vote," Dilip said.

"That means Operative Fleischer will not be keeping her active status and will be placed on immediate suspension without pay. Turn in your ring." Dmitri held out his hand. "And pray the evidence doesn't sentence you to Sector A."

Chapter 31

I slid into some numb place where I couldn't feel the tips of my fingers or toes and the voices around me were blurry wah wah wahs.

No wonder the entire council had flown here. Dmitri wanted me out. This vote was rigged, worded in such a way that Secretary Pederson's lack of focus all but guaranteed Kozlov's desired outcome.

Beads of sweat trickled down my forehead and I was gripped with the fear that if I removed this ring, the very essence of my identity would slip away, leaving me adrift in a world that no longer made sense.

I clenched my right hand, the smooth golden band digging into the sides of my fingers. It radiated warmth and weight, a reminder of the heavy vow that came with it. "Tikkun olam. My personal responsibility as a Jew, and as a Maccabee to fix the wrongs in the world. I'm not the one who should be removing her ring. You are."

I'd grown up with my kind feared and despised. It was the reason I'd dedicated myself to doing good in the first place. But I didn't want to be part of a group where our values held no weight.

"You arrested Silas, hoping to force Ezra into leaving the Copper Hell so you could strike out at him," I said. "You don't care about justice or fairness, just remaining entrenched in your power, no matter what ethics or basic rights it violates. This Authority is a joke. A horrible one." I wrestled the band off, but it anticlimactically got stuck on my bottom knuckle.

Michael placed a hand over mine and I tensed. "Have you learned nothing from history, Dmitri? The original Maccabees were the underdogs. The ones who kept fighting and whose faith kept a flame burning for eight days and nights. But you're acting like a self-righteous villain. Suspend Aviva, or discipline her *in any way*," her voice darkened, "and you'll have a rebellion on your hands."

My jaw hit the floor.

Michael said it herself just this morning over coffee; she didn't do preferential treatment. The only reason she'd speak up—*talk back*—to them like that was because she believed me. Believed *in* me. She hadn't silenced me or tried to keep me safe while preserving her own position. She'd thrown her lot in with me and there was no going back.

"Speak a word of what happens in this room," Dmitri said, "and your career will be on the line as well."

Michael gave a mean little laugh. "I don't need to say a damn thing. You've been too removed from operatives for too long. They're notorious gossipers and I assure you that their speculation will be far worse than the truth."

Dr. Olsen smirked. "She's got a point. Michael, let's hear *your* proposal."

"It's the same as Aviva's," she said.

Dilip chuckled, the sound ripe with condescension, and stroked the hair on his arm. "Probably want your daughter to spearhead it."

"Not at all," she said.

I rubbed my hand over my heart, knocked off-balance by the certainty in her voice. Had I misread everything she'd just said out of false or foolish hope? Michael's next career move was the Authority and for that, she required an opening. Was I her way of achieving it?

"She'll have enough on her plate policing Vancouver as a level three operative." Michael winked at me.

Promoting me wouldn't further her own career goals in any way. On the contrary, given how she'd gone about it. The wash of relief and incredulity at her confidence in me left me flapping my hands like I couldn't contain all these excessive and unfamiliar emotions bouncing around inside.

"You are not—promoting her," Dmitri sputtered.

I held my breath, carefully gathering my joy to me, lest this moment turn to Elmer Fudd having his dream of hair within reach, only for it to turn to flowers.

Or Sector A.

"Let's take this to a vote," Zhengyu said. "All in favor of acting like grownups in the face of adversity and moving forward as a unified whole determined to keep our vow no matter what, raise your hands. That also means Operative Fleischer gets her promotion." He raised his hand.

Dr. Olsen joined him before he finished speaking.

Dmitri crossed his arms and Dilip hurriedly followed.

Everyone looked at Secretary Pederson. She bit her lip, twisting her hands in the hem of her sweater. "There's been so much death already…" Her voice was barely above a whisper.

She was scared, too broken by her nephew's death to remember that at the bottom of the Pandora's box lay hope. I tried not to blame her, even as I dug my fingernails into my palms to keep any trace of fear from my expression, because I tasted my heartbeat and the hair at the back of my neck was plastered to the skin in icy sweat.

Dmitri smirked. "Secretary Pederson abst—"

Her hand rose slowly into the air.

Dmitri blinked at her. Twice.

"That's a clear yes to me," Zhengyu said. "My motion passes."

I let out a deep breath, savoring the flavor of victory. My elation wasn't the blast of a cannon radiating happiness, it was the gentle unfurling of a delicate flower, a quiet and contented sigh that filled my heart with warmth and satisfaction.

Dmitri looked like he'd bitten into a sour lemon. He didn't argue further, but the baleful stare he gave me before leaving with Dilip promised that I'd made a powerful enemy.

I accepted my congratulations from Zhengyu and Dr. Olsen.

Between them, they scooped Secretary Pederson into their care and left.

Then there were two.

"When did you decide to promote me?" I said.

Michael smiled. "The other night at the pedestrian overpass."

"Because of my brilliant sleuthing?"

"That and you didn't offer to use Sire's Spark to suss out shedim magic on other locks. Maccabees need leaders, not martyrs." She reached for my hand like it was a snake that might strike. "You don't need healing, Aviva, or fixing. You're perfect as you are."

"You gave me the promotion, Michael." I crossed my arms. "You can spare me the bullshit."

She chucked her ballpoint pen at me.

"Excuse me?" I threw it on the table.

"What I said about you being perfect. It's not bullshit.

342

There's only one thing I love more than being a Maccabee, and if I could heal the stubbornness out of her, I would in a heartbeat, because I swear, Aviva Jacqueline Fleischer, you try my patience. In my desire to protect you, I..." She took a deep breath. "I may have overreacted—"

I snorted.

"I'm sorry I made you feel like you weren't enough." Her voice and pose were stiffly formal, but no less sincere.

It wasn't the big declaration of my amazingness that I'd longed for, but that wasn't Michael's way. Besides, words were easy. Actions were what mattered, and Michael had stepped up.

"I just want you to know, I hope that you get on the Authority sooner rather than later, because an organization under your top leadership is one I'd be proud to serve in."

"Thank you." She actually blushed. "I spent thirty years making sure no one finds out about you, but I realize it's your life and your truth to share with whomever you like."

"Ezra knows," I blurted out.

"Yes, well, he should never have broken up with you over that."

"*You knew that too?!*"

She shot me an "are you dim?" look. "Since I'm your mother, and also not a total idiot, yes. How about this? From now on, we don't keep secrets from each other. I swear that I'm not keeping anything else from you about the murdered half shedim or what the vamps are after or Sire's Spark or anything involving you."

"Delacroix is my father." I blurted it out, gauging whether this was a surprise.

"I—well—huh." Michael looked around with the desperation of a person wishing a bottle of whiskey would manifest in front of her. "He didn't use that name when I…we…huh."

"Are you all right, Mom? You're blinking scarily fast."

"What's he like now?"

"Horrible."

Her expression hardened. "Did he hurt you?"

"Don't worry about it. Though I may have told him he should work with the Authority to expose this operation and kill the shedim behind it so that he can stay in power and keep any harm from coming to Maud Liu, who's his other kid."

"Please tell me that's everything." Michael blotted her forehead with the back of her wrist.

I tilted my head, then nodded. "Yup. That about covers it. Damn, it feels good to let all these secrets out."

"A veritable breath of fresh air," she said faintly. She squeezed my shoulder as she headed for the conference room door. "Mazel tov, Operative Fleischer. Now go do good in the world."

Sachie was the first person I shared the news with, and I was profoundly relieved when she texted me back a congratulations message saying we'd go out to celebrate. It didn't mean she'd forgiven me, or I her, but our foundation hadn't crumbled away either.

I replied that it was a date, to which she said that she planned to drink her body weight in booze since her dad was recovered enough to harp on her choices again and her mother just chastised Sachie any time she defended herself for stressing out her dad. Oh dear. I offered to buy the first round.

The second person I itched to tell was a certain dark-haired vampire, so I was somewhat confused when, heading for the café with the city's best mocha lattes (double shot of espresso, double heaping of whipped cream), a limo pulled up alongside me, and the window rolled down to reveal Ezra sitting in the far back seat.

I did a double take.

No, the features were the same, but this man's hair was medium brown and straighter, and his light blue linen shirt tucked into white trousers like a *Miami Vice* extra fit a slimmer frame. Most telling, though, were his eyes. There was none of the mercurial silver in them. These were cornflower blue, deceptive in their sunniness until you saw that the color was a sham. They held no warmth from the smile that the man wielded like a mask.

Or wore like a costume piece, same as the kippah he had pinned to his hair. Religious jew, my ass.

"Mr. Cardoso." I refrained from flinching as his driver got out of the idling limo and stood off to my side.

She was a slender woman, but she was also a vampire with very pointy fangs and a cold stare.

Her boss chuckled. "I shouldn't be surprised you recognize me." Unlike his son, Natán hadn't lost his Venezuelan accent. He said something about having met me when I was a baby, but I was too busy getting over the shock of his similarity to Ezra to do more than nod.

Natán had been changed when he was in his thirties. I'd read that fact more than once, but until now, it had never hit me that he wasn't some aging mobster. He looked like Ezra's brother. At the moment, they were of a similar age, but Ezra would slowly get older, while Natán would forever be preserved in his prime.

He watched me expectantly.

I had no idea what I was supposed to respond to, so I cast about for a neutral topic. "What brings you to Vancouver?"

He mentioned a family-run Italian restaurant that I was very familiar with, since Michael and I had eaten there a ton when I was growing up, and I'd introduced Sachie to it later.

"How do you— Oh. Michael took you there?"

"Sí. Your mother introduced my wife and me to Nonna Rosa back in happier times."

I didn't buy his wistful look for a second. "Is there something I can help you with?"

"I was in the city, and I heard the good news. ¡Felicitaciones! Level three at such a young age."

That news was less than twenty minutes old. I clasped my shaking hands behind my back. "Thank you."

"I've followed your career for some time," he said. "You're a tried-and-true Maccabee, just like your mother."

Was that a threat? He'd killed Roman. Had he come here for me? For Michael?

I cast a sideways glance at the café. Fifty feet to safety. And the world's greatest mocha, but that was very much secondary right now. "I'm actually on my way to an appointment and—"

"I'll only take up a moment of your time." Natán raked his gaze over me. Not in a creepy sexual way, more like he was placing me on a set of scales to see if they'd tip in his favor.

Perhaps in three weeks when I'd dug up every last piece of dirt on him and then arranged the meeting somewhere I couldn't be taken to an undisclosed secondary location, we could schedule something.

His driver stepped forward, presumably to open the door for my convenience, but in practicality, boxing me in.

Like it or not, this was happening.

I smiled pleasantly, taking the path of least resistance but also, calling on Cherry to help keep my heart from hammering too crazily, and got in the car. "What can I do for you?"

The door closed with the gentlest of clicks, but it

reverberated in my body like a gunshot. I braced myself for a subtle threat couched in whatever outcome he sought.

"Do you light the Hanukkah candles?" he said.

I blinked. "Yes, actually. I'm not super observant, but I do the major holidays."

"Then you understand the importance of fire to Jews." Natán kissed his fingers and touched them to his kippah.

Religious jews kissed mezuzahs and their tallit, the prayer shawls, but kippah-kissing wasn't a thing. Did he not expect secular Jews to know that? Regardless, this was another piece of theater enacted for an audience of one.

I settled back against the leather seat, curious about where all this was leading. "I do understand its importance."

The limo pulled into traffic, the glass divide rising into place to assure our privacy, and Natán gestured for me to continue.

"The fire within us," I said, "that spark of life that is snuffed out in death or undeath, is one of the reasons our people fought against being changed. No disrespect intended. I simply meant it as it pertained to the founding of Maccabees as a modern police force."

Natán regarded me with an inscrutable expression that was more unsettling than if he'd run his tongue over his bloody fangs. Did he even experience genuine emotion or was everything a mask or a game to this psychopath? It was a minor miracle that Ezra wasn't stunningly emotionally stunted.

"Fire, when harnessed, provides great power," Natán said. "Consider the Hebrew word for man: 'ish,' spelled 'aleph,' 'yod,' 'shin.' Remove the yod and what remains is aleph and shin or the word 'eish,' for fire."

Gosh, really? Eish is fire? I would never have guessed,

being Eishei Kodesh, one of the holy fire people. I nodded, trying half-heartedly not to grind my teeth.

"Woman, on the other hand," he continued, "is 'ishah,' spelled 'aleph,' 'shin,' 'hay.'"

Someone shoot me, the lecture wasn't over. "Remove the letter 'hay' and you're left again with the word 'eish.'"

Natán narrowed his eyes. "Yes."

I pressed back against the seat. Do not interrupt the teacher with the fangs. Noted. "This is all fascinating, but..." I paused to reframe "is there a point to this?" to something less bite-inducing. "Is there a connection to a bigger picture?"

That earned me a smile. The same one my kindergarten teacher bestowed upon me when I glued the macaroni to the paper for some art project, instead of sucking on the dry pasta.

"That lack of fire within is what brings me here," he said. "Vampires want it back. They are obsessed with the idea, because unless they reignite that fire, they can't achieve the one thing that would ensure their legacy."

My pulse fluttered against my throat like a moth trapped in a jar. Legacy. That was the whole solution to this mess. Natán could no doubt hear my pulse and there wasn't a damn thing I could do, but I didn't care, because suddenly the final crucial piece of the murdered infernal puzzle snapped into place.

"Invincibility, being untouchable. Vamps aren't seeking it by becoming stronger." I shook my head in disbelief. "They want to continue their blood lines, but biologically as opposed to through turning people. They seek to procreate."

"Blood calls to blood," he said.

I shivered. The phrase applied to Sire's Spark, but Roman had said it about others knowing who I was.

Blood didn't just call to blood, it colored the waters I

currently swam in, hunted by a shark. Sorry, being driven through the streets of Vancouver by the shark's minion who contrived to hit one green light after another.

The shark leaned forward with a shrewd look. "You've heard of the concept."

"Blood calls to blood. It's catchy." There was no point in pretense. "Roman shared it. You remember him, right? The operative you killed?"

"I'd never kill a Maccabee." Natán touched his right index finger, where he'd once worn his ring.

No. You'd have someone do it for you, like Alastair. My father was a literal sea serpent, but Ezra's had an impressive ability to be slippery.

"You don't want vampires to achieve this, do you?" I couldn't magically illuminate this vamp, but his reasoning was textbook simple to determine. "Why let the riffraff have what only you possess? The world's sole Prime as your son. The one vampire capable of procreation. Of legacy."

Oh gross. Did Natán want me to breed with Ezra?

"*Ezra* is my legacy," his father said.

"What about grandchildren?" I said warily.

"I'm immortal. Grandchildren are of no interest to me. I have Ezra. That is all I require."

That? Ezra's your son, not a thing for you to use.

It took all my self-control to remain calm. "What do you want from me, Mr. Cardoso?"

"To keep the world free of any more Primes. Should vampires gain the ability to procreate and make more of them, humanity's time on this earth has an expiration date."

Let them get in line with the battery-toting shedim.

"That sounds like something you should speak to the Maccabees about," I said.

"I am."

"Officially. Not during a visit with the daughter of an old friend." My smile was bland, but Cherry hissed at him inside my head.

"You never found the blood taken from the murdered infernals," he said.

"You have it?" I braced my hands flat against my thighs so I didn't lunge across the limo and search his person.

"I have a lead on it. One that might uncover the ritual necessary to restoring that fire within and giving vampires procreation abilities."

This was everything I'd wanted on a silver platter. An icy drop of sweat ran down the back of my neck. "You'll give it to me in exchange for what?"

"Your promise to stay away from my son."

Chapter 32

Asshole fathers. I was done with all of them. "Your son is a grown man. Go get his promise to stay away from me."

Natán laughed like I was a particularly amusing child. "Ezra doesn't always know what's good for him."

I rested my hand on the door handle. "You raised him to be a killer, so forgive me if I have my doubts about your suitability as a parenting expert. Besides, I'm not dating him." Technically true.

"Then why did he stay in Vancouver after the investigation into those murdered infernals wrapped up?"

"Another Prime was killed and Ezra was in a unique position to help us."

Natán met my gaze, brow raised, as if to say *Is that how we're going to play this?* When I didn't back down, his expression iced over. "Half-breed dhampirs are like rattlesnakes on a path. A lot of noise, and a danger to some, but an eagle can swoop down, ensnare the rattler in its grasp and crush its head." He clenched a hand into a fist. "They are a weakness, unbefitting of my family."

"Difficult as it is to ignore the cries from my ovaries," I

said snarkily, "I have no plans to make dhampir babies with Ezra."

"Perhaps not now, but as for the future?" He gave a one-shouldered shrug. "You distracted him once from his proper path, Ms. Fleischer, I'm asking you not to do it again."

I unclenched my jaw, pushed past any ability to shrug this off. Natán could do nothing more than bluster or verbally intimidate me. Well, at least right now. I'd gotten into the car in a public place. I'd be missed.

Any reprisal was a problem for another day.

"If Ezra and I did choose to be in a relationship, that would be none of your business." There was a bladed edge to my pleasant smile. "That said, if he's distracted by anything, it's his duties at the Copper Hell."

Natán dismissed my comment with a wave of his hand. "It places him in a unique position."

Oh, don't you dare quote me back to me, asshole.

"One that is beneficial to my line of work." Natán's brows knit together. "There's no conflict of interest if you two get involved, is there? That's an eternal dilemma for young women, isn't it? Having to choose between love and a promising career."

Sexist and threatening, a two-for-one special. Lucky me. "I may not have your power, Mr. Cardoso, but I'm no pushover and I don't take kindly to threats."

"This isn't a threat. I have the utmost respect for what Michael has achieved, and I'd like to see her daughter soar to those same professional heights. Eva, may her memory be a blessing, would have wanted the same thing."

This piece of shit was invoking his dead wife? I dropped my now-prickling eyes to my lap before Cherry went full throttle on him.

"That's why I'd like to help you find the missing blood," he said. "An easy feather in your new cap."

"I'm good." I rapped on the dividing glass. "Stop the limo."

The driver gunned it through a yellow light.

I crossed my arms and met Natán's stare. "If you plan to keep me here, at least hit up a drive-through. Buy me a milkshake."

Natán knocked twice on the ceiling and the limo pulled over to the curb.

The driver didn't get out to open my door, so I opened it myself.

"Good luck," Natán said.

He didn't specify with what: finding the blood, dating his son, saying no to his proposal—and I didn't ask.

It took the trifecta of the great song playing inside the café, a double shot mocha, and a chocolate brownie for the sugar rush to contravene the ragey adrenaline in my veins, and when I crashed, I crashed hard, utterly wrung out by the time I got home.

Craving the soothing ritual, I placed all eight candles in the menorah, with the shamash in the center to light them on this final night. While I was hunting in the kitchen for a new book of matches, Sachie came home.

I exited the kitchen. "You're just in time to light the— Fuck me."

She sported a hell of a bruiser on her left eye.

"You should see the other guy," she said.

"That's not funny." I returned to the kitchen and got her a cold pack from the freezer.

She took it with a nod of thanks. "I wasn't kidding." She smirked. "I made Olivier's ears ring."

Tuesday. The boxing gym. Right.

I straightened a listing Hanukkah candle. "You have a strange idea of foreplay."

Her smirk widened. "He doesn't seem to think so."

"Nope. Don't need to know."

She sniffed herself then grimaced. "I'm going to shower."

I struck the match then stared at it. Tonight was the last night of Hanukkah. The last night I could hope for a miracle.

Or the best time to step out of the shadows and illuminate who I truly was to my best friend.

The flame almost burned my fingers and I quickly snuffed it out. "Before you go?"

"You want to light the candles? Sure thing."

"No. I mean yes, but…" I let my eyes turn from brown to toxic green, my horns popping onto the top of my skull, and the fingers of my left hand shifting to claws. I didn't bring out my scales, though I did change my hair to crimson.

Sachie didn't say anything, her expression unreadable, and her arms crossed.

My heart pounded in my chest, and I couldn't help but fidget with the hem of my shirt, my claws clicking against each other in a nervous patter.

Her silence stretched on, each passing moment feeling like an eternity as I searched my best friend's face for any sign of what she might be thinking. Was she afraid? Shocked? Disgusted? I held my breath, bracing myself for whatever was to come, and yet, I didn't regret my decision.

Sachie narrowed her eyes. "Your hair is the same color as the sweater Ezra made you."

"Is it?" I said lamely, running my fingers through it.

She smacked me. "You really told him first? Is *that* why he dumped you?"

Attuned to her fury via my training, experience, and because her glare was hot enough to incinerate, I dropped into fighting stance. "Yes. Sort of. Where's your weapon?"

Sachie gestured around the kitchen as though to say, *Everywhere?*

"Okay," I said, not particularly loving what was about to happen next but bracing for it. "I'm ready."

"Ready for what, you weirdo?" She shook her head. "Although you do match our curtains really well. Damn."

"Ready for you to attack me for deceiving you all this time?" I said.

"It sucks that you kept it a secret, but you didn't deceive me."

I did a double take. "You were so pissed I lied about Maud, but not telling you I'm an infernal is okay?"

"Actually, the correct term is half shedim."

"What is happening here?" I peered into her eyes. "Did Olivier concuss you? Should I call a doctor?"

She pushed my head away. "I could have lost my dad, okay? No. I'm not thrilled you didn't tell me, but I also thought a lot about what you said. About how Maud lived her life in fear. I don't want that for you. Especially not from me."

Without this confluence of events, Sach might not have been able to accept my truth as easily as she was now. But I hadn't tried, hadn't spoken up, preferring instead to live with my preconceptions of what she'd think, just as I had with my mother and Ezra.

Without those other relationship shifts, how long would I have continued to justify keeping my secret from her? Ten years? Twenty? The rest of our lives? It had taken some hard acknowledgments that I wasn't always the wronged party to allow me to be honest. But that pain, that growth, had been worth it.

I squeezed her hand.

Sach worried her bottom lip between her teeth. "I've spent the past few days in tense silence with my parents. I don't want us to become that. Besides, I know who you are. You're a good person. I may not be able to say that about all half shedim, but I can say it about some. And the rest I'll judge on a case-by-case basis like I do with every other person on this planet." She grabbed the matches. "Are we doing this or what?"

I exhaled, a weight floating off my shoulders like a helium balloon. "Yeah. We are."

"All right then." She lit the match.

As easily as hope was extinguished, it could be rekindled. But the thing that was even better than hope?

Living in certainty, in the light.

There was still a lot of darkness in the world and a lot of challenges ahead, but standing around these nine dancing flames, with my best friend at my side, everything was peaceful, warm, and for the first time in a long while, absolute perfection.

THANK you for reading BETTER THE DEMON YOU KNOW.

If you enjoyed this book and want to be first in the know about bonus content, reveals, and exclusive giveaways, become a Wilde One by joining my newsletter: http://www.deborahwilde.com/subscribe

You'll immediately receive short stories set in my various worlds and available FREE only to my newsletter subscribers.

Now, are you ready for Aviva's next page-turning adventure in DEMON IN DISGUISE (Bedeviled #4)?

Welcome to Vancouver, where the coffee's strong, the magic's stronger, and the murders are getting personal.

With tensions between the magic and non-magic communities already at a breaking point, Aviva goes undercover on a high-profile murder case that could shatter the city's fragile peace. As if that weren't enough pressure, she uncovers a deadly connection to demons—and her own past.

But why have one code red crisis when you could have two? Enter the Shepherd: a shadowy figure convinced a vampire breeding ritual is a good idea.

Spoiler alert: it's not.

And forget juggling stolen moments with Ezra between supernatural smackdowns. Fed up with her work-life chaos, Aviva realizes that sometimes, the best disguise is no disguise at all.

Cherry Bomb is ready for her close-up.

<u>Get it now!</u>

About the Author

Deborah Wilde is a global wanderer and hopeless romantic. After twelve years as a screenwriter, she was also a total cynic with a broken edit button, so, she jumped ship, started writing funny, sexy, urban fantasy and paranormal women's fiction novels, and never looked back.

She loves writing smart, flawed, wisecracking women who can solve a mystery, kick supernatural butt, banter with hot men, and still make time for their best female friend, because those were the women she grew up around and admired. Granted, her grandmother never had to kill a demon at her weekly friend lunches, but Deborah is pretty sure she could have.

"Magic, sparks, and snark!"

www.deborahwilde.com

Made in the USA
Coppell, TX
04 October 2024

38186330R00215